The Festival Murders

D0383254

Mark McCrum began his career as a travel writer, with well-received books about Southern Africa (*Happy Sad Land*), Australia (*No Worries*) and Ireland (*The Craic*). He is also the author of the UK Top Ten non-fiction bestsellers *1900 House* and *Castaway 2000*, the UK number one bestseller *Robbie Williams: Somebody Someday*, and *Walking With The Wounded*, which told the story of four wounded soldiers and their successful attempt to reach the North Pole. *The Festival Murders* is his debut novel.

@McCrumMark markmccrum.com

'A marvellous set of unsavoury suspects . . . good, nasty fun with a ring of truth'

Mail on Sunday Thriller of the Week

'A rollicking read'

London Evening Standard

'A wicked send-up of literary festivals . . . the eventual winding up of the mystery is ingenious'

Suzi Feay, *Independent*

'An old-fashioned murder mystery with neatly disguised clues . . . and a satisfyingly unexpected culprit'

Literary Review

'An informative and delightful gem for international travellers'

Library Journal on *Going Dutch in Beijing*

CHOSEN FOR *INDEPENDENT ON SUNDAY*'S
'ALTERNATIVE 2014 BOOKER PRIZE LONGLIST'

First published in Great Britain, the USA and Canada in 2019
by Black Thorn, an imprint of Canongate Books Ltd,
14 High Street, Edinburgh EH1 1TE

Distributed in the USA by Publishers Group West and in Canada
by Publishers Group Canada

First published in 2018 by Severn House Publishers Ltd,
Eardley House, 4 Uxbridge Street, London W8 7SY

blackthornbooks.com

1

British Library Cataloguing-in-Publication Data
A catalogue record for this book is available on request
from the British Library

ISBN 978 1 83885 030 2

Typeset by Palimpsest Book Production Ltd, Falkirk, Stirlingshire, Scotland

Printed and bound in Great Britain by Clays Ltd, Elcograf S.p.A.

MIX
Paper from
responsible sources
FSC® C018072

The Festival Murders

MARK McCRUM

BLACKTHORN

For Jo,
with love

MOLD-ON-WOLD LITERARY FESTIVAL

In partnership with *The Sentinel*

Saturday 19th July

3 p.m. Big Tent. £10
DAN DICKSON
The iconic author of *Dispatches from the E Zone* and *The Curious and the Damned* reads from his new novel *Otherworld* and discusses the challenge of creating a convincing futuristic dystopia.

Sunday 20th July

3 p.m. Big Tent. £10
The Sentinel Keynote Talk
BRYCE PEABODY
CELEBRITY AND HYPOCRISY
The legendary literary critic launches *The Poisoned Pen*, a new collection of his dazzling reviews. He reflects on our obsession with celebrity and considers how ill-founded these public myths often are.

3 p.m. School Room. £10
VIRGINIA WESTCOTT
The author of *Entente Cordiale, A Fine Imagined Thing* and *The Useless Boyfriends Club* reads from her latest novel, *Sickle Moon Rises*, and discusses the role of romance in contemporary fiction.

3 p.m. Small Tent. £10
FRANCIS MEADOWES
THE AMATEUR SLEUTH
The creator of the acclaimed George Braithwaite series of crime novels considers the history of the amateur detective in crime fiction, from early beginnings in *The Thousand and One Nights* to TV's Jonathan Creek and Jackson Brodie.

Monday 21st July

2 p.m. Big Tent. £10
FAMILY MAN
Everyone's favourite countryman and smallholder, Jonty Smallbone, talks frankly about the ups and downs of life on Peewit Farm, the joys and challenges of bringing up three kids in a rural setting, and the problems he faced as he researched and wrote his latest book, *Wild Stuff*.

6 p.m. Middle Tent. £10
TO HELMAND AND BACK
Ex-Royal Marines officer Marvin Blake discusses the experiences that lie behind his extraordinary memoir of a life in combat, culminating in his being seriously wounded in a firefight with the Taliban in Afghanistan. He is joined by ghostwriter Anna Copeland, in an unusually frank discussion of how his real-life adventures were brought to the page.

ONE

In the bathroom of Room 29, Bryce Peabody leant in close to the mirror above the sink. Through steamed-up glasses, he was working on the hairs in his nose and ears with the electric wand that his new girlfriend Priya Kaur had bought him for his birthday. It had been a shocking moment when he'd realized that he could no longer see to trim his nasal hair without his specs – if that wasn't a definition of middle age, what was? But Priya, rather than pronounce him 'past it', as his ex Scarlett would have done, had gone onto the Net and found him this wonderful tool, which buzzed and whizzed around his nostrils and lobes and rendered him in a minute as clean-cut (almost!) as some far more appropriate squeeze of her own age.

There was a light double knock at the door of the main room.

'I'll get it!' Priya called.

As a man who had passed the grim milestone of fifty, you came in for a lot of flak for dating a woman in her twenties. But it wasn't all about physical attractiveness, as people endlessly implied. Part of it was the sheer energy and freshness of outlook.

1

Could he imagine Scarlett – or Anna even – leaping out of bed to meet room service?

There was a loud crash from next door.

'Oh no, sorry. Now I must clear . . .'

Glancing through, Bryce saw that the skinny, dark-haired waitress who had brought in the breakfast tray had spilt the coffee.

'It's OK, love, we can mop it up.'

Bryce smiled as he heard Priya's forgiving laughter mixed with apologetic Eastern European murmurs. Compare and contrast what Scarlett would have done to the poor creature. Minced her.

There were several reasons why Bryce had decided to eat in this morning. For one, this was a very nice room. The festival had done him proud, getting him, he reckoned, the best in the hotel – and where did you stay for Mold if not at the White Hart? Room 29 had its own staircase, a four-poster bed, and a view down the sloping garden to the woodland at the bottom; beyond that, the river glinted through the trees. For two, he loved the rare ritual of breakfast in bed, the decadence of munching bacon and sausage while lying back on soft pillows, the newspaper sections spread out before you. For three, when those pages contained a coruscating – and, one hoped, a defining – attack on one of the country's most irritating writers, it was fun to be able to savour one's prose in private. Having done so, to toss it across to one's youthful paramour with a casual, 'This might amuse you.'

Of course it would amuse her! Bryce was under no illusions about that. Nor, really, about what Priya saw in him. He was the literary world's number one hatchet man, the guy to whom all the others looked to set the agenda. Bryce knew full well the impact his attack on Dan Dickson would have. When he emerged later, into the festival crowds, he would be the centre of attention. Mold wasn't a pop concert, so no one would mob him. But they would all notice him, and mutter about him, all those earnest nobodies who bought the *Sentinel* on a daily basis, who lapped up its liberal, left-leaning views like mother's milk. He was their naughty chancer, the guy that showed you didn't have to be dull to be right-on. Tomorrow afternoon they would throng to the Big Tent, longing for more. And boy were they going to get it. Bryce couldn't help but chuckle at the thought of that great big stick of dynamite lying at the bottom of his briefcase. *Celebrity and Hypocrisy*. Bring it on!

As Bryce strolled back in from the en suite, Priya was carrying the trays across from the table.

'That scatty cow spilt half the coffee,' she said, in the Midlands accent that Bryce still found strangely sexy. 'But it's OK, there's enough left for both of us.' Priya nodded at the *Sentinel*, which had mercifully escaped the mess. 'You got anything in this morning, love?'

'A little bombshell, though I say it myself.'

'Let me see.'

'Shall we eat our brekky first? It would be a shame to let it go cold.'

They climbed between the sheets together, lifted up the steel plate covers and got stuck in.

'Well, well,' said Bryce, examining the spread. 'White pudding. You don't often see that outside the Gaelic fringe.'

'It looks disgusting.'

'Taste it. If you don't like it, I'll have it.'

She did so. 'Yuk,' she said, making an exaggerated grimace.

Bryce laughed. 'Famous Scottish delicacy. Oatmeal and pork fat.'

'Should you really be eating that, Bryce? It must be a hundred per cent bad for you.'

'Too late,' he grinned, popping the gleaming slice into his mouth with the expression of a naughty child.

'You silly man! This breakfast really is a heart attack on a plate. Why couldn't you have had the Loch Fyne haddock?'

'I expect I'll live a few more years yet. Whatever I choose to eat.' Bryce forked up a rasher of bacon and chewed it thoughtfully. 'For such a deeply rural bit of England,' he said, 'this is an exceedingly good hotel.'

'Didn't you stay here before? Oh no, I suppose you didn't.'

The subject was closed before it was even opened. For festivals gone by, Bryce had of course stayed at the cottage. This year, for the first time, Scarlett was out there with the twins on her own; this year there would be no sneaky texts from Anna, popping up at awkward times on his mobile, requiring an answer, or at least the practised lie that he was 'out of range'. At one level, he was sad, about the awful mess he had left behind; at another he felt so much better. This was the place he was in now, this was the future. Who was to say that he and Priya wouldn't be at the cottage themselves next year?

Tray pushed aside, Bryce sank back on the pillow, savouring the last irresistible flakes of his *pain au chocolat* and keeping a weather eye on his undeniably gorgeous girlfriend as she read his piece. Anna and Scarlett, Anna and Scarlett, he mused, as those penetrating blue eyes of his roamed from the floral-patterned satin curtains of the four-poster and out round the room. How had he let it all go on for so long? He didn't feel so bad about Scarlett, they had been falling apart for years, it was a relief to have finally achieved closure. But abandoning Anna so abruptly had been cruel; especially as she was now forty-three and had been banging on forever about wanting a baby.

'Very mean and very funny,' said Priya, tossing down the Review section and snuggling in to his side. 'Just like you, my love.'

'You didn't laugh much.'

'More smileworthy than laughworthy.'

'Silly tosser's had it coming.'

'Let's hope he doesn't turn up at your talk and make a scene.'

Bryce chuckled. 'All the better if he does. Anyway, this is just the starter. By the time the punters leave the Big Tent tomorrow, they'll have forgotten all about the preposterous Dickson.'

'Really? Who's next?'

'Never you mind.'

'Oh go on, tell me . . .'

'Got to promote my bloody book somehow.'

Priya reached out to the bedside table and opened the festival programme. '*3 pm, Sunday 24th July, Big Tent*,' she read out loud. '*Bryce Peabody*. CELEBRITY AND HYPOCRISY. *The legendary literary critic launches* The Poisoned Pen, *a new collection of his dazzling reviews. He reflects on our obsession with celebrity and considers how ill-founded these public myths often are.*

'Give us a clue, Brycey,' she said, loosening her dressing gown as she stroked the grey stubble on his chin with those always-arousing fingers of hers. 'I'm assuming a huge star.'

'Are you now?' he gasped, rolling in to her. 'Make it worth my while and maybe I'll tell you.'

TWO

Five miles out of town, at Wyveridge Hall, they rose later, having been up, some of them, till the sky had started to lighten and high above the silhouetted battlements the clouds were tinged with pink. The old mansion had about fifteen usable bedrooms and these were crammed with festivalgoers; in some, the youngest members of the house party, those fresh out of uni, lay ten to a floor in sleeping bags, all paying forty quid a night for the privilege. But Ranjit Richardson, their dreadlocked host, was an astute Master of Ceremonies. He liked to have a few luminaries around too, to spice things up and give his satellite scene some glamour. And they, the younger crowd joked accurately, got special treatment. If you were published, you would, for the same price, be in a room with just one other. If you were famous, you'd have private quarters.

Unusually, Ranjit was one of the first down to the kitchen this morning. It was a wonderful old room that had surely changed little since the days when the Delancey family had been waited on by a butler and a team of servants. An ancient range took up the best part of one wall. Under the mullioned window were three big stainless steel sinks. Huge saucepans, encrusted with years of black grease, hung from the ceiling. Off to one

6

side was a pantry, with shelves of slate and a musty smell of old vegetables.

'See what your rival's come up with,' Ranjit said, yawning as he passed the *Sentinel* Review section across to the travel writer Conal O'Hare, who sat the other side of the big, wooden-topped kitchen table, eating a bacon sandwich of his own design – four slices of well-crisped bacon, a slew of grainy French mustard, two hunks of wholemeal brown bread.

'He's not my feckin' rival,' Conal replied, tugging with his spare hand at one of the dark curls that straggled down below his left ear. None the less he took the paper. Still munching on his sarnie, he speed-read Bryce's review.

'Such a twat,' he said when he'd finished. 'Dan Dickson's not that bad. And what has Bryce-effing-Peabody ever written that's worth reading?'

'A lot of brilliant reviews,' said Ranjit. 'One has to say.'

'Does one? "Have to say"?' Conal put on the exaggerated posh English accent that he'd been using to tease his friend since the day they had first met, at Trinity College, Dublin, a decade and a half before. 'And what else?' he continued, back in his well-maintained brogue. 'Nothing. Except a crappy little biog of some barely remembered critic of the last century.'

'Is that fair? Did you actually read the Leavis book?'

'I did, as it happens. I went to the launch party. You forget, we used to be friends before the bastard betrayed me. Insofar as that tosser has any real friends.'

'Don't get obsessed, mate. What happened wasn't entirely his fault.'

'That's not what I heard,' Conal replied. 'Dinners, flowers, presents. When he knew she was involved with me. I mean, that's the thing that gets me.'

'All's fair in love and war. You'd have done the same.'

'No, I wouldn't.'

'Don't be ridiculous,' said Ranjit. 'Of course you would.'

'He's twenty years older than her. Why can't he pick on someone his own age?'

'He's at the top of his game, he can have who he wants.'

'He already has a wife. And a girlfriend. It's just gross.'

'He doesn't have a wife, actually. Bryce and Scarlett were never married.'

'Whatever. They've got kids. That's as good as married.'

'Not in the eyes of the law.'

'Screw the eyes of the law. As far as I'm concerned he's a professional c-u-next-Tuesday, and if I could cause him serious harm I would.'

Ranjit laughed. 'Oh yes, whatever happened to your "public revenge"?'

Conal let out a bitter chuckle. This was an idea that had been cooked up one drunken evening at the Frontline Club in Paddington, just after he'd returned from his long research trip to Somalia and was still in the stunned mullet stage of rejection. A tableful of friends had offered him suggestions as to what he should do to Bryce to make his point. Pouring a glass of wine on his head at a launch party was one option, but somewhat clichéd; in any case, Scarlett had already done that. 'Kick him really hard on the shin,' someone had suggested, 'that'll hurt like buggery but it won't do him any damage.' 'But I want to do him damage!' Conal had cried. 'Seriously, I'd like to strangle the bastard.'

'It's still pending,' he said now. 'Maybe I'll break his nose at one of the festival parties.'

'D'you know what, mate? Leave it. The very best form of revenge is to be happy with someone new. Cruise past the pair of them with some cutie-pie on your arm—'

'In fairness,' Conal cut in, 'it's as much to do with me as anything else. It was hard core in Africa and I was eejit enough to keep Priya in my head like some feckin' talisman. Something certain in an evil world. And then to come back and find . . .'

'Yes, well, these things happen,' Ranjit replied with a yawn. 'There are plenty more fish in the sea. What d'you make of the Grace/Fleur combo?'

'Lovely.'

On Ranjit's suggestion, Conal had given these two young women a lift from London the day before. By the time they had arrived in the long and beautiful valley that led down to Mold, the three of them had been laughing together like old friends. This was typical of Ranjit. He was forever trying to stir things up, get things going.

'More than just lovely,' Ranjit replied. 'Has Fleur shown you any of her films?'

'We talked about them. And Grace's "novel-in-progress".' He made the quotes with his fingers.

'Don't be so patronizing, you arsehole. The films are excellent. Quirky and funny.'

Conal shrugged. 'Grace has a boyfriend.'

'Who's in New York and on the way out, by all accounts.'

'So I'm supposed to do to him what Bryce did to me?'

'For Christ's sake, Conal! Grow up. If you like her, go for it. You may find you've got competition.'

'You?'

'Certainly not. I'm cool with Carly. No, strictly *entre nous* Rory McCarthy has the hots for her.'

'Does he now? That's OK, because strictly *entre nous* I prefer Fleur.'

'What are you waiting for? Tasty as a very tasty thing and currently single. I can't guarantee she'll remain so all weekend.'

But Conal's eyes remained moodily on the floor. 'I still love Priya. That's the trouble. Can't get the stupid creature out of my system.'

THREE

By a quarter to three that afternoon the Big Tent was buzzing. On the screen above the stage was a huge black and white photo of Dan Dickson in trademark pose. Facing sideways, but looking straight out at the audience, the ageing *enfant terrible* of English letters almost personified the word sardonic. A sneer curled on his lips; above that proud Roman nose, his dark eyes met yours with disdain. But there was insecurity there too. *You are all scum,* his look seemed to say, *and yet, somewhere deep inside, I'm a teensy bit scared of you.* The forehead was as long as one would expect from such an intellect; above it, the receding hair was cropped to a no. 2 – a good strategy, as otherwise he would have been in line for a disastrous comb-over. Below his short neck came surprisingly muscled shoulders, shown off to effect in a skin-tight black T-shirt; he looked more like a scaffolder or a squaddie than most people's idea of an author. Over this portrait, in a chunky crimson typeface, was superimposed the single word:

dickson

Paradoxically, Bryce's attack on him in the *Sentinel* had made Dan's talk a sellout. The punters wanted to know how he'd react

11

– if he reacted at all. And then of course there was the tantalizing question: would Bryce himself appear?

He did. Fantastic! At two minutes to three, up the creaking steps at the back of the marquee to take his place with Priya at the end of a row. The noise in the tent doubled. Heads turned to observe the famous critic, and then, embarrassed to be so naff, turned hurriedly back. 'That's him all right,' they said. 'The short guy in the pink jacket' . . . 'Next to the pretty Asian girl' . . . 'That's his latest' . . . 'Can't stop himself, it's like a reflex' . . . 'She was his PA, apparently'.

Five rows from the front, Conal felt sick at the sight of his ex with her new man. Priya was wearing a tight purple top that set off her deep brown skin perfectly. The last time they'd spoken he had been on his knees in front of her, begging her to rethink. She had looked down at him with an indifference that had seemed heartless, but surely on reflection masked more turbulent feelings within. Now, watching her chatting with Bryce, he felt a rush of hope. She was showing her teeth in that familiar nervy laugh, but it was hardly, he decided, the look of love. With that he felt calm again. Maybe there was room for a few Ranjit-style tactics after all. Just in case Priya might notice him, he leaned forward and engaged Fleur on his other side – launching into a loud and visibly entertaining riff on the subject of the 'dickson' image.

Priya hadn't, in fact, seen Conal. But Bryce had spotted Anna's dark bob, ten rows in front of him at the bottom of the raised section of seating. Beside her sat a brawny-looking black guy with a missing arm. This was presumably Marvin the Marine, wounded in action, whose book about operations in Afghanistan and Iraq Anna had been ghosting and was up at the festival to help publicise; the gossip was that they were now an item. Seeing him with her, Bryce was surprised at how little jealousy he felt. Good on you, girl, he thought, for not sitting around moping about the might-have-beens; and double good on you for not dating someone from your social comfort zone. In a funny kind of way her choice reflected well on him too. He was the kind of guy that Anna Copeland dated: cool, contemporary, possibly a bit dangerous.

Bryce ran his eyes on over the crowd, looking out for his other ex, Scarlett. He couldn't see her anywhere. Perhaps she'd decided to stay in London after all. Absolutely bloody typical. Make a huge fuss about having sole access to the cottage, 'the twins' first week of holiday', etc., etc. Then not turn up at all.

The crowd hushed. Out from the wings came Dan in person, dwarfed by his photo. Behind him, auburn hair flowing loose, gleeful in a cream and blue dirndl skirt, was Laetitia Humble, the director of the festival. Bryce had known her since the earliest days of Mold, when the whole shebang had been run by her dad Henry. At that point Laetitia had still been trying to make it as an actor, settling for ever dimmer parts in ever grimmer fringe shows. Bryce remembered one particularly dire performance Scarlett had dragged him along to at the Man in the Moon pub theatre in Chelsea: Laetitia as Titania in a five-woman Midsummer Night's Dream with an 'alien theme'. But she'd seen sense eventually. She wasn't Kate Winslet, and once over thirty the statistics were against her. As Henry Humble became increasingly frail she promoted herself from assistant to organizer. Since his death she had made the festival her full-time job. She had moved to the area, shacked up with the drummer of a once famous punk band, and was now indisputably the Queen of Mold.

'Good afternoon ladies and gentlemen,' she shouted over the gathering hush. 'We are very privileged to have with us in the Big Tent today one of the country's leading writers . . .'

And off she went, overdoing it as usual. Absurd and ghastly though she was in many ways, you couldn't help but admire her PR skills. Finally Dan was allowed to approach the microphone and greet his fans. Four minutes into a reading from his new novel *Otherworld* Bryce squeezed Priya's arm.

'Can you stand it?' he whispered loudly.

'Oh Bryce! It's interesting.'

'Is it?'

'Since we've come, we might as well stay.'

So he sat, patiently, through the sesquipedalian prose, wondering why people liked this kind of wilful obscurity. Because it made them feel clever? Because it made them feel stupid? Probably a bit of both. If even he were stumped for some of these definitions, what chance the rest of these dutifully nodding heads?

At the end of the reading there was the usual applause, totally over the top for the passage 'dickson' had treated them to. Now he moved on to discourse on why he'd wanted to create his futuristic dystopia and the issues he hoped he might be tackling. Climate change, yawn. Overpopulation, double yawn. The fight for dwindling resources, treble yawn. The man was as modish as he was unoriginal.

Finally it was time for questions. 'I always enjoy interaction with my readers,' Dan said, 'so I've left a good twenty minutes for us to chat.' With some fumbling, and accompanying laughter from the tent, he replaced the mic on its stand. Then he sat down on his chair and leant forward in a matey way. 'There is,' he went on, 'at one level, something rather hideous about these festivals.' Across the stage, perched on her chair, the director tittered a bit too loudly. 'Sorry Laetitia, nothing personal. What I mean by that is this making of writers into public figures, into stars, if you like, when what writers should really do is to keep things as normal as possible, to insinuate themselves seamlessly into the warp and weft of ordinary life . . .'

'Pretentious arsehole,' muttered Bryce. 'If he really wants to insinuate himself into the warp and weft of life, what's he doing at an event like this?'

Beside him Priya giggled.

'As those who've heard me talk before know,' Dan was saying, 'there are three questions I don't allow at festivals.'

'Time to go?' said Bryce.

'Bryce! Come on. We're here now.'

In the row in front of them a woman with a face that looked as if it had been scrubbed pink by a Brillo pad turned round and glared. 'Shsh!' she hissed, eyes like gobstoppers through her thick specs.

'Question one,' said Dickson. '"Where do you get your ideas?" From my frigging head, of course. That's why I'm a writer.'

'God, he's smug,' said Bryce.

'Question two: "What is your routine?" Answer: My routine is irrelevant. And let me tell you a secret. Even if you followed my routine to the minute, you wouldn't be me. So make up your own routine. Whatever works for you.'

'So arrogant too. Under that man of the people pose.'

'Ssshh!' The Brillo pad woman glared again; Bryce was amused that she was taking notes. He couldn't see whether she'd written down 'from my frigging head, of course'.

'Question three: "Do you use a pen or a word processor?" Answer: Never you mind. Sometimes I even use a pencil.'

From the back of the tent came the sound of some female who seemed to be approaching orgasm as she laughed, so thrilled was she at every word that dropped from Dan's lips.

'OK,' Dan continued, 'with those strictures in mind, let's begin. The first question, please.'

Four hands shot up. 'Girl, young woman I should say, five rows in. With the short blonde hair.'

'Whoops,' muttered Bryce with a chuckle. 'Not quite as PC as you'd like to be, eh, Dan?'

'I'd like to ask a question about reviews,' asked the blonde. 'Do you read them? And if you do, and you get a really awful one, how does that feel?'

There was a collective intake of breath across the tent. In the magnified image on the screen, Bryce could see the cogs of Dan's mind whirring, wondering how to play this.

'I imagine you're talking about the pasting I got in the *Sentinel* this morning,' he said.

'Well, yes. I suppose I am.'

'Here we go,' said Bryce. He was aware of heads turning.

'You know,' said Dan, 'there are always two quotes I remember when it comes to reviews. The first is Somerset Maugham's. "Don't read your reviews, dear boy, measure them." The second is Evelyn Waugh's. "You may let a bad review spoil your breakfast, but don't let it spoil your lunch."'

'Ya-a-awn,' said Bryce. 'Such old hat.' But he was drowned out by the laughter that rang through the tent.

'So no, you'll be glad to hear that I ate a hearty ploughman's for lunch today. And also, when I receive a pointless stinker like that, I always think: at least I'm trying. While what is *he* doing?'

There was sporadic clapping; presumably, Bryce thought, from all the sad wannabe creatives in the place.

'You wonder what motivates these people,' Dan went on. 'Professional critics.' He spat out the word. 'Is it because they have little or no talent themselves that they need to keep savaging the efforts of others? The funny thing about reviewers, if you get to know them, is that they know exactly how hard a road it is writing fiction. D'you know why? Because most of them have had a crack at it themselves. And failed.'

On the screen, Bryce could see Dan pause, wondering whether to hammer home this tired point. He knew him well enough to know that he would. He remembered the first time he'd met him, at a squat in Belsize Park, way back in 1983. Dickson, just down from Oxford, lying on the floor cradling a bottle of Bulgarian red, a huge Camberwell carrot of a spliff in his mouth, sounding off about the newly published list of Twenty Young British Novelists. 'What the frig is Adam Mars-Jones doing there? He's not even a novelist. Three short stories, that's all he's done.' No, Dickson could be as vicious as any of his critics when it suited him.

'I happen to know,' Dan went on, looking straight at Bryce, 'that the *Sentinel*'s reviewer wrote a couple of truly shocking novels a couple of decades ago which never even saw the light of day.'

This was a bit below the belt. Bryce hadn't published his early fiction; to his knowledge, Dan had never seen it. As the heads of the audience turned towards him, Priya squeezed his arm and looked supportively up at him.

'So who do you like, Bryce?' Dan taunted, in the grating, cynical tone that was his trademark. 'I sometimes get the feeling, reading your reviews—'

Bryce had had enough. 'So you *do* read them?' he yelled back across the crowd.

'Wait, please, Bryce,' came Laetitia's voice. 'We can't quite hear you up here. Just let Holly get to you with the roving mic. For any of you who don't know, this is Bryce Peabody, ladies and gentlemen, literary editor of the *Sentinel*.'

The work-experience was now at Bryce's side, holding out the bulbous microphone. 'I said,' he said softly, taking it, enjoying the sudden power of his amplified voice, '"So you *do* read them?" Your reviews. From the quotes you just gave us, Dan, I imagined you'd be out there with your ruler.'

'Oh yeah,' said Dickson, 'I read them all right. And some of them aren't bad, for what they are.'

'Very gracious.'

'I wasn't talking about yours. D'you know what your problem is, Bryce? You don't inhabit the modern world. From the endless historical comparisons you make, I get the feeling that, deep down, you don't like anything written after about 1950. Correct that, 1850. You're always banging on about Tolstoy and Conrad and Proust. I mean, who do you like from now?'

'Tolstoy died in 1910, Conrad in, I think, 1924. The last volume of *À La Recherche* wasn't even published until 1927 . . .'

'My point exactly.'

'What's sixty years between friends? But they were *better*, don't you think? Than most of the stuff we're forced to read now.'

'No one's forcing you to read anything, Bryce.'

'Oh, but they are.'

'OK then, Bryce, tell us. Who do you like from this century? That we happen to live in? The twenty-first. As opposed to the nineteenth.'

'Anybody who reads my column knows that I regularly applaud contemporary authors,' Bryce fired back. 'But yes, I'm not ashamed to say I like writers who give me a story, who present me with characters I can at least half-recognize from this twenty-first century that you treasure so much, a few real-life human dilemmas I can start to try and empathize with . . .'

Dan was laughing, but you could feel the anger vibrating in his voice. 'So what precisely do you know about real-life dilemmas then, Bryce? What do you actually see of the world outside the *Sentinel* offices and your cosy little launch party circuit?'

'Let's make this *ad hominem*, shall we?'

'La di dah, bring on the Latin tags, mate. Seriously, what *do* you know about what it's like to be . . . I don't know . . . a farmer in Mold or . . . a . . . a dustman in Warrington.'

Bryce's amplified gurgles of amusement rang through the hall. 'A bit more than you, apparently,' he replied. 'I think the word "dustman" went out about twenty years ago. The refuse in Warrington is probably collected by women these days. Romanian women most likely. If someone wrote me a good story about a feisty female garbage disposal operative from Bucharest I would be the first to give it the thumbs up. I'm longing to be transported from the parochial world I live in, to feel the impact of something powerful from elsewhere. Just so long as it's convincing. Unpretentious. Dare I suggest *well-written*.

'Look Dan, nobody likes criticism. But that doesn't mean that it isn't valid for a critic to express his opinion. He must be honest to what he feels, otherwise what is the point? Can you imagine a world in which writers received non-stop adulation? Their egotistic bonces would be even more like watermelons than they are already. Sometimes, if someone produces a piece of shit, it has to be said. It *is* said, by most of the people reading it. You just don't hear those conversations in kitchens at parties, see those paperbacks being hurled across bedrooms. Someone has to have the courage to express these feelings publicly. To help the ordinary reader discriminate in the face of the tidal wave of manure that appears every week in print. To say nothing of the tsunami of e-crap out there. And that's my job. For which I get paid, I might add, a lot less than Dan Dickson. As for my own attempts at fiction, which were, by my own choice, never published, I long ago accepted I didn't have that particular talent.' Bryce paused for a second, to give heft to his final punch. 'Unlike some people I was sensible enough to admit it.'

Shocked laughter rang through the tent.

'Are you saying I have no talent for fiction?'

'Everything's relative, Dan. You're not Tolstoy, I think that's pretty clear.'

'Here we go again. Ranking everyone, marking them out of ten, like some bloody schoolmaster. Creativity doesn't work like that, bro. Tolstoy was writing in a different century, in a different country. It would be strange if I were frigging Tolstoy.'

There was a momentary pause, during which Bryce could be heard scornfully repeating the word 'bro'. Then Laetitia, who had been rooted to her chair, a studied look of fascination on her face, seized her chance, rushing for Dan's microphone and pulling it from its stand. 'Thank you both,' she interrupted, 'for that absolutely brilliant little dialogue on the subject of creativity and criticism. It's at moments like this that I count myself truly privileged to be running this festival, to be able to bring together such mighty talents as we've heard battling it out today. Sadly, Dan Dickson's time is now up and we have to clear the tent for Alan Titchmarsh, our next wonderful speaker this afternoon. I should just point out before we go that many of us are looking forward to Bryce's talk tomorrow afternoon, in this very same tent, on the fascinating-sounding subject of "Celebrity and Hypocrisy", and there are still a few tickets left for that, so I'd hurry along to our lovely girls and boys in the box office if I were you. And now, if I might ask you all to join me in a hearty round of applause for Dan Dickson, for a really very enjoyable . . .'

Bryce leant in to Priya. 'Come on, let's make a dash for it, before I'm surrounded by effing gossip columnists.'

FOUR

The *Sentinel* party was the most prestigious gathering of the festival, held every year in the Council Chamber of Mold Town Hall, a splendid late-Victorian room with tall windows and a fine wrought-iron balustrade at one end. Commencing at 6.30 on Saturday evening, the event was reserved for those who were giving talks or interviewing; any other big names who were in town; key publishers, agents and TV people; partners of all of the above; and finally, any journalists who were definitely going to file copy to a national newspaper. Laetitia was strict about the guest list – had to be, otherwise the thing would be swamped by hangers-on, guzzling the wine, scoffing the canapés, and diluting the glittering crowd she had so painstakingly assembled.

For yes, there was Stephen Fry, head thrown back, laughing at some bon mot of Sandi Toksvig (resplendent in a boating blazer). There was Bob Geldof, jabbing a long finger at Ian Rankin as Caitlin Moran looked on. There were Kevin McCloud and Hugh Fearnley-Whittingstall, each sampling a mini sushi roll they had taken from a plate held by Jonty Smallbone, aka Family Man (and where else but at Laetitia's would you get a major TV star handing round the nibbles?). For those more in the know, there was Kirsty McWhirter, CEO of Hephaestus, chin-wagging with Amit Chaudhary of the *Independent* and legendary agent Julian Blatherskite; there was Rachel Lightfoot, senior fiction editor at Caliban, tête-à-tête with Sarah Sproat-Fanshawe, who selected the chosen reads for Channel Four's *Book Camp*, and had recently been named by *The Bookseller* as the third most powerful woman in British publishing.

Though Mold was sponsored by the *Sentinel*, this party was Laetitia's show. She glided among the guests, making sure that famous names didn't get stuck with some tedious partner or other nobody bending their ear. Her eyes flashed as she flirted, flattered, or just listened dutifully as this or that author sounded off on the shocking lack of coverage for serious books in today's newspapers, the deleterious effect of supermarkets on the bestseller lists, the dearth of decent editors, the paltry size of the average advance, the temptations of e-publishing, the fear of piracy in the digital world, and other such hot, writerly topics.

In the wider crowd there was talk of the festival and its progress; talk that was mostly focused this evening on the continuing ding-dong between Bryce and Dan. 'Surely he's had it coming' . . . '*it actually is completely awful*' . . . 'only ever had one book in him, in my opinion' . . . 'but have you *seen* her, she looks about sixteen' . . . 'poor Scarlett, is she here?' . . . 'and what about the other one?' All this muted, as both Dan and Bryce were in the room, steering well clear of each other. Any further denigration would be done in print, to a larger public, at a later date.

Bryce was, in any case, in a mellow mood. After Dan's talk, Priya had insisted that the pair of them go out for a drive, which had become a walk, then a glorious alfresco shag in a cornfield, during which his delectable consort had been even wilder than usual, at one point sinking her teeth into his neck so hard that he'd been left with a visible love bite, which he'd now had to conceal (deliciously) with a black polo-neck. This serendipitous session had been marred only by the fact that Bryce had got some grit behind his contact lenses, which had left him rather red of eye. But now, as he truncated a conversation with a good-looking black crime writer called Francis Something-or-Other to give his full attention to a blonde gossip correspondent who worked, apparently, as a stringer for his newspaper, he was exuding, he imagined, the animal magnetism of the freshly post-coital. Even as he did his best not to stare at Grace's delightfully perky breasts, Bryce chose his remarks carefully, mindful that they might end up in tomorrow morning's Muckraker. But he couldn't help but be indiscreet, as he always was with pretty women.

'Today is nothing, believe me,' he told her. 'Tomorrow's the big one.'

'How do you mean?'

'In terms of having a go at so-called celebrities . . .'

'Really,' said Grace, moving closer.

'Yes,' said Bryce. 'I have one very big fish in my sights—'

He was saved by his beloved, appearing just in time with two flutes of champagne.

'Gulp that down,' Priya said, gesturing to his glass of wine. 'This is the real thing. Present from Laetitia. She only gives them to her star writers, she says.'

'Thrilled I make the cut.'

'Sorry,' Priya added to Grace, flashing her a challenging smile. 'I'm Priya. Bryce's partner.'

'Grace Pritchard. Nice to meet you. We work for the same newspaper.'

'Do we?'

'I rarely go into the office.'

'Be warned, dear heart,' said Bryce. 'Grace is a gossip hound. Anything you say may be taken down, changed, and used in evidence against you.'

Grace giggled as Priya rolled her eyes. 'Take no notice of him,' she said.

'You were saying,' said Grace, returning to Bryce, 'about tomorrow being the big day.'

'Oh nothing,' Bryce replied, looking sheepishly over at Priya, 'I was talking out of turn.'

'Oh come on!' Grace joshed. 'You can't leave me with that.'

'Yes, he can,' said Priya, sharply.

'You see,' said Bryce. 'I can. Tell you what, make sure you come along to the Big Tent tomorrow afternoon and I promise you a red hot story. And not just for Muckraker either.'

Meanwhile, out at Wyveridge Hall, those who hadn't managed to blag their way onto Laetitia's guest list sat around pretending they didn't care. The after-party was the thing, they told themselves, and that was here. The tradition had started three years ago, when Ranjit had found himself, at the end of the *Sentinel* shindig, among a crowd of frustrated revellers looking for somewhere to go on to. The pubs of Mold were packed and even during the festival closed at eleven. 'I'm renting a big place just outside of town,' he'd announced. 'We've got booze and food, why not grab a bottle at the offy and join us?' That first impromptu thrash had been legendary. Those lucky enough to be present still talked of the excesses: the drink, the drugs, the skinny-dipping in the fountain, the couple who had been found, at dawn, copulating by the embers of the fire in the morning room, oblivious to a circle of onlookers, one of whom was providing a running commentary. Each year since, the louche and young-at-heart had returned, hoping for a replay.

The first cars started pulling up on the gravel circle at the front of the house at about eight. In the double drawing room the more active of the young people stirred themselves, tidied up and uncorked a bottle or two. Eva Edelstein, the American poet, her curly dark hair falling fetchingly over a lavender sarong, wandered around offering 'shroom tea', a murky, soup-like brew which she was carrying with her in a glass Kenco jug.

'Lift your evening to a whole new level,' she said with a conspiratorial grin. The mushrooms in question were liberty caps that she'd found in the big 'pasture' below the house. 'It's only, like, late July and already they're fruiting. That's one of the cool things about all this rain you get over here in your British so-called summer. In the States we have to wait till September.'

Over by the fireplace, a big, bearded guy called Adam read his short stories out loud to anyone who would listen; for the moment he had found an audience in a bird-like Australian in a flimsy green tulle dress. Just along the couch, Conal O'Hare continued to work on his laptop. He would socialize when it suited him. The *Sentinel* party was a waste of time, he had told Fleur, who had gone into Mold with her friend Grace but been turned away at the door. It was hardly a writers' party any more anyway. Laetitia was so up the arse of agents and publishers and

TV people it was ridiculous. If Fleur wanted to film real creative people, she would do better to preserve her energies for later.

Around eight thirty the host himself appeared, along with Carly his girlfriend and various others of the Wyveridge gang who had made it to the *Sentinel* bash. Striding in, Ranjit hurried to get things moving, clicking his iPod into the Bose portable system and flicking on the first track of a Prince CD. 'Conal, you dickhead,' he cried, 'get with the programme, we're having a party now.'

'I thought this was supposed to be a writers' retreat.'

'Not after eight o'clock.'

'Bryce and Priya coming by any chance?'

'No idea. Of course they're invited.' Seeing the expression on his old friend's face, Ranjit went over and leant down towards him. 'I couldn't not, could I?'

'Couldn't you?'

'If I took everyone's shagging history into account we'd never get the party started. Anyway, this is the perfect chance to piss her off. Seriously, mate, make her realize what she's lost. Get Fleur or someone on your arm and get out there.'

Ranjit could be such an insensitive prat sometimes, Conal thought, as he headed upstairs to his room to change. But maybe this time he was right. He didn't imagine Priya would have the gall to show up, but if she did, perhaps he *should* do the ignoring and making her jealous thing.

As he walked down the circular front staircase ten minutes later, he heard his ex's laughter in the main room. That bubbling, upbeat gurgle was unmistakable and it shot straight to his heart. He strolled in as casually as he could, to see Bryce and Priya making their number with Ranjit. He ignored them, grabbed a glass of sparkling wine, and dived through the French windows. He might get exceedingly drunk tonight, he thought. And then *do* something to that smug, short-arsed twat that would really put him back in his box.

As the sun set and the dusk thickened, the terrace was crowded with chattering figures. Unlike Laetitia, Ranjit had an open guest list, so people came from all over the festival. They were enjoying the balmy late-July evening, the chance to mingle with their literary heroes, as well as feeling part of the controversy that everyone was talking about. Dan Dickson was at one end of the terrace; Bryce Peabody at the other. What price a midnight tussle?

But Bryce was weary. All these bright young faces, expecting him to be catty and witty. You couldn't keep that pose up indefinitely, could you? Especially as they were half-cut now, most of them, desperate to engage with him, to show off in front of their peers and potential shags how awfully clever they were. It was a great game. But not for Bryce. Especially as some bird with a video camera kept hovering, trying to catch his embarrassment on film. He'd have told her to clear off if she hadn't been so cute.

One wild-eyed character called Rory, who was definitely high on something, had announced himself as an 'indie novelist and poet who utterly rejected traditional publishing' and then spent five minutes haranguing Bryce about why he didn't review ebooks, concluding that he was 'an outmoded parasite on the tree of creativity'. Yeah right, Bryce thought. At least I'm on the effing tree, not grubbing around in the dirt below it. But though he was famous for putting the boot in in print, it wasn't his style to highlight the failings of a tragic nobody like this to his face.

At one point he perked up briefly, as he and Priya found themselves in a group with Jonty Smallbone. Priya was trowelling on the charm, telling the sun-tanned TV tosser he was the best thing on the box – she'd just loved his recent series on food from the wild. Family Man was lapping it up, visibly irritating the dour-looking wife beside him. *Enjoy your fame, you glossy fraud, because it ain't going to last a lot longer.* Despite Priya's best efforts at persuasion Bryce hadn't yet told her who his next victim was; it wasn't that he didn't trust her, but it was essential to his purpose to keep the spectacular denunciation he was planning a total surprise.

He yawned again. He had definitely lost his mojo tonight. What he fancied now was a cup of herbal tea and his bed; one of those nice White Hart home-made biccies; his script for tomorrow's talk propped up in front of him; a few addenda, then blissful oblivion.

Just before nine thirty he touched his girlfriend's arm.

'D'you want to stay?' he said.

'Don't you?'

'I'm exhausted. And rather weary of this "controversy".'

'You started it!'

'It was only a review.' He put his arms round her and nuzzled in to her neck. 'I've got my talk tomorrow. I don't want to be completely knackered. So anyway, I called a taxi.'

'I hope you're not taking her home already,' said Family Man, now back on the scene without his wife. 'Things are just getting going.'

'Yeah, stick around,' said a large American creature whose heaving mammaries were barely restrained by a loose mauve sarong.

Bryce managed his cheesiest smile. 'No, really,' he said, 'I ought to get some beauty sleep. Before my event tomorrow. Which I do hope you'll all be coming to. Three o'clock in the Big Tent. Revelations galore.' He couldn't resist giving Jonty a wink. 'But you stay, darling,' he added to Priya. 'Enjoy yourself. You can get a taxi back in a bit.'

He hoped this would do the trick. Priya would have won her little battle and would now agree to return to the hotel with him. Such a wheeze would have worked with Anna. And even his nightmare of a long-term partner. But no. He had underestimated his latest woman.

'OK then,' Priya replied, stretching up to peck him on the cheek. 'You pop off and get your beauty sleep. I'll come and wake you up later.' She raised a single eyebrow, so flirtatiously he was tempted to stick around. But Priya had already turned back to Family Man.

'I'll do that,' Bryce heard himself say. He paced off through the chattering throng. Priya was a complete dreamboat, but did she actually give a shit about him? Or was it just his status, his notoriety she was after? Sometimes he really didn't know. He loved her, that was his awful secret, not to be confided, yet, even to her. As he crossed the gloomy hallway, he saw himself in the huge mirror, a jowelly figure hurrying away to bed. Hell, he was well over fifty now. He had to accept it, Priya was half his age; he was lucky to have her, on whatever terms.

Outside, his eyes were dazzled by a headlight's beams. ACE TAXIS MOLD 5555. His cab. Bryce rushed towards it, past that same lovely creature with the video camera who now seemed to be filming the arriving and departing vehicles. Crazy youth!

How he wished he were twenty-five again, his life ahead of him, that sense of endless time, of huge if unfocused talent, of anything and everything being possible. 'Hey, wait a mo!' he shouted, running in front of the car, waving his arms. He puffed up to the driver's window. 'Are you going back into Mold?'

'Yes, sir. But I've already got my fare.'

'I just called you. Ace Taxis, yes? I'm Bryce Peabody.'

'Sorry. I thought he was Bryce.'

Bryce looked in the back. It was Dan Dickson. 'Are you trying to nick my cab?' he said.

Dan shook his head slowly and smiled. 'Hop in, mate. All roads lead to Mold.'

Ranjit looked down the terrace. Oh dear. There was a very public row occurring.

'It wasn't forever,' Conal was shouting at Priya. 'Couldn't you wait for me for three months, you slag?'

'It wasn't about you, Conal.'

'You social-climbing whore. You told me you loved—'

'Conal, Conal,' said Ranjit, pacing up. 'Stop this right now.'

'Fuck off!'

'Conal, please, you've had too much to drink—'

'I have not – had – too – much . . .'

'Ranjit . . .' Priya's eyes were begging him to stay.

'Leave us A-LONE!'

'No mate, you heard the lady. Come with me and cool off.'

Ignoring the circle of watching partygoers, Conal met the eyes of his friend with a scorching stare. 'Traitor,' he muttered. He clenched his big right fist, pulled back his arm and then, as Ranjit ducked out of the way, fell face forwards onto the gravel.

With the strange dignity of the very drunk, he got up, dusted off a shower of little stones, and walked off ten yards or so. 'I'll kill the bastard,' he shouted. 'Bryce feckin' Peabody. As of now he's a dead man.' Then he turned and strode purposefully away, down the steep grassy bank and on across the lawn, towards the ha-ha and the dark fields beyond.

Ranjit turned to Priya. 'You OK?'

'Just about.' There were tears in her eyes.

'Silly idiot,' said Ranjit. 'He's arseholed. Where's Bryce?'

'He went back to the hotel,' Priya replied. 'I'd better go too. It's getting late. Have you got a taxi number?'

Ranjit pulled out his wallet and handed her a card. 'But don't leave us yet. The night is young. Come on. Let's get you another drink.'

'You poor darling, are you OK?' It was that gossip columnist, Grace, hand on Priya's arm. Followed by the American, Eva, who enfolded her in a crushing hug.

'I must apologize for my friend,' Ranjit was saying. 'He's like that. Highly emotional and volatile. It's the Celtic blood.'

'I did go out with him for six months,' said Priya. 'I know what he's like.'

'What a jerk!' said Eva. 'He should offer you an apology, at the very least . . .'

So Priya, more rattled than she wanted to be, found herself accepting a large glass of wine and following Grace and Eva up the stairs, past the huge stag's head on the landing, to Ranjit's room, where a relaxed crowd sprawled out over the chairs and double bed and carpet, retreating every ten minutes in more select groups to take cocaine in the bathroom. Why they bothered to retire wasn't clear. This wasn't a public place and everybody knew what was going on. Perhaps it was part of the ritual around a Class A drug that you had to keep it a little bit secret, even if you were in a private house. Priya waved away Ranjit's offer to join them, then Eva's suggestion that she try some 'shroom tea'. Grace, squashed up on her other side on the little yellow settee by the door, was also refusing the narcotics; instead, she was trying to get Priya to reveal what Bryce's big talk was going to be about.

'He hasn't told me,' Priya said. 'He always keeps his cards close to his chest.'

'I'll bet you know, though.'

'Honestly,' Priya laughed, 'I'm not that bothered. I'll find out tomorrow anyway.'

'I don't believe you for a moment.'

Later they were interrupted by that Rory guy who'd been so rude to Bryce, swerving down towards them in a black velvet jacket and artfully torn jeans. 'Who wants to come to my room for a magical mystery tour?' he cried, eyes wide as they spun lecherously from Grace to Priya and back again. He was accompanied by a cackling sidekick called Neville, whose little round spectacles were wobbling with excitement.

'Screw you, Rory,' said Eva. 'Nobody's interested.'

Priya stayed up there until it was almost 1 a.m. It was time to head home, she told herself. Quite apart from anything else, Eva's hand was resting on her thigh and she wasn't sure what to make of that.

'I really ought to call a cab,' she said. 'Get back to the hotel.'

'Oh, don't be a party pooper,' said Eva. 'You only live once.'

FIVE

In his room at the White Hart Francis Meadowes couldn't sleep. He had been at the *Sentinel* party earlier and was now regretting drinking so much white wine. Once it wouldn't have mattered; he would have crashed out and slept through to breakfast time. In the past few years, though, things had changed. Wine now did this to him: woke him at 3 a.m. and kept his mind dancing around all sorts of pointless subjects. It was as if his own body were saying to him, 'OK, Francis mate, let's make sure you're really *not* on form tomorrow.'

What did it matter? He was only a minor crime writer. A junior genre man. Not a big draw like Dan Dickson or one of those telly celebs. That afternoon, having attended the 'dickson' talk and witnessed the bust-up with Peabody, Francis had popped into the festival office to see how his own ticket sales were going. Yes, said the young woman at the computer, he was still in the Small Tent, though it was possible that could change. To the School Room. 'Only twenty-eight sold so far, I'm afraid.' She made a face. 'Sorry.' So now he knew: it was going to be one of those grim sessions where he had a couple of rows of punters and had to keep looking upbeat while everyone thought, *Who is this loser? Why did I sign up for this?* As if it were his fault that his audience was so paltry. Which in a way it was.

The main problem was that he was scheduled opposite Bryce Peabody – at 3 p.m. How very unfair was that? After the events of this afternoon, who was going to want to miss Bryce in full spitting form? Laetitia herself had bustled in at that moment and Francis had made the mistake of bothering her about his concerns, going over to her desk while she was on her mobile, then waiting patiently as she made another call on the land line.

'Hi, I'm Francis Meadowes,' he said, when she was done.

'Of course you are.' Laetitia flashed him a worn smile; then gazed hopefully at both her phones, as if someone more interesting might rescue her.

'Your assistant told me you could be moving me. From the Small Tent to the School Room. Is that likely? I just want to know as I like to check the venue before the talk.'

'I seriously hope not, er, Francis. But I'll make that call tomorrow morning. Sorry, I've got to dash.' And she was off, punching numbers into her mobile as she went. Rude cow, Francis thought. You asked me down here. You charge punters ten pounds each to listen to me. The least you can do is be civil.

Now, at 3 a.m., this encounter whirred pointlessly round Francis's head. He shouldn't have gone over. If anything were going to go wrong it would be the thing he least expected. His laptop wouldn't work, like that time at Dartington, when his visuals had been continually interrupted with Windows updates. Or he would get in there and clam up. Be unable to go through with the ordeal of standing up, just him, for fifty minutes, spouting on about himself. He would stop mid-sentence and break into a Tourette's style string of obscenities. He would pick on the one person he knew in the audience and reveal their intimate secrets to the crowd at large. He would break down in tears . . .

Come on Francis, he told himself, pull yourself together. His talk, his saner self knew, was perfectly well-structured and entertaining, an historical canter through the subject of the amateur in crime fiction: from the very earliest examples in *The Thousand and One Nights* and the Chinese detective fiction of the Ming dynasty, through European beginnings, Voltaire's *Zadig*, early nineteenth-century Danish and Norwegian writers, Poe, Sherlock Holmes, the 'Golden Age' of Wimsey and Poirot and Marple, right up to contemporary television's Jonathan Creek and Jackson Brodie. It was of course a way of showcasing his own series hero, George Braithwaite, a retired professor of forensic science, and his feisty wife and sidekick Martha, who had done well for him over a run of seven books. Though to be perfectly honest, he was a little sick of them now, was wondering if the time had come to kill at least one of them off. Having said that, his publishers loved the idea of more of the same. At a recent lunch, his ever-upbeat editor Nigel had pretty much begged him to keep the pair alive. No, a new detective would not be a good idea. Nor would Francis's ambitious plan to abandon the genre altogether and attempt something more like literary fiction.

'I'm never going to win the Booker Prize with George Braithwaite,' he'd said. To which Nigel had sighed deeply and replied: 'So, how d'you feel about a pudding?'

Let's face it, if he got really stuck, there were always questions.

Now Francis leaned over and switched on the bedside light. He got out of bed and wished he were back home in his flat in Tufnell Park, where he could make himself some hot milk, with honey and nutmeg, his sure-fire cure for small hours insomnia. As it was, there was a bizarre choice of coffee and tea: Nescafe Instant, Kenco Smooth, Clipper Decaffeinated, Yorkshire Gold, Tetley's Green, Twinings Digestif and Tranquillity. Only that last one offered even the vaguest promise of sleep. Perhaps he should risk going downstairs, finding the kitchen, raiding the fridge. But what if there were a fire alarm?

Whoo-ooo-ooo-oosh! How loud the little kettle sounded at this time of the morning. Francis tiptoed to the window. Even the last revellers had gone to bed now. It would be dawn soon. Out here in the country, the noise would begin early.

As the kettle clicked off, he heard a footstep in the corridor outside. Then, 'Shit!' – a man's voice. 'Shit, shit, shittety-shit!' Somebody back late from one of the parties, he presumed. The celebrated Bryce Peabody perhaps. Francis had been introduced to him at the *Sentinel* do, then run into him half an hour later in the hotel lobby, pacing up and down like the White Rabbit, staring at his watch. He had looked at Francis as if he'd never seen him before.

Now, overcome by his usual curiosity, Francis opened his door a crack and peeped out. Nothing. Just the green carpet stretching away to the steps at the end of the corridor and the arrow pointing, one way, to ROOMS 26–8, FAMILY SUITE and the other, ROOM 29. That was where Peabody and his pretty young girlfriend were staying. You had to wonder what the attraction was for her: fame, presumably, or fortune. Perhaps she just wanted to get on in journalism. Maybe – who knew? – she was escaping from an arranged marriage. When Francis had been researching his last but one Braithwaite novel, *A Matter of Honour*, he'd come across many extraordinary examples of what young Asian women would do to get away from the unions the more traditional of their families still demanded of them.

Francis got back into bed with his tea and the chocolate that had been left on his pillow earlier, which was decorated with a tiny purple sugar rose. Then he pulled out the stack of cards on which he'd typed his talk. Was he really only going to scrape thirty punters? When he'd made a special effort to do more than the usual festival dreariness of a reading from the book you were promoting followed by a Q&A? Oh well, he decided, however many there were he would do them proud. That was the key to being professional in these situations. Even if it were just a handful, you had to treat them as if they were the centre of your world.

SIX

A piercing scream rang through the room. A girl in a green tulle dress ran in and threw herself down on the hearth rug.

'*Healp! Healp!*' she cried, banging her head on the floor like a toddler. 'That Rory guy just tried to kill me. With a *noyf*.'

'Cool it, Birgit,' said Eva, who was still at Priya's side. They were downstairs now, with the last few survivors, strewn on armchairs and settees in front of the dying log fire. 'It's fine. He's just had too much coke or something. He's like that. He goes a bit psycho when he's overdone it.'

'A bit *soyko*?'

Her accent was Australian, Priya thought; that or Kiwi – she never could tell the difference. 'He's in the kitchen waving a *farking* Global *noyf*. D'you know how dangerous those things are? I'm going, back into town. Anyone want a lift? I'm driving *nye-ow*.'

'I'll come with you,' Priya said, leaping up. She had discovered – an age ago, it seemed – that both Mold's taxi firms packed up before one o'clock. That this had left her stranded at Wyveridge hadn't seemed to bother her host one jot. 'You can always crash on a sofa,' Ranjit had said, genially. 'Be my guest.'

'Let's go then,' said Birgit, 'my car's out back.'

Eva looked disappointed, but Priya gushed her way out of

any awkwardness, pecking her new friend on the cheek, squeezing her hand and promising to hook up with her tomorrow at the festival site. Then they were gone, bumping down the potholed drive in Birgit's gleaming red Mini.

It was 4 a.m. and just starting to get light. The birds were singing their hearts out in the empty fields. Over the river was a long low sliver of mist. A big ochre moon sank towards the horizon.

'Thank *fark* for that!' said Birgit, whose hands were trembling on the wheel as she drove. 'What a bunch of drongos.'

'What happened?'

'That Rory freak only tried to kill me because I wouldn't root him in the larder. What a dag. What was he thinking? One moment I was snogging him, the next he had a *noyf* out.'

'Why did you snog him in the first place?'

'I was only doing it as a *thenk you*. He gave me a couple of lines of coke, which was nice. But then he got all horned-up and tried to give me, like, acid. He had these tabs right there in his wallet. Little white postage stamps with strawberries on them. He told me the last time he'd had a trip he'd seen Mylene Klass playing chess in the nude with Lily Allen – and they'd both ignored him. I was laughing my head off. But then he was going on about how, like, really nice I was and how awesome it would be if we were tripping together at sunrise, especially if we were up on the roof, where there's some amazing view over five counties or something. When I said I wasn't interested, he told me not to be so uptight, so I told him to eff off. Then he flipped.'

'How did you get away?'

'Kneed him in the goolies and ran for it. He was well gone

anyway. He just groaned and crashed to the floor. But he's a big bloke. He could have done what he'd liked with me if he'd been a bit more together.'

'It does seem like a rather decadent scene.'

'Posh Pommie weirdoes, if you ask me. Now I've got to wake up this other guy who's after me and beg to sleep on his floor.'

'Out of the frying pan . . .?'

'Donald wouldn't dare. But I'll still have to put up with him hanging around me all tomorrow.'

Soon they were driving down the long hill into Mold; then over the quaint little stone bridge and right round the mini-roundabout onto the empty main street, straight to the White Hart on the bend.

'This is me,' said Priya. 'Thanks so much. I thought I was stuck there for the night.'

'No worries. You're well out of it.'

'Maybe I'll see you around the festival site?'

'If I don't head straight back to London. I'll see how I feel in the morning. I tell you what, though. I never want to clap eyes on that Rory jerk ever again.'

Reaching the hotel, Priya rummaged around in her big red Mulberry bag for the front door key. There it was, at the bottom, under her make-up. But when she tried it in the lock it wouldn't turn. Shit. That kooky waitress must have given her the wrong one. She was going to have to ring the bell.

She had to press three times before anything happened. Finally a light clicked on in the hallway and a face appeared at the door. It was the hotel manageress, in a hairnet and black silk dressing gown. She didn't look happy.

'I'm so sorry,' said Priya. 'I stupidly let my boyfriend come back with our key. This one doesn't fit.'

The manageress took it from her. 'Who gave you that?'

'The Eastern European girl.'

'How much more can I take?' she muttered. Then, to Priya, almost as if it were her fault: 'This is the key to the *back* door. Come on in then. Quick as you can. You're the third tonight. Some of us have to be up at six.'

'I'm really sorry,' Priya repeated, even as she thought, Stupid cow, no need to get stroppy with me; if you don't want to answer the door yourself, get yourself a night porter.

'Thanks again!' she called, as she hurried on up the green carpeted stairs.

Along the corridor she went and turned right for Room 29.

SEVEN

Francis was back with the love of his life. He was in a dark street and Kate was right beside him. 'Come on,' she said, tugging at his hand, 'let's go home.' She leant in to kiss him and he was crying with happiness to think that she was alive and they were still living in that tiny basement in Kennington.

It was where they had rented when they first came to London, two English grads fresh out of York. Kate had been doing a conversion course to become a lawyer, and Francis had taken a bar job in Soho while he struggled to get going as a writer. They had lived on nothing, vegetable soup and bread and cheese and the occasional bit of marked-down meat past its sell-by date. Towards the end of that happy time, they had got married, exchanging their vows in a sunlit, wood-panelled room in Totnes Town Hall, ten miles from where Kate's parents lived, in a lovely old house on the river Dart. Kate had worn a slinky white sheath of a dress that had looked just perfect; he could still see her dancing by the rose bushes in the twilit garden.

Then he had a terrible thought. Hadn't she drowned? In that felucca in Egypt he had tried so hard to stop them going on. Hadn't he seen her naked body laid out, as dead-eyed as a fish, on the brown Nile mud?

But no, no, she hadn't, she couldn't have, because she was still there with him. 'Come on!' she cried, eyes bright, her hand tight in his. 'I want to show you something.'

Now the sky was darkening and people around them were running for their lives. A woman screamed, loudly.

'Oh my *Go-od*!'

'Kate! Kate! Come back!' She was sprinting away from him now, far too fast for him to catch up with her, down towards the river. He was right by the dark water, which swirled powerfully past the concrete bridge supports. Where was she?

'Oh my *Go-o-od*!'

Francis woke abruptly, his eyes wet with tears. He wasn't in London with his long-dead wife. He was in a room with the curtains half open. Outside birds were singing. It was getting light. He was at the Mold-on-Wold literary festival. Where he was due to talk. Tomorrow. Today. This afternoon at 3 p.m.

Even as his heartbeat slowed, the scream came again.

'Oh my *G-o-o-od*!'

It was coming from inside the hotel. A woman was being attacked, right outside his room. Francis leapt from his bed and ran for the door in his pyjamas. Outside, at the end of the corridor, the pretty Asian girl was collapsed on the stairs.

'What's happened?' he asked, running to her. She was in a crimson silk dress and sheer black tights, no shoes. She smelt of alcohol, perfume, sweat, smoke.

'I – I – I—' she gasped.

'Come on, you're all right,' he said, kneeling to hold her. 'What's happened?'

'He's *dead*. My – my – boyfriend. Bryce. He's out cold on the

44

bed. He came back early. I was at the party. At Wyveridge Hall. I couldn't get a taxi. I just got back. He – he's lying there, on the sheet, dead.'

She was shivering, uncontrollably, like someone out in the cold.

'Now calm yourself,' said Francis. He took her hand between his. 'You're OK. Breathe deeply. That's it. Did you manage to check his pulse?'

'There's nothing.' She looked up at him, her eyes desperate. 'He's gone.'

Another woman had now appeared from the end of the corridor, in a long white nightie. Her shoulder-length hair was distinctive: shiny black with a thick streak of white in the middle of her fringe, like a badger.

'What's happening?' she asked. 'All this screaming.' Her voice was fluting, old-fashioned, upmarket.

'It seems there's been a death.'

'Not . . . Bryce?' she replied, looking towards Room 29.

'Apparently, yes.'

'Heavens above! Let me see.'

'No!' said Francis, surprising himself by the force of his reply. He held up a hand. 'We mustn't go in there. The police will want things left as they are.'

'What are you saying? That it's not a natural death?'

'Please,' Francis interrupted, gesturing with his eyes at Priya, who was shaking with silent sobs, white snot dribbling from her nostrils. 'I'm not saying anything. Just that, whatever has happened, we must follow the correct procedures.'

'What's going on?' It was the hotel manageress, clutching a torch, though the lights were all on in the corridor.

'There appears to have been . . . a fatality,' said Francis. 'We need to call an ambulance. And the police as well.'

'An ambulance isn't much use if he's dead,' said the badger-woman. 'Anyway, how far away's the nearest hospital? Dewkesbury?'

'This is standard procedure,' said Francis. 'Trust me.'

'Who are you, anyway? Telling us all what to do?'

'Please,' said Francis. 'This young woman's in shock. Can somebody get her a cup of tea with several sugars in it.' He turned to the manageress. 'Are you OK to do that? I can call the emergency services from my room.'

'I'll do that,' she replied. 'And we can sort out some tea for her, that's fine.' She turned to a dark-haired girl who stood in blue and white striped pyjamas right beside her. 'Irina, can you get that, please. Cup of tea, three sugars. Quick as you can. Don't forget to switch off the fire alarm before you go into the kitchen.' She hurried past several more guests who were now crowding down the corridor, in dressing gowns or the hotel's white robe. Among them were the TV celebrity known as Family Man and a sour-faced woman who was presumably his wife.

'What's going on?' he asked.

'There's been a death,' said Francis. 'This young woman's partner. The manageress has gone to phone for an ambulance now. I think the most constructive thing would be if everyone went back to their rooms. At least until the police have arrived. I'm quite happy to take charge in the meantime.'

'We can see that,' said the badger-woman. 'Has anybody even been in his room yet? Or taken a pulse? I happen to know Bryce.'

'Bryce Peabody?' asked Family Man.

'Yes,' said Francis. 'Now please . . .'

'Ms Westcott.'

'Ms Westcott, I hardly think this young woman is making it up. I can go and check everything in a moment, once we've got her settled.'

'*You* can check, can you? None of us even know who you are.'

'My name is Francis Meadowes. I'm a crime writer. I do have some understanding of how to deal with sudden or suspicious deaths. Now can we please be grown up about this.'

'But you don't even know Bryce. I've known him for years. I'm also a writer—'

'Oh shut up, you stupid woman!' It was the Asian girl. 'He's my boyfriend. He's dead, OK. As a doornail. He's straddled across the bed with his arms outstretched. And no pulse. Now why doesn't everybody do what the man says and return to their rooms.'

'Oh kay,' said Ms Westcott slowly.

There was the sudden clanging of an electric bell.

'Oh dear!' she yelled over it, needlessly. 'The fire alarm.'

Thirty seconds later it stopped.

'Now *everyone* in the hotel will be awake,' she said.

'Whatever the cause of death,' said Francis, taking advantage of the silence, 'the police will want as little disturbance as possible. Fifteen new sets of DNA trampling all over the place is not going to help.'

'Whereas one set is perfectly fine,' said Ms Westcott. 'OK then, I shall do as I'm told and go back to bed.'

'I think you're right,' said Family Man. 'Less is rather more in this situation. I suggest we all take your advice, Mr Meadowes, and return to our rooms.'

There was more muttering among the assembled guests, as they realized there was nothing more to see and started drifting back up the corridor.

'Did someone say it was Bryce Peabody?'

'Yeah, seems so.'

'What did he die of?'

'Nobody knows.'

'Maybe Dan Dickson bumped him off.'

'That's just silly. And offensive in the situation.'

'Oh lighten up.'

'A man's just died, for Christ's sakes!'

The manageress was back. 'Sorry about that. One of my staff accidentally set off the fire alarm. Right, I've spoken to the emergency services. They're sending police and ambulance. There'll be someone here within the hour.'

'Where's that tea?' asked Francis.

'Irina's just getting it.'

'Would you like to come and sit in my room?' Francis asked the Asian girl. 'I don't imagine you want to be in the same room as the body.'

'Yes,' she replied, in a thin voice. 'That would be . . . better. I mean, d'you mind?'

'Not at all,' said Francis.

The waitress had arrived holding out a mug, which read HAPPY on it in large red letters.

'Tea. Three sugars,' she said.

'A miracle,' said the manageress, checking the contents. 'Thank you, Irina. You can go back to bed now. Normal start time, though: six thirty.'

She handed the mug to the Asian girl, who cradled it grate-fully.

'You may find it rather sweet,' said Francis. 'But you're in shock, so you need the sugar.'

'Is there anything else I should do before the police arrive?' the manageress asked. 'Otherwise I ought to get dressed and ready for them.'

'Perhaps you could sit with . . . with—'

'Priya,' said the Asian girl.

'Priya, thank you, just for a couple of minutes, while I check over the room. If that's OK with you?' This last addressed to Priya.

'Whatever,' she replied. 'You seem to know what you're doing.'

'Fine by me,' said the manageress. 'Remind me which your room is?'

'I'm right here. Twenty-one. I'm Francis, by the way. Francis Meadowes.'

'Cathy. Tyndale.'

'Priya Kaur.'

They all smiled, despite themselves. It seemed an odd time to be making introductions, but necessary all the same. Tyndale – that was an unusual name, Francis thought. Hadn't some famous medieval printer or someone been called that? Kaur, by contrast, was a common, even generic Sikh name, the female equivalent of Singh. He showed the two women through his still open door, then backed quietly out, scooping up his key with its oblong blue plastic tag from the top of the chest of drawers. He walked up the steps at the end of the corridor, then turned right into the short passage that led to Room 29. The door was wide open, and through it came the light of early morning, a paler version of the brilliantly rosy sky outside, which deepened towards crimson and yellow streaks by the dark treeline above the river.

The body was on the bed, an antique four-poster in the middle of the room. The eiderdown, blanket and top sheet were pulled back and Bryce was stretched out for all to see, his head resting on two pillows. His upper torso was naked, though a pair of pale green pyjama bottoms covered his lower half. Francis turned and pushed the door to, then he tiptoed closer.

The celebrated critic was dead all right, but his expression was peaceful enough: his eyes closed, his mouth in repose, almost as if he'd just drifted off in sleep. Only two things suggested that the situation might not be so simple. There was a fresh bruise on his upper right cheek, and on his neck a prominent love bite.

Francis felt sick. It wasn't as if he'd never seen a corpse before. But though he'd written seven crime novels, this was the first time in his life he'd been present at the scene of a sudden death. Much as he would have liked this to be a murder, he didn't for a moment think that it was. That sort of thing was strictly for the books. Most likely this was a heart attack, though it must have been serious to knock Bryce out before he was able to call for help. Then again, perhaps it was a stroke or other brain breakdown: such things were more common than people realized. As for the marks on Bryce's body, the love bite was easily accounted for. That bruise, however, was fresh, and definitely raised questions. Had Bryce been in a fight? Was it possible that the blow that had bruised him had led to his death?

So what would George Braithwaite have noticed, he wondered, pacing slowly round the bed, hearing each footstep loud in the silence. In his books, Francis drew his readers' attention to significant details (as well as the odd red herring). But here, in the real world of this silent room, there were countless things to take in – and which would have caught the attention of the scrupulous investigator? The window half open to the garden below – surely there was nothing unusual about that? Bryce was a man who liked fresh air when he was sleeping. The pink jacket thrown across the back of a chair, below that the black polo-neck and T-shirt, blue jeans, dark green boxer shorts – Bryce's party gear, discarded on his return. Then the laptop on the low table by the window, its lead stretching across to a power point in the wall, the tiny oblong light on the transformer glowing blue; the contact lenses, soaking in a little dish by the bed, a bottle of solvent and another of Optrex alongside – what was sinister there? Next to that was one of the hotel cups, in which sat a herbal teabag, Twinings Tranquillity, still marinading in half an inch of yellow-green liquid. Beside that was a silver Parker 45, with an inscription. Unwilling to move it, Francis bent down and looked closely.

dd. V.R.C.W. Memento mori. 7.5.79.

Now what did that mean? *dd* stood, Francis rather thought, for 'given by', though he couldn't remember the exact Latin it was short for. The two words after the initials meant 'Remember your mortality', something like that. Whatever, Bryce had hung onto this writing instrument for an impressively long time.

Here was another intriguing detail. There was a single pillow chocolate on Priya's side of the bed, complete with a tiny pink sugar rose. But it wasn't on top of her two plumped, untouched pillows, which is where the staff would have left it when they serviced the room, it was on the table by the phone. Bryce must have eaten his and put his girlfriend's there for her return. How touching!

Francis cast his gaze back to the body. He had written often about rigor mortis. He knew that this post-death hardening of the muscles happened because aerobic respiration ceased; that rigor set in after three hours, moved from the head down through the body and reached its full effect after twelve hours, when a corpse became, as the Americans put it so graphically, a stiff. Now Francis reached out a thumb and forefinger and gently squeezed the muscles of Bryce's upper arm. They were no harder, surely, than they would have been in life? And the body was still warm. Gingerly he ran a finger up the neck to the face, which wasn't cold either, nor drained of colour, though the lips were an eerie pale purple and the eyes were closed. Francis was no pathologist, but his strong suspicion was that rigor had not yet set in, which meant that Bryce must have died sometime within the last three hours. It was five to five, he noted, glancing at his watch.

In the bathroom there were two washbags. Nothing madly unusual in either. The larger one, in fake leather, with brass rings at each end, contained half-used blister packs of Imodium, a sleeping pill called Zimovane, and Galpharm Non-Drowsy Allergy Relief (a hay fever remedy?). There was also a battered box of Alka Seltzer, a round plastic dental floss dispenser, and a small bottle of shampoo from another hotel – the Crown at Southwold. The smaller bag had Liz Earle Body Cream, Miss Bollywood GLAM-X liquid foundation and Sunora Deep Shine Shampoo alongside a half-used, shiny green pack of contraceptive pills. On the floor was a towel; another, still damp one was slung over the shower rail, drying. And that was it. There were – that Francis could see anyway – no stray hairs on the sheets, no fragments of unusually coloured fibre on the fawn carpet, no mugs of cocoa laced with strychnine on the side.

It was time, he thought, to head back and offer some comfort to the primary witness.

EIGHT

Priya and Cathy were sitting side by side on the blue couch by Francis's window.

'Well?' asked Cathy, as he walked in.

'I'm afraid he's dead all right, no doubt about that. I'm sorry, Priya.'

She nodded dumbly.

'What's your verdict?' Cathy asked.

'I've no idea,' said Francis. 'But he looks peaceful enough. Almost as if he died in his sleep.'

'He does,' muttered Priya.

'Maybe it was a heart attack. Or a stroke or something. I mean, how old was he?'

'Fifty-four,' said Priya.

'I had a college friend,' said Francis, 'who died in his sleep at forty-two. Perfectly fit guy, went to the gym regularly, drank moderately, never smoked. An aneurysm, they said it was.'

'And what's that when it's at home?' asked Cathy.

'Sudden breakdown in the brain. Like a stroke, only more severe.'

'Bryce did have high cholesterol,' Priya said. 'He was supposed to be changing his diet, but he was way too greedy for that.'

For a moment, the expression on her face was almost a smile, then she lapsed back into blank seriousness.

'So what now?' asked Cathy. 'There's not much an ambulance crew can do for him, is there?'

'Except pronounce him dead. Legally speaking, of course, you still need a medic to issue the death certificate.'

'The ambulance crew can't do that?'

'No. They'll have to send for a doctor. Or the police will. One of their own surgeons, more than likely.'

'Out from Dewkesbury?'

'I should imagine so. Or further afield.'

'So what's the point of the ambulance?'

'It's procedure. They have to check there's nothing more they can do.'

There was silence. Then Priya said: 'D'you mind if I use your toilet, Francis?'

'Please . . .' As Francis waved in the direction of the en suite, Priya ran. The door was hurriedly pushed to, then came the sound of retching. Francis looked at Cathy, who made a face.

'The shock . . . kicks in,' he said in a whisper.

'What if I called Dr Webster in town here?' Cathy asked. 'To issue the certificate.'

'You could do. Is he likely to come out at five on a Sunday morning? I thought those days were over.'

'No, no, Roger won't mind. He's a friend and he does pretty well by us. It might get things moving. To be perfectly honest, I don't really want the customers to be watching police vans and ambulances coming and going all day. This is our busiest weekend of the year.'

'I guess they'll have to know there's been a death on the premises.'

'It's the difference between knowing and having your face rubbed in it, if you're with me.'

She let herself out. A couple of minutes later Priya emerged from the bathroom. She looked pale and was trembling visibly. 'Sorry about that,' she said.

'Don't be silly.'

'Delayed reaction, I guess.'

'Now you sit down,' said Francis. 'What can I get you? Another cup of tea? Or something stronger from the minibar?'

'No, no, I'm fine.' She sat, one hand clasping the other in her lap, staring out across the room. 'Thanks, by the way, for taking charge like this.'

'Not a problem. Make the most of the lull, I should. It'll all kick off again once the police arrive.'

'How many will they send?'

'It'll be a couple of uniforms probably, in the first instance. They may want to call out CID.'

'Detectives?'

'It's fairly routine when you get a sudden death like this. Especially of somebody who seemed so . . . fit and well . . .'

'Yes.'

'I'm sorry, Priya. This must be a terrible shock for you.'

She had got to her feet. 'Actually, I might just go back up there for a couple of minutes. To get some things. And say goodbye. If you don't mind.'

'Take your time. I'll wait here for you.'

Francis pulled off his pyjamas and slipped into the en suite for a quick shower. It was one of those rickety plastic jobs, which produced a narrow stream of water with no effective temperature regulation: it either scalded you or, when you turned the dial, went suddenly cold. Strange that a hotel that paid such attention to detail in other areas should have such a crappy unit as this. Towelled dry, he slipped into fawn chinos and a pale blue cotton shirt. Then he lay back on his bed. Outside he could hear the birds chirruping away fit to bust. The occasional car passed along the road.

He had almost dozed off when there was a light double knock on the door.

'Come in.'

It was Priya, changed out of her party dress into jeans and a brown polo-neck. She was carrying a big red handbag and a scuffed leather overnight case.

'I brought a few bits along. Hope that's all right?'

'Make yourself at home. You OK?'

'Actually, if you're offering, I might have something from your minibar, after all.'

'Brandy?'

'Sure.'

'No ice, I'm afraid,' he said, as he unscrewed the top.

'That's fine.' She took the tumbler from him and drained it in one.

'Better?'

'Thanks.' She grimaced. 'He's left us all right.'

'Yes . . .'

'I've only ever seen one dead body before. My granddad. It's the same as it was then. Everything's there, all the things you recognize: the mouth, the hands. But *they're* not there.'

'I know what you mean. The spirit's gone.'

'And yet, there's still the bit of stubble on his chin he missed shaving yesterday. It's just so weird.'

And the love bite, Francis thought; but he didn't mention that.

Outside in the road beneath the window, they heard a vehicle stopping suddenly. Blue light flashed on the ivory brocade curtains. 'Hey ho,' he said. 'Looks like one of the emergency services.' He went to the window. 'Ambulance.' He watched as the crew of two, in bulky fluorescent yellow jackets, climbed out of their cab and approached the front door of the hotel: a squat woman with dark hair and a skinny, older guy with a shaved head and a neat white beard.

Two minutes later Francis heard them pass in the corridor.

'You want to go back up there?' he asked.

Priya shook her head.

'They'll have to run through their standard checks. I might go and see what's happening, if that's OK with you.'

Up in Room 29, Francis found the pair leaning over the body. The female technician had a hand on Bryce's pulse. 'Zilch,' she said, turning. 'I'm afraid he's a goner.'

'This is the gentleman that was one of the first on the scene,' said Cathy, who was watching from a few feet away, a finger pressed to her lips.

'Oh, sorry,' said the female technician. 'He wasn't a friend of yours, I hope?'

'No,' said Francis. 'I met him for the first time last night.'

'He's beyond anyone's help now. There's nothing for us to do here except move the body. And we can't do that till the police have been and we've got the doctor's certificate.'

'So what d'you reckon happened?' asked Francis.

'Looks like a heart attack to me. At a guess, eh, Phil?'

'Yep,' her colleague agreed.

'But a pretty severe one, because it doesn't look as if he had time to call for help. Sudden cardiac death is the technical term for it. I expect the police'll want a thorough look-see, though.'

'Yes?' said Cathy.

'Youngish fellow like this. You know, they might want to check for der-rugs.' She lowered her voice. 'Coh-caine. Ecstasy. Ketamine. Down from London for the book festival, was he?'

'Certainly was,' said Francis. 'A distinguished literary critic.'

'Is that right?'

Way down the corridor a bell rang. 'Front door,' said Cathy. 'That'll be Dr Webster now, I expect. Or the police. I'll go.'

'We'll stick around shall we, Phil? See what they've got to say.'

'Yep.'

There was a slightly awkward silence. Francis paced quietly across the room. Priya's party dress and tights were slung loosely over one of the chairs. While she'd been up here, she had also turned the laptop off at the mains and – he noticed with a lurch – the pillow chocolate on her side of the bed was gone.

Cathy returned with a short, red-faced man with unkempt grey hair. 'This is Roger Webster, our local GP.'

'Morning, everyone. Now what have we got here?' The doctor approached the body on the bed and put his black case down. 'Any loved ones present? No. OK then. We can all relax.' Putting his hand around Bryce's right wrist, he turned to the ambulance crew. 'You're not going to be wanting to rush him off to A&E, I shouldn't imagine?'

'No, doc.'

'No,' he said, after ten seconds or so. 'I fear it's all over for our friend here. At a glance I'd say a coronary. Then again, he does look very peaceful, doesn't he?'

He reached down and pulled back one of the eyelids. 'A little bloodshot. Hm,' he muttered, when he'd examined the other eye.

'Significant?' asked Francis.

'I doubt it. Probably just tired. I see he had contact lenses. Maybe some irritation from them.'

'Aren't red eyes a symptom of suffocation?' asked Francis.

Dr Webster gave him a sharp, surprised look. 'They certainly are. Also, for the record, conjunctivitis, uveitis and Sjögren's syndrome. But in the case of suffocation, you would generally expect the eyes to be open. More to the point – what's this?' He was peering at the bruise on Bryce's cheek. 'Looks like he might have been in a scuffle of some kind.'

'That wouldn't have been responsible, would it?' asked Francis.

'For his death? I very much doubt it. Not directly, anyway.' Dr Webster had reached the love bite. 'Now here's an interesting-looking flesh wound.' He chuckled. 'Am I right to assume there's a woman in the case?'

'His girlfriend's in my room. Down the corridor.'

'Lively lady, is she?'

'Quite a bit younger. Like twenty, twenty-five years.'

'Very nice. That may explain a good deal. I hope he wasn't overexerting himself.'

'Not last night, no. She was out at a party. Came back and found him like this.'

'That's what she told you, anyway.'

'What are you saying?'

'If she said she did, I'm sure she did. But it wouldn't be the first time I've seen this kind of thing, believe me. Poor girl. Don't suppose she'll be going for the father figure again in a hurry. Well, the autopsy will reveal all. Though I imagine the police will want the coroner's officer out here. Before we can move him—'

He was interrupted by the doorbell, ringing again way down the corridor.

'That'll be the police now, I expect,' said Cathy. She slipped out through the door. Dr Webster, Francis and the ambulance crew were left with the corpse.

'Up in town for the festival, was he?' the doctor asked, after a moment.

'Certainly was,' said Francis. 'I was just telling our friends here, he's one of the country's leading book critics.'

'Name of?'

'Bryce Peabody. Literary editor of the *Sentinel*?'

'Never heard of him. Sorry. But then I can't say I ever read the *Sentinel*, so why would I have done. More of a *Telegraph* man myself. But the *Sentinel* sponsor the festival, don't they?'

'They do. Bryce was due to give their keynote talk this afternoon.'

'They're going to miss out on his pearls of wisdom now.'

Heavy boots up the stairs announced the arrival of the constabulary: a lumbering, ginger-haired twenty-something with round wire specs accompanied by a bright-eyed blonde. Cathy was behind them. What was that saying about getting old? You knew it was happening when the policemen started to look young. To Francis, this pair hardly looked grown-up enough to have left school, let alone be coming out to remote hotels in the small hours to check on dead bodies.

'Morning,' said the PC, a little stiffly. He approached the bed and stared at the recumbent Bryce for several long seconds.

'This is our local doctor, Dr Webster,' said Cathy. 'Who's just been examining him.' She handed him a mug. 'There's your coffee, Roger.'

'Thanks.' The GP took a long swig, then let out a satisfied sigh.

The policeman turned. 'Beyond your help, by the look of him.'

'I'm afraid he is.'

'Hotel guest, was he?'

'Yes,' said Cathy.

'I'd imagine he would be, Stuart,' said the WPC. 'Since he's in a hotel room.'

PC Stuart nodded, unsmiling. 'You got his name?' he asked, pulling out a notebook.

'He's a Mr Peabody,' said Cathy. 'Bryce Peabody.'

'Brice,' said the constable, pen poised. 'Never heard that one before. Is that an "i" then, in Brice?'

'No,' said Francis. 'A "y". B-r-y-c-e.'

'On his own, was he?'

'No,' said Francis. 'He had his girlfriend with him.'

'As you can see from the female clothing,' said the WPC. 'Lying all over the place. Also the love bite on his neck.'

PC Stuart ignored this. 'And where is she?'

'We took her along to my room. I thought you'd want this place left as untouched as possible.'

'And who are you, sir?'

'I'm a fellow hotel guest. Staying just down the corridor. I was woken by the screams.'

'The screams?'

'Of his girlfriend coming back and finding him. She'd been out at a party and returned in the small hours.'

'What time was that then?'

'Just after four o'clock,' said Cathy. 'I had to get out of bed and let her in to the hotel, because she'd been given the wrong front door key. Five minutes later there was this unholy yelling.'

The PC turned to Francis. 'So you came straight up here, did you, sir? When you heard these screams?'

'I only got as far as the corridor. The young lady had collapsed on the stairs. Then Cathy here appeared, and quite a few other hotel guests who'd also been woken.'

'And where did they go?'

'We sent them back to bed and took Priya into my room.'

'Priya. That's the girlfriend's name, is it?'

'Yes. P-r-i-y-a.'

'Not heard that one before either.'

'It's Asian,' said Francis. 'Of Asian origin anyway.'

'I see,' said the PC. He noted this down too. Then he turned back to Dr Webster and the ambulance crew. 'What d'you reckon this is then? Heart attack?'

'Looks very much like it,' said the doctor. He chuckled again. 'Unless he's been poisoned by a rare South American plant extract that no one's ever heard about.'

'You think he might have been poisoned?'

'No, bad taste joke, sorry. It's almost certainly a heart attack. Or possibly a brain event. Both would be consistent with his facial expression which, as you can see, shows no alarm, no indication that he was consciously aware that anything was wrong.'

'And what about this bruise?'

'Wouldn't have killed him. My guess is that it was sustained earlier.'

'So you're saying there's no chance of him being poisoned?' said the PC.

The doctor looked despairingly across from the PC towards Francis and Cathy and back again.

'I can't say there's no chance. It's also possible he was strangled. By a very expert murderer. Using a silk scarf which has left no obvious mark.'

'You think he might have been strangled?'

'Please, constable. The point I'm trying to make is – no, I don't think he was either poisoned or strangled. If there was, by any remote chance, foul play, it would most likely be suffocation.'

'You think he might have been suffocated?'

'No! I'm ninety per cent sure he had a heart attack – a myocardial infarction, if you want to get technical. Though obviously I can't rule anything out until we've had an autopsy.'

'And in the meantime we have to decide whether to call in CID.' The constable looked back over his notes. 'Shall we have a word with the girlfriend now, Wendy?'

'Let's do that.'

'Might not be a bad idea for me to see that she's all right too,' said the doctor.

'We'll just have a quick chat with her first, sir, if you don't mind,' said the PC.

'As you see fit. We'll wait here, shall we?'

'Unless there's another room you could all go to,' said the PC. 'We may need to seal this one off shortly.'

At Cathy's suggestion, Dr Webster, the ambulance crew and Francis repaired downstairs to the little guest lounge that backed onto the terrace, where newspapers lay scattered on a central table and a chess board was set up ready for play between two straight-backed, green velour armchairs.

'Tea or coffee anyone?' Cathy asked.

'Why on earth did I say all that about him being poisoned or strangled,' said the doctor, when she'd gone. 'I might have known that idiot would take me literally. Now he's going to want to cover his arse and call in CID. The body'll be here for days.'

Cathy arrived with mugs of tea and a fine array of biscuits: shortbreads and chocolate Bourbons; round Jammie Dodgers and Rich Tea. Ambulanceman Phil munched his way silently through no less than three Bourbons. A little later, the two PCs had joined them.

'We've spoken to the young lady and we've decided to call in CID,' said the constable. 'So we'll be sealing off the deceased's room in a minute. I'll remain up there until they arrive.'

Cathy was trying hard to conceal her disappointment. 'D'you really think that's necessary?'

'I'm afraid we've got to follow procedures,' said the PC.

'What about Priya?' asked Francis. 'It is her room too.'

'She won't be able to go back in there now,' said the PC.

Francis turned to Cathy. 'I don't imagine you've got any spare capacity this weekend, have you?'

'Completely fully booked. I've even got someone in the box room, which is where we put people in emergencies.'

'She'd better stay with me,' Francis said, 'for the time being. I can sleep on the sofa. Could you provide us with some bedding?'

Ten minutes later the ambulance crew had gone. Dr Webster had examined Priya and found her to be in shock, but coping fine. Now she sat on Francis's sofa, lit from one side by the early sunshine, sipping a freshly made cup of Tetley's green tea.

NINE

'So what did they say to you?' Francis asked.

'Oh, just as you'd imagine. How had I found him? Where had I been? All that sort of thing.'

'You were at that party in the country house, weren't you?'

'Yes. Bryce came out too, for a bit. But he was tired and wanted to come back. I should have left with him. But, you know, it was a beautiful evening and it's an amazing place. Spreading lawns and hedges clipped like giant birds and animals. I was having a good time. Then I got involved in a stupid argument with an ex who's staying out there. I had a drink to cheer myself up and the next thing I knew it was one in the morning and all the taxis had stopped. They don't do them after midnight in Mold, apparently.'

'Even during the festival?'

'As I said to one of the girls, they need a few immigrants up here. With a bit of a work ethic.'

Francis laughed. She was offering some racial solidarity, but also probing gently; he'd pass on all that for the time being.

'So how did you get back?'

Priya explained about the Australian girl; about Rory's attack and their escape in the dawn.

'And when you got up to the room?'

'I let myself in, very quietly, so as not to wake Bryce. I saw him lying there, you know, *Oh, Bryce is asleep*. I was just starting to undress when I realized he wasn't snoring, which is unusual for Bryce. Then it dawned on me that he wasn't making any noise at all. So I ran over and saw that he wasn't breathing. I pulled back the duvet and there he was, just sprawled out.'

'Yes,' said Francis.

'For a moment I thought he might be unconscious. So I slapped him.'

'On the cheek?'

'Yes, hard, two or three times.'

'It wasn't you that gave him that bruise, was it?'

'No, that was already there. Then his head lolled over and I knew he was dead. That's when I freaked out and ran away.'

'Which is when I found you?'

'Yes.' Priya had kicked off her flat leopard-skin pumps and her bare feet were sunk into the beige carpet. The nails of her long toes were painted a shiny crimson. 'What will happen now, d'you think?' she asked.

'They've called in CID,' Francis replied, 'so probably some kind of duty detective will come out and make another judgement. They're covering themselves basically. Couple of young PCs, three, four, five years on the clock, they don't want to make a mistake. If our GP friend hadn't started going on about poisonings, they might have left it for the coroner.'

'How come you know about all this?'

'Police procedure?' Francis smiled. 'I'm a crime writer. For my sins.'

'Oh. I see. So do you think it's possible, that somebody might have' – Priya looked up and met his eye – 'done something?'

'Anything's possible, Priya. That's what the professionals in the world of crime always end up saying. I personally think it's unlikely. Bryce was a literary critic. It wasn't as if he were a drug dealer in his spare time, was he?'

'Not that he ever told me about.'

'Or an immensely rich man with penurious relatives who stood to be set up for life by his will?'

'Not immensely rich, no.'

'He had money?'

Priya shrugged. 'More than he liked to let on. His dad was some kind of Midlands building magnate. When he died, Bryce came into quite a bit. And he'll come into much more when his mother goes.' She closed her eyes. 'I'm sorry. He *would* have come into much more . . . I'm not very good at this, am I?'

'You're still in shock, Priya. Take your time.'

'If you're a literary type you don't boast about money, though, do you? I mean, the thing to be is as broke and bohemian as everyone else. Although obviously you are allowed to live in a beautiful house.'

'Which he did?'

'Up in Hampstead, in a leafy street just off the Heath. And then he had this bachelor flat in Bloomsbury he kept on as an office.'

'You've been there?'

'To the flat, yes, of course. I only ever went to the house once. Every summer he threw a bash in the garden. For the literary world and assorted extras. You'd see them there, all the big names.'

'Even though he regularly damned their work?'

'That's the funny thing about that scene. They lay into each other in print and then six months later you see them chatting away merrily at a party. Secretly, I think they're all suckers for punishment. But Bryce was pretty canny. He never went for the really successful ones – at least if they were still up there. He waited till there was a whisper against someone, then got his strike in quick. That's the truth about him, despite his reputation for fearlessness.'

'So Dan Dickson . . .?'

'Classic case in point. People have been sick of Dan and his posturing for ages. Just nobody's dared say anything. Until recently. But *Otherworld*'s a bit crap, so there've been a few mutterings and tweets and so on, and now it's open season.'

Francis smiled and looked over towards the window, where the morning sunshine was now streaming in.

'What other enemies did Bryce have?' he asked.

'Apart from the paper tigers of the literary world?' Priya shrugged. 'The mother of his children, Scarlett. I think she hates him, pretty much, these days.'

'His children?'

'Twins. Identical girls. They're eleven. He adores them. They've been a little tricky with me, but who could blame them?'

'They live with their mother?'

'Yes.'

'Were they married then, Bryce and Scarlett?'

'No, they had the weirdest set-up. They lived together for years and kept up this sort of family life for the kids, but then they both had other things going on on the side as well. It was like an open marriage, but not really, because from what I can work out Scarlett got jealous of Bryce's shenanigans and I think Bryce got more action than she did. I mean, when he met me, he already had another girlfriend on the go as well.'

'Besides Scarlett?'

'Yes. Anna Copeland. She's a ghostwriter.'

'It all sounds a bit complicated.'

'It was.'

They sat quietly for a moment; birdsong floated through the open window.

'So d'you mind me asking: why did you . . .?'

'Get involved?' Priya sighed and her intense, dark eyes flashed downwards in the direction of the floor. 'Good question. I didn't mean to. But, you know, I was working with him, on a daily basis. Bryce has – had – this huge charisma. He knew everything . . . had read all the classics . . . and despite everything that Dickson said yesterday he was really up to speed on all the new stuff too. That applied to the visual arts and music as well. His frame of reference was astonishing. To cap it all he had this effortless writing style . . .'

'I see,' Francis said, in that quiet way of his that always invited more.

'He could sit down, in a crowded newspaper office, with all the crap going on around him, and bang out a thousand words of fantastic journalism. He was like Dr Johnson, writing a *Rambler* article while the delivery boy waits in the pantry. Then he was a great companion, always entertaining, but kind and thoughtful too. You know, funny little presents, dinners out . . .' Suddenly Priya's face had crumpled and she was in tears.

Francis reached out and covered her hand with his. 'It's OK,' he said.

'I'm sorry.'

'For goodness' sake, don't be.'

Eventually she looked up at him. 'Go on then,' she said. 'Ask . . . whatever. I don't mind.'

'I was wondering how exactly . . . you managed to replace Scarlett . . . and, er—'

'Anna.' Priya grinned. 'I gave him an ultimatum. I told him I wasn't prepared to be another of what his therapist called his "satellites".'

'He had a therapist?'

'Yeah, God knows what she did. She was like a mother confessor who imposed no penance. Bryce told her everything and she validated the whole lot, as far as I could see. Anyway, I wasn't having any of that shit, so I gave him a deadline to sort himself out. He had a week to leave that sham home of his and finish it with his mistress too, otherwise I wasn't interested.'

'Tough terms. Did you think he'd manage it?'

'No, I was gobsmacked when he told me. On day six. He hadn't been in to work for a couple of days, so I thought it was over. Then he turned up with a bunch of flowers and a big smile on his face to say that he'd moved out. He was staying at his friend Rob's place and Anna was history too.'

'Did you believe him?'

'I did, as it happened. I made him show me emails.'

'Very thorough.'

'I didn't want to be messed around. I had a boyfriend myself.'

'Right.'

'But you know, he was a bit younger, more on the make, had less and less time for me, so it was time to move on. He's here, actually.'

'At the festival?'

'Yes. He's staying out at Wyveridge Hall.'

'This is the ex you had the row with last night?'

'Yes. Conal O'Hare. He's a travel writer. That's one of the reasons why I stayed so late. To prove a point to him. That I wasn't going to let his histrionics put me off enjoying myself. Not that he noticed. He buggered off into the woods, like the drama queen he is.'

'So what happened to Anna and Scarlett in all this?'

Priya filled him in. 'Anna and Marv are here at the festival actually,' she said when she'd finished. 'Promoting the book they've been working on together.'

'So it's a real gathering of the clans,' said Francis. Looking over at the window, he saw pale flashing blue again, mingling now with the glow of sunshine on the curtains. 'Uh oh. More fuzz, by the looks of it.' He got up and Priya followed him. They peered out to see a man in a casual jacket and grey jeans emerge from the front of a marked police car. From above, his round pate stood out against a corona of dark brown hair. Perhaps they should paint a number on it, Francis thought, as they do with the cars. 'This one looks a bit more senior,' he said.

'They're taking it seriously?'

'So it seems.'

TEN

Breakfast at the White Hart was a surprisingly lively affair. Newspaper headlines were left unread as individual experiences of the night were relived and the developments of the morning discussed. Some of the guests had slept through the whole drama; others had clearly been craning out of windows to keep up. The ambulance had long gone, but there were now two police cars and a van parked outside the side door that led up to Bryce's wing. There was blue and white scene-of-crime tape sealing off this entrance and the gate outside. A uniformed policeman was standing guard and men and women in protective white forensic suits came and went, looking like so many spacemen getting ready for a moon landing.

Twenty minutes after Francis and Priya had spotted the balding guy emerging from his car, he knocked on Francis's door and introduced himself as Detective Sergeant Brian Povey, CID. After a quick chat with the pair of them he asked to see Priya alone.

'The same questions all over again,' she said on her return. 'I think they think I did it.'

'You were in a relationship with him and you were first on the scene,' Francis said. 'In police terms that puts you firmly in the frame.'

'I suppose it does.'

Since then DS Povey had been joined by an important-looking female with a younger man in tow. 'It's the West Country version of *Prime Suspect*,' Francis joked to Priya. Not that the police-woman looked anything like Helen Mirren. She was shorter, for a start. And younger. Early forties, Francis reckoned, with shoulder-length dark hair and a crimson lipsticked smile. Her companion looked as if he could keep her out of trouble, though; he was a burly prop-forward type, with cropped curly blond hair.

Now Francis and Priya sat together at a table in the corner of the dining room, Francis wolfing down a full English while Priya toyed with a kipper and a torn-off half of brown toast. There was a hush and the clatter of cutlery being put down. The policewoman and her sidekick were at the far end of the room, with Cathy Tyndale next to them.

'Good morning, ladies and gents. If I could just introduce myself, I'm Detective Chief Inspector Julie Morgan and these are my colleagues Detective Sergeant Brian Povey and Detective Sergeant Steve Wright – no relation to the Radio Two DJ, I'm afraid. I'm sorry to disturb your breakfast but I have an impor-tant announcement to make. As you all, I'm sure, know by now, there was a death upstairs during the night. We have no reason to believe at the moment that this was due to anything other than natural causes, but as the gentleman in question was rela-tively young, and there are a couple of other factors to be taken into account, we will be keeping the part of the hotel where the fatality occurred sealed off. Once an autopsy has taken place we should have a clearer picture, but for the time being my team will be taking statements from everyone who stayed here last

night. So if you could please make yourselves available to one
of the officers sitting downstairs in the guest lounge we would
be grateful. This is particularly important if you are checking
out this morning. Any questions?'

'Are you in fact saying that this is now a formal murder investigation?' It was that unmistakable fluting voice: the badger-
woman, Ms Westcott.

'Absolutely not, madam. As I said, we're keeping an open
mind on the fatality until we get the results of the autopsy.'

'Taking statements from everybody staying in the hotel
doesn't sound like a terribly open mind.'

'At this stage, it's a formality we need to go through. Once
people have left the area, it becomes a whole lot harder to gather
the information we need.'

'So you do need to gather information. That hardly suggests
a simple death from natural causes.'

'And what about all these people popping in and out in forensic
suits?' piped up a man at a central table.

'Do you actually suspect foul play?' came another voice.

It was at this moment that Dan Dickson strode into the
breakfast room. He was accompanied by a tall blonde in a
crimson pencil skirt and fishnet tights. There was a hush. Dan's
eyes darted nervously around the occupied tables until his gaze
settled on Cathy the manageress.

'Are we too late for breakfast?' he asked.

Involuntary laughter rippled across the room. Dan looked
taken aback. 'Sorry,' he said, 'have I missed something?'

Whatever they were saying in public, Francis knew the police
had serious suspicions. Rapidly and efficiently, particularly for a

Sunday morning deep in a rural area, a Major Incident Investigation was clearly under way. As he looked out of his bedroom window at half nine in the morning, he could see that the place was swarming with all the characters associated with serious crime: forensics people, photographers, scene-of-crime officers (SOCOs in the jargon). That last, grey-haired guy who had emerged from the blue BMW with a heavy black medical bag looked suspiciously like a pathologist, almost certainly from the Home Office recommended list.

For the time being Francis held off from giving his statement. It wasn't as if he were leaving today, and he didn't particularly want to waste good coffee-drinking time in the shuffling, politely grumbling queue that had formed outside the guest lounge downstairs; in which, at twin green baize card tables, sat two officers taking statements, WPC Wendy of earlier and DS Brian Povey. He would pop along later, when the smoke had cleared. Maybe at that point he might get a chance to talk to DCI Julie Morgan herself.

Not that any of this was Francis's business, even if he did have the girlfriend of the deceased camping in his room. But there was no way it wasn't intriguing. What lay behind all this activity, he wondered, as he drained his coffee cup and strolled off down the garden. Was it just a string of police officers covering their respective arses? Was it down to that bruise on Bryce's cheek, the unusually red eyes, or even the love bite? Had somebody – Priya perhaps – said something untoward? Or maybe DS Brian Povey had turned up something else suspicious in the room?

There were lots of people who disliked Bryce, and plenty of

them were here in town this weekend. But who, seriously, hated him enough to want to kill him? In a traditional murder mystery, of course, Dickson would be the main suspect, bigged up at the start, only to be replaced further on with less obvious characters, until finally the least likely person of all would turn out to have done it. But in mundane reality the idea that one writer would do away with another because of a bad review was so ridiculous that of course Dickson wasn't in the frame. A spat with Bryce was just what he needed. A diary item in the *Sentinel*, followed by an amusing five minutes on the *Today* programme on literary feuds – it could do him nothing but good.

If George and Martha had been on the case, Francis thought, who else would they have wanted to speak to? Bryce's two previous partners, for sure; but thinking through what Priya had told him earlier, Francis reckoned it would be interesting to talk also to her jilted boyfriend. Was being spurned in love enough of a motive for murder? In the books, yes. But in real life? Allied with something else, who knew?

Francis's talk wasn't until three that afternoon. Unless he was going to listen to Alain de Botton on the news or Jennifer Saunders on her life in laughs, he had the rest of the morning to kill. What the hell was the harm in satisfying his curiosity? Probably Conal O'Hare would refuse to speak to him and that would be that. But at least he would have tried.

ELEVEN

Crunching up in his Saab onto the big circle of gravel at the front of Wyveridge Hall, Francis smiled to himself. This was more like the setting for a traditional murder mystery; the kind of old English country house that had battlemented towers, tall windows in elegant bays and inside probably still a library and billiard room, if not a length of lead piping or a revolver to hand.

The front door was eight feet of solid oak, complete with decorative brass studs, set inside a little arched porch. Francis let himself into a stone-flagged hallway area, where coats were piled on hooks and wellington and walking boots stood haphazardly by the wall. Beyond, through another, smaller oak door, was a central hall, dark with mahogany panels. On the left was the main staircase, with an elaborate wrought-iron banister, painted pale green under a polished wooden rail. At the far end, up against a faded tapestry of some classical scene (a half-naked maiden either being rescued or set upon by warriors) was a grand piano, its top still covered with a scattering of last night's wine glasses. Francis walked through into a big drawing room, where French windows opened onto a gravel terrace. Beyond and below that was a croquet lawn surrounded by thick green hedges, embellished with the topiary Priya had mentioned – doves, dogs, rabbits, even a small, squat horse. On the far side was a ha-ha and beyond that open countryside.

There was no one around. A couple of half-burned logs in the fireplace indicated a fire, quite something for the end of July. There were more dirty glasses on the mantelpiece and a stale smell of alcohol and tobacco.

Francis heard a sound behind him and turned. It was a short, white-haired woman in pink overalls, carrying a dustpan and brush and a black plastic rubbish sack.

'Good morning,' he said.

'Morning, sir. I'm just going to get this room straight and then it'll all be done for you.'

'Oh no, I'm not staying here. I came out looking for a friend.'

'They're still in bed, most of them. They had one of their parties last night, as you see.' She gave him a nervous smile. 'I don't know. Mr Ranjit is a very nice young gentleman, but they don't half leave a mess for me to clear up in the morning. It's lucky he's such a good tipper, else I might have something to say about it to the boss.'

'Who is the boss?'

'Mr Delancey, sir.'

'He lives here?'

'Oh no. Mr Gerald lives in Berlin. That's why the Hall is rented out. We get all sorts. Wedding parties, house parties, shooting parties, conferences, even, since they installed that Wi-Fi thingy.'

'And how long have you worked here, if I may ask?'

'Fifty-eight years, sir. I started as a parlour maid. Of course, Mr Digby, that's Mr Gerald's father, was the master in them days. We had a butler and a cook and a proper household.'

'And you're the last survivor?'

'Me and Gunther, sir, yes. The German gardener. He came over in the war and never went back.' Her lips pursed. 'A prisoner,' she whispered.

'He must be getting on a bit now.'

'Ninety-two. Still clips the hedges himself. Most of them, anyway. Now I'd better be getting on or I'll never get finished. If any of them are up, sir, you'll most likely find them in the kitchen. Through that door and along to the end.'

Francis was in luck. There was a smell of bacon wafting down the corridor and a couple of house guests already up and about. A skinny blonde, yellow dress over jeans, diaphanous blue scarf slung round her neck, was bent over a cafetière, making coffee. Up at the Aga was a young woman with a mane of dark hair and a Gibson Girl figure in a green and white floral tea dress. She was stirring scrambled eggs with a wooden spoon. A laptop was open on the side, with a little video camera plugged into it and a picture on the screen of partying youth (outside this very house, it looked like).

'Good morning,' said Francis.

'Hiya,' said the dark-haired girl, turning to reveal a pair of thoughtful hazel eyes. 'Would you like some breakfast?'

'No, no, I'm OK, thanks. I've eaten already.'

'We're having a quickie before we shoot. We've got tickets for Hilary Mantel at eleven.'

'Right . . .'

She yawned extravagantly. 'Sorry, bit of a late one last night. Then we're going to see Stephen Appleby at one and the big attraction at three.'

'Which is?' Francis didn't for a moment think she'd say, *Francis Meadowes, the crime writer*. She didn't.

'Bryce Peabody. Didn't you see his piece in the *Sentinel* yesterday? Slagging off Dan Dickson?'

'I did.'

'And then there was, like, this big row between them at Dan's talk.'

'Which I witnessed.'

'Wasn't it great? So Grace and I are hoping that this afternoon is going to be the rematch. Dickson's just the type to want to turn up and make a scene.'

'I think that's unlikely,' said Francis.

'Why?' asked Grace, with just a touch of youthful scorn.

'Because the talk won't be taking place. Bryce Peabody was found dead in his hotel room at four o'clock this morning.'

This piece of information had the desired effect. Two mouths gaped open.

'Oh my God!' said the dark-haired girl; the wooden spoon stalled in the pan.

'You're joking,' said Grace.

'Sadly not.'

'What happened?'

'Nobody knows. It looked at first like it might have been a massive heart attack. But the police are out in force, so . . .'

'Not . . . suicide?'

Francis shrugged and made a face.

'*Murder?*'

'All I can tell you is that the cops seem to be checking every angle. All the guests in the hotel are being asked to give statements, there are forensics people everywhere.'

'Oh my God!' the dark-haired girl repeated, looking sideways at her friend, her hand over her open mouth.

'But he was out here last night,' said Grace. 'With his girlfriend. He seemed fine. Didn't he, Fleur?'

'Actually,' Fleur replied, 'he looked shattered. He was yawning his head off. Then Rory had a big go at him and he left the party.'

'Rory being one of your fellow housemates?'

'Yuh. Drug-crazed barrister cum wannabe novelist prat who's staying out here.' Grace looked round at the kitchen door, presumably in case the prat in question was about to make a sudden entry. 'But no, you're right, Bryce went home early. Because it was only after he'd gone that Priya had that huge row with Conal.' She looked over at her friend. 'We'd better scoff these eggs. I need to get into Mold right away. I'm going to have to forget Hilary Mantel. This is a real story.'

Fleur looked disappointed. 'Won't the *Sentinel* be covering it anyway? I mean, didn't Bryce work for them?'

'Yuh, but still . . . I need to be there.'

'I was looking forward to Mantel. Conal said he was going.'

'Then you'll have him all to yourself, won't you, darling.'

'Don't be silly.'

'Fleur, if I can get something the others can't this could be a real break for me.' She turned to Francis. 'I don't suppose you're driving back into Mold now?'

'I'm sorry, no. I was hoping to talk to your friend Conal.'

'He's probably asleep upstairs,' said Fleur. 'He's not like a suspect or anything, is he?'

'Not as far as I'm aware. Should he be?'

'No,' she said, with a little giggle. 'It was just last night. After his row with Priya he shouted at everyone about how he was going to kill Bryce. Then he vanished.'

'He was totalled, Fleur,' said Grace.

'But he really hates Bryce.' Fleur turned back to Francis. 'We drove down from London with him on Friday and he bent our ears about it for ages. I thought it was quite sweet.'

'Like, er, how?' said Grace.

'Because he's like this battle-hardened foreign correspondent type, doing these mad, dangerous expeditions round the West Bank and Somalia and places, and then he comes back to the UK and he's really upset about his girlfriend.'

'Wounded pride,' said Grace.

'You think?'

'Definitely. Thought his little woman was there for him whatever he did and then was terribly piqued when he discovered she had a mind of her own.'

'He was only away three months. She could have waited.'

'Little Miss Devoted here would have done. She's basically in training to be a Stepford wife.'

'Ha ha, Grace.'

'You said he was asleep upstairs,' said Francis. 'Does that mean you saw him again last night?'

'This morning,' said Fleur. 'He reappeared right at the end of the party. We were all on the terrace as the sun came up.'

The door opened and a curly-haired, dishevelled, slightly chubby figure appeared. 'Hi,' he said, holding out a hand to Francis. 'I'm Conal O'Hare. Who are you?'

TWELVE

'So the bastard's dead,' said Conal, when the young women had gone, taking the laptop with them. 'I can't pretend I'm unhappy about that. After everything he did to screw things up for me . . .'

Francis said nothing. He stayed sitting at the kitchen table while Conal got on with making his breakfast. Then: 'You really felt as if he'd stolen Priya from you?' he asked.

'He knew perfectly well I was her boyfriend. I introduced them, for Christ's sake! This time last year, here at the feckin' festival. The next thing I knew she was working for him.'

'Whose idea was that?'

'Priya wrote to him, got herself an interview, and then, lo and behold, he took her on as his PA. He probably couldn't believe his luck.'

'And then you went away?'

'For three months. It was hardly a lifetime.'

'To Africa?'

'Somalia, yes. To research my current book. I didn't imagine for one moment that when I got back the old walrus would have enticed her into his bed.'

'It does take two to tango.'

'I appreciate that. But he was on her case non-stop, by all

accounts. Taking her out to the smartest places, introducing her to his big name chums. She's an amazing woman, Priya, but she's as susceptible to flattery as any other bloody female.'

'So what happened last night?' asked Francis.

Conal didn't reply. He forked his rashers out of the pan, one by one, switched off the gas, and took a long swig of his coffee. 'What's it to you?' he said eventually.

'I had a long chat with Priya this morning and I wanted to hear your side of the story,' Francis replied. This was stretching it a bit, but he had enough understanding of heartbreak to know that it might do the trick.

'What did she say?' Conal asked, after a few moments.

'I'm not sure it would be fair to repeat it.'

'She thought I was being ridiculous, I suppose, a jealous twat?'

'I really don't think I ought . . .'

'Fine, I respect your discretion.' He sighed. 'I'd been drinking tequila shots on top of sparkling wine, never a good idea. When Priya arrived at the party with Bryce I ignored her. But then I saw her standing all on her own at the end of the terrace. She looked lovelier even than I'd remembered, all shining-eyed in this long red dress, like some sort of Hindu goddess. I was drunk enough by then to think that if I told her I loved her she would admit it had all been a horrible mistake with Bryce and fall back into my arms. So when she started putting up objections, I lost it. Then I realized I was making so much noise that everyone was watching. So I ran off, across the lawn and into the fields. I kept going until I got to the river, then I climbed a tree and sat high up in the branches. I was crying like a baby. It was a full moon, the river was lit up silvery white and the shadows in the trees were as black as ink. I was just wishing that we could have been there together. Sharing the beauty, like we did last year.' Conal smiled ruefully across at Francis. 'Pathetic, eh? But that's how I felt.'

'Nothing pathetic about true feeling,' said Francis, quietly. 'Not in my book, anyway.'

'Once I'd sobered up a little and got over my anger,' Conal went on, 'I realized there was no point crying over spilt milk. If Bryce really was what Priya wanted, good luck to her. She was heartless when she binned me, and I'd told myself she needed to be like that, to make things clear to me. But I don't think that now. I saw a dark side of her last night.'

'You can hardly blame her for defending herself. By all accounts you did come at her out of the blue.'

'Maybe I did. But where was the humanity? Where were the womanly tears?'

'Do you remember shouting at her about how you were going to "kill Bryce", just before you walked off?'

'No. What did I say?'

'Exactly that, apparently. That you were going to kill him – you didn't specify how.'

'And now he's dead. Oh dear.' Conal laughed. 'No one's going to take that seriously though, when I was off my face.'

'There were plenty of witnesses.'

'It was an explosion of justifiable feeling, m'lud. I thought I was over her. That was part of the reason why I came up to Mold. I knew she was going to be here. With him. I thought I could handle it. I was all set to have a meaningless fling with one of the other literary lovelies that my friend Ranjit invites to this place. Instead, as soon as I set eyes on her, I was finished.

What was she doing with this old turd who's over twenty years her senior? For whom she's just a trophy.'

'You don't know that. Presumably he loved her too.'

'Do your research. The man was a serial philanderer. When he met Priya he had a wife and a girlfriend. She was just the latest notch on his bedpost. Something Asian for a change. What was it going to be next year? Jamaican? *Oirish*?'

Francis laughed. 'So what were you offering that was any more than that?'

Conal didn't reply. He took the last corner of his bacon sandwich and wiped it into the remains of the dollop of mustard he'd put on his plate. He slid it into his mouth and chewed it slowly, washing it down with a long gulp of coffee.

'I was going to marry her,' he said eventually. 'If you must know. It was something I thought about a lot while I was away and I'd made my mind up. Seeing all that chaos and horror out in Somalia made me realize I wanted to build something for myself here. She really loved me, you know. Before I went. Before he put his decrepit snout in the trough . . .'

'How long were you with her?'

'Five, six months. We got it together in July last year. I went off to Africa in January.'

Francis let the silence surround them. Outside the bay window, footsteps crunched across the gravel. A car door slammed, an engine started, the noise dwindled away down the drive. Perhaps Grace had got her lift into Mold.

'Did you ever get to meet any of her family?' Francis asked.

'No. Her dad's dead and her mum's up in Derby or somewhere and Priya doesn't see her much. They don't really get on.'

'So you never met her?'

'No. It's no big deal. She hardly ever goes up there.'

'And what about you? Did *you* ever invite her home?'

'Home home, you mean? No, we hadn't got to that stage. My folks are back in County Wicklow, heavy duty Catholics. If I'd taken her there they'd have assumed we were heading up the aisle.'

'Would they have had a problem with that?'

'Are they typical Irish racists, d'you mean? No, they take great pride in their charitable Christian open-mindedness. If anything they'd have gone over the top the other way. Cooked her a curry to make her feel welcome, that sort of thing.' Conal chuckled.

'How long did you stay up in your tree?' Francis asked, after a few moments.

'No idea. An hour maybe. I lost track of time.'

'And then what?'

'I came down.'

'And . . .?'

'I headed over the fields to the house. I sneaked in the back way and went up to my room. I knew I'd made an arse of myself and I didn't want to discuss it with anyone. I crashed out for awhile, then I was woken by a high-pitched scream in a room right below me. It was some Aussie girl who thought she was being attacked by one of the other lunatics in this house party. She'd already left by the time I got down there. The rest of them were wasted, sitting around on benches on the terrace watching the dawn.'

'Who was there?'

'Four or five of them. My friend Ranjit, who organizes this

whole thing; his girlfriend Carly; then Eva, who's this American poet; Fleur, who you just met . . . I was mainly talking to Fleur.'

It was a pretty feeble alibi, Francis thought, as he drove back into Mold. Yet Conal *had* been seen heading down towards the river and then again on the terrace in the dawn. It didn't make a lot of sense that he'd somehow got into Mold, done away with Bryce and got back in time for the end of the party – especially if he'd been drunk. Having said that, it was perfectly possible. There were several hours around the critical time when there was only Conal's word for it that he'd crashed out; and of course he could have been acting drunk.

THIRTEEN

The police had now closed down the bar, restaurant, terrace and garden of the White Hart. Resident guests were being allowed to stay in their rooms, but had to keep to the front entrance and main staircase and make arrangements to drink and eat elsewhere. Just down the road The Coffee Cup on the corner was busy with festivalgoers leafing through Sunday newspapers. But it wasn't the headlines they were talking about. 'Dead on the bed' . . . 'statements from *everybody*' . . . 'but at the peak of his career' . . . 'come off it, would he really stoop to . . .?' . . . 'well, the body's gone off now, unless that was a giant breadstick I saw' . . .

Back in Francis's room, there was no sign of Priya. Just the soft leather bag she'd brought along from Room 29 earlier; inside, visible, were her washbag, a couple of colourful T-shirts and a pair of black, shiny plastic trousers. Next to this on the bed was a transparent blue scarf that – hey, hey – was exactly like the one Grace had been wearing when Francis had seen her at Wyveridge, barely two hours before. It looked like she'd already got her interview – and he hadn't even told her his room number!

Francis found the note cards for his talk on the chest of drawers by the TV. They were exactly where he'd left them, still bound by the lilac rubber band that had once held a bundle of Peruvian Fairtrade asparagus. Was it his imagination, or were they ever so slightly out of kilter? Francis scooped the little package into his man-bag and headed off downstairs. The bar and dining rooms were empty and silent. The queue for giving statements had abated, so he went in and made the acquaintance of Detective Sergeant Brian Povey, who was sitting alone at a card table in the corner of the guest lounge.

Francis hadn't given a police statement before. He found it an intriguingly old-fashioned procedure, with DS Povey writing notes in longhand, then compiling a draft and reading it back, before finally getting the necessary signature. It reduced what had actually happened to a few bland sentences, and how helpful would they be in catching a murderer?

At four twenty a.m. I was woken from sleep by loud screams outside my bedroom at the White Hart (Room 21). I came out to find Ms Priya Kaur sitting on the stairs at the end of the corridor in a state of considerable distress. I comforted her in the corridor and when other hotel guests appeared took temporary charge of the situation . . .

Povey was throughout admirably polite and patient.

'Funny, isn't it,' said Francis, at the end, 'I'm a crime writer by profession and yet I've never even seen anyone give a police statement, let alone given one myself.'

'What kind of crime writing is that then?'

Francis explained; and was then gratified to discover that not only had DS Povey heard of George Braithwaite, he was a fan. 'I love your denouements,' he said. 'Never quite what you expect.'

'I do my best.'

'And the way,' DS Povey went on enthusiastically, 'that wife of his, what's she called . . .?'

'Martha.'

'Martha, yes, keeps getting in the way with her bright suggestions. Truer to life than you'd imagine, especially round here.' He raised his eyebrows suggestively. 'I tell you what though. Her nibs likes your stuff too.'

'Your boss?'

'Yes.'

'I'm flattered.'

Really, he was. Two real police personnel, approving of his work.

'Of course it bears no relation to the shit we really have to put up with!' Povey laughed and Francis somehow managed a smile in return.

Outside, the uniform on the front door was the same sharp young blonde – Wendy – whom Francis had first met at five in the morning.

'Hello again,' he said. 'You're having a long day.'

'Looks like it, sir.'

'They've moved the body now, I understand.'

'I'm afraid I'm not allowed to discuss operational details, sir.'

Francis turned right down the road out of town, which led past a row of neat bungalows and then a long, dense hedgerow, with a muddy ditch in front and an open field behind, until he came to The Sun Rising, a quaint-looking old pub whose sign featured a cheery yellow orb winking as it rose over the edge of a cartoon-book green hill. The inside lived up to the promise of the exterior: wood-panelled front and back bars, no games machines, and only discreet modernisation. Outside, picnic tables ran down a pretty garden to apple trees at the bottom. The barman was rather a splendid specimen: bald as a billiard ball, with greying mutton-chop sideboards, and an accent that was a little too strainedly posh to be convincing.

'Yes, sir, and what can I do *you* for?' he repeated to each customer in turn, like something out of a bad sitcom. Eventually he came to Francis, giving him the sort of super-polite reception that he often got from rural people, to show that whatever might be said elsewhere about the denizens of the English countryside, there was absolutely no racial prejudice here. Francis returned the compliment, giving his host the benefit of his best received English accent as he asked for a pint of ginger beer shandy.

'That's half ginger beer and half bitter, is it, sir?'

'Yes, thanks.'

'Any particular bitter?'

'Something good and local?'

'I'll give you the Dewkesbury Demon then.'

'Not too strong?'

'Three point eight. That do you?'

'Fine. It sounded rather stronger.'

'Oh no, sir, he's a relatively puny demon, the Dewkesbury one.'

Traditional taproom relations happily established, Francis ordered fishcakes and chips. If you wanted to eat outside, you were given a wooden bird with a number on it, which you placed on your table of choice; but today, he saw, there wasn't a single one left. He was about to find a dark corner indoors, when a grey-haired couple started to get up from one of the tables down by the apple trees. Francis shot over and asked if they were leaving. They were.

'OK if I join you?' he asked the other pair who were sharing. Even as he noted the milky-blue eyes of the woman with tightly curled dark hair, and the muscly black guy in the yellow T-shirt beside her, his stump neatly wrapped in a tailored sleeve, he realized that this must be Anna the rejected mistress and her new boyfriend, Marvin the Marine. What a beautiful coincidence; you really couldn't have made it up.

He put his bird down next to their drinks. 'Thanks,' he said. And then, after a few moments, 'Bit packed today, isn't it?'

'Yes,' said the woman. 'They've had to close the bar at the White Hart, so I think a lot of people have decamped here.'

There was another pause. Francis contemplated the dappled sunlight filtering through his pint of shandy and Anna's adjacent ginger beer. Then, with a jolt, he noticed that Marvin's good hand had no thumb. Just four fingers and a mini stump.

'Are you staying there too?' he asked.

'Yes,' Anna replied. 'And we were really enjoying it. Lively bar, nice restaurant, quite funky rooms, but it's all gone a bit spooky now . . . after the events of last night . . . which we pretty much slept through, being right at the other end of the hotel.'

'Didn't the fire alarm wake you up?'

'Only briefly. You?'

'I was in a room right next to the action, I'm afraid.'

'Oh *really*.'

She was as inquisitive as Francis himself. Bit by bit he fed her the key elements of the morning and his place in them, wondering if and when she would fess up to the reason for her interest. After a bit they exchanged names and Francis's suspicions were confirmed. He shook Anna's delicate, artistic hand and, in as natural a fashion as he could muster, Marvin's chunkier fingers, and explained what he was doing at the festival.

'Sorry to be so curious about everything,' Anna said with a light laugh. 'The thing is, I knew Bryce . . .'

'Really?'

Beside her, Marvin frowned. 'Sweetheart,' he began, his voice a gravelly bass with a strong Midlands accent.

She put a hand on his good arm, which rippled with well-defined muscle. 'It's fine, Marv. No, the thing is,' she went on, turning to Francis, 'I was his girlfriend for a while.'

'No wonder you're interested . . .'

She shrugged. 'So what about all these *polizei* everywhere?' she asked. 'Do they know something we don't?'

'Since they're not talking to anybody,' Francis replied, 'my guess is as good as yours. They may be erring on the side of caution, what with Bryce being the age he was and apparently healthy. Which was the case, as far as I can understand. I mean, he didn't have any underlying conditions that you knew about, did he?'

'He had high cholesterol. Of the wrong sort. That he refused to even attempt to reduce. Apart from making the occasional half-hearted jog across Hampstead Heath.'

'No special diets then?'

She laughed. 'He used to sometimes buy that Benecol spread to put on his toast. As if that was going to make much difference to a man who ate out in restaurants all the time.'

'What about drink?'

'Plenty of that. Every now and then he'd have these stints of trying to give up for a month, usually in January, but then he'd get so grumpy he'd be back on it after a fortnight.'

'Drugs?' Francis asked.

'Sweetheart,' Marvin growled again.

Anna gave him a swift, uncompromising look. It was clear she wasn't going to be told what to do by anyone, least of all her new boyfriend.

'Bryce wasn't a spliffer, put it that way,' she said.

'Something else?'

'Maybe.'

'I'm guessing coke.'

Her smile gave her away. 'He didn't do it a lot,' she said. 'But he wouldn't turn it down and yes, he did buy the occasional wrap for special occasions.'

'And that was it?'

'He did a bit of ecstasy in the Eighties, I believe. But he'd packed all that in by the time I met him. We had a couple of Es right at the start, but then he started worrying about his age, you know, the effect it might have on his heart.'

'Fair enough. And you'd never have put him down as the suicidal type?'

'Bryce? God no!'

Francis laughed at her reaction. 'Why not?'

'Too much vanity.'

'Don't vain people ever kill themselves?'

'I'm sure they do. But not here, not now. It might be a possibility if he were miles from anywhere with nobody to look after him and laugh at his jokes. But at the start of a literary festival. With a brand-new girlfriend. When he was about to give one of his talks. To a sold-out tent. I don't think so.'

'When it comes to his enemies among the literati,' Francis asked, 'can you seriously imagine any of them wanting to bump him off? Getting something into *Private Eye* would surely be easier.'

'Believe me,' Anna said, 'there are plenty of writers who wouldn't mind seeing Bryce dead. But no, you're right, they'd be more likely to try and murder his reputation than murder him.'

'Who were his particular enemies?'

'Dan Dickson is up there. Especially after yesterday. As for the others, Bryce writes a big review every week. Many of them are negative. But that's his *schtick*. I suppose the interesting thing about all this is that a literary festival is the one time where quite a few of his victims are gathered in one place. If it is murder, it's a murderer with a sense of humour.'

'And what about you? How did you feel about him?'

'You think I did it!' She laughed and glanced sideways at Marvin, whose scowl had deepened further. 'No, I have plenty of good reasons to be cross with Bryce. But murder isn't quite my style. I have subtler ways of operating.'

'Such as?'

'Never you mind.'

'Number seventeen,' a waitress up the garden was calling.

The arrival of his fishcakes gave Francis an excuse to change the subject to the neutral topic of pub food: how pretentious it so often was in the countryside, and how the spread of gastro-pubs had all but destroyed the traditional old boozer. From there they segued on to literary festivals and their proliferation. What had begun with Hay and Cheltenham had now grown to the point where there was barely a charming rural spot left in the UK without its own little litfest.

With each step away from a discussion of the newly deceased ex, Marv's facial expression relaxed, until by the time they were onto festivals he was laughing out loud. Francis had realized that there was no way he was going to get anything significant out of Anna while her personal protection detail was around. If he wanted to know more, he would have to try and get her alone later.

FOURTEEN

An hour before his talk, at two o'clock, Francis made his way down to the main site through the big car park, where groups of festivalgoers loitered between talks, chattering excitedly, studying programmes or just hanging out. He passed the fluttering purple banners proclaiming 22ND MOLD-ON-WOLD LITERARY FESTIVAL and paced on through the gates into the community school which was the centre of events. It was an unworthy thought, but with the competition removed, perhaps he'd picked up a few more punters for his talk. As he hovered by the entrance to the festival administration office, no less a personage than Laetitia Humble rushed up to him.

'Francis!' she cried. She flashed him a wide, toothy smile and though she didn't quite meet his eye, her mascara-laden lashes fluttered madly. '*So* glad you're here,' she gushed. 'There's been such a lot of interest we've had to move you into the Big Tent. In fact, I think you're going to sell out. Holly,' she called to one of the festival helpers, who was bent fetchingly over a nearby photocopier, 'could you be a darling and check with ticketing how Francis Meadowes is doing.'

'I guess Bryce . . .' he began.

'Poor Bryce.' Laetitia's face switched in an instant to tragic mode. Francis remembered people saying she had once been an actor; clearly she hadn't forgotten her skills. 'It's such dreadful news. We're all in deep shock.' Now she took his arm and smiled up at him confidingly. 'I gather you were one of the people who found the body.'

News travelled fast in this place. 'Not actually found,' he said. 'But I was in the room just along the corridor, so I was one of the first on the scene.'

Laetitia's phone trilled. She glanced at the screen and did a half-roll of her eyes. 'Sebastian Faulks. Now what does he want all of a sudden?' She clicked it off and her gaze returned to Francis. 'So do you think you'll want to talk about that at all?'

'Bryce?'

'Yes. Finding him and . . .'

'I wasn't intending to.'

'It's almost certain to come up in questions. So you might feel you wanted to address it upfront. I'm sure people are genuinely dying – I mean, er, gagging – to know what you think. As a crime writer. I know I am.'

'Laetitia.' Holly was back again. 'Francis Meadowes is sold out.'

'Fabuloso!' She grinned at Francis. 'What did I tell you? Holly, darling, this is Francis Meadowes.'

'Oh. Wow. Hi.' Holly's eyes widened in excitement.

'Hi,' Francis replied; he could get used to this. 'So how many is sold out?' he asked Laetitia, as Holly scuttled back to the photocopier.

'In the Big Tent. Five hundred.'

'Goodness. And only yesterday . . .'

'You had twenty or something. I know. We offered people who were booked for Bryce either a straight refund or a swapsie with you and the other three o'clock. Fortunately we've had quite a lot of swapsies. At least for your event.'

'Remind me what the other one is?'

'Virginia Westcott. She writes kind of upmarket romantic fiction. Masquerading as something more significant.'

'Oh yes. I met her briefly earlier . . .'

'Not my cuppa char, to be absolutely frank with you, but she is very pop. Anyway, *so* can't wait for your thing. Gotta dash now, but you know where the Green Room is. Get yourself a coffee and chillax . . .'

'Thanks. And perhaps I'll see you—'

'At your event. Of course you will. I'm introducing you.' Laetitia's phone rang again and she glanced down at the screen. 'Andrew, darling, sorry, I was just chewing the fat-bat with Francis Meadowes . . . the crime writer, where've you been? Too busy penning those wonderful poems of yours for your own good. Anyway, he seems to think . . .'

She was out of earshot. Francis cut through the busy ticketing hall where a SOLD OUT banner was now pasted over 3 PM. FRANCIS MEADOWES ON CRIME. He found the Green Room round the back: a small marquee filled with comfy armchairs and low tables. The Sunday newspapers were scattered about, and there was a sideboard with an urn of tea and a Kenco coffee machine stewing away by a stack of white china cups and saucers and a tin of assorted biscuits. Further along were plates of sandwiches and bottles of beer and wine. Francis was tempted to have another beer, but opted for tea instead. *Five hundred people.* He needed to be on tip-top form. There was nothing worse than getting up in front of an audience after a drink or two and realising your reactions had slowed. He had done that once, thankfully in Shetland, where the three dour rows of punters had appeared not to notice, but it wasn't an experience he wanted to repeat.

He contemplated a Sunday paper, but the headlines seemed irrelevant now. On a side table there was a pile of blue photo albums. A printed sign read MOLD FESTIVAL PHOTO ARCHIVE – NOT TO BE REMOVED. This last instruction was a bit unnecessary, as each of the books was attached to a central ring with a length of brass chain. There was one for each year, stretching back to Mold's beginnings in the early 1990s. Francis picked 1998 and was rewarded with snaps of a much younger Laetitia, with high cheekbones and hair cut short like a pixie, arm round a genial-looking old boy with a neat white moustache. *LAETITIA AND HENRY HUMBLE, FESTIVAL FOUNDERS*, read the handwritten caption (though '*LAETITIA AND*' and the '*S*' of *FOUNDERS* looked as if they'd been added later). Francis flicked on, through pages of famous literary names in earlier incarnations. How young they all looked, these Ackroyds and Amises and Barneses and Bainbridges and Bakewells and Dicksons and Drabbles and Motions and Weldons and . . . here was an interesting one. *Young Guns! Bryce Peabody, Scarlett Paton-Jones, Dan Dickson, Tilly Bardwell*. The four of them were posing in front of a tumbledown stone cottage half submerged in brambles. So that pretty bob-haired blonde between Bryce and Dan was Scarlett. And Bryce and Dan had been friends . . .

Enough of that! Francis had work to do. He took the cards for his talk from his bag and sank into one of the battered sofas, just along from – oh no, it was his competition! As he caught the badger-woman's eye, she smiled.

'Francis Meadowes.'

'Yes.'

'We meet again.' She held out a bony-fingered hand. 'Virginia Westcott. I think we're on at the same time in the slot that poor Bryce has conveniently vacated. Though by all accounts you've done rather better out of him than I have.'

'So Laetitia was saying. Yesterday they were talking about moving me to the School Room because I'd sold so few.' He laughed.

'And now you're in the Big Tent.'

'So it seems.'

'While I'm in the School Room.'

'Oh no, I'm sorry.' Francis's face fell. How obtuse of him not to spot that one coming.

'Obviously the vulgar hordes are bound to be attracted to a crime writer who everybody now knows was first at the scene.'

'Do they?'

'The gossip at this festival is toxic. People have been tweeting about it all morning . . .'

'I'm afraid I'm not on Twit—'

'Though actually, if people understood anything about this particular story, it would be me they'd be coming to see.'

'I'm sorry, I don't follow you.'

'Bryce and I . . . go back.' Virginia paused. 'As undergraduates at Cambridge we were great friends.'

'Really. I didn't realize . . .'

'That the old shit was that ancient. Were you going to say?

It's amazing how some of these chaps get away with it, isn't it? No, Bryce had clocked his half-century all right. One can only hope he didn't have any problems in the bedroom department with pretty little Preeta . . .'

'Priya.'

'That's the one.'

There was a pause. Virginia met his eye, then flashed him a rather awkward, artificial smile.

'So you met Bryce at college?' Francis asked.

'University, please. Cambridge has many colleges. But yes, in our first term. At one of those fresher meetings, you know, when you go along and wonder whether you're going to join the Christian Sky-Diving Society or what-have-you.'

'And did you?'

'What?'

'Join the Christian Sky-Diving Society?'

'Don't be absurd! There wasn't one.'

'But you met Bryce?'

'I did. He was very taken with me, I can tell you. I had the power at that point. For a start I was a woman, and in the late Seventies in Cambridge there were something like nine men to every one woman, so getting a girlfriend at all was quite a challenge, unless you wanted to go out with a nurse or someone from one of the secretarial colleges.'

'I see . . .' Francis kept his thoughts to himself; the snobbery of this remark was so throwaway it was almost unwitting.

'And then I'd been to a co-ed school in North London which I'd loathed, but had somehow made me *reasonably* trendy. My stockings were purple, rather than blue, put it that way.'

'What about Bryce?'

'What about him?'

'How "trendy" was he?'

This made Virginia laugh. 'Not very at all. Rather an earnest, spotty little fellow with dreadful National Health specs. He'd been at a grammar school in Solihull and still had a bit of that horrible Birmingham twang. Cambridge was terribly public school in those days, so poor Bryce didn't know anyone. He was very happy to be friends with me.'

'More than just friends, though?'

'What an inquisitive chap you are. Yes, we did get it together. But not immediately. I was a virgin, would you believe? Very concerned about what I should do with my much-prized cherry. Just lose it in a mad one-night stand so I could be like all the others, or keep it for someone special. I liked Bryce, and I could see he was terribly clever, but I wasn't sure that he was The One.'

'So he persisted?'

'He did. That's – that was one of the things about Bryce. He was highly persistent.'

'But it didn't last?'

'Evidently not. No, two years later he'd suddenly made good. He was editor of the student newspaper, *Stop Press*, and was starting to get known for his brutal theatre reviews. He didn't need me any more.'

'So he left you?'

'For the inevitable brilliant fresher. In the summer term before my finals. I took it all much worse than I should have done. Totally messed up my exams and barely scraped a 2.2.'

'When by rights you should have got a First?'

'I would have done if he hadn't messed me around so dread-fully. Promising me things he then went back on. The sad thing is I was far too young to realize how much more important a First is than a silly student love affair.'

'Is it? Once I left York, nobody ever mentioned my degree.'

'It's there, though. On your CV. All the key employers take note of it.'

'Don't tell me, Bryce got his First.'

'Course he did. His double First. He worked bloody hard for it, don't think he didn't. I watched him swotting and sweating. Under that newly debonair exterior was the same old grammar school boy, who worked late and got up early and never let himself go too much.'

'It wasn't you that murdered him, was it, Virginia?'

In Francis's books, George Braithwaite often used the direct-question technique to shock his suspects into surprising revelations. Now Virginia laughed, Francis thought, just a bit too loudly.

'What! Get my revenge thirty years later? Perhaps I should have done.' Her eyes met his quite candidly, but in her lap, he noticed, her hands were trembling. 'So do you seriously think there was foul play, Francis? You were the one who saw him this morning. Wouldn't let anyone else in the room, would you?'

'A herd of guests trampling around in dressing gowns and slippers wouldn't have helped the police very much.'

'You haven't answered my question. What was in there to arouse your suspicions?'

'Nothing much.'

'What does that mean?'

'There was one item I was rather intrigued by. A silver Parker 45, with the initials V.R.C.W., a date from the Seventies, and a Latin tag, *memento mori* . . .'

Virginia's face was a picture: of excitement mixed with . . . was that sadness, or something more sinister?

'And where was that?' she asked.

'Right by the bed.'

She was looking into the middle distance, almost as if in a trance. 'So he kept it . . . all these years . . .'

'I was going to ask you your middle names, but I guess . . .'

'. . . there's no need. Ruth Constance. No, I gave him that pen. For his twentieth birthday. A week before he took his part ones.'

'And garnered the first part of his First?'

'Indeed.'

'Remind me exactly what *memento mori* means?' Francis asked.

Virginia pursed her lips. 'Literally,' she said, '"Remember, you must die." But metaphorically, more like, "Don't take your life for granted." The sort of motto that seems terribly sophisticated when you're nineteen.' She looked away across the tent for a moment. 'I can honestly say I had no idea he still had it, let alone used it. Perhaps he hung onto it for luck. He was always oddly superstitious. So what else did you find?'

'That was about it. As far as I could tell it could easily have been a heart attack that killed him.'

'What did the police say?' Virginia asked, eyes narrowing.

'The police were a pair of rookies. Luckily there was a medic there too. Local GP. He seemed to think a cardiac arrest was the likely picture. That or some kind of brain event. Hopefully the post-mortem will confirm.'

She sighed deeply. 'Poor Bryce. A completely inadequate shit of a man, but generally an intelligent read. In a strange way I shall miss my weekly dose of viciousness.'

'Did he ever review you?'

'Funnily enough, he left my first novel alone, but he couldn't seem to bear it when I looked set to repeat my success. I was too much of a threat to him, I suppose. You know he always wanted to be a novelist too?'

'I didn't.'

'When we were at Cambridge we were going to be George Eliot and Henry James. Reimagine the great Victorian novel for the modern age. A simple enough task it seemed to us then. But in the real world Bryce's efforts never got anywhere. His talent was too flashy, I suppose. Brilliant at the one-line put down, but he never had the stamina for the lonely long haul. Anyway, yes, he ignored *Entente Cordiale*. But when it came to *A Fine Imagined Thing*, he couldn't help himself. Actually, it was embarrassing, because the sheer level of vitriol made it clear to anyone with half a brain that it wasn't about the book at all. None the less, at the time, it was a shock. I was foolishly upset. It seemed like adding insult to injury.'

Injury being binned ten years before, presumably. 'Did you say anything to him?' Francis asked.

'I did. Against everyone's advice. You're not supposed to bleed in public in the literary world. I didn't care. I wrote a letter to his stupid newspaper, pointing out the various errors of fact he'd made, and followed it up with a personal missive. Didn't stop him, though. Every time I've put my head above the parapet since he's shot me down. It's pathetic.'

'And face to face. How was that? Did you stop speaking?'

'We barely spoke anyway. Just a nod or the occasional surface exchange at launch parties. Sad, isn't it, when you think how well I once knew him. So much better than the long string of floozies he's had since.'

'Better than his long-term partner, Scarlett?'

She ignored this quiet reality check.

'Who's to say?' she replied. 'I do think that if you get to know someone intimately when they're nineteen or twenty you under-stand them in a way that others can't. Before they've had a chance to put on all those adult airs and graces that fool the world so convincingly.'

'And what about you?' Francis asked.

'What about me?'

'Did you ever find anyone to match Bryce?'

Virginia looked straight back at him and for a moment the sadness in her eyes spoke volumes; then she recovered herself and the ironic twinkle returned. 'My my, you do love the direct question, Mr Meadowes. I'm surprised you didn't try for a career in broadcasting. You'd have given Paxman or Harrumphrys a run for their money. No, as soon as I left Cambridge I was heartily relieved I'd got rid of Bryce. I was free to do all sorts of things I'd otherwise never have done. Travel. See the world. In my twenties I lived for five years in Paris. That experience was the basis of *Entente Cordiale*. If I'd stayed with Peabody I'd have been buried in nappies, more than likely. I seriously doubt if I'd have been published. I've seen too many of my clever female friends swamped by the demands of procreation. Whatever they say about the march of feminism, it's still the women that bear the brunt of making a family. And always will be, in my view. Until they invent wombs for men . . .'

'So you've a new novel out this summer?'

'This week. To tie in with the festival. *Sickle Moon Rises*. It's in the bookshop if you're interested.'

'When was your last one? I'm afraid I can't remember.'

'How sweet you are, Mr Meadowes. There's really no reason why you should know about my work. I'm hardly a name to be conjured with. But no, it was almost nine years ago.'

'And Bryce had his usual go?'

'Savaged it in a couple of paragraphs. In a round-up of what he offensively called "hag-lit" . . . I'd given the Aga Saga a new meaning for the over-fifties . . . I was to Joanna Trollope what she was to Anthony . . .'

'Trollope?'

'Of course. Silly, sexist nonsense like that. I'm afraid I've forgotten most of it.'

'Nine years is a long gap. Did you hit a block?'

'Well, after that review, and, hardly surprisingly, rather poor sales, I was dropped by my publisher. Too "midlist", apparently, though they never said that when I was selling well. Nor did they ever consider that their appalling jacket design or their near-comatose marketing department might have had something to do with it. Then my agent died. Run over by an Ocado van while chatting on his mobile phone on Highgate Hill. I couldn't find another decent one for ages. Either too ancient and grand or too young with no experience or contacts. The old story. I ran through an alcoholic ex-BBC producer and the fantasist daughter of a famous actor before I found darling Harriet.

'Then my mother had a hideous battle with cancer, which she lost. Father of course was hopeless without her. Could barely boil an egg. Tried to teach himself to cook from the *Good Housekeeping* book I gave him, but failed miserably. He was always calling me up, saying things like, "What does it mean, *fold* sugar into the mixture, they don't explain." We had exploding coffee percolators, the works. Then one day he fell down the steep stone stairs I'd been warning him about for ages. Two funerals in two years. A relationship I was in at the time didn't survive the fallout. So all in all not a terribly fun time.'

'I'm sorry.'

'Don't be. Life has its little surprises. But it's all grist to the mill for us authors, isn't it? And fortunately Father left me enough to keep writing, regardless of whatever sales I might achieve.'

Francis nodded thoughtfully. 'And are you pleased with this one?' he asked.

'As a matter of fact, I am. I can honestly say it's the best thing I've done. Whether it will storm bestseller lists and win prizes remains to be seen.'

'And Bryce can't diss it now, whatever happens.'

'Indeed.' Virginia looked down at her watch. 'Oh my giddy aunt, it's ten to three. We'd better get to our respective publics, Francis.'

'Yes.' Francis felt the familiar rush of nerves at the thought of that packed Big Tent. 'I suppose we better had.'

FIFTEEN

Conal had made a special effort to be at Francis Meadowes' event. After that odd encounter this morning he'd found himself wondering why exactly he had opened up so much, to this total stranger, about stuff that he was under no obligation to share. Now he took his place in the Big Tent, near the back on his own. Involuntarily, he looked around for Priya, but he couldn't see her. Down near the front he spotted the Wyveridge lot: dread-locked Ranjit, swan-necked Carly, bearded Adam, cute Fleur, Earth Mother Eva, that madman Rory and his speccy pal Neville. Only Grace was missing, which was puzzling, as she'd been so vocal earlier about how interested she was in Bryce's death. Perhaps, like him, she was on her own, elsewhere in this jostling, expectant crowd. As the tent hushed, and Meadowes came on, two steps behind Laetitia Humble, Conal leant forward.

'Good afternoon,' Meadowes began, once Laetitia's rather OTT intro was out of the way. 'I must say it's great to see such a full tent. Yesterday when I checked, I had just twenty-eight signed up. Now, I believe, it's closer to five hundred and twenty-eight. So first off I'd like to thank those original supporters, wherever they are. Of course I am aware that this audience, the biggest I've ever faced at a literary festival, is down to two related things. One, simply, that the talk scheduled for Bryce Peabody has had to be cancelled. And two, the reason for that cancellation: that Bryce was, as I'm sure you all know by now, found dead in his room at the White Hart in the early hours of this morning.' Meadowes looked around slowly and for five seconds you could, as they say, have heard a pin drop. Just a couple of coughs from the crowd and far away, across town, the bleating of sheep.

'Because my room was adjacent to his,' Francis went on, 'I was first on the scene, so I got to see the dead body *in situ* and was there when the emergency services turned up. Laetitia Humble has asked me if I'd be happy to say a few words about all that, and the answer, Laetitia, is yes, a few words. But if you don't mind I'll leave that to the end of my talk, when I'd be happy to take questions too . . .'

Clever bastard, Conal thought, as an excited buzz filled the tent. Nobody was going to get up and leave now, were they? They had to quieten down and listen as Meadowes moved on to his chosen subject – the amateur detective in literature. He traced the development well, making interesting links across the genre and being funny about the danger of these non-professional know-alls coming across as smug or otherwise irritating. 'I don't want to upset any Dorothy Sayers fans, but I'm afraid I've always thought Lord Peter Wimsey was infuriatingly pleased with himself. I also find Poirot a bit too effing twinkly at times. And don't get me started on Jonathan Creek . . .'

Though the audience were enjoying it, laughing in the right places, not exhibiting the restlessness that afflicted some sessions, it was clear they were also longing for the end – and questions.

When the time came, these weren't about Conan Doyle, Chesterton or Christie.

'Yes,' said Laetitia, who had taken charge, 'the hand in the middle, the woman with the long dark hair.'

'Hi, Francis.'

'Hi.'

'I'm a big fan of the George Braithwaite books, I've read them all, and I'm one of the twenty-eight you talked about at the beginning who were going to come anyway.'

'Thank you.'

'That was a fascinating talk.'

'Thank you again.'

'But what I wanted to ask you, perhaps a bit cheekily, was what George would have made of the scene you encountered in the White Hart this morning.'

'I can see I'm not going to be let off the hook on this one,' said Francis.

'No you're not!' shouted someone.

'OK then, now let me see. I think George would have been, as he always does, checking everything carefully, looking out for those unusual clues that other people might have missed.'

'Such as?'

Francis's face assumed a sober expression. 'There were a couple of intriguing details in that room this morning, but I can honestly say that Bryce himself did look as if he'd passed away in his sleep. But seriously, even if all this is bound to be the subject of gossip around the festival, I don't think I should be speculating in public about what I personally might or might not think.'

'Hear hear!' said a man with long blond hair and a big nose

who was sitting down near the front. It was that TV chef guy, Conal realized, who did the *Family Man* show. There were other mutters of approval, as well as a couple of loud groans.

There were five hands up now. 'Yes,' said Laetitia, 'the man about ten rows back, with the thick black specs.'

'Are we to intuit, from this coyness of yours, that you do in fact suspect foul play?'

Francis smiled patiently. 'I think I've just answered that.'

'But you haven't. At all. You were there in the bedroom. What are these "intriguing details" you titillate us with?'

Up on the big video screen behind his head, you could see the feeling in Francis's face. Irritation in the furrows of his forehead, quelled with a tight smile. 'As anyone who's been near the White Hart today knows,' he said, 'the police are following their own investigation into the death of Bryce Peabody. I've already given them a short statement, and as one of the first on the scene I expect to be interviewed in due course by the officer in charge. That's really all I want to say about this. Now are there any questions on the rest of my talk?'

'Is that really all you're going to give us?'

'I'm afraid it is, yes.'

'Was that why I listened to your potted history of crime-writing for forty minutes – what a frigging let-down!' Having spat that sentence into the microphone, the man in black specs got to his feet and stalked towards the exit. But even as the audience sighed with excitement at this little storm-out, Francis was rescued; a woman with a colourful length of cloth tied into her hair wanted to know what George Braithwaite thought of Francis Meadowes.

Francis chuckled. 'I'm not sure he's that aware of me. He doesn't, like many detectives, have much time for crime fiction. He sees enough horror on the job without wanting to read about it. Plus I suspect that he thinks most crime novels are a bit artificial anyway.'

'Why?'

'Because he knows that most murders in the real world are committed by desperate, vicious, or crazy people in squalid circumstances. While murderers in crime fiction, even of the more realistic kind, tend to be altogether more glamorous figures.'

'Are you saying your books don't contain lifelike characters?'

'No, I'm not. I sincerely hope they do. Which is precisely why George would never read one. Yes, the woman in the pink specs. Down towards the front on the left.'

'This might be a bit of a cheeky question. But I'm interested in the fact that you are of mixed-race origins, while George Braithwaite is a white man. Weren't you ever tempted to create a detective hero who could tackle some of the issues around race that you yourself must encounter all the time?'

As Francis paused, you could see the tent wondering which way he'd go.

'I am, yes,' he said, 'an individual from a mixed-race background, but as those of you who've looked at my website or read interviews with me know, I was adopted at a young age by white parents, and brought up in a pretty white world. The grammar school I went to in Kent had only one other person of colour all the time I was there, so it would have been much harder for me to get all the little wrinkles of, say, a London

Afro-Caribbean or a Bradford Pakistani background right, and I didn't see the point, because there are other writers who understand about those things far better than I. As for your point about race, I hate to say this, but we really are all much the same under the skin. I do quite often think like a white man, you know. My biological mother was white. As someone said about Barack Obama, in other circumstances he could have been the first white President of Kenya.'

There was laughter at this, mixed with a general hum of approval. The audience were loving Meadowes and there were now ten or fifteen hands waiting like schoolchildren to be picked upon.

'Yes, the lady five rows back,' said Laetitia. 'With the purple top and the, er, white hair.'

'Are you saying that you're a coconut?'

Oh no, thought Conal. There was always one, wasn't there? Meadowes had put on a studiedly puzzled face, though surely he knew what she meant.

'I'm sorry,' he said. 'Could you elucidate?'

'A *coconut*,' she repeated loudly; and you could almost hear the audience wince. 'I'm told it's someone who's black or, erm, coloured on the outside and white on the inside.'

'I thought you might mean that. It's an interesting expression, isn't it? And one of several of a similar type, often used by black or brown communities about their own kind. "Oreo" is another example, which you come across in the States, referring to the chocolate biscuit with the white filling. I believe some people use "Bounty" in a similar way over here, although I can't say I've ever heard it. In Hong Kong they say "banana".' Meadowes smiled and looked out over the tent. 'It's a concept that I find both puzzling and a little racist in itself. To be white on the inside. What does that mean? That I'm fastidiously punctual, or crap at dancing? You tell me.'

More laughter, of the relieved variety. Meadowes had saved her and people were grateful for that, whatever they thought of the question. Down the front Laetitia had spotted her moment and was up on stage thanking him with the usual festival clichés. After the extended applause, Conal got to his feet and joined the surge of people making for the exits. He had said more to Francis than he'd intended this morning, and then regretted it. Now he felt better about the whole thing.

He headed down the front to join the Wyveridge crew. Fleur was standing to one side, looking slightly at a loss. As she spotted him, her face lit up with a wide smile.

'Not got your camera out, Fleur?'

'I lent it to Grace for the day. She wanted to do interviews with people about the whole Bryce thing. It must be going well, because I haven't seen her since.'

'I thought she was a newsprint journalist.'

'She is. But she's keen to break into the online side of the paper, so she was hoping to get some sample video interviews with well-known people. All of which is cool for my film.'

'So you are going to do something about the festival?'

'After that whole Bryce–Dickson fallout yesterday I thought it might be fun. And now of course . . .'

'It's morbidly fascinating.'

She nodded. 'D'you think I'm a terrible person?'

'No.'

'It's just, I got such a lot of good footage last night. We'll have to see what Grace comes up with today.'

'Loads, I'm sure.' Conal shifted awkwardly from foot to foot. 'Hey, what are you up to?' he asked.

'How d'you mean?'

'Right now.'

'Not a lot. I thought I might go to that Joe Sacco talk later.'

'Definitely. That's a must for me.'

'I hoped you might be going.' Her eyes rested on him encouragingly.

'Look, d'you fancy getting out of here for a bit?' he said. 'Head for the hills for a couple of hours. All this high-octane literary bollocks gets quite exhausting after a while, don't you find?'

SIXTEEN

Back in the Green Room Francis poured himself a large glass of white wine. It was only four thirty, but what the hell, it had been a long day. And he had done it, got through his talk in one piece, despite some outright rudeness and a couple of tricky questions. His queue at the bookshop afterwards hadn't been enormous, but it was perfectly respectable and, he couldn't help but notice, longer than Virginia Westcott's. Oh God. Here was Laetitia again. Now he couldn't keep the bloody woman away from him.

'Francis. That was terrific. It's the kind of event that makes me glad I do this festival.'

Francis was aware of Dan Dickson sliding quietly past. But not so quietly that Laetitia hadn't spotted him. 'Dan, Dan!' she cried. 'Do come and meet Francis Meadowes.'

Dickson stopped in his tracks. Close up, hailed like this, the celebrated iconoclast looked almost shy. He probably liked this sort of forced introduction as little as Francis did. But that's what women like Laetitia were put on the planet to do. Oil the wheels.

'Francis has just done the most wonderful talk about, well, the history of crime-writing really.'

'*The Amateur Sleuth*,' said Dan. 'I was there.'

'Oh were you?' said Francis.

'Very informative, mate. I knew that Holmes had a French antecedent, but I didn't know about the Oriental roots. Or realize there was anything in the Arabian Nights.'

'Ja'far ibn Yahya, the first fictional detective.'

'Diverting questions . . .' Dickson raised a quizzical eyebrow.

'What about that "coconut" woman!' said Laetitia. She waggled her fingers into quote mode, protecting herself from any taint of political incorrectness. 'What was she *on*? I'm surprised you were so nice to her.'

'I was just wondering whether I'd been a bit mean. Making her say what she meant like that.'

'*So* not. Don't you think, Dan?'

Dickson shrugged. 'I guess it's up to Francis how offended he wants to feel.'

Laetitia laughed, a trifle uncertainly.

'I was more interested in the other questions,' Dickson continued. 'They were desperate to know about Bryce, weren't they?'

'I was ready for that.'

'So we noticed. You were marvellously obstructive.'

'I'm sorry you didn't say more,' said Laetitia.

'There's a police investigation going on,' said Francis. 'I can hardly start adding my own suspicions to the mix.'

Laetitia's mobile trilled – a snatch of hip hop. 'Sorry, guys, got to get this. But I'm coming back. Yes, Rupert,' she said, as she marched off across the tent.

'Murdoch, d'you think?' said Dickson.

Francis chuckled. 'She is quite something, isn't she?'

'A legend in her own Green Room.' There was a pause, as Dickson lowered himself onto the tatty armchair vacated by Laetitia. 'So you do have some suspicions?' he said. 'About Bryce?'

Francis met his gaze. Close up, Dan had fine, frank eyes; chestnut brown irises, ringed with a thin line almost as dark as his pupils. It really wouldn't do to share his private thoughts with 'dickson', would it? And yet he was flattered, and tempted.

'How well did you know him?' he countered.

'Bryce? I've known him for years.'

'Don't tell me you were at Cambridge with him?'

'I was at the other place, mate. For my sins.' Francis did his best not to laugh out loud. Dickson's image was hardly Oxbridge, but why would it have been? The tweedy whiff of elitism didn't sell books these days. Dickson had wisely cultivated a much more streetwise vibe, even if he talked about 'the other place' in private. 'But we were both knocking around London in the Eighties,' Dan went on. 'Bryce was a ubiquitous figure. Supposedly working on his magnum opus while contributing reviews to this or that little publication.'

'And what happened to the magnum opus?'

'Never appeared. Bryce claimed he never submitted it. Anyway, by then he'd found his *métier* as a critic, tearing into established names. He was used by more and more editors, got a little gig on the *Indie* when it started, carried on writing reviews while teaching media studies, finally scored the Lit Ed's job on the *Sentinel*. He's been there ever since, growing ever more papal in his pronouncements.'

'So were you pissed off by that review?' Francis asked. 'I wouldn't have blamed you.'

'Of course I was! I mean he wasn't content just to trash *Otherworld*, was he? Which I've spent five years on. He had to go for my entire *oeuvre*. The thing that gets me is that so much of his bile is about him. He can't do it himself, so he has to keep taking it out on the rest of us who are at least trying. It's pathetic. Was pathetic, I should say.'

'So you don't regret his passing?'

'His passing. Very quaint, Francis. When to all appearances you seem to think he's been rubbed out. Actually I'm going to be honest and say I don't. Obviously I feel sorry for his nearest and dearest, though the truth is he'd managed to piss most of them off too. But professionally speaking, I'm afraid he'd become a Grade A shyster. He was just so destructive – to the culture. Week after week, putting people off this or that struggling author, making them feel good and clever about being philistines. Until the only thing his public were going to be allowed to read was Jane Austen, Henry James, Joseph Conrad or possibly Bryce-frigging-Peabody himself.'

'What about his women?' Francis asked.

'What about them? If they were stupid enough not to see what he was like, more fool them.'

'As far as I can gather, he had a long-term partner and a girlfriend and dumped both of them simultaneously when he met Priya.'

'The "Asian babe"?' Dickson didn't need to use his fingers to make the quotes; his rich, ironic tone did all the work for him. 'You really are quite the amateur sleuth yourself, aren't you? I'm afraid I'm not that up to speed on Bryce's complex private life these days. But yes, what I heard on the grapevine was that the incumbent doxy found out she'd been binned at some dinner party, when someone said, "Have you heard the news about Bryce Peabody? He's left his partner for a younger model." She thought it was her, and then freaked out when she discovered the truth: that she'd been out-younger-modelled.' Dickson cackled throatily.

'So what about his long-term partner?' Francis asked innocently. 'Did you know her too?'

'I've known Scarlett for years.'

'Well?'

'You really are quite something, aren't you?' Dickson paused and stretched. For a moment Francis thought he was going to get up and walk off. But then he seemed to think the better of it. 'I doubt whether it's possible for anyone to know Scarlett very well,' he said. 'There's a basic standoffishness at her core. Even Bryce struggled, poor fellow.'

'But he stayed with her, none the less?'

'He did.' Dickson yawned noisily. 'Always a mystery what motivates people in relationships, don't you find? My guess is that despite all his infidelities, she offered some kind of basic security. But you can't discount the children either. He did love those little girls – and why wouldn't he? Have you met them?'

'I haven't met Scarlett.'

'I speak as a man too selfish to get involved in the rearing of another generation, but there is something entrancing about them. Bright, funny, beautiful – the kind of children you'd dream of having, if that was your dream. As for Scarlett, although she did endlessly complain about Bryce, she always lit up in his company. She could also be very jealous. In a way you perhaps shouldn't be if what you'd agreed to was an open marriage . . .'

'An open, common-law marriage?'

Dickson's grin acknowledged the absurdity. 'But look, if you went round there at weekends, which I did on a couple of occasions, it felt like a perfectly normal family scene: kids running around, Mum and Dad bickering over the Sunday roast, everyone getting pissed together. But then, come Monday, they went their own way. You'd see Bryce in the Groucho with the latest star-struck student or sub. The word was that Scarlett reciprocated, and for a while I think there was a reasonably serious man. But it was like a lot of these situations. You got the feeling that the bloke had the best of it, really.'

'And where is she now? Still in the family home?'

'In London she is, yes. But if you mean right now, she's up here too. Out at their cottage with the children. I saw her yesterday, at the Michael Rosen gig. She didn't make mine, sadly. Otherwise, who knows, she might have pitched in.'

SEVENTEEN

Francis was glad he'd followed his instincts and brought the Saab rather than accepting the festival's offered alternative, a 'limo' from Dewkesbury station, some twenty-five miles away. The joke among the festival's participants was that said limo was actually a bog-standard minicab, but then authors hardly expected to be treated like film stars. They were grateful for the chance to promote their books; happy enough with the proffered payment of half a case of English wine and a few extra goodies that Laetitia had conned out of local enterprises: a round of Dewkesbury Camembert, a jar of organic honey from the Dewkesbury Bee Centre.

Now his sleek blue chariot was winding up a narrow lane between high stone walls, thick with luxuriant undergrowth: long grass, nettles, brambles, bracken, wild flowers you would never see on Hampstead Heath. At a glance these barriers looked as soft as hedges; but try getting too close and you soon realized what an illusion this was, how rock solid they were underneath. SINGLE TRACK WITH PASSING PLACES was written on the sign at the bottom of the hill, and the best plan was to bolt along, getting as far as you could before you ran into someone coming the other way. Hopefully not literally.

As part of their strange non-marriage (Dickson had explained), Bryce and Scarlett jointly owned a cottage, ten miles outside Mold.

'I think I've seen a snap of it, in the festival albums,' Francis said; but even if Dan was aware which one he was talking about, he wasn't going to be drawn.

'You might well have done,' he replied. 'They've had it for years.'

Francis found it easily enough. The nearest village, Tittlewell, was clearly signed, as was the Black Bull pub two miles beyond. FREE HOUSE. OPEN ALL DAY. DRAUGHT HEADBANGER AND DEMON ON TAP. SIMON'S SCRUMPY. MARGE'S HOMEMADE PIES. GAGGIA MACHINE. That was a nice touch. If all went well, perhaps he'd drop in for a coffee on his way back. Down the long hill, up a slope, and there was the stony track on the bend, right by the *Gnarled Tree* of the sketch-map Dickson had drawn on the back of a press release.

Francis bumped slowly upwards, keeping carefully to one side of the grassy ridge down the middle. There were big, suspension-busting rocks in there too, as well as deep, puddle-filled dips. You needed a 4×4 for this kind of thing, not a low-slung Saab. He stopped to open and close a cattle gate, stepping carefully over the clanging metal bars, remembering childhood walks on Bodmin Moor. Driving on, he could see the view in the mirror getting better and better, a green and pleasant England spreading away to the east. Finally he reckoned he'd arrived. If this was the cottage, it was quite something, a long low stone building with a pond out front and a big garden running up the hill behind. Two little girls were playing on a swing to one side. At the sound of the car, they stopped and ran for the front door, shrieking for their mother.

She appeared a moment later, in a flowery apron over white blouse and blue jeans. She was more lined than in the Young Guns photo, but still beautiful in a fey kind of way. Slighter in the flesh than Francis had imagined, and now with long hair down her shoulders. For a moment he wondered if he should have come at all; he had no role here whatsoever. Curiosity and a gut instinct had driven him on, away from the afternoon party developing in the Green Room. Who – what precisely – did he think he was?

'Good afternoon. Scarlett . . .'

Now he couldn't remember her surname. Idiot. He could hardly say Peabody.

'Paton-Jones, yes.'

He held out a hand. 'My name is Francis Meadowes. I've come out from the festival. I'm one of the writers who's speaking . . .'

She was laughing. 'Sorry. I thought you were the police. They told me to expect a Family Liaison Officer.'

'So you know?'

'Yes.' She made a warning face in the direction of her two girls, who were standing to one side, staring at him. Identical twins, mini-me versions of their mother, apart from those big, thoughtful brown eyes. Francis could see what Dan had meant; they were a rather magical-looking pair. 'Girls. D'you want to go and play for a bit? And then Mummy'll make you some supper—'

'With striped ice cream?'

'Yes, Perdita. With striped ice cream.'

This seemed to do the trick. The girls took one more look at the intruder, then ran off, screaming and giggling, round the side of the house.

'I'm afraid I haven't told them yet. I thought I'd wait for the police and find out exactly what happened first.'

'What do you know?'

'Just that Bryce died suddenly in the night. A friend phoned this morning. Then, later, the police, though how they got this number I've no idea, as we're ex-directory. I suppose I'm being naive. They're probably watching us as we speak from some satellite. I'm afraid I haven't been in . . . to the hotel. It was OK for his new bird to identify him, apparently. So what's your role in all this, may I ask?'

As Francis explained, he watched her interest growing.

'So perhaps I can offer you a cup of tea,' she said when he'd finished. 'As you've nobly trekked all the way out here.'

He followed her inside the 'cottage', which was done up to the highest contemporary standards. There was polished slate on the kitchen floor and varnished boards in the long sitting room that led off it. Central was a big open fireplace with stylish sofas and chairs grouped around it. The walls were hung with original paintings and prints, while on tables and stands were a number of carved figures: two Buddhas; a Ganesh; various African bodies in dark wood.

Scarlett came through with a tray: Clarice Cliff teapot, two matching mugs, biscuits.

'What a beautiful place you have here,' he said.

'Thank you.' She looked around, proprietorially. 'It is rather special, isn't it?'

'When people said "cottage" I imagined something a bit more basic.'

'We've put in quite a bit of work over the years. It was pretty basic when we started out, believe me. Damp up all the walls, no big windows, pre-war kitchen, outside loo. But when we saw the location we just had to have it.'

She sat down and poured tea for them both. 'So what's going on?' she asked.

'How d'you mean?'

'With the police and everything. Aren't they happy with the doctor's verdict?'

'I've no idea. Not having spoken to them in any detail.'

'Do *you* think Bryce had a heart attack?'

'He might well have done.'

'But you're not sure, are you?'

'This is an odd situation for me. I'm a crime writer by profession. I've imagined and written about scenes like the one I saw today many times. And yet this morning was the first time in my life I'd seen a dead body *in situ*. So I have to admit to being intrigued.'

'What exactly did you see?'

'Apart from a single bruise on his right cheekbone, there was nothing at first glance to indicate any foul play. And yet my gut feeling now is that this wasn't as simple as a straightforward heart attack.'

'Why's that?'

'I suppose I don't believe Bryce wouldn't have had time to call someone. Surely some kind of pain would have woken him up. There's a phone right by the bed.'

'These things do happen.'

'I know they do. But how likely was it that Bryce would have died so suddenly? Is there a family history of heart disease? That you know about? I know he'd had his cholesterol checked out recently, hadn't he?'

'Who told you that? Priya?'

Francis nodded; he didn't think it would be tactful to mention Anna too.

'Very thoughtful of her to care,' said Scarlett sarcastically. 'Well, he had a high count of LDL, low-density lipoprotein, bad cholesterol as it's called. Which, being Bryce, he did bugger-all about, despite my nagging. At one point a couple of years ago I almost got him to start taking statins, then he read some blog that was dead against them, so he decided not to.'

'Forgive me for being nosy,' Francis asked, 'but until recently you lived together most of the time. Or all the time?'

'All the time. Your informants have clearly told you it wasn't a conventional partnership. So what else did they say? That I was some downtrodden little mouse who sat waiting for him to waltz home from his latest mistress?'

Francis smiled. 'Nobody seemed to understand the dynamic at all.'

'It's good to know that we kept them guessing. The simple truth is that we're both quite headstrong people. A couple of years after the twins were born we just woke up one day and realized that we'd stopped having sex. We discussed it and there seemed to be a few limited options: we went to some kind of therapy and tried to work things out; we did what a friend of mine in LA did and spiced things up with naughty accessories;

133

we became celibates; we split up; or we stayed together, but took other lovers as and when.'

'Highly logical.'

'Practical, I suppose. Bryce was always that. The bottom line was that neither of us wanted to leave the girls. We didn't want some bossy outsider telling us how to fancy each other. Then Bryce brought home some bits and pieces from a sex shop in Soho, but once I'd handcuffed him to the bed and got the whip out I got the giggles, so that was a no-go.'

Francis wasn't sure how literally to take this scenario. Was this woman always so open? Or perhaps this was just a reaction to the shock of her ex's sudden death.

'So you chose the last option?' he said. 'How did that work?'

Scarlett smiled; almost nostalgically, Francis thought. 'It was fine for a year or two. Novelty factor, I suppose. We both had quite a bit of fun and for a while it actively improved things, gave us back our frisson. But the problem with that sort of set-up is that, Sod's law, things never happen at the same time. One of you has always got the hot new thing going while the other's just been dumped or whatever. Inevitably, you get jealous. So the temptation not to be honest creeps in. Then it becomes impossible, because you can't trust each other . . .'

'Which is where you got to?'

'You're a very sympathetic man, Francis, and I've no idea why I'm telling you all this, but basically Bryce started fibbing to me. Lying, actually. About Anna. The one before Priya. She had started as one of his little summer flings. Then she became more and for some reason he couldn't give her up . . .'

There was a shriek from the kitchen and the twins were upon them. 'Mummy, Mummy, Perdita won't get off the swing.'

'I just got off, you total spastic.'

'Perdita! I've told you never to use that word.'

'But I did get off the swing.'

'Mummy, when are we going to have supper?'

'Girls, please! I'm having a talk with Mr Meadowes. As soon as Nurjan gets back, we'll eat.'

'She might be ages.'

'If she isn't back in fifteen minutes I'll start cooking. How does that sound?'

'Six thirty?'

'Six thirty, yes.'

'We'll hold you to that, Mummy.'

'OK.' Scarlett rolled her eyes at Francis. 'Hold me to it then. But only if you run off and play right now. And never use that word again.'

'Daddy uses it.'

'I know he does. He's being silly.'

'When are we going to see Daddy?'

'Tomorrow, darling.'

'OK!'

They were gone, back out into the garden. Scarlett sighed deeply and picked up her BlackBerry.

'I'm going to have to tell them tonight,' she said, looking down as she tapped out a text. 'God knows how they'll take it. They adore their father.' Francis said nothing, as Scarlett wiped the corner of her eye with the end of her little finger, then looked down at the painted wooden princess that sat on the glass table next to her, as if contemplating the blue, green and magenta beads implanted so delicately into her cuffs and trousers, the smile on her lips that was so artfully rendered. 'Beautiful, isn't she?'

'She is.'

'That one's Burmese. Bryce and I found her at a magical place called Inle Lake, where all the hotels are on stilts over the water. That was one of our happiest trips. Before the girls were born. Now where were we?'

'Bryce had started lying to you about Anna.'

'Oh yes. He lied to me. And from what I can gather, he lied to her too. Started to tell her that he was about to leave me and shack up properly with her, which was terribly mean of him, because she was over forty and wanted a baby and I don't think he ever had any intention of giving her one. Actually, by the end it suited him pretty well. Family weekends at home. Social life and sex with Anna in the week. And me still doing all his bloody laundry.'

'But then, in the end, he did leave you – all.'

'He did, didn't he?' Scarlett swallowed hard and for a moment Francis thought she might be about to break down, but then the steely calm reasserted itself. 'And I never thought he would. Have the guts. Or the ruthlessness. Because he loved the girls. So much. But she gave him an ultimatum, pushy little Priya, didn't she? All or nothing. And he was so cunt-struck he couldn't bear the thought of nothing. But perhaps you knew that already?'

'She did say something along those lines, yes.'

Scarlett sighed. 'These young girls going for these middle-aged men, I really don't get it. When I was that age I never fancied anyone more than five years older, max.'

'There are other factors, though, aren't there. He was a big cheese. She's ambitious.'

'I guess that must be it. What fools women are.'

'And what about Anna?'

'What about her? I'm afraid I thought it served her right. She knew we had kids. Her stated ambition was to split up this family. If she lost the chance of a family of her own then tough titty.'

'Did you hate him after he left?'

Scarlett turned and met his eye. 'I'm not sure "hate" is quite the right word. I thought Priya would soon tire of him and he'd come running back. It wasn't the first time Bryce had fallen for an Asian bird. There was another one when he was teaching at Birkbeck a while back. One of his students, naughty man. He had to let her go in a hurry when her brothers found out.' She laughed. 'I suppose at the back of my mind I thought something similar might happen with Priya, but I guess the world has moved on since then. Anyway, I really didn't see how it could last. Once she realized what a crusty old shit Bryce could be on a day to day basis, she'd wake up and want someone of her own age. At that point I would have the luxury of deciding what to do with him.

'But yes, at the same time, when I thought about it, I wondered whether all along I hadn't been a fool. Agreeing to an open marriage when we weren't even married. My trouble is that I always see the best in people. And Bryce and I go back such a long way. I know him better than almost anyone else. I know his weaknesses, his ambitions, his phobias.'

'Yes,' said Francis; he was thinking of Virginia, another woman who claimed to have known Bryce better than anyone else. 'I didn't see you at the *Sentinel* party last night, did I?' he asked.

'You most certainly didn't. My alibi is firmly intact.'

'I didn't mean . . .'

'I'm sure you didn't. But no, I was here with the kids all evening. NFI, I'm afraid.'

'NFI?'

'Not Effing Invited. Why would Laetitia want me now? I only ever got asked because of Bryce. I was aware of that. But to be off the list on my first year as a dumpee. There's female solidarity for you. Have you met the silly bitch?'

'Briefly. She came to a talk I did this afternoon.'

'Lucky you. She must rate you. She's basically the most appalling intellectual snob. Made worse by the fact that she's so stupid herself. But because she does her festival and mixes with all these top literary types, she's kind of half-kidded herself that she's on the same level as them. When she's basically a failed actress who was lucky enough to inherit a festival. You know about her dad?'

'I heard something . . .'

'Henry was the brains behind all this; and, I may say, the charisma. Unlike her, he believed in the writers.'

She spoke with such passion that Francis began to wonder how objective her view of the flame-haired organizer was. Don't say that Bryce had been involved with her too? It was hardly a question he could ask directly. 'You don't think she believes in the writers?' he said.

'She believes in success. In putting her long slimy tongue as far up the sphincter of the latest award-winner as she can. Booker, Costa, Baileys, she's not fussy. What she's not interested in is the grubby struggles of writers *per se*. While they're suffering in their garrets to produce their marvellous confections. It's actually funny. Because when people are obscure they get ignored and then they don't know how to deal with her when they become flavour of the month and she's all over them like a rash.

'The sad thing is that when Henry was running the festival, it was a great week. Not only did he love writers, he understood what insecure egotists they all are. If anything he preferred failure to success. I think he thought that winning gongs was rather vulgar. Not that there were so many gongs back then. No, in the old days you'd find yourself in the pub with all kinds of people. The latest Booker Prize winner alongside some midlister who'd been jogging along quietly for years.

'And people talked about ideas, not who'd won this, and who'd won that, and have you heard about this huge advance with this amazing agent? The party was a writers' party. Not guarded at the door by dolly birds with clipboards asking you which TV company you work for. I remember when my girls were tiny, taking them along in their double buggy and letting them run around while we enjoyed ourselves. Julian Barnes feeding them crisps, Margaret Drabble patting their curly heads. But every year since Henry died it's got worse.'

'The party or the festival?'

'Both. Half the people in the programme are off the telly, as far as I can see. She's even got Family Man this year. Did you see that?'

'Hard to miss, since he's on the cover. But I suppose he is pretty famous, and he does sell an awful lot of books.'

'That's it, isn't it? Where our culture has got to. Volume equals quality. Come to our literary festival and load up with recipes and gardening tips.'

'If you hate it so much, why do you still bother to come?'

'A good question. One I was starting to ask myself. But we have this place. And I love it up here at this time of year – whether I go into Mold or not. It's like the end of term, start of the summer hols. We always used to stay on for a week or two. While Bryce tried to do what he called his "serious writing".'

'Bryce was out here with you?'

'Of course. It was always a good time for the two of us. We've done it for so many years that in a way we used to relapse into a happier mode. Bryce's girlfriends *never* came to Mold.'

'And then this year was different?'

'Certainly was. He and Priya even stayed here for a few days last week.'

'I don't imagine you were happy with that.'

'Bugger all I could do about it, but no, it was pretty thought-less of him.'

'Was this the first year he hadn't been at the cottage for the festival?'

'It was. And look what happened. To tell you the truth, Francis, I so nearly didn't come this year. But then I thought: stuff it, it's my house too, why shouldn't I? And I suppose I wanted to prove something to him as well. That he couldn't just trample over all our memories like that.'

There was the sound of a car drawing up outside. Scarlett rose to her knees on the sofa to look out of the window. 'It's only Nurjan. Our au pair. I sent her into town to get some bits and pieces.'

Francis rose. 'I must leave you in peace. It's been good talking to you. One final little question, which only someone who knew Bryce intimately could answer.'

'Shoot.'

'When he took out his contact lenses at night, did he generally do it in the bathroom or the bedroom?'

'In the bathroom, why?'

'Always?'

She paused for a moment. 'Yes. I guess so. I never really thought about it.'

'Thanks. I don't suppose I'll see you in Mold.'

'Not tonight you won't, certainly. I've got to wait in for the police. If they ever turn up.'

Francis reached inside his jacket for his wallet. 'May I give you my card?'

She looked at it, then made as if to toss it away. 'What am I supposed to do with this?'

'Keep it. You can always call me if you need to.'

As Scarlett stuffed the card into her front jeans pocket, the au pair appeared, though she wasn't carrying any shopping bags. Nurjan was stocky and dark, with muscly arms either side of her sleeveless black T-shirt, and breasts like poached eggs. Francis wondered if Bryce had ever had a dalliance with one of her predecessors; unless he had a taste for the Amazonian, there was little temptation for him here.

EIGHTEEN

The Black Bull was quite a find. Down through a sloping garden a creaky wooden door opened onto a tiny, stone-flagged bar. There were other rooms off to left and right, with low ceilings and real beams. A bell hanging by the crisp packets summoned a teenaged barmaid with spiky black hair and an uncomfortable-looking bolt through her nose. There was a blackboard with a good list of draught beers chalked on it, along with strength and price. And there was the promised Gaggia machine, authentic if somewhat ancient.

Francis had fancied a coffee, but the early evening sun was shining, so he thought he'd treat himself to a proper drink. Strangely for a Sunday – and during the festival – the place was all but deserted. Three stout women in wind jackets sat around a table on the little terrace by the door. At the far end of the lawn a young couple were visible in silhouette, canoodling behind the backlit fronds of a willow tree. Having ordered himself a pint of Headbanger and a packet of goat's cheese crisps, Francis found an empty bench at the top of the garden. Below the hedge at the bottom the hill dropped away sharply; beyond was the perfect patchwork of countryside that he'd seen in the rear-view mirror earlier. His iPhone had lost its signal,

142

which was a relief; no one could bother him and he had time to think.

Hmm. If this had been a George Braithwaite mystery, now would have been the point at which the detective paused to consider the suspects in the case. With his beer in front of him, Francis took out his notebook and jotted down a few thoughts. George's list, perhaps, would have looked something like this:

Dan D – most obvious susp – with real reason to hate B. But: no clear motive bar literary revenge, best satisfied through print anyway? Despite his fearsome rep, seemed nice enough in a one to one. Then again: most obv, least likely character turns out to be a double bluff?

Conal O'H – threatened publicly to kill B. Since said he's happy he's dead. No secret that he hates him for stealing (as he sees it) Priya. Vanished at critical time last night. Nobody saw him return to room. Could have been pretending to be drunk, driven to Mold, done deed, and got back before 4 am, which was when Fleur saw him again. But likely? Hardly.

Priya K – in textbook theory, prime suspect, in that she discovered B and apart from taxi driver (and maybe random guest at hotel?) was last to see him alive. But why would she want to do away with brand new boyf + key patron at Sentinel? Also: Cathy saw her come into WH at 4 am. Would have had to bump off B v. quickly indeed, with zero resistance, because 2 minutes later was screaming on the stairs. 2 niggles tho: why did she switch laptop off when she went back to the room? What happened to pillow choc?

Scarlett P-J – ex non-wife! Definitely a poss, esp if she's going to inherit B's money and property. 'It's my house too,' she said of cottage. What about London gaff?Must be worth £££s. And what would have happened if Priya's claim on B had got stronger – as in, say, marriage?

Scarlett stood to lose everything. Has alibi in that someone had to be there to look after the twins last night – but what about Nurjan?

Anna C – dumped cruelly after several years of waiting for B to leave S. Furious when she found out, but quickly found replacement. Does that mean she stopped hating him? Even if she didn't, is that enough of a motive? On other hand, new boyf Marv certainly has experience to do away with someone. And he didn't seem at all amused when I was quizzing her. Also staying at White H, so easy access. Joint alibi down to anyone who saw the pair of them out at Wyveridge last night – how late did they stay?

Virginia W – dark horse ex-love of a million years ago. Quite obviously never got over B. Resents him deeply, for all her talk of enjoying travel and other boyfriends, etc. Has clearly been struggling with career and is hanging everything on latest offering. Is it credible that part of a (deeply twisted) motive could be that she didn't want B to slag her off again in review? And what about that pen?

That was it, then. And under the unwritten rules of classic detective fiction, in a George Braithwaite mystery it would have had to be someone the reader had been introduced to reasonably early on (i.e. one of those six) – unless of course this was a Roger Ackroyd style story, and for as yet undisclosed reasons, it was I, Francis Meadowes, what had done him in, ha ha ha.

Back in the real world, though, if Bryce really had been the victim of foul play, then it would, most likely, have been someone outside this cosy circle. This was why police procedure was so different from Poirot-style antics. Solving a case like this involved the painstaking business of checking and eliminating all possible suspects. TIE was the police acronym. Trace, Interview, Eliminate. There were no short cuts.

As he sat deep in thought, Francis's gaze settled idly on the couple under the willow tree. He could half see in, so could they half see out? Probably not. Now, after a long slow snog, and some touchy-feely stuff involving hands and hair, they had pulled apart. Then the woman's head sank back onto the man's shoulder. They were obviously a very recent item. A passionate meeting of minds, followed shortly afterwards by bodies – typical of many a festival. Now the man stood up and edged his way through the curtain of green fronds and out into the sunlight, carrying two empty pint jugs.

It was Conal O'Hare.

Francis looked hurriedly down at his notebook. If Conal spotted him, then he might not want to say hello. Out of the corner of his eye, Francis watched the Irishman cross the garden and lower his head to enter the bar. Francis looked back at the willow. The young woman was half hidden by the trailing greenery, but he could see enough of her now to work out who it was. Fleur. So Grace had been right. She *had* liked Conal. And Conal seemed to have overcome his heartache about Priya at double-quick speed. If, that is, he'd had any heartache about Priya.

When he saw the pub door swing open again, Francis returned to his notebook. Conal paused in his tracks for a couple of seconds, then turned and headed over to where Francis was sitting.

'Francis . . .'

'Oh hello, Conal. What are you doing here?' The travel writer looked flushed, almost high.

'Escaping from the festival bullshit. Like you, I expect.'

'It's a beautiful spot, isn't it?' Francis said. 'I came across it by accident.'

'One of those little gems that can't possibly stay the same forever. Somebody's bound to buy the old crone out and turn it into a gastropub. Anyhows, just thought I'd say hello. I enjoyed your talk, by the way.'

'You were there?'

'It was interesting. And the questions – you did a fine job of keeping them off the one subject they all wanted to know about.'

He paused, but Francis wasn't going to be drawn. 'I'll leave you in peace,' Conal said. 'Come out to Wyveridge later, if you've nothing better to do. Ranjit's having another of his parties. Starts about eight. Should be excellent crack.'

'I might just do that.'

Conal sloped off. He hadn't mentioned Fleur, but Francis was amused, looking up, to see that his presence hadn't intimidated them. He finished his drink and headed back to the Saab. The bottom line was that this wasn't a George Braithwaite story. Thinking about his dubious list of suspects Francis could only conclude that it was unlikely that any of them had done Bryce in. The few oddities in the room this morning almost certainly had simple explanations.

He had no idea why the police had decided to send in forensics. Had the love bite and the bruise been enough to set the whole investigative process going? Then again, it was perfectly possible that there was a Chinese whispers effect from the doctor's other jokey remarks. Green young copper mutters to DS, DS summons DCI, till everyone's covering their arses and the full rigmarole of TIE is under way. The post-mortem would probably confirm a heart attack or aneurysm. And that would be that. Bryce just another one of those who fell in their fifties. There were more of them than you realized, as a wander round any graveyard would confirm.

Returning to Mold, Francis easily found a parking space in the yard at the back of the hotel. The police activity, he noticed, was visibly reduced. The marked cars and vans had gone, even the WPC on the front door had been stood down. Ah well, perhaps that was it. Drama over. With a good conscience he could retire for a quiet meal at the Rising Sun.

At the end of the main corridor he saw Cathy, working away under the bright beam of an anglepoise in the little reception booth.

'Police left you to it, have they?'

She looked up. 'Haven't you heard?'

'No. What?'

'There's been another death. Out at Wyveridge Hall. One of the people staying there. Fell from the roof, apparently.'

'God help us,' said Francis, quietly. 'D'you know who it was?'

'A young woman, apparently. Grace somebody-or-other. Roger Webster's already out there.'

NINETEEN

Francis found the gravel circle at the front of Wyveridge crowded with police vehicles, not all of them marked. That sharp-eyed humorist WPC Wendy was stationed by the front door. An altogether heftier PC, whose ballooning beer belly made you wonder how many criminals he'd chased recently, stood guard by the blue and white scene-of-crime tape which blocked off the gravel path that ran round the side of the house to the terrace. POLICE DO NOT CROSS POLICE DO NOT CROSS.

Francis decided that the direct approach was likely to work best. 'We meet again,' he said, walking up to Wendy.

'Yes, sir.'

'There's been another death . . .'

'Yes, sir.'

'A young woman who was staying here?'

Wendy started to nod agreement; then she recovered herself and said: 'I'm afraid I'm not allowed to discuss the incidents with the general public, sir.'

'Fair enough, you have your procedures. I've come out in the hope of seeing Ranjit Richardson, the young gentleman who's hosting the house party. D'you think you could you let me in?'

'Only house guests are allowed in and out, sir. And they have to be cleared.'

'What does that involve?'

'I'd need to talk to my superior, sir.'

'DCI Morgan?'

'Yes sir. Though she's just left. It's DS Povey now.'

'Now DS Povey I met this morning. Perhaps I could have a word with him?'

Ten minutes later, Francis was inside. It was lucky, he thought, that Povey was a Braithwaite fan. Francis did as he was told and kept away from the police activity on the ground floor. He found a shattered group of the house party's remnants in a room at the end of the long upstairs corridor, huddled round a low, glass-topped coffee table in front of the empty fireplace: host Ranjit; a lithe young woman with high cheekbones and catlike green eyes; and a big, bearded fellow in an untucked denim shirt.

'Francis,' said Ranjit, rising to his feet. 'What are you doing here?'

'I'm so sorry.'

'It's a hell of a thing . . .'

'What exactly happened?'

'She fell from the roof. So it seems. Over by the tower. None of us can work out what she was doing up there. See for yourself, if you like. It's pretty grim.' He gestured towards the bay window at the end of the room.

Francis walked over and looked out. Down below, poor Grace was still prone on the terrace, surrounded by forensics people performing various intricate tasks. One moved around the body taking flash photographs while another crouched over the gravel, picking up individual stones in a white-gloved hand. Another was finishing the job of marking out her position with white tape. Grace's arms and legs were akimbo, but otherwise she could have been sleeping, enjoying the last rays of the sun, which cast a slanting parallelogram lengthwise from the gap between the hedges at the end of the terrace. She was still in the yellow dress and blue jeans combo she'd been wearing at breakfast.

'She had a video camera with her,' Ranjit said, at his shoulder. 'You can see it on the bank a few yards away to the right. Totally buggered by the looks of it, though the police obviously haven't let us anywhere near.'

'That's Fleur's, right?'

'We think so. Grace must have borrowed it off her. So how did you manage to get in, Francis? We're under strict orders that all visitors are banned.'

'I'm afraid I dropped your name with DS Povey. Told him that I was moving out here from the White Hart, so was technically a house guest.' Francis walked back towards the window, craned his neck round to look up at the battlements. 'Is it likely,' he said, 'that Grace would be up there, on her own, in the middle of the afternoon? And if so, could she really have slipped?'

'No,' said the green-eyed girl. 'I went up there with Fleur yesterday evening and the battlements are a good three feet high. You'd have to physically climb over before you could jump.'

'You were on the battlements with Fleur?'

'Yes.'

'Doing what?'

'She was filming the start of the party. And the view . . .'

'I see,' said Francis. 'So if Grace couldn't have slipped, how on earth did she go over? Unless she was suicidal . . .'

'Which she so wasn't. Rushing around getting copy off the celebs for her gossip column.'

'Or, I suppose, tripping?' Francis looked meaningfully from one to another of the silent trio.

'Implying what?' said Ranjit.

'It's hardly a secret that there are drugs out here.'

'Not any more there aren't.'

'The police have confiscated them?'

'Hell no. What d'you take us for?' Ranjit made a face and mimed a toilet chain being pulled.

'You didn't try and ship them out somewhere?'

'My friend's just, like, er, died,' said green-eyes, in a sarcastic voice, 'so excuse me delaying calling the ambulance while we hide our illegal substances for use later.'

She was as tiresome as she was beautiful, this one, but it was clear she was close to Ranjit, so Francis bit back any response in kind. 'So who found her?' he asked.

'We did,' said Ranjit. 'Got back here just after your talk.'

'You and . . .?'

'Carly was with me.' He gestured at his girlfriend. 'We let ourselves in and went straight into the drawing room . . .'

'Then I saw her through the French window,' said Carly. 'Just lying there. In the sun. For ten seconds I thought she'd crashed out. Her head was turned away.'

'Then we realized she wasn't moving,' said Ranjit. 'We ran out. And there she was, with this thin line of blood running down onto the gravel from her mouth. We shook her and rolled her over and slapped her, but her head just lolled back, eyes wide open. She was absolutely gone.'

'Shocking,' said Francis quietly.

'It was. Is. I can't get my head around it.'

'I was sick,' said Carly. 'On the bank. I've never seen a dead body like that before. Let alone a friend.'

She was crying now. Ranjit went over to her, held her as she slowly calmed down. From outside came the voices of the professionals, the crunch of boots on gravel, surprisingly loud.

'Was there any way Grace might have taken something that could have led to this?' Francis said eventually. 'I mean, were any of those drugs you got rid of hallucinogenic?'

Carly looked up, eyes glinting. 'No,' she said fiercely.

'Even if they were,' said Ranjit, 'Grace wouldn't have taken them. She didn't do drugs.'

'You're sure about that?'

'In confidence,' said Ranjit, 'she was up here in this room when we were doing coke last night. She didn't touch a single line.'

'Rory was trying hard enough to persuade her,' said the bearded guy.

'She barely drinks,' said Carly.

'So if she wasn't suicidal,' said Francis, 'and she wasn't tripping, and she couldn't have slipped, someone must have pushed her.'

This stark assessment brought silence.

'D'you think that's likely?' said Ranjit.

'There she is,' said Francis. 'Dead on the gravel.'

'So – what? You think she came back with someone?'

'Or someone followed her.'

'But if they wanted to bump off Grace why on earth would they come all the way out here to do it?'

'Because if you could persuade your victim up onto the battlements,' said Francis, 'it would be relatively easy to push them off. And make the whole thing look like an accident. While other forms of murder are harder to conceal. This way, you don't have to worry about getting rid of the body, nor what might turn up in the post-mortem. All you've got to do is sneak away unseen.'

'Almost sounds as if you did it,' said Carly.

'Unfortunately,' Francis replied coolly, 'I have an excellent alibi. In that I was giving my talk at the time.' He turned back to Ranjit. 'The other possibility, of course, is that the murderer was here all along. You don't happen to know who was in residence at half three this afternoon, do you?'

'Sorry,' said Ranjit, 'I don't keep tabs on my guests. Or their visitors. It's always been open house here.'

Not any more, thought Francis. He turned back from the window. 'So what's going to happen to you lot now?'

'The police are taking statements and contact details,' said Ranjit, 'and we're supposed to stick around till they let us go. But the party's over. I might go back to London tomorrow. It feels a bit spooky staying on.'

'Too right,' Carly agreed. 'I want to get out of this hideous place as soon as possible. Don't you, Adam?'

The bearded guy nodded agreement.

'Thank you all for your collective time,' said Francis. 'Now tell me, where am I likely to find that housekeeper I met at breakfast time?'

'Mrs Mac?'

'Small, bright-eyed old biddy? Been here since the Fifties or something?'

'That's Mrs Mac,' said Ranjit. 'She'll probably be at her cottage, which is up the back, beyond the kitchen garden, which runs behind the sheds and greenhouses you see as you come in on the right. There's a row of three. Gunther the German gardener lives in the near one, and she's in the middle.'

'Who's in the end one?' Francis asked.

'Some Ugandan friend of the owner's.'

'Mr Gerald?'

'Yeah. He's quite something, if you see him. Very tall and rather beautiful. Likes to dress as a woman. Which suits him, because he's a dead ringer for Grace Jones. He's an artist, paints funky abstracts. A local character.'

Francis left the house the way he'd come in. He walked down past the greenhouses and found the kitchen garden, a big oblong with crumbling brick walls. It was dilapidated: bare earth, brown grass, brambles and long trails of bindweed with its distinctive white, bell-shaped flower. Up in the top left corner were a few rows of vegetables marked out by bamboo canes. Beyond this he came to the little row of cottages, up against the six foot high estate wall that ran along the main road. It seemed a shame that in all this peaceful space, the staff living quarters should be here, right by the traffic. But then these pretty, ochre-stone buildings dated from a time when the noisiest vehicle passing by would have been a coach and four.

Francis saw no sign of the cross-dressing Ugandan, but a sturdy old figure with a bushy white moustache and thick eyebrows was digging in the front garden of the end cottage.

Gunther, presumably. Francis smiled at him and received a grunt. He gestured at the second cottage. 'Mrs Mac?'

Another grunt and a nod. Francis opened the gate, walked up a crazy-paving path to the front door and pressed the bell push, which rang inside with a quaint suburban ding-dong.

'Oh, it's you,' said Mrs Mac, peering out from a dark hall. 'You'd better come in.'

They sat opposite each other in a gloomy front room, which was crowded to the ceiling with ornaments: porcelain, plastic, wood, wicker, cloth; fairies, shepherds, dogs, dolls, you name it, lined up on the shelves of the bookcase, on the mantelpiece above the old-fashioned gas fire, and on the white tablecloths and doilies that covered the four occasional tables.

'You've heard about the accident?' Francis said.

'I found out when I went in just now. I'm supposed to be giving a statement, though what I'll say I can't think, except that she seemed a very nice young girl, a lot better than some of them, I can tell you. Always a pleasant word, helped me clean the place up one morning, wouldn't take no for an answer. We haven't had a death here for years. Not since Miss Alison's riding accident, and that was in the 1960s.'

'So you weren't in the house yourself this afternoon?'

'Not after two o'clock, no. That's when I knock off, come back here for my break. Then I go in again, generally about six, tidy round, light the fires in winter, put the drinks tray out and what have you. I don't stay long. I don't cook any more and I don't like to get involved in their high jinks.'

'I imagine not. Was anyone else there when you left this afternoon, Mrs Mac? That you were aware of?'

'There was. Three of them. In the kitchen. Still having their breakfast at lunchtime. I wouldn't know their names. There's so many in and out.'

'You couldn't give me a description?'

'I could. It's the tall young gentleman with the haughty look. And that black velvet smoking jacket what he's always wearing. Looks like he's stepped out of one of them TV costume dramas. And his little friend, with the spiky hair and the coloured glasses. And that American girl, bare feet and bows in her hair. Hippy chick, they call them, don't they?' She gave Francis a mischievous smile.

'I think they might. But you'd gone before they left for town?'

'I didn't know what that they had left. They were still having their breakfast, as I say, because I couldn't finish in the kitchen, which I like to do before I go. Still, if Mr Ranjit doesn't mind a dirty kitchen I dare say I'm not fussed. Leave them to it.'

'And you didn't see anyone else around?'

'I was over here after. As I said, I don't go back in till six.'

'And when you went back over today?'

'There was police everywhere. Most of them in them white shell suits, forensics, is it, like that *CSI: Crime Scene Investigation*. They wouldn't let me through. I know they've got a job to do but I was shocked. It's the first time in sixty years I've not been allowed in that back door.'

'Did you see the body?'

'Couldn't, could I? Not allowed round there either. Though I wouldn't want to. Poor girl. What was she doing up on them battlements, that's what I'd like to know. You wouldn't catch me climbing out that window.'

'What's that then? The access to the roof?'

'By the stairs to the tower, yes. You have to hoist yourself up to get through it. Then you can walk along. You can go all round the house, if you want. When Mr Gerald was younger he was always out there. Frightened the life out of his mother. Liked the view, he said. But he went to smoke, didn't he? And not just ordinary ciggies either, though I never let on about that. They say you can see five counties from up there.'

It was 9 p.m. now and through the treeline the sun was setting, a fiery orange ball. Down in the gardens the wood pigeons cooed on, oblivious. The police were still everywhere, looming white ghosts in the gathering gloaming. Francis didn't see the point in staying out at Wyveridge. He had been back up to the room where Ranjit, Carly and Adam had been joined by other house guests, all sitting around on the floor like shocked zombies. There were no drugs in evidence, but a couple of bottles of wine had been opened and chillout music emanated from the sleek white sound dock that sat on the side. Francis had checked with Ranjit the identity of the three people Mrs Mac had remembered from lunch. The tall guy in the velvet jacket was almost certainly Rory, especially if he were with his little friend Neville. The American 'hippy-chick' could only be the poet Eva Edelstein. The three of them had gone to the festival, Ranjit thought, to see Joe Sacco, the cartoonist who made picture books about Palestine and other political subjects. 'They almost certainly went on to the poetry slam afterwards,' Ranjit said. 'Rory fancies himself as a bit of a poet.'

'He is a poet,' said Carly. 'And a bloody good one. I don't know why you two have to put each other down the whole time. It's so childish.'

Francis ignored this. 'Have you phoned them?' he asked Ranjit.

'We were just discussing that. I thought the best thing might be to go into town and look for them. Break it to them in person. I'm not sure I can stand spending the rest of the evening here.'

As Francis drove back into Mold he recalled an incident from his school days. A boy who had taken LSD and jumped from the roof of Block B onto the tarmac car park below. He had, people said, decided he was an angel and could fly. He had broken his neck and died instantly. Luke Cooper. Francis could still remember his name. The tragedy had overshadowed the end of Francis's last summer term, Speech Day and all.

But no, on balance, he didn't think this latest event was an accident – or a drugs-related freakout. Two unlikely deaths, so close together; his gut instinct was telling him that this had to be foul play. If his suspicions were well-founded, whoever was responsible was moving with care and intelligence. God, was he even in danger himself, sniffing around in the way he was?

TWENTY

The scene back at the White Hart was low-key. The bar and restaurant were still shut. Cathy was working at her screen in the corner of the little reception area. The hatch was open, but Francis didn't disturb her.

Up in his room, there was no sign of Priya, but she'd unpacked some of her stuff and moved her case onto the stand next to the wardrobe. On the glass shelf in the bathroom was a make-up bag, and next to that her trio of lipsticks: purple, cherry-red and maraschino. Francis sat down at the desk and wrote her a note on White Hart headed paper.

9.25 p.m.
Hi Priya,

Hope you're OK. I've come back hungry to find the hotel bar still closed so I'm going out to forage for some supper. Mobile number below if you want to join me – even for a pudding! Otherwise I'll see you later. If you get back first, please help yourself to the bed. I'm fine on the sofa.

You might have heard there's been another death. Out at Wyveridge Hall. Grace, the gossip columnist on the Sentinel. *Fell off the roof, it seems. I've just been out there – shocking,*

awful – another reason why I need a drink and some sustenance.
Talk about all this later, I hope.

He hesitated over the sign-off, then wrote:

All best,
Francis

He left the hotel and walked down the road towards The Sun Rising. The sunset was almost over now; the fleet of brilliant pink ships, monsters and will o' the wisps sailing across the sky had faded to a dull grey, though a deep crimson gash lingered in the heap of dark cloud by the western horizon. High above, in the trees by the road, the stark silhouettes of leaves trembled in the breeze. Francis shivered as he thought of Grace: her young, bright life, full of hope and expectation, cut off so suddenly. No way had she taken acid – or even drunk alcohol – and jumped off that roof.

Yellow artificial light spilled out through the pub's front door. Francis was glad to get inside. The front room was packed with festivalgoers, a jostle of faces up at the bar. What a day it had been. All he wanted now was a soothing pint and one of those shepherd's pies from the specials board. That empty corner table would do him fine. That and a crumpled copy of the *Sunday Sentinel*. But when he got to the front and caught the eye of the plump barmaid with the livid spots of red at the centre of each of her paper-white cheeks, he was told he'd missed the chance of supper.

'Sorry, sir. Last orders are at nine thirty.'

'It's nine forty-five,' he said. 'I've been queuing for over fifteen minutes. Couldn't you manage *something*?'

'Sorry, sir. Chef goes at ten. He's just plating up a few puddings and then he'll be off.'

'Even during festival time?'

''Fraid so. Sorry.'

'I'm sorry too,' Francis said, turning tetchily on his heel.

'You could try the Purple Pomegranate up the road,' she called after him. 'They've got a restaurant licence.'

'Thanks.' He turned back and managed – just – to flash her a smile; it was hardly her fault if Mutton Chops didn't want to make money.

He paced up the lane towards the lights of town, scanning the dark bushes to his left as he went, jumping at a sudden noise. But it was only a startled pheasant, making a break through the undergrowth. *Pull yourself together, Francis.* He didn't seriously think he was in any immediate danger. But then neither had Bryce or Grace. What was it, he wondered, that linked them? They both worked on the *Sentinel*, but it couldn't be that, could it? A lunatic with a grudge against a newspaper. Hardly.

Fifty yards beyond the darkened ground-floor windows of the White Hart, he found the Purple Pomegranate, a smart-looking place with a handwritten menu and a wine list to each side of the front door. There was a touch of the Heston Blumenthals here: an array of alarming-sounding dishes at – frankly – London prices. Did he really want Locally Shot Duck Liver Pâté with Home-Made Blackberry Compote, Baby Gherkins and Toasted Brioche or Pecan Pie with Beetroot Ice Cream? What the heck! He was hungry now. He pushed through the door and stood on the mat inside, watching two teenaged waitresses in green spotted aprons service the tables. The customers were festivalgoers, one and all, guzzling their food and yelling noisily at each other (none of them, it seemed, had yet heard the news from Wyveridge). There were performers too. In one quick scan Francis spotted Julie Myerson, Howard Jacobson and Caitlin Moran. And hey, who was that across the room but ghostwriter Anna and her consort Marv dining with Jonty Smallbone (aka Family Man), today resplendent in an eye-catching purple floral shirt. His wife, beside him, looked as grim as ever. Francis flicked his gaze away before he should be caught staring.

Finally the baby-faced maitre d' with the pudding bowl haircut stopped shooting the breeze with the customers he'd been serving ice cream sundaes to and came over. Sorry, sir, they were fully booked. No, there was no chance of a table later.

'My apologies,' he said, with a weary, slightly smug smile. 'It's festival time. You could try the Old Bakery, I suppose. Up the road. They might have something.'

On account of their atrocious food, Francis thought. He paced on up the hill, still feeling edgy. Little bands of festivalgoers drifted past him, chatting away innocently about talks they'd been to: 'simply love his drawings' . . . 'such an original way to deal with the subject' . . . 'it's not poetry, it's verbiage' . . . 'cut and pasted, really'. As he passed a hot dog van, the smell of onions, fried in old fat, simultaneously tugged at and turned his stomach. If necessary, he supposed, he could make do with that. A slimy orange frankfurter in a processed roll. A squodge of cheap mustard from the yellow plastic squirter. It was often the way at these festivals that after your starring role in a session, ego stroked to the max, you ended up alone in a KFC or McDonald's.

On the corner, by the steep road down to the river and the bridge, he was relieved to see the lit-up hanging sign for the Old Bakery. There was a waitress at the door who looked like a young starlet from the Fifties – albeit with a silver ring through her dainty upturned nose. Did they have a table for one? 'Not a problem,' she sang.

She led Francis through the crowded room to a place by the wall. He sat and studied the menu and the wine list; then, having made his choice, gazed absently around. The owners clearly had a taste for mixing it up. A ship's wheel hung below a moth-eaten fox's head. A copy of the famous Warhol screen-print of Marilyn, with yellow hair, blue eye shadow and pink lips, was right next to a black and white photo of what looked like Mold High Street early last century. Shelves, inset into the roughly rendered wall, were crowded with odd objects: dusty, cloth-covered old hard-backs, china Toby jugs, a framed bus timetable.

Away on the far side, he spotted another lone diner, head bent over a book. It was badger-woman Virginia Westcott, no less! Even as he glanced over, she looked up and caught his eye; then smiled, shyly almost, before returning to her reading.

The waitress came over to take his order. He settled on a half bottle of Chilean Cab Sav to wash down his meal; even though he badly needed a drink, he didn't want to be waking in the small hours tonight. He took out his notebook and studied it with a contemplative air. Across the room he was aware of Virginia waving at the waitress, then gesturing towards him. The girl was back; she looked almost embarrassed.

'Sorry, sir. That lady over there said that if you cared to join her at all that would be fine by her.'

'And would that be fine by you?'

The girl was blushing. 'How d'you mean?'

'Bill-wise, table-wise . . .'

'Oh right. We can transfer your bill, sir, no problem.'

It would be rude to refuse; Francis got to his feet and went over.

'Sorry,' Virginia said as he joined her. 'That was terribly forward of me. You probably wanted to cogitate on your own.'

'Not at all. I could use some company.'

'I've been in these situations before. At literary festivals. Where you have all the writers staying in the same hotel and they sit tight at their own tables throughout dinner. Seems a shame to me, missing the chance to interact with another mind that's probably a cut above the ordinary. We're alone enough with our screens as it is.'

'We are.'

'My event is over but I booked for another night. I always think it's a pity to come all the way to these things and then rush off straight after one's finished. Other people's talks can be so interesting. So how did yours go?'

'OK.'

'Don't be so absurdly modest, Francis. Your tent was packed out. I'm sure it was a great success. Did you spill the beans?'

'About?'

'Everything you saw early this morning.'

'Not really, no. I think some of them might have been a bit frustrated. Sitting through a history of the detective novel and then not getting the juicy details they wanted. As it's turned out, I'm glad I didn't say more.'

'How d'you mean?'

'Haven't you heard? There's been another death.'

'What? Who? Where?' Either Virginia was a magnificent actress or she was genuinely shocked; her eyes were alive with alarm.

'Grace Pritchard. She's one of the gossip columnists on the *Sentinel* . . .'

'Short-haired, blonde little piece?'

'You got her.'

'She spoke to me about Bryce.'

'Did she?'

'Just this morning. Cornered me on the terrace of the White Hart while I was having a coffee. She'd somehow found out that we'd been an item, years ago.'

'I'm impressed.'

'So was I. It's not as if it's common knowledge. She even wanted to film me talking about it. I'm afraid I declined. Unlike that poser Jonty Smallbone. He couldn't wait to get in front of her camera and opine about the situation. So what happened to the poor child?'

'She fell off the roof of Wyveridge Hall. Apparently.'

'What on earth was she doing up there?'

'Nobody knows. Although she was carrying a video camera with her. So it's possible she may have been trying to film the scenery.'

'And now she's dead?'

'I'm afraid so. It's a good thirty feet up to those battlements.

She'd have been lucky to have survived a fall like that. Even if she'd landed on grass.'

'You're telling me she hit the terrace?'

''Fraid so.'

'How horrible!' Virginia drained her glass of wine in a single gulp and poured herself another. 'This rather changes the picture, doesn't it?'

'You think?'

'To paraphrase Oscar Wilde: one sudden death at a literary festival could be regarded as a misfortune, two looks dreadfully suspicious.'

'It does put a different complexion on Bryce's death, doesn't it?'

The waitress was upon them, carrying Francis's starter.

'Eat up,' said Virginia. 'It's actually rather good in here. Despite the bizarre decor.'

As Francis forked up a lightly browned scallop and a gleaming lump of black pudding, Virginia rummaged in her handbag. 'But how on earth is Bryce linked to this unfortunate young woman? There's your conundrum.'

'Grace was a gossip columnist. And a more assiduous one than most. She was trying to find out what had happened to Bryce. Maybe she stumbled on some evidence.'

'But wouldn't she have told somebody? If she had. If not the police, her newspaper?'

'Maybe the murderer got to her before that could happen.'

'The oldest one in the book,' said Virginia, pulling out her iPhone. 'You of all people should know that.'

'Just because it's a cliché doesn't make it any the less likely.'

'I suppose not. Let's see what the Twitterati are saying on

the subject. Bloody typical, now the signal's gone. And this place doesn't even have Wi-Fi.' Virginia stared crossly at her screen, then took another swig of wine. 'So, are you going to tell me who your suspects are?'

He wasn't, not in any detail; but it would be good to play along. 'OK,' he said, 'so we have to start with our first victim. Assuming, of course, that there *was* foul play, why would anyone want to do him in?'

'Easy. Bryce aroused intense feelings, like all very special people. He'd just abandoned two women, at least one of whom may have stood to gain financially. Hell hath no fury, especially if there's spondulas involved.'

'You think . . .?'

'He and Scarlett were together for a heck of a long time. I doubt he left her with nothing, especially as he had plenty to spare. Anyway, for all his emotional callousness, Bryce had a weird sentimental streak. Look at how he held onto my pen.'

'And Anna?'

Virginia shrugged. 'Don't rule it out. He might well have left her something. Out of sheer guilt, if nothing else. And she has that ex-Marine with her. Who presumably knows how to do someone in in any number of expert ways.'

Francis laughed, with relief that someone had been thinking along similar lines to him.

'I'm not joking,' she said. 'So who else are you fingering?'

Francis smiled. 'I have some thoughts . . .'

'He says, cryptically. But he's certainly not going to share them with an inquisitive middle-aged novelist he barely knows.'

Francis ignored this tack. 'What do you think?' he asked.

'Besides the women in the case, I've no idea. I suppose he was frightfully rude about Dan Dickson. Though if there were a murder every time there was a literary assassination our stock of writers would be sorely depleted.'

'I don't think Dan is terribly likely.'

'Me neither. Though I should perhaps share with you an interesting vignette I came across during my post-prandial stroll last night. Dan and Bryce, engaged in old-fashioned fisticuffs, down by the bridge.'

'You're not serious?'

'I am. It was an odd little scene, so odd I was wondering at first whether I'd had too much to drink at Laetitia's party. The pair of them piled out of a taxi together, arguing, then sort of squared up to each other, almost like a staged fight. Dan launched a punch, Bryce tried to retaliate, then Dan knocked Bryce over. Onto the road. At which point they must have realized how silly they were being, because as Bryce struggled to his feet again, Dan held up his hands and they stopped, quite suddenly. Then they walked off together and sat on the bridge, where they engaged in a very intense conversation.'

'Did you get any idea what it was all about?'

'None at all. I was a good fifty yards away.'

'The review presumably. Though would they really come to blows just about that? It's a shame you weren't closer.'

She pouted her lips and made a mock-contrite face. 'Sorry.'

'Why didn't you say anything about this earlier?' he asked.

'I did. To the police. My attempts to get involved with you were rather rebuffed, weren't they?'

Silly woman. Taking umbrage because Priya had told her to

shut up, five minutes after she'd found her boyfriend murdered. 'But you never mentioned this when we chatted in the Green Room,' he said.

'You never asked.'

They sat there considering the case for a while longer. Having finished their wine, they succumbed to digestifs: a sambucca for Virginia and a grappa for him. The novelist pursed her lips to blow out the flickering purple flame. 'One other little thing you might like to consider,' she said, with a twinkle in her eye, 'is that Dan and Scarlett were once an item.'

'You're not serious.'

'I'm afraid I am.'

'As part of the famous open marriage?'

'No, it was before all that. I don't think Bryce ever knew about it, even though the affair nearly broke him and Scarlett up.'

'So what happened?'

'In the end, heaven only knows. It fizzled out. Maybe Dan lost interest. You have to remember, when his first novel came out, he went from being a nobody to suddenly very successful.'

'Remind me what that was.'

'*Dispatches from the E Zone*. It was a *succès fou*, as they say.'

They talked on, or rather Francis listened on, intrigued by quite how much Virginia knew about Bryce and Scarlett's lives. Finally, two digestifs each down the line, they were alone in the restaurant. Their bills were paid and up by the door to the kitchen the waitress was wiping down the last of the tables.

'I do feel I can trust you,' Virginia said. She wasn't quite slurring her words, but she was sucking her tongue in a decidedly tipsy fashion.

'Thank you,' Francis replied.

'Can't think why. But on condition you keep this totally to yourself, I'll let you into a secret about Peabody and me.'

Francis guessed what it was before she said it.

'Years ago, when we were together, he got me' – her voice dropped to a whisper – *'up the duff.'*

'When you were students?'

'Undergraduates, please. Yes, that's why I messed up my finals so badly.' Virginia looked round to make sure the waitress wasn't anywhere near, then mouthed: 'I . . . had to have . . . the abortion . . . a week before . . . my first exam.'

'Was that your choice?' Francis kept his voice low too.

'Obviously, at one level. But no, you're right, it wasn't. If Bryce had wanted it I'd have had that baby like a shot. I was completely mad about him at that stage. But he didn't, did he? He'd already moved on, the little shit. And I wasn't prepared to be a single parent at twenty-one. So that was the end of that.'

There was a long pause. Francis took a throat-burning slug of his grappa. 'Did you regret it?' he asked.

Her sigh was deep and powerful. 'At the time I had no idea what I was doing. Abortion – hah! That's what you did. Don't tell your parents, bit naughty, but a woman's right to control her own body, all very fashionable then, bing bang, into the clinic and away you went. There was always going to be another chance. But life isn't like that, is it? It races on and suddenly it's all too late. I often think about that child now. He'd have been in his thirties. University well behind him, established in his career. I wonder what he'd have been. A writer, like his mother, a critical genius like his father, or nothing much at all, like so many of the children of the unusually talented.' Virginia pressed her lips together in a grimace and her eyes glistened. 'It's crazy isn't it, the things we let ourselves do when we're young.'

Francis held out a hand and covered hers. 'I'm sorry,' he said.

'*Please* don't offer me sympathy,' she said, 'or I really shall break down and I'm sure you wouldn't want that. Look, I'm a grown-up. There are worse tragedies in this world than the mistake of a silly lovestruck girl.' She looked up and wiped her eyes with the corner of her napkin. 'Come on, I'm sure this pretty little thing wants to get off home.'

They walked to the White Hart side by side. Back in his room there was a light on by the bed. Priya was fast asleep on the sofa, still fully dressed, snoring quietly. Francis's note lay on the desk by the window, untouched. Unnoticed?

He took a blanket from the cupboard and spread it carefully over her. He stood for a few moments, watching her, her chest rising and falling as she slept. She was a beautiful young woman and he could easily understand how Bryce had thrown his life over for her. He tiptoed into the bathroom and flossed and cleaned his teeth as quietly as he could. Then he turned the room key in the lock, leaving it there with its plastic tag dangling, in case Priya woke before him and wanted to get out. He slid between the sheets of the big double bed and clicked off the light. Am I going to be too tired and tipsy to sleep, he wondered, regretting the grappas already; but even as the thought recurred, oblivion swept over him in a wave.

TWENTY-ONE

Monday 21st July

Francis woke early, with a dry mouth and a stinging headache. It was barely light, though outside the birds were serenading the little town with another noisy dawn chorus. It had rained in the night, and heavily, because he could hear drops still falling from the leaves of trees in the garden outside. He thought about boiling a kettle to make tea. But Priya was still asleep on the sofa, hands clasped tightly in her lap. It wasn't fair even to risk waking her. So he took a sip of water from the glass by the bed, then lay still, staring up at the ceiling, doing stretching exercises with his toes, thoughts about the case racing around his brain.

His main problem was this. If the two deaths were related – and surely they had to be? – Grace's 'accident' had drastically narrowed the field of suspects. Conal, for example, had to be struck off; at the critical time Francis had seen him with his own eyes out at the Black Bull. Unless his appearance there was some kind of elaborate alibi; but then how could he have known that Francis was going to visit that pub? He'd only dropped in on a whim. Then Virginia: even if her confessions of last night had given her more of a motive, the simple fact was that she'd been doing her event from 3 to 4 p.m. Was it possible that she'd hung around the Green Room afterwards to create an alibi before racing out to Wyveridge to do away with Grace? Hardly. Scarlett, too, was surely out of the frame. Not only had Francis been with her at the time of the second death, it wasn't clear that she even knew of Grace's existence. Which left three candidates from his original list: Dan Dickson, who had always seemed unlikely (even if the fight on the bridge offered an explanation for that bruise on Bryce's cheek); Priya, first on the scene, but despite that traditional indicator of guilt, surely another long shot, with a watertight alibi and no obvious motive (though that missing chocolate still bothered him); and finally (and most likely?) Anna Copeland, with or without the assistance of four-fingered Marv. But however badly he'd treated her, Bryce's behaviour hardly justified *murder*, did it? Even if she was completely broke and he'd left her money in his will. No, almost certainly, in a non-Braithwaite world, the real-life killer was someone else entirely. With some proper motive that had nothing to do with literary rivalry or being scorned in love.

Outside, down the street, he could hear the electric hum of a milk float, the clink of bottles being left on a doorstep. What on earth was he *doing*, he wondered. Curiosity had got him started on this quest, now he felt emotionally involved. He had barely known Grace, talked to her for what, ten minutes at the outside. But the thought of that bright young spirit snuffed out for no reason – or rather, for some all too compelling reason – had stirred him up horribly.

He knew why. Grace had reminded him, from the first moment he'd spoken to her, of his wife Kate. Not only did she have the same boyish figure, she had her attitude too: questioning, enthusiastic, always up for something different. Grace was Home Counties to Kate's Devon, but it was the same essential personality.

Six years after she and Francis had got married, they had been on holiday in Egypt when they had decided that now was the time to start trying for a family. Neither of them were earning much, but, as the Peruvians say, and Kate liked to repeat, 'every child brings a loaf with them'. It had been an intensely romantic time, touring Cairo, seeing the spooky mummies in the museum, laughing about the Pyramids being in a suburb of the city, being taken round on camels by a guide who refused to drink water in the heat of the day (it being Ramadan) but then strained every sinew to sell them overpriced perfumes back in his shop. From there they had headed on up the Nile, with Kate so enthusiastic about the people and the country she had been talking about Egyptian names for the baby they probably hadn't even conceived yet. At the end of their first week they had decided at the last moment to go for a three-day cruise on a felucca. It was a dodgy-looking craft and the youthful, bearded captain didn't exactly inspire confidence, but hey, wasn't that all part of the adventure?

'Don't be so uptight!' Kate had said to him, and Francis had gone against all his instincts and acquiesced. They were abroad, she was right, he should stop being so English and careful about everything. On their second night on the river, a freak storm had swept in – terrifying lightning zig-zagging across the black sky, a tree-bending desert wind bringing with it sand that stung your cheeks. It had been thrilling for an hour; then the boat had flipped over in a second and they had found themselves trapped under-water in their cabin. They had fought like wild animals to get out, but it had proved impossible to shift the door. Francis remembered all too vividly the choking panic as his lungs filled with water, then the strange sense of acceptance that came over him once he realized there was nothing more he could do. In that moment he thought they would die together and he squeezed his wife's hand tight as it went limp in his. When he came to, strange men were yelling at him. There was bright torchlight in his eyes. He was being dragged by his arms through the shallows to the shore. Choking, vomiting up river water on the reeds, he had screamed for Kate. But she hadn't made it. He knelt beside her pale, naked body on the stony mud, weeping incoherently.

That had been twenty years ago. There had been several attempts to replace her, but none had worked out. Now Francis was more or less reconciled to being on his own. He simply wasn't prepared to compromise with any relationship that didn't give him what he'd had with Kate; a mutual understanding that felt so easy, yet so complete.

When Francis woke again the sun was shining on his face. It was nine forty. Damn! He had missed the hotel breakfast and now he'd have to make do with coffee shop pastries. Priya had woken and gone; though her electric toothbrush was still in the bathroom and her lipsticks were lined up in a row on the glass shelf, so she hadn't left town.

Francis stood for a couple of minutes under the puny shower, trying unsuccessfully to establish a mean temperature. Towelled dry, standing in the soothing warmth of an oblong beam of sunlight, he pulled on a khaki T-shirt and matching shorts.

Outside it was a beautiful day. The sky was that lovely blue of late July, the soft-edged clouds tinged with an ochre that spoke already of the end of summer. There was the lightest breeze, tickling the hair on Francis's bare arms and legs. Even at ten in the morning, the festival crowds thronged the narrow pavements, ambling between talks in a fine variety of summer gear – everything from fluorescent crop tops to grey wind jackets and back again. One man was dressed as a fairy, complete with pink ballet shoes and wings; if his outfit was a joke, he wasn't smiling, as he paced along alone, intently studying his programme.

Pausing at the newsagent's Francis saw that Mold was now headline news. He bought a *Times* and stepped into The Coffee Cup two doors along, scanning the front page as he waited in line for a latte.

MYSTERIOUS DEATHS AT LITERARY FESTIVAL
Detectives investigating the deaths of two journalists at the annual Mold-on-Wold literary festival are now treating both as suspicious. Bryce Peabody, 54, was found dead in his room at the White Hart Hotel early on Sunday morning. He was the Literary Editor of the Sentinel *and a well-respected reviewer and commentator on literary affairs. Later yesterday, the body of Grace Pritchard, 24, a junior reporter on the same newspaper . . .*

Having got his coffee, Francis found a stool by the window and read on. Further down the piece Bryce was described as 'a literary hatchet man' and 'a legend in the world of books'. The picture editors, meanwhile, had done a number on Grace. They had clearly found an old photoshoot where she had been modelling various eye-catching outfits. The sexy pics gave the story the glamorous edge it needed. Seasoned, disreputable-looking writer and bright-eyed totty in a catsuit, what more could you want? Francis wasn't surprised, looking round the café, to see that the tabloids had gone big on it too. The same pictures, Grace's full lips in a pout that had presumably been ironic, were everywhere.

He sat, soaking up the criss-crossing conversations around him. Amid the discussion of the talks people had been to or were about to go to, one subject predominated: 'got to be a link' . . . 'maybe she *will* have to cancel' . . . 'all kinds of drugs out there' . . . 'but you'd have to be seriously off your face to jump' . . .

He looked up from his paper to see, at the front of the queue, Anna the ghostwriter, a *Daily Mail* tucked under her arm. She smiled and gave him a wave; then, latte glass in hand, came over.

'Mind if I join you?'

'Out on your own?'

'Marv's off on his training run. Likes to do ten miles before breakfast. And about five thousand sit-ups and squat jumps. Not to mention the hundred one-armed press-ups.'

'I'm impressed.'

'You should be. He likes to make the most of what he's got left.' She waved her *Mail* at him. MURDER, THEY WROTE was the three-quarter page headline. 'So what d'you make of all this?'

'Hadn't you heard?' Francis asked. 'About Grace?'

'Not until I saw this, no. Marv and I had an early night last night. We've got our talk later.' She was shaking her head solemnly at the paper. 'It's appalling. I can't quite believe it.'

'Actually, I was on the point of deciding yesterday that Bryce had had a heart attack—'

'You knew about this yesterday?'

'I went out there. Saw her body . . . spreadeagled on the gravel.'

'How awful.'

'It was.' The image of that broken rag-doll came back to him forcefully. He gritted his teeth, fighting back a sudden wave of emotion.

'So what d'you think?' she asked. 'That this is related . . . somehow . . . to Bryce?'

'Has to be. Doesn't it? Why else would someone want to do away with a blameless young woman like that?'

'Unless she did fall. Or had a freakout and jumped or something. It is a pretty druggy scene out there.'

'So everyone keeps telling me,' said Francis. 'But from what I can gather, Grace wasn't into that side of things at all. She was just a smart young cookie who was staying out at Wyveridge because it was fun and, presumably, a hub of the kind of gossip she was after.'

'So what . . . you think she found out something about what had happened to Bryce?'

'She was certainly out and about, asking questions.'

'As were you.'

'Not as successfully as her, obviously.'

'You don't feel in any danger yourself?'

'I'm certainly watching my back. But then I haven't found anything out yet, have I?'

'Haven't you? They don't know that, do they?'

'I suppose not,' he said. *They*, he thought. That was an interesting usage.

'You've let me off the hook, I trust.'

Francis acted surprised. 'What d'you mean?'

'Oh come on! I'm sure you weren't quizzing me yesterday

out of idle curiosity. That was why Marv was so pissed off. He thought you were trying to pin something on us. He might have helped me out or something . . . bit of military expertise?'

Francis laughed, he hoped convincingly. 'Oh dear. I suppose if you've been taught how to kill people for real it would make you a bit sensitive about stuff like that.'

'It's one of his big things. That the training he's received means he'd be far more disciplined than most if he ever faced a crisis in Civvy Street. It's like karate: you school your body to be a weapon, but simultaneously learn how to control your aggression.'

'I understand.'

'Do you?' she said, with a sharp look in her eye. 'Marv suffers from PTSD, so he has real problems in that area.'

Francis let the pause hang in the air, as they sipped at their matching lattes. 'So you've been helping him with a book about his time in Afghanistan?' he asked.

'And Iraq, yes. Among other places. *To Helmand and Back* it's called. We're promoting it together. The Marine and the ghost-writer. It was Marv's initiative. He wanted to be totally open about how it came into being. Very keen on giving me credit. It's unusual.'

'And the publishers are happy with that?'

'Not initially they weren't. They thought it would confuse the picture. Readers don't want to know about the process, they want an image, a brand they can identify with. But when we presented it to them as a publicity angle, us going out together and all that, they went for it. Black warrior and white ghost. It seems to be working well.'

'I hope you sold the book for a shedload.'

'More like a rabbit hutch. It's a tough time at the moment.'

She smiled. She was a good-looking woman, Francis thought, with a lovely aura: thoughtful, obliging, though in some way damaged (there was something about her eyes).

'Presumably,' he said, 'you must have been pretty angry with Bryce when he told you that he wanted to be with Priya?'

There was silence. Anna held his gaze. For a moment he thought he'd pushed it too far.

'He didn't tell me,' she said eventually. 'Spineless creep. I found out at a dinner . . .'

'Party?' he said to fill the silence.

'No, no, it was one of those sessions after a book launch. You know, where everybody's a bit pissed and you go on to some restaurant and then wonder why you've bothered. As you find yourself sitting between the two most tedious people at the event.'

Francis chuckled; he recognized the scenario all too well.

'It was some bash at Daunt's in Marylebone High Street. Afterwards about fifteen of us descended on this cheap Turkish place over the road. Souvlakia and shevtalia and red wine that gives you a hangover before you've finished your glass. Anyway, I found myself next to this chatty American who writes about fashion for the *Sentinel*. Skinny little creature with beady black eyes like a dachshund. Over the table was some enormous old hack who'd worked on the paper before they had their latest cull, wheezing as he crammed his face with kebab. Right in front of me they started gossiping about Bryce, neither of them obviously aware of my involvement with him. So I kept schtum and listened in. And the fashionista was full of this story that was apparently halfway round the office. That Bryce had finally left his long-term partner and run off with his girlfriend . . .'

'You didn't think they were talking about you?'

'For about half a minute, yes. Typical Bryce, I thought. Finally gets it together to leave home and then doesn't even bother to tell me. I was all set for the sketch of me, the siren who'd lured him away. Then came my shock. It wasn't me at all. It was this "Asian babe". My stomach just turned over, because I knew all about Priya. I'd even teased Bryce about fancying her, because he'd started repeating funny things she said to him at work, always a bad sign. Not that I ever thought she would look in his direction for more than a second. I listened for five minutes, just to be sure I hadn't got my facts wrong, then I left the table and called him. He cut me off, the coward, then switched his phone off. I was sorely tempted to go straight to his house, but I couldn't face Scarlett, so I waited till morning and turned up at the *Sentinel*.'

'You bearded him in his lair?'

'Had to. He wasn't answering my calls. I knew it was press day and he'd be there. He was pretty cross actually.'

'But not as cross as you?'

'I was off the register. It was a wonder to behold. I really didn't care who knew. Here was a guy who'd been promising me for five years that he was imminently going to leave his wife . . .'

'I thought she wasn't his wife?'

'As good as. You're right, though. The bastard never gave her a commitment either. Not that that ever bothered me when I was with him. I was in love with him and he'd managed to fool me that he really was waiting for the right moment to go . . .'

'Worried about the children?'

'Of course. He wasn't inhuman – and nor was I. I come from

a broken family myself, so I knew what I was going to put those girls through. But he kept telling me how his relationship with Scarlett was a completely busted flush, she didn't love him, they hadn't had sex for five years, blah blah, and I believed him. So we were waiting for the twins to get into this school, some C of E place that meant he and Scarlett had to go to church together, present a united front; then we were waiting for them to be settled; then this, then that, on and on it went. Meanwhile, I'd put my own future on hold. I was forty, forty-one, forty-two . . . Was it time to secretly bin the contraceptives and present him with the baby he'd promised me? But you know, silly me, I didn't want a relationship like that. I wanted it all. The honesty and the beautiful house.'

'And who was going to pay for that?' Francis asked ingenuously. 'Presumably Scarlett would require maintenance of some kind.'

'Don't be fooled by the scruffy boho act. Bryce had more dough than he let on. I don't know the exact details, but his *Sentinel* salary was pocket money basically.'

'Was that part of the attraction?' Francis asked.

'Honestly?'

'Yes.'

'No.' Her full lips cracked into a sly grin. 'And then again, maybe yes.'

'Which was it?'

'"No" to start with. When I was still infatuated with him and knew nothing about all that. Other than thinking that he must have a bit of cash if he could afford to keep a flat to work in as well as a house. But then, as I stayed with him, and waited, and waited, it *was* probably a factor. We could have had a nice life together, if that's what the silly twit had actually wanted. A nanny for the baby, holidays abroad, the full Monty.'

'I don't suppose,' Francis said casually, 'he'd made any provision for you in his will?'

Anna looked him slowly up and down. 'What an innocent question, Francis. As a matter of fact, he had. So yes, I do have an extra motive.'

'An extra motive?'

'Come on, don't play the naïf with me. Other than mere revenge. Isn't that what the abandoned harpies in the books usually do it for?'

'Had he left you a lot?'

'I've no idea. But he used to say, "I'd hate it if I got run over by a bus one morning and you got nothing." So yes, I reckon I was in for something.'

'You've no idea how much?'

'No.' Her expression was unbending; if she knew more, she certainly wasn't going to tell Francis about it.

'So was the baby always part of the picture?' he asked, after a moment.

'We talked about it a lot. Particularly in the early days. He wanted to have a child with someone he loved, he said.'

'Ouch,' said Francis.

Outside the café window, a picture-perfect toddler was standing on the pavement, trying to go one way while her mother went the other. She had curly ash-blonde hair and big blue eyes. She was wearing a denim dress, white tights speckled with stars, and shiny crimson shoes. 'Maya, come *on*!' called her mother. 'We're going this way.'

'No, we're *not* going this way,' Maya cried, waving a finger. 'We're going *this* way.'

Eventually the mother shook her head in desperation, swooped and grabbed her child and carried her off, screaming, under her arm. Had Bryce said yes, or Anna thrown the Microgynon to the winds, this little darling could have been hers; such was the unspoken thought that passed between them, as Anna met Francis's eye, then gave him a surprisingly indulgent smile.

'So why didn't it happen?' Francis asked.

Anna sighed. 'Bryce liked the idea in theory,' she said, 'but in practice he kept stalling, just as he did about leaving Scarlett. Didn't I realize how disruptive it would be having a child? It would come between us. We'd never be able to jump on the Eurostar for a dirty weekend in Paris ever again. And so on. But then, when I threatened to leave him, he always came round. Yes, he said, he understood how important it was to me, just give him another couple of months. One interesting thing about him, though. He was never flippant about it. He never took any silly risks. I always thought he must have had a bad experience with a girlfriend in the past . . .'

'Like?'

'Having to go through with an abortion or something.'

'He told you that?'

'Never in so many words. But I got that feeling.'

'Didn't you ever ask him straight out?'

'Of course. But he could be terribly uncommunicative. When it suited him. The bottom line was that he was very clever. He had this way of making you feel, when you were with him, as if you were the centre of his world and everything was going to be all right.'

'I'd heard that. So you met Marvin soon after your bust-up with Bryce?'

'I was already working with him. Bizarrely, before the Priya thing kicked off it was Bryce who was jealous about Marv. Or at least pretended to be. He used to make stupid jokes about how I fancied him. And I encouraged that thought, I have to admit.'

'So how was he when you finally did go off with Marv?'

'I don't think he gave a toss. He was so besotted with Priya I could have brought Marv into his office and shagged him on the desk and got no reaction.'

'You two got together quite quickly?'

'The classic rebound.'

'I didn't say that.'

'You were thinking it. Everyone does. But Marv has been a revelation to me.'

'In what way?'

'In every way. He's strong. Principled. He's there for me. He puts me on a pedestal, and that's quite refreshing.'

'Is it refreshing that he's not from your world?'

'By which you mean, "What on earth do you talk about?" Since he's an ex-Marine who likes watching footie on telly and you're a literary type happiest curled up with a book.'

'I didn't say that.'

'All but. Marv is highly intelligent and very receptive. The fact that he's not been lucky enough to have my particular kind of education means that there's more, not less, for us to talk about, especially when we're in a place like this. His take on the book world is great. How it's basically just a bunch of middle-class poseurs trying to prove how right-on and clever they are to each other.'

Francis laughed. 'Is that what you think too?'

'When I'm in a jaded mood. The other great thing about Marv is that he's a great noticer. He sees everything, all the time. From the colour of the eyeshadow you're wearing to the guy on the corner who might have a knife in his shoe. It's an education walking the streets with him.'

'Where's he from?'

'Nottingham, originally. He used the military to get himself away from a pretty shitty situation. As he says, if it hadn't been the Marines, it would have been a gang . . .'

'And now?'

'He's no use to them now, is he, so he's out on his ear like all the others. Actually, that's the thing that pisses him off most. Not so much losing his arm as his career. As he says, fighting's what he was trained to do. It's what he loved.'

'So what are his plans?'

'We're hoping the book will do well.'

'You can't live on that, though.'

'Andy McNab does. Anyway, there's no reason why, with a bit of help, Marv mightn't branch out, write a novel, even.'

'No reason at all, Anna.' Francis smiled. 'With a bit of help. But that's hardly going to pay the bills, is it?'

'It might. With luck. In our game you never know, do you?'

'That's true. So you're not planning a baby just yet?'

'Francis! We've only been stepping out together for five months. Give us a chance!'

TWENTY-TWO

Letting himself into his hotel room half an hour later Francis found Priya slumped on the sofa. Her eyes were red; she had clearly been crying.

'You've heard the news?'

'Last night,' she said. 'I ran into Rory and some of the Wyveridge lot at that Joe Sacco talk, and we went on to the poetry slam and ended up in the pub. Then Ranjit phoned to say he had something terrible to tell us. When he turned up, some of them thought he was taking the piss. The rest of us were too stunned to take it in. Then they started ordering bottles of wine. A wake, they said, though I thought it was a bit early for that. That Eva woman was crying. Really howling. It was all too much for me, so I came back here.'

'You didn't see my note?'

'Not till this morning. I was knackered. I lay down flat on the settee and the next thing I knew it was breakfast time.'

Francis stared out across the room, watching the bright particles of dust dancing in the sunbeam that fell across the beige carpet in a narrow strip, the triangle at its tip reaching high up onto one of the wardrobe doors. Come to think of it, 'dancing' was entirely the wrong word; if this was a dance, it was the slowest, gentlest, swirling waltz.

'What's going on?' Priya asked.

'I wish I knew. So what did you think? About Bryce? Before this? That he'd been murdered?'

'No, not to start with. But then, as the police stuck around, I was beginning to wonder. You?'

'I thought they might find something.'

'Like what?' asked Priya.

'That he'd been poisoned. Or suffocated.'

'Poisoned! Why?'

'He just looked so peaceful, lying there. He didn't look like a man who'd suffered a heart attack – or a stroke . . .'

'But poison! Wouldn't he have been rolling around in agony?'

'Not necessarily. There are some very sophisticated products out there these days.'

'But who on earth would have given it to him? And when? Considering that he came straight back here after the party and went to bed.'

'He made himself some herbal tea.'

'Yes,' said Priya. 'He made *himself* some tea. From one of the sachets in the room. Who could possibly have known that he'd pick Tranquillity?'

'Someone who knew him well.' Francis gave Priya a searching look. 'There are other possibilities. Someone might have done something to the home-made biscuits. Or the pillow chocolates.'

'In that case I'd be dead too.'

'Why?'

'Because I ate one.'

'What! When? You told me you went in there, saw him and immediately started screaming.'

'I did. But then when I went back up to the room to say goodbye I saw there was a second chocolate. On my side of the bed. Which I'm embarrassed to say I polished off.' She smirked guiltily. 'It sounds a bit macabre, doesn't it, but I needed that fix.'

'I see.' That explained that then – unless this was a brilliant double bluff.

'It never occurred to me,' she muttered. 'I could have bought it too . . .'

'I'm glad to have that explanation.'

'What, you mean . . .?'

'I thought it was possible you'd thrown it away,' Francis said. 'Or hidden it. While you were up there, changing.'

'Why?'

'To cover up the evidence.'

'You thought I was . . .?'

'The first person on the scene is always a suspect, Priya. You know that.'

'You seriously thought I might have *had something to do with it?*' Her voice had dropped to a whisper.

'The one rule of thumb in this business is that you can never rule anything out.'

She laughed bitterly. 'I'm surprised you let me stay in the same room as you, Francis. I might have slipped you a poisoned choccy too. What was my motive supposed to be, by the way?'

'I had no idea. Unless you'd managed to get Bryce to change his will with the same speed that you sorted out every other aspect of his life.'

'What! So I targeted him from the start. Knew he was rich. Talked myself into a job as his deputy. Seduced him. But why Bryce? Why didn't I go for – I don't know – a hedge funder? Why didn't I marry a hedge funder, come to that? Get myself the man and the lifestyle without the hassle of killing someone.'

'I'm sorry, Priya. I was trying to keep an open mind.'

'And how about poor Grace? How do I fit into that?'

'Second murders usually happen because someone discovers something the murderer of the first victim doesn't want them to know. Grace was looking for answers yesterday. The first person she spoke to when she got into Mold was you.'

'How d'you know that?'

'She left her scarf here, on the bed.'

'Did she now? I hate to disillusion you, Francis, but she was buzzing around talking to everyone. Virginia, Jonty, Dan, she was like a bitch on heat. So what was I supposed to have told her that was so incriminating?'

'I've no idea. But then again I've no idea what you were up to yesterday afternoon.'

'Meaning?'

'In theory, it's entirely possible you drove out to Wyveridge with Grace . . .'

'Yeah, right. "Oh do please show me the famous view from the battlements, Grace." Push. Bye bye. I was at your event, Francis. In case you didn't notice. I was about to tell you how interesting I found it. All that stuff about the Chinese and Dupin being a model for Holmes. After which I came back here for a snooze and then went out to hear Joe Sacco talk about graphic novels. The rest you know.'

'Did anybody see you come back here?'

'Not you, obviously. Hey, where were you after your talk? Perhaps it was you who was out at Wyveridge?'

'Don't be silly. I was in the Green Room.'

'Apart from anything else I don't see what my motive could have been. I owe my job on the paper to Bryce. Now he's gone, I'll be lucky to keep it . . .'

Suddenly she was in tears; and Francis felt terrible. He had been trying to be straight with her, but it hadn't come out well. He sat down next to her on the sofa.

'I'm sorry, Priya. That was very inconsiderate of me.'

'No, no, it wasn't.' She looked up at him with gleaming eyes. 'Why shouldn't you suspect me? As you said, I was first on the scene. It's just . . . well . . . I thought we were working together on this. I thought we trusted each other.'

'We do . . . we are. I'm sorry. I was thinking aloud. I didn't mean it.'

'But you clearly did.'

'I suppose I'd decided that someone had done it and my list of suspects is lamentably small. I mean, unless these two incidents were unrelated accidents, which seems unlikely, we're still left with the basic question – why on earth would someone want to murder Bryce? A nasty review just isn't enough of a motive.'

'No.' Priya pulled a tissue out of her pocket and wiped her face. 'But what,' she said, after a few moments, 'if it were more than a review? What if it was an actual exposé? Would that be enough, d'you think?'

'What d'you mean?'

'I'm not sure I should tell you this. I promised Bryce I wouldn't breathe a word.'

'About what?'

'*Celebrity and Hypocrisy.*'

'The talk he never gave?'

Priya nodded. 'But how am I supposed to trust you? Especially after all you've just said.'

Francis stayed cool. 'That's a call only you can make,' he said. He got to his feet and walked over to the window, looked out at the perambulating festivalgoers in the sunshine. Just below him, a young man in a white Australian-style hat was laughing at two female companions as he dodged theatrically out of the way of a slowly passing car. 'Hey,' he said, turning to her with a smile. 'Shall we go up the road and grab a sandwich from the pub? I'm starving.'

At The Rising Sun, Mutton Chops was back behind the bar in person. Faced with two brown-skinned punters, he was on exaggeratedly courteous form.

'And what can I get you and your, er, friend?' he asked Francis. In a moment, Francis thought, he's going to ask us where we originate from.

After a little deliberation, Francis and Priya ordered baguettes, then took their drinks out to an empty table under the apple trees.

'The *Sentinel* Review attack on Dan Dickson was just part one,' said Priya. 'Of Bryce's promotional plans . . .'

'For *The Poisoned Pen*?'

'Exactly. The main event was going to be his talk on Sunday afternoon. It was a full-blown assault on the phenomenon of celebrity publishing. How spineless and cynical editors are commissioning this stuff when privately, so often, they despise it. How tragic that the decision makers are almost all highly educated, yet continue to push out this crap that swamps any decent writing that might occasionally appear. Bryce was passionate about it. He'd been devious too, worming quotes out of leading publishers and agents to back him up. He was going to juxtapose those with extracts from some of the worst of these kinds of books. I think it would have brought the house down.'

'So he let you see it?'

She nodded. 'I was sworn to secrecy, though, because I think quite a few of the publishing types would have been seriously upset.'

'That was the point, presumably. Nothing career destroying, though?'

'Probably not in that bit. But then he moved on to the celebs themselves. How fraudulent they are in that often they only want one side of their story told, so each of these kinds of books is really just a huge vanity project.'

'He had examples?'

'Of course. Then he was going to talk about other aspects of the scam. Celebs who insist on saying they've written a book when they hardly even read. Not everyone is as honest as Jamie Oliver . . .'

'I'm sorry?'

'He stood up in front of four hundred children's writers and told them that despite his success as a bestselling author he'd never actually finished a book. Reading one, that is.'

Francis laughed. 'To be fair, I did read somewhere that he was dyslexic,' he pointed out.

'Then the kind of distortions that follow from all that,' Priya continued. 'So, like, people start to think that writing is easy. From there he went on to the real hypocrisy. Whereby a personal myth is invented and sustained by a book, when the reality is something completely other.'

'Such as?'

Priya leaned forward. 'His star example was someone who's headlining at this very festival.'

Francis thought hard, his brain spinning through the big names in the programme. Priya looked round conspiratorially, though there was no one within ten yards of them.

'Jonty,' she whispered.

'What, Family . . .'

'. . . Man, yes. The idea of this wholesome guy who lives with his family and his pigs and chickens on a smallholding in Somerset is total bollocks. Apparently he spends most of his time in Soho snorting coke and shagging waitresses. His poor wife looks after the farm and he just turns up to film . . .'

'It all sounds a bit libellous, Priya.'

'Bryce's argument was that proof of the truth is a defence in libel. He had evidence to back up everything he was going to say. Sworn affidavits from girls Jonty had dumped, one he'd got pregnant.'

'Spare us, not a love child.'

'Little Amelie. Aged two and a half. And this is the really shocking bit. Jonty doesn't want to see either her or her mother and he pays the mother the absolute minimum required by law . . . Family Man.'

'Goodness . . .' muttered Francis. Here at last was a real motive. 'So why hasn't this come out in the press?'

'Jonty had all that covered, according to Bryce. Point one, he's a national treasure, so unless the evidence is incontrovertible people won't believe it. Point two, he's got an immensely powerful PR who offers up the misdemeanours of lesser celebs in return for hands off Jonty. Point three, just to sew it up nicely, he's got a super-injunction.'

'And how was Bryce going to get round that?'

'By claiming he wasn't aware of it. Jonty's lawyers had served the super-injunction on the newspapers but hadn't thought of serving it on authors like Bryce.'

'But would the papers be able to print what he'd said?'

'They'd find a way. Probably by getting someone to repeat the allegation on Twitter. Once the cat was out of the bag, their lawyers would be able to advise that publication was fair game.'

'He'd worked it all out, hadn't he? Why didn't you tell me all this before?'

'I swore to Bryce that I wouldn't say anything about it to anybody.'

'While he was alive. But obviously this makes his death so much more suspicious. Quite a few people stood to lose if that talk went ahead. Not just Family Man.'

'D'you really think Jonty might have had something to do with all this? But he's such a huge star . . .'

'All the more reason,' said Francis. 'If his brand goes down in flames there's one heck of a lot to lose. For him, the publishers, the TV company, the associated merchandising operations, the annual Family Man exhibition at Earl's Court. It's an awful lot of dough. Now and in the future. Because his career would never come back from a revelation like that. It's not as if he's some Jack-the-lad, like Gordon Ramsay or Boris Johnson, who can just say, "Yeah, I did it, sorry, bit stressed at the time" – and then everyone forgets it. This is central to everything he stands for. The question we need answering now is: had Jonty somehow found out what was in this talk? If he had: how and when? Presumably recently, otherwise he would surely have tried to scupper Bryce earlier. I mean, is this something that someone might have gossiped about at one of the parties? On Saturday night, even?'

'But that was the night Bryce died.'

'I know. So maybe earlier on Saturday. Or Friday night?'

'But how could they have done? I was the only one who knew.'

'Are you certain about that?'

'Not completely certain. I mean, Bryce could be indiscreet.'

'I should say! At the *Sentinel* party he nearly spilled the beans about his talk to Grace, right in front of you.'

'How d'you know that?'

'I was there. I'd just been chatting to him.'

'Were you? I don't remember that.'

'You breezed up with some champagne from Laetitia and cut him off just as he was about to say something. He was going on about having a big fish in his sights. He must have been talking about Jonty.'

'You're right,' said Priya thoughtfully. 'You don't think he was just teasing her?'

'It didn't look like it to me . . .'

'Because he swore me to *total* secrecy. And I didn't get all this out of him easily.'

'I'm sure you didn't. But I'm afraid, from what I saw, that doesn't mean he didn't tell someone else what that Sunday session was going to be about. Who then told Jonty. Or one of his people.'

'If you say so . . .'

'We need to get to Jonty somehow,' Francis said, excited now. 'And/or the people around him. Discreetly suss them out about all this. So how are we going to do that?'

'I suppose we could do worse than go and listen to him talk. He's on in twenty minutes.'

Priya passed over the festival programme, open at that afternoon's page:

2 p.m. Big Tent. £10
FAMILY MAN

  Everyone's favourite countryman and smallholder, Jonty Smallbone, talks frankly about the ups and downs of life on Peewit Farm, the joys and challenges of bringing up three kids in a rural setting, and the problems he faced as he researched and wrote his latest book, Wild Stuff.

TWENTY-THREE

As they walked down towards the festival centre, Francis couldn't help but notice the increased media presence. By the gates to the school, where the banners flapped in the strengthening breeze, there were two full TV crews as well as a gaggle of paparazzi, burly, shaven-headed men carrying cameras with enormous lenses, who looked as if they would stop at nothing to get the picture that paid. None of this seemed to have set the festival back, though. *Au contraire*. The site was packed and Family Man's event was sold out.

'Sorry,' said the plump young woman at the ticket booth. 'It's returns only now.' She pointed at a long queue of hopeful punters: mums and dads with kids, older couples in matching anoraks, even a sprinkling of funky-looking young singles, one with a wicker basket over her bare shoulder containing a fresh cabbage. God help us, thought Francis. The power of the TV image. Realized in devoted followers.

'I'm going to have to call in a favour,' he told Priya. He turned to another of the festival elves, a skinny creature with huge teeth that she seemed to be constantly trying to swallow. 'Excuse me. Could you possibly get Laetitia Humble for me?'

'She's, like, *reelly* busy at the moment.'

'I appreciate that. Could you tell her that Francis Meadowes is extremely keen to see the Family Man talk as he wants to write about it for a national newspaper. I spoke yesterday,' he added, as the young woman stood looking at him and Priya open-mouthed. 'In the Big Tent. Sold out.'

'OK.' She scurried off.

'Sorry,' said Francis. 'I don't usually pull rank, but . . .'

'Don't worry. I'd do the same if I could.'

A minute later Laetitia appeared, today in a magnificent William Morris style floral skirt, all greens and oranges and pale blues.

'Francis, darling. You're still here. How wonderful.' She dropped her voice and pushed him and Priya away from the returns queue. '*Of course* we can get you in to see Jonty. And you must come to the Green Room afterwards. It would be good for you two to meet. He'll doubtless have a few books to sign in the bookshop, but we'll all be there straight after.'

'I'd like that. Is there any chance you could squeeze in my good friend Priya Kaur as well?'

Laetitia's eyes were on stalks. You could almost hear her whirring through her mental Rolodex trying to place this possibly significant Asian female.

'Priya was Bryce Peabody's partner.'

'Of course! I knew I knew the name.' Laetitia's grin switched to an appropriate mask of tragedy. 'I'm so sorry about Bryce. I was one of his greatest fans. Such a huge talent.'

'Thank you,' said Priya.

Laetitia shook her head. 'This weekend has been ghastly. First Bryce, and then this poor girl out at Wyveridge. I don't know what's going on. And now we've got totally the wrong kind of press crawling all over the place.' She glanced imperiously at the waiting elf. 'Two for the VIP row, please, Victoria. D'you mind taking them in?'

So Francis and Priya were ushered into the packed tent and shown to seats five rows from the front. On the big screen above the stage was projected the jacket cover of *Wild Stuff*: nettles, sorrel, seaweed, samphire, with a fine array of mushrooms and berries Francis would have struggled to put a name to.

'If we do get to talk to Jonty afterwards, will you do me a favour?' he said.

'What's that?'

'I'm going to bring up the subject of Bryce's talk and ask you, in front of him, if you had any idea what was in it. Will you please deny all knowledge?'

'Why?'

'Partly because I want to gauge his reaction; and partly to protect . . . you,' he said, dropping his voice because the tent had now hushed. Up on stage, Laetitia had come out from behind the entrance screen, bringing with her the genial, grinning, always slightly shambling presence that was Family Man. Jonty was casually but fashionably dressed, in a green and white checked shirt, faded blue jeans and brand-new Converse trainers. His long, trademark blond hair covered what his public knew all too well were his rather large ears. To either side of that famous beak his eyes sat perhaps a fraction too close together. Francis had of course been aware of him; how could he not be, straddled as he was across all media in a way that only the biggest celebs are. *Home Cooking*, the show that had made his name, was still a weekly fixture on BBC One. More recently, there had been spinoffs. *Family Man's Big Adventure*, for example, in which our hero had left the comfort zone of Peewit Farm and gone off round the world examining 'family values' while doing a bit of cheffing on the side. Francis had caught half of a programme in which Jonty had been learning how to make a yak curry in Nepal. 'We have so much to learn from simple Asian families like this,' he'd said, as he sat in the dirt with some toothless matriarch, now his new best friend.

'Good afternoon,' said Laetitia, casting admiring looks in her guest's direction. 'Jonty Smallbone is one of those wonderful people who's so famous he barely needs an introduction. Certainly not to you lot. But what we love about him, in addition to his cooking and his farming and his writing and everything else he does so well, is how reassuringly down to earth and unpretentious he remains. He really is, always has been, so refreshingly himself. So now, without further ado . . .'

You had to hand it to him, Francis thought, watching Jonty swing into action. His thank you to Laetitia was charming and sincere, yet somehow managed to convey that her gushing welcome was a bit on the ridiculous side. Then he moved on to his audience, thanking them for coming, making them feel special, to the point where you almost started to feel it was just you and him in here; and his family, of course, whom he introduced from the front row: wife Amber, sons Ethan and Milo, and baby daughter Jasmine, a bouncy-looking creature in a shiny pink frock, with red-spotted bows in her pigtails. No sign of little Amelie, though.

'I suppose,' Jonty said, 'you'd like to hear about the new book.

Since this is a literary festival.' It was called *Wild Stuff*, he went on, when the laughter had died down, because that's what it was about. 'And the great thing about wild stuff, particularly in these straitened times, is that most of it is also free stuff. Nettle soup, for example, costs nothing and is absolutely delicious. If you try and buy samphire in Primrose Hill it'll cost you five pounds a bunch. Go up to the marshes of North Norfolk and, as my sons here will tell you, at this time of year it's literally sprawling across the mud.'

The book was about all the natural nourishment you could find, he continued, in the hedgerows, the woods, the fields, the rivers, the sea. There was even a chapter on road kill. 'If you get to it quick enough, there's really no reason to throw it away. I remember once, driving home to Peewit, knocking down a pheasant on a back lane. We scooped it up, plucked it, cleaned it, and had it roast for lunch the next day . . .'

When the session was over Francis and Priya walked through to the bookshop. Francis didn't join the long queue waiting for the precious signature; instead, like Priya, he picked up a copy of the lavishly illustrated hardback from the big stack on the central table and glanced through it, starting with the blurb on the inside front flap:

When Jonty Smallbone left the Navy to start his own smallholding in the 1990s, little did he realize he was on the way to becoming a national treasure . . .

After a cursory look at the chapter on road kill (Badger Casserole with Wild Garlic and Field Blewit mushrooms looked surprisingly tasty), Francis looked over and caught Priya's eye. Her dark eyebrows flicked upwards as her forefinger tapped the title of a chapter called 'Wild Highs'. This was certainly intriguing, going in some depth into the properties of wild (lettuce) opium, magic mushrooms (fly agaric and liberty cap), salvia, betel nut, jimson weed, qat, peyote and yerba, amongst others.

PSILOCYBE SEMILANCEATA, or liberty cap as it's more often known, is the classic 'magic mushroom' or 'shroom'. It's a tiny, bell-shaped fungus, typically with a pointed umbo (see photograph), like the French 'liberty cap'. It grows abundantly in grassland: on lawns, in parks, on playing fields and in wilder pastures too. The fungus fruits in late summer and autumn, and is common after heavy rain. Once offering a legal high, the liberty cap is, since the Misuse of Drugs Act 2005, a Class A drug, which means that any preparation involving it is illegal.

Dried shrooms are more powerful than fresh ones and are often made into tea. Some people experience nausea when taking shrooms; sensory changes kick in after about forty minutes and can last for several hours. These range from a general feeling of wellbeing to hallucinations, very similar to those experienced by takers of LSD . . .

Having glanced through the rest of this section, Francis went on to a chapter entitled 'The Dangerous Wild: Poisonous Plants in Our Hedgerows and Gardens'. This had similar informative paragraphs alongside colourful photos:

People generally know about things like deadly nightshade, ivy and yew, but less often about azaleas, delphiniums, foxgloves and lilies. The list goes on, not all of them easy to recognize. The toxic red berries of black bryony and bittersweet are awfully similar to rosehip or rowan, which you might make wine or jelly from . . .

At the back of the book, Francis found the Acknowledgments,

which was mostly a list of Jonty's famous and influential friends. Right at the end, however, was a telltale sentence: *With special thanks to Anna Copeland, without whom – or is that without who, Anna? – words don't come easy.*

As he turned to Priya, he was smiling.

'Interesting?' she asked.

'Certainly is. Shall we see what's going in the Green Room?'

Forty-five minutes later Jonty finally came through, his family and Laetitia in tow. They took a seat on a sofa complex in the corner while Laetitia bustled around, organising refreshments. Francis kept glancing in her direction; but after five minutes, it didn't look as if her promised introduction was going to materialise.

'Time to be proactive,' he said, getting to his feet. 'Let's put her on the spot.' He winked at Priya and headed across the room, wine glass in hand.

'Laetitia,' he said, and watched with amusement as her face re-registered him, realized the position she was in, then, like a recalibrating satnav, switched into welcoming mode.

'Francis Meadowes, how lovely, you're still here.' She turned to Jonty. 'The well-known crime writer,' she added. 'Francis, I'm sure you know Jonty, by reputation if nothing else, but maybe not his lovely wife Amber, and their three amazing kids, Ethan, Milo and, er, Jasmine. And this is Priya, oh gosh, sorry . . .'

'Kaur.'

'Of course, apologies, festival brain overload, shoot me please. Priya was Bryce Peabody's partner.'

'We've met,' said Jonty. 'On Saturday night.'

'At my party?' said Laetitia.

'It was actually out at Wyveridge afterwards.'

'Oh.'

'And then again yesterday morning,' said Priya.

Jonty flicked a rapid sideways glance at his wife. 'Yes, indeed,' he said.

'You were very consoling, thank you,' said Priya.

'The least I could do. Such an awful shock for all of us.' Whatever else he was, Francis thought, Jonty was an impeccable performer. Next to him, Amber's features were hard to read: her lips tight together in a slight downwards curve, her eyes expressionless. Seeing her in the flesh explained why you saw so little of her on the TV, even as her children were shaping up to be little stars. 'Bryce's reviews were like my wicked indulgence,' Jonty was saying now. 'Always so funny. Even if they could be a tad cruel at times.' He shook his head again. 'But such a terrible thing to happen. To one so . . . relatively young. He wasn't particularly old, was he?'

'Fifty-four,' said Priya, and Jonty's look was priceless as he focused all too obviously on Priya, in the beige dress that hugged her figure as tightly as a T-shirt.

'Only five years older than you, darling,' said Amber. Her voice was a posh, no-nonsense drawl.

Jonty ignored this wifely dart. 'So do we know what happened yet?' he asked.

'The police are still waiting for the post-mortem,' said Francis.

Jonty looked from Francis to Priya and back again. 'And do they seriously suspect . . . *murder*?' he asked, his voice dropping to a whisper. 'Or is that just gossip?'

'It seems as if they might,' said Francis.

'When for all we know the poor man may have had a heart attack.'

'Or an aneurysm,' said Francis. 'Which the doctor seemed to think as likely.'

Jonty nodded thoughtfully. 'Did he? Trouble is, the local constabulary probably don't get much going on down this way. If something like this happens, they get overexcited, start to think they're in an episode of *Midsomer Murders*.'

'But this second tragedy has rather changed the picture, don't you think?' said Francis.

'Now that does sound like a ghastly accident,' said Jonty. 'The story I heard was that they were all high on drugs out there.'

'But you were out at Wyveridge yourself, you said?'

Jonty didn't blink. 'Yes. Amber came with me. Seemed like a pretty lively scene, didn't it, darling? We didn't stay long.'

'Did you see evidence of drugs?'

'Can't say I did. But you'd hardly expect to. People tend to pop into toilets and upstairs rooms to do these things, don't they?'

'I believe they do,' said Francis. 'So you don't think the two deaths are linked?'

Jonty seemed almost thrown, but only for a couple of seconds. 'Do *you*?' he returned.

'Two unexplained deaths in twenty-four hours,' Francis replied. 'It does seem a bit . . . surprising, to say the least. How many other incidents like this have you had over the years, Laetitia?'

'We've had heart attacks and so on, but always of much older people – and never of one of our performers. Nothing like this. I mean, front page news and all that.'

'I guess if you're a crime writer,' Jonty cut in, 'you're bound to be trying to find a story here. But d'you know what? I hate to be controversial, but here's poor Bryce, whose death – with respect, Priya – the entire festival has been gossiping about, but could very well be from natural causes. By the same token, I'd say it was perfectly possible that this unfortunate girl was high on some drug or other and thought she could fly off this tower or whatever.'

'Magic mushrooms, perhaps,' said Francis. 'Though maybe it's too early in the season to find them out in the wild?'

Family Man shrugged. 'Hard to say . . .'

'I noticed you had a very interesting chapter on "natural highs" in your book.'

Jonty laughed, perhaps a little too loudly. 'You've actually read it! I'm flattered.' If looks could kill, Francis thought, I would be the third victim of this festival. 'No,' Family Man went on, 'since you ask, it's a fascinating area, rather vexed of course since the change in the law of July 2005, which means that technically you could get seven years for picking a bag of liberty caps and taking them home. Meanwhile, equally scary things remain legal: fly agaric, for example, the other kind of magic mushroom, the crimson one with white spots, the toadstool of the children's stories, which can make you seriously ill. Or *Salvia divinorum*, which is a kind of sage, and could give you a trip to put mushrooms – or even LSD – in the shade . . .'

'You've tried it?'

'Salvia, lord no! You wouldn't catch me with any of these things. But you've only to look on YouTube. There's hundreds of videos of young people freaking out on this stuff. Terrifying to watch, some of them.'

'I enjoyed your chapter on natural poisons too.'

'Did you?' Jonty looked slowly round the little group and his face cracked into an uneasy smile. 'Looks like I've got a fan here. No, that's a whole other subject which, and don't let my publisher hear this, I could have done much more on.'

'Do I feel another book coming on?' said Laetitia.

'Now there's an idea!' said Jonty. 'But seriously, you couldn't do a book like *Wild Stuff* without pointing out that not everything in our fields and hedgerows is harmless.' He turned to his children. 'I remember when you guys were little, having to keep a jolly careful eye on you when we were out on country walks. You in particular, Milo, used to love shoving anything and everything into your greedy little gob. Holly berries, yew berries, the works. It was a constant worry.'

'Yes, Dad,' said Milo, eyes glazing over.

'I think I'd like to have you with me in person,' said Laetitia, 'before picking the ingredients for any wild meal I tried to have.'

There was polite laughter in the circle.

'You can always read the book,' said Jonty. 'The photographs are pretty accurate. And you're hardly going to get into trouble with nettle soup or nasturtium salad.'

'The very best of luck with it,' said Francis. 'I'm sure you'll do well.'

Laetitia pointed two fingers at Jonty's head. 'Number five as we speak.'

'Congratulations,' said Francis. 'And climbing, I hope? D'you get time to write the books yourself?'

'Of course. Like to be hands-on. Obviously I have researchers to help with some of the boring detail, but no, at the end of the day, it's my golden prose.'

'So refreshing to hear that,' Francis said. 'Priya and I were just saying, earlier, so much of what's out there now isn't written by the people whose name's on the cover. Particularly when it comes to busy celebrities. She was telling me that that's what Bryce's talk was going to be about. The one he sadly never got round to delivering.'

Francis's accomplice laughed nervously; she was acting her part well. 'That's what he hinted,' she said. 'But he never let me read his speeches before he delivered them.'

'Is that so?' said Family Man.

'You knew the title, though,' Francis prompted.

'*Celebrity and Hypocrisy*. Hardly a secret, it's in the programme.'

'Shittety-shit!' said Jonty. 'That sounds interesting.' He fixed them all with a tigerish grin. 'Did he really not tell you what it was about? I run *everything* past Amber. She's like my in-house editor. She'll always tell me if I've made a joke that's a bit off-colour or whatever. And she certainly knows how to trim me if I'm being boring.'

'Shall I trim you now then?' said his wife, and despite, or perhaps because of her deadpan tone, there was laughter from the group. For a second, a tiny acknowledging smile flickered on her thin lips. Francis reckoned the time had come to move on.

'I hope I gave you the answer you wanted,' Priya said to Francis as they crossed the room.

'Perfect. The subject of Bryce's talk was raised and there was a reaction.'

'He gave the impression he knew nothing about it?'

'Exactly. And simultaneously we got across that you didn't either, which hopefully will make you a little safer.'

'You really think that Jonty . . .?'

'I'm keeping an open mind, Priya. So you spoke to him again yesterday morning? You didn't tell me that.'

'I ran into him on the terrace of the White Hart. When Grace was there filming, after breakfast. He came straight over and gave me a hug. Which was nice of him, considering we'd only chatted for a few minutes the night before.'

'Very nice of him,' said Francis. 'I'm sure his motives were entirely pure. How long a hug was it?'

'Long enough.' Priya made a 'yuk' face and Francis laughed. 'So why were you asking all that stuff about mushrooms?' she asked.

'Why indeed?' said Francis, looking at his watch. 'Now what time is it? I'd quite like to shoot out to Wyveridge. See if we can't find Rory and his posse. And see what the police are up to. You coming?'

TWENTY-FOUR

Arriving at Wyveridge shortly after four, Francis and Priya found the police presence substantially reduced. The vans and cars crowded onto the gravel circle at the back of the house had gone, leaving just one marked car behind. There was a single uniformed PC stationed at the front door, the big-bellied fellow they'd seen earlier. Yes, he confirmed, the young lady's body had gone off to post-mortem early that morning, though even if he knew the results, which he didn't, he wouldn't have been able to give them out, as a matter of policy. Was DS Brian Povey still around, Francis asked. No. Where was DCI Julie Morgan? That was confidential information, but yes, he could confirm that she wasn't here. Could they pop into the house to look for someone? No, they couldn't. He had a list of eight resident guests he was allowed to let through and they weren't on it. Were any of those people currently in the house? That he couldn't say.

'I was here yesterday,' Francis said. 'Detective Sergeant Povey gave me permission to go in and see my friend Ranjit Richardson, who's the organizer of the house party here.'

'That was yesterday, sir. I'm afraid I have to stick to my orders.'

'Are we even allowed to go round the front?'

'I can't stop you walking in the gardens, sir. But strictly not within the areas marked off with tape. The terrace is still a crime scene.'

'What a knob,' said Priya, as they walked off.

'Only doing his job,' said Francis. He winked. 'Doesn't mean we can't get what we want.'

He led her round to the top of the grassy bank that flanked the terrace, which was completely outlined by blue and white scene-of-crime tape. Above them, the Hall looked haunted in its emptiness. There on the gravel was the taped-off body shape of poor Grace, now damp with gleaming rain droplets and slightly askew. Priya shuddered visibly.

'That's where she was . . .?'

'Yes.' Francis, right beside her, put a comforting arm around her shoulder. 'Horrible, isn't it?'

'Poor, poor girl,' she said. 'She was younger than me.'

'I know she was.'

Suddenly she had broken down in tears.

'Come on,' said Francis, ushering her to a nearby bench. 'That's it, take your time.' He pulled a clean handkerchief from his pocket and gave it to her.

'I'm sorry,' she said eventually, dabbing at her face. 'I barely knew her.'

'None of us did,' he replied. 'Doesn't mean we're without feeling, does it.'

Now she looked up at him with an expression he'd not yet seen; more open, yet simultaneously more helpless. 'I didn't tell you,' she said, 'but I had a sister who died young. She was almost exactly the same age as Grace.'

'Priya, I'm sorry. I had no idea . . .'

She shook her head. 'Don't worry, it was a long time ago. It's just like . . . all this . . . has brought it back. I feel so vulnerable. I'm sorry, you really don't need to hear . . .'

'Don't be silly.' He sat quietly with her, then took her hands between his. 'Tell me about her,' he said.

'She died in a fire. At my parents' house in Derby. We'd all gone out for the evening to see some cousins, and Chinni stayed behind to do some course work. When we got back the place was ablaze. You could see the flames from three streets away.'

'And why didn't she get out?'

'I don't know. None of us knew. We thought she must have fallen asleep . . .'

'I'm so sorry.'

'Chinni was like my role model growing up,' Priya went on, eyes gleaming. 'She always stood up to my parents, told them she wasn't going to listen to their stupid ideas about what Punjabi women were born to do, look after their families, cook, clean, and when the time came marry some man they didn't know and probably didn't like or fancy either. She managed to get her A-levels and go to college. So many of the sisters of my friends were the total opposite of that, would go along with their parents, let them enforce the old traditions. But Chinni was always different, always said what she thought, what *she* wanted, she was so cool . . .'

Priya trailed off and there was silence. Her lip was trembling. 'She was pregnant,' she said quietly. 'That was the worst of it . . .'

Francis looked out over the terrace, to the garden and big field that sloped down to the woods below. Heavy grey cloud was moving in right above them, but down the hill, beyond the gleaming snake of the river, that patchwork green and ochre quilt of English countryside stretched away in the sunshine to distant blue hills.

'For what it's worth,' he said, eventually. 'I lost someone very dear to me, in my twenties.'

'Who was that?'

'My wife, Kate.'

'I'm sorry,' said Priya. 'How?'

Even as he told Priya the story of the felucca and the storm, Francis could hardly believe he was doing it. He had been through whole relationships and not shared this. But there was something about this woman that pulled it out of him.

'It probably sounds a bit ridiculous,' he said. 'But Grace reminded me of Kate. This death has brought it all back to me too.'

'I get that,' said Priya, squeezing his hand.

They sat in silence for a while. 'So why exactly did you bring me here?' she asked.

Francis shook himself and got to his feet. 'You up for a short stroll?'

'OK.'

He led her across the lawn and – via a quaint little bridge with a cattle grid – over the ha-ha that separated it from the field beyond. At the bottom of the valley was a herd of black and white Friesians, which now started to lumber up the pasture towards them.

'I'm frightened of cows,' Priya said.

'Don't worry. As long as they've got udders they're all right. It's bullocks you need to watch out for.'

The foremost animal was now approaching, wide eyes watching in a slowly turning head, at the front of a clutch of its peers.

'Boo!' shouted Francis, holding up both his arms like a scare-crow. The cow jumped back, then turned and loped off, pursued by its gaggle of supporters.

'Very impressive,' said Priya. 'Now what?'

'I just wanted to see what magic our thoroughly miserable summer might have worked.'

Leaving Priya close to the bridge, he paced down across the field, pausing every now and then, stooping, then returning to the upright.

'Eureka!' he cried and came running back towards her. He arrived, breathless. '*Oh ye of little faith.* Just as I was starting to think I was on totally the wrong track, I find not just one, but two.' He held out a browny-white mushroom with a head like a little bell. 'This, Priya Kaur, is the liberty cap, known colloquially as the magic mushroom. Odd-looking chap, isn't he? I have now, by plucking it, committed a criminal act. But I expect we can get past PC Intransigent without him searching us and sending us to Dewkes-bury nick.' He slipped it into his jacket pocket. 'That wasn't so far from the house, was it? Easy enough to spot on a casual foray.'

'So what are you saying? You think Grace had one?'

'I don't think anything,' said Francis. 'For sure. But it's a possibility, isn't it?'

'That Eva woman was offering magic mushroom tea at the party on Saturday.'

'Was she?' said Francis. 'You didn't mention that before.'

'I didn't think it was important. There were drugs everywhere that night.'

Francis paced on, back over the ha-ha and the lawn, with Priya following. At the end of the terrace away from the body shape, he bent down and picked up a handful of gravel. His arm swung up in a circle and a spray of fine stones hit at least two of the first floor windows.

'What on earth . . .?' Priya said, but her question was answered by a familiar face, peering out from the side window of the mullioned bay; which was then pushed open.

'Francis!' shouted Ranjit. 'And Priya. What are you two doing here?'

'Not allowed in, I'm afraid,' said Francis.

'That effing copper?'

'Yes.'

'Silly arse. I'll come down.'

A minute later he was striding towards them in a full-length purple coat. 'I can't think what he's so worried about,' he said. 'Most people have left now anyway.'

'Back to London?'

''Fraid so. The whole thing's been altogether too traumatic. We're down to a hard core of eight, and not for much longer.'

'And where are they? Inside?'

'They've all gone into town. I don't blame them, really. It's a bit spooky out here. And Rory wanted to see that SAS guy that was wounded in Afghanistan.'

'Marvin Blake? He was actually a Marine.'

'Same difference. I was about to call a taxi. Thought I might join them. I don't suppose . . .'

'We're driving back in? Yes, we are. We're going to the same talk.'

'Sounds interesting, doesn't it?' Ranjit said. 'The soldier and the ghostwriter. What kind of relationship is that, I wonder?'

TWENTY-FIVE

As the rain drummed down outside, Priya and Francis sat squashed up round a table in the noisy back bar of the Barrow and Turnip with Ranjit and his friends: tall, cadaverous Rory, in his trademark black velvet jacket; spiky-haired, bespectacled Neville; and American Eva, today in a voluminous flowery dress. Francis had hooked up with them as they came out of Marv and Anna's talk and suggested hitting the pub. Once ensconced, a lively discussion had ensued. Eva had found Marvin's testimony scary. 'Like, all that stuff about "slotting the Taliban" and "getting good kills". I mean, what expressions! I was amazed he was so open about it all.'

'That's what soldiers are like,' said Rory. 'Bottom line, they're killing machines.'

'Don't be ridiculous,' said Ranjit. 'They're doing a necessary job. Anyway, I liked his honesty. Particularly the way he talked about the shock of being wounded, how you never expect it to happen to you . . .'

'That was moving,' said Eva. 'And PTSD. He really got that across, didn't he? Terrifying, what he's had to deal with . . .'

'He was cool,' said Neville. 'I really liked the fact that he hates to be called a hero. And he wants everyone to know he uses a ghostwriter.'

'Yeah,' Eva agreed. 'That *was* cool. And Anna was great, wasn't she? So modest and understated.'

'And sexy,' said Neville.

'Did you think so?'

'*Yeah.*'

It had been a powerful interview, no doubt about that. Chair Dan Dickson had done well drawing the pair of them out; at moments it seemed like a soldier's discipline was all that was holding Marv together, for all the blokey banter on the surface.

But now Francis had this gang together, he didn't want to waste his opportunity. After a couple more minutes, he steered the conversation away from the intriguing relationship of Anna and Marv and on to Grace. 'So who was the last person to see her alive?' he asked. 'I mean, were any of you guys out at Wyveridge when she got back there yesterday afternoon?'

'No,' said Rory. 'We came into Mold around lunchtime, didn't we?' He fixed Eva with a look that seemed to carry a load of extra meaning.

'So what time's lunchtime,' Francis asked, 'in your schedule?'

'I don't know, one-ish, something like that.'

'And you didn't see Grace when you got into town?'

'No,' said Rory.

'And then you were here for the rest of the day?'

'Yeah. Later we went to Joe Sacco's talk about Israel/Palestine. Where we ran into you, Priya.'

'I can vouch for that,' said Priya.

'Then we all went on to the poetry slam together. And after that the pub, where we were having a great time until Ranjit turned up and broke the news to us . . .'

'May I ask what you were doing between one thirty and five,' Francis asked, 'when the Sacco talk began?'

The three of them looked at each other, their faces suddenly a picture of uncertainty.

'You weren't at my talk, I don't think?'

'No.'

'Or Virginia Westcott's?'

'Who's she?' asked Neville.

'A doyenne of romance, who was speaking at the same time as me.'

'No,' said Rory. 'We weren't.'

'That's quite a long time,' said Francis, 'to be hanging around a festival site.'

'I suppose it is,' said Rory. 'But I guess that's the point of going to a festival – to hang out. What were we doing, Eva? I can't really remember. Drinking coffee, chilling in the Relaxation Zone . . .'

'I'm sorry to be pernickety,' said Francis, 'but the Wyveridge housekeeper, Mrs Mac, told me you were still having breakfast when she knocked off at two o'clock.'

Rory didn't miss a beat. 'Christ,' he said angrily. 'I can't remember precisely when we left for town. One o'clock, two o'clock, who's counting? Anyway, what's it to you? You're not the police.'

'I appreciate that,' said Francis. 'All I was trying to find out was when Grace got back to Wyveridge and whether she was alone when she did. It's an important question, because the poor girl died in a horrible way that may well not have been an accident. I don't for one moment think any of you were involved in her death but I am trying to establish the facts. If she was alone, we need to confirm that. If she was with someone, even if it was a friend of yours, we need to know that too. So if any of you want to answer my question truthfully, that would be a real help.'

The trio were silenced by this. The chatter and clatter from the rest of the pub sounded loud in Francis's ears. 'I've gotta say this, given the circs,' said Eva, eventually. 'In confidence, Grace did come back before we left.'

'I see,' said Francis. 'And when was that?'

'Middle of the afternoon. We didn't go into town straight after our breakfast, because we went for a walk first. By the time we'd got back and had, like, tea, it was probably getting on for four, because we arrived in Mold with just enough time for a coffee before the Sacco talk, which as you said was at five.'

'Was Grace alone?' Francis asked.

'I think so, yeah. She popped her head round the door. She was in a rush to get some work done, she said.'

'Thanks Eva, that's very helpful.'

'Yeah, thanks Eva,' said Rory. 'I've already given the police my statement. Saying we left at half one. I thought we'd discussed this.'

'Do stop obsessing about yourself, Rory. Someone's died here. As you said, Francis isn't the police.'

'If any of this turns out to be relevant, d'you imagine for one moment that he won't go to the police?'

'It's more important that he knows about it than not.'

'Why? Who is he? Sherlock Holmes? I signed a statement this morning. I think you forget I'm training to be a lawyer. If I'm done for perverting the course of justice that's the end of my career. It's lucky Francis isn't the police, because you've basically just stitched me up, Eva. So perhaps it's my turn to do a bit of stitching myself and point out the reason why I fibbed about the time in the first place. The reason, Francis, we went for our walk was to look for mushrooms – of the magic variety. Surprisingly, it still being July, we found quite a few, and you, Eva, being the world freaking expert, found more than most. Then, when we got back to the house we made some shroom tea, which Eva offered to Grace. Maybe that will be relevant to the inquiry.'

Eva was shaking her head. 'Rory,' she said. 'There was no need for that.' Then to Francis. 'She didn't even want it.'

'Fortunately,' said Rory, 'as Eva says, Grace refused our funny tea.'

'But she knew what it was?' Francis asked.

'Oh yeah,' said Rory. 'Eva was trying to talk her into forgetting her work, getting high and coming into the festival with us. I wonder why that was.'

'Rory,' said Eva, with a clear note of warning.

'Did she say what this work was?' Francis asked.

'Something to do with the diary column she contributed to on the *Sentinel*,' said Eva. 'She thought she had a scoop.'

'She didn't tell you what it was about?'

'She said it wouldn't be a scoop if she did. Then she ran off upstairs to write it.'

'And you're sure nobody was with her?'

'We didn't see anybody else, did we?' said Eva.

'No,' Neville agreed.

'So did you finish off this shroom tea?' Francis asked.

'Hey, good question, Sherlock,' said Rory. 'No, we didn't. We had a cup each, but there was a good two inches left in the pot.'

'Which was still there when you came back?'

'If you must know, the pot was empty.'

'Washed up? In the machine?'

'No. Where we'd left it, on the table.'

'Completely empty, or with the remains of the mushrooms in the bottom?'

'Jesus Christ, what is this?'

'These details could be important, Rory.'

'OK, with the mushrooms at the bottom. It was like someone had drained the liquid in the pot, but no, it hadn't been washed up.'

'So what was this?' Francis asked. 'An ordinary teapot?'

'No, it was like a glass coffee pot thingy. From the filter machine.'

'And the police hadn't found it?'

'They were all busy up the other end of the house. When I saw it was still there, I got rid of it immediately. Just flushed the dregs down the bog. Psilocybins are illegal. Class As, in fact, since—'

'July 2005.'

'Correct.' For a moment Rory looked almost impressed with his inquisitor.

'So you washed it up,' said Francis. 'Was there anything else there to do?'

'Just a couple of cups and saucers, plates, that kind of thing.'

'So: two cups and two saucers and two plates?'

'Does it matter?'

'It very well might do. Was there anything on the plates?'

'I really can't remember.'

'Try.'

'I don't know. Some crumbs, maybe, from, like, a cake.'

'From a cake? How did you know that?'

'Because they looked like cake crumbs, doh. And also, since you ask, half of it was still in the larder. It was a fruit cake the girls brought with them from London.'

'"The girls" being Grace and Fleur?'

'Yes.'

'So this little washing-up session must have been quite late, Rory. By the time you got back to Wyveridge from town?'

'It was, yeah.'

'And what kind of a state were you in by then?'

'Pretty shitfaced. Upset, too, for obvious reasons. But not so far gone that I can't remember what I did.'

Francis turned to Ranjit, who had been listening quietly to this exchange, sipping thoughtfully on a pint of Abbot's Finger. 'You didn't treat yourself to tea and cake, Ranjit? When you came back with Carly?'

'We didn't even go to the kitchen. We let ourselves into the house, went to the drawing room, looked out and saw Grace on the gravel. As soon as we realized what had happened, we phoned the police and went straight upstairs.'

'So how long does it take, Eva,' Francis asked, 'for this funny tea to take effect?'

The American shrugged. 'Depends on the individual. You usually start to feel something after ten minutes or so. Then it builds.'

'Lasting in total?'

'A few hours, maybe. Though sometimes it can seem longer. It's weird. It starts to feel like time itself is distorted.'

'How else does it affect you?'

'It hits different people different ways. For me, it's always amazing. I get this, like, spiritual vibe. Like everything is more vivid, more real somehow. You see these trails of warmth coming off people, then sometimes you see sounds as colours. Like birdsong becomes a dappling of colour, which is pretty wild.'

'And a bad trip?'

'I never had one. On shrooms. But yeah, some people can get a bit paranoid, I think.'

'Is it possible,' Francis asked, 'that you could get into such a crazed or unhappy state, in forty-five minutes, that you might want to jump off a roof?'

'I wouldn't say so.'

'Though there was that guy in America,' said Neville, with a sudden mad cackle, 'who cut his friend's heart out while on shrooms. Thought he was the devil incarnate or something.'

'That's really helpful, Neville,' said Rory.

The group was joined at that moment by Carly and Adam, who had come fresh from a seven o'clock session on 'Reinventing British History' with Lucy Worsley and Tristram Hunt.

'OK,' Francis went on, when more drinks had been bought and the new arrivals had squeezed in round the table. 'So if this account of yours finally is the truth, it sounds as if Grace was only alone at the house between four o'clock, when you three left for town, and shortly after the end of my talk, when you,

Ranjit, told me you returned with Carly and found her dead on the gravel. What time was that exactly?'

'I don't know,' said Ranjit. 'Your talk finished when?'

'Four.'

'So we came out, had a coffee, didn't we, Carl, then drove back. So maybe five, five thirty by the time we walked through the door.'

'Doesn't leave an awful lot of time for Grace to get high on your shroom tea, does it?' said Francis. 'Even assuming she finished filing her piece and decided to change her mind, go against the habits of a lifetime and help herself to your leftovers.'

'Doesn't leave an awful lot of time for a murderer to chuck her off the battlements, either,' said Rory, looking pointedly at his watch. 'Now d'you mind if we leave you to it? We were planning to catch the Boomtown Rats gig. Which starts in five minutes.'

'Charming fellow,' said Francis, when he'd gone, taking Neville and Eva with him. 'Doesn't like being put on the spot, does he?'

'He's always been like that,' said Ranjit. '"Angry man", we used to call him at college. But he's got a lovely side, too. Very loyal to his friends. He's just got a problem with authority.'

'Francis is hardly authority,' said Priya. 'He's just trying to find out what happened.'

'I know that,' said Ranjit, 'but the bottom line is that Rory's terrified of getting a drugs conviction. It would totally mess up his career.'

'Perhaps he should stop taking drugs then,' said Francis.

Priya laughed, but she was on her own.

'I do understand where he's coming from,' Francis continued. 'One moment he's at a festival, with a load of friends, in a place where you'd be unlucky to run into an off-duty Community Service Officer. The next he's at the centre of a police enquiry. But in a situation like this he's his own worst enemy. If he behaves with the police like he just behaved with me he's going to get himself into trouble. It's classic guilty suspect stuff. Which is unnecessary . . .'

'Unless there's something he's not telling us,' said Priya.

'Meaning what?' asked Francis.

'I don't know. Grace turned down their funny tea. Is it possible Rory offered her something else?'

'Such as?'

Priya shrugged. 'I don't want to dump him in it, but when I left Wyveridge early on Sunday morning, it was with a seriously upset Australian woman. Birgit was her name. She told me she'd been nearly raped at knifepoint by Rory. More to the point, that this was after she'd refused a tab of acid.'

'OK,' said Francis, slowly. 'Is that likely, Ranjit?'

'I honestly don't know. Rory's a law unto himself.'

'Why would she make it up?' said Priya.

'Drama queen,' said Carly, dismissively. 'She turned in quite a performance that morning.'

'Hardly surprisingly,' said Priya, widening her eyes. 'Like, er, attempted rape, excuse me? I believed her anyway. She described to me exactly what Rory's tabs looked like. Postage stamps with strawberries on. It's not the kind of detail you invent.'

'Isn't it?' said Carly. 'Everyone knows what a tab of acid looks like.'

'Ranjit,' said Francis, 'level with me. D'you think it's possible that Rory was offering people LSD?'

The dreadlocked host shrugged. 'Anything's possible. With Rory. But if Grace turned down Eva's funny tea, why on earth would she have taken acid from Rory? It doesn't make sense.'

'Maybe he slipped it to her,' said Priya. 'In a cup of ordinary tea. Or a piece of that cake you were talking about.'

'Why on earth would he do that?' said Carly.

'Why d'you think?' said Priya. 'Having tried and failed with Birgit . . .'

'Oh come off it!' said Carly. 'He's not that desperate.'

'Ranjit?' asked Francis.

'As I said, with Rory . . .'

'Some friend you are,' said Carly.

'It would certainly explain why he's so jumpy,' said Priya. 'And why he felt he needed to lie about when the three of them went into Mold.'

TWENTY-SIX

The rain continued unrelentingly, splashing off rooftops, bubbling along gutters and into drainpipes, running in streams down the steep hill to the river. An hour and a half later Francis and Priya met up again in the Old Bakery.

'Any joy?' Francis asked, as he ran his fingers through his wet hair, then sat down opposite her at a table by the wall.

Priya grinned. 'Well,' she said, 'I got through to the *Sentinel* and managed to speak to Grace's boss on Muckraker. Matthew Ashcombe.'

'And?'

'He's in a state. Wondering if he shouldn't talk to the police himself. Basically, Grace phoned in yesterday afternoon at about quarter past three to say she had a scoop.'

'Did she tell him what it was about?'

'She couldn't get hold of Matt personally, because he was in a meeting, but she did tell his assistant that it was something big to do with a major TV celebrity. Matt never got the email. By the time he phoned her back, around five, she wasn't picking up.'

'He should definitely talk to the police. Hang on. Maybe this could be our way in.'

'To . . .?'

228

'The police, of course. I imagine DCI Julie would be extremely interested to hear about this.'

'So you really think,' Priya said, her voice dropping, 'that Family Man did it? *Murdered* Bryce . . . and then Grace?'

Their waitress was upon them; it was the same nose-ringed starlet as the previous night. 'Hello again, sir,' she said warmly.

'Jonty may not have been personally involved,' said Francis, once they'd placed their order and young Marilyn was out of earshot, 'but I'd say it was perfectly possible, considering everything he stood to lose.' He sat back and took a swig of wine. 'Imagine for a moment,' he continued, 'that having arrived at the festival, Jonty – or possibly one of his associates – got to hear about what Bryce was planning to reveal on Sunday. It wouldn't have taken him – or them – long to decide that this was really, really serious for him. In fact, in order to save the Family Man brand Bryce had to be silenced before things could go any further. Now, Bryce is well-off, as a literary journalist he hardly has a respectable position he needs to uphold, so neither bribery nor blackmail are options. However, he is most definitely staying at the White Hart for the weekend. So it wouldn't be impossible to get to him in a more serious, shall we say final, way, if such a desperate course of action could be countenanced.'

'OK . . .'

'He's fifty-four years old and a celebrated party animal, no stranger to the kind of recreational drugs that wiser people stop taking before they hit middle age. So maybe his sudden death could be disguised as something altogether more natural, such as a heart attack or a stroke. We already know that Jonty is an expert in poisons from the wild . . .'

'But surely anything like that would turn up in a post-mortem?'

'So maybe he tried something less visible.'

'Such as?'

'Strangling is a possibility . . . as is suffocation.'

'Strangling would leave a mark, surely?'

'It's amazing what you can do with a silk scarf. Suffocation could be even more discreet, and one of the symptoms of that is . . .' Francis held up a finger.

'Yes?'

'Bloodshot eyes. Which Dr Webster remarked on when he was examining the body.'

'Did he? I should have been there. I could have told him that Bryce was already red-eyed on Saturday evening. We went for this walk and he . . . fell over and got some grit behind his contacts.'

Francis nodded thoughtfully. 'Is that so? Doesn't rule it out, though, does it? Now just imagine for a moment that Jonty and/ or the people around him did decide that something drastic had to be done about Bryce; that a plan was hatched and actioned; that the murderer – or murderers – did the deed, then snuck away from Room 29 in the small hours. When Bryce is discovered, they've told themselves, most likely by his girlfriend returning late from the Wyveridge party, his death is going to seem entirely natural. With any luck, they're going to get away with it. However. When the police arrive and look at the body, they are, for some reason, suspicious. Soon scene-of-crime officers are crawling all over the place and the whole festival is jumping to the wrong – that is, the right – conclusion. Meanwhile, to compound our man's problems, a keen young hackette is running around asking awkward questions and seems to have found something out.'

'About what? The truth about Jonty's private life or . . . Bryce's death?'

'Both, probably. Jonty gets to hear about this or, more likely, realizes what's up when Grace interviews him, which we know she did on Sunday morning. Now he's got a new problem. If he doesn't stop her, it's all going to come out. So she has to be dealt with too – and quick. But what's he going to do? Grace is far too young for the heart attack/aneurysm trick, and in any case that could hardly be repeated. She's most unlikely material for "suicide". But what is there out at Wyveridge that everyone already knows about?'

'Drugs?'

'Exactly.'

'Your starters, sir?'

Francis looked up to see their waitress right above them, her blue eyes wide; her timing was uncanny.

'So,' he continued in a low voice, once she'd put their plates down and was well out of the way again, 'everyone knows about the drugs at Wyveridge.'

'I guess so.'

'It's general gossip that this is what's fuelling the parties out there. There's people openly spliffing on the lawns, mountains of coke in the bathrooms, and for those who fancy something a bit more organic, magic mushrooms too. So if our killer can make it look as if Grace had a few shrooms before she jumped from the battlements, when the post-mortem finds traces of psilocybin in her bloodstream, it's the perfect explanation.'

'So you're thinking . . . that's where the rest of Eva's funny tea went?'

'It had to go somewhere.'

'But how would Jonty or whoever have known she was going to make it in the first place?'

'You said yourself that she was offering it around on Friday night. Jonty was there then, wasn't he?'

'But on Sunday afternoon?' said Priya. 'How on earth could he have known that that gang were going to be there, let alone go for a walk, find some shrooms and randomly brew up another jug?'

'Perhaps he didn't.'

'How d'you mean?'

'Perhaps you were half right earlier. Perhaps our murderer had planned to give Grace something else, a tab of Rory's acid maybe, and then came across this tea instead.'

Priya looked puzzled. 'So you're saying . . . Rory's involved too?'

'Not directly. But he might easily have sold Jonty – or an accomplice – one of his tabs. Then again, one might have been pinched from him.'

'Either of which would explain why he's acting so oddly.'

'Exactly. Especially if it's the selling option. Which would mean that Rory knows who the murderer is, but in order to out him he's got to admit to dealing Class A drugs. Not the nicest dilemma for a young man training to be a barrister.'

'No,' Priya agreed. 'OK, so then what – in your theory? Jonty arrives out at Wyveridge . . . with a tab of acid he's already somehow got from Rory . . . but then finds the shroom tea . . .'

'Already brewed and waiting on the table. Now this is a much more natural and likely alternative. So he dumps the acid idea and runs with that.'

'And what time is this?'

'After Rory and co. have gone into town. Unless he came with Grace and somehow made himself scarce. Or unless Rory and co. are covering up and they knew he was there all along.'

'D'you think that's likely?' said Priya.

'I don't. I think Eva is honest enough that she would have said something.'

'I agree. OK, so Jonty gets out to Wyveridge once the coast is clear?'

'Yes,' said Francis.

'But how would he persuade Grace to drink this tea? When she'd already turned Rory and the others down?'

'Perhaps he didn't need to persuade her.'

'What d'you mean?'

'Maybe he gave her the tea after she fell.'

Priya's hand flew to her mouth. 'What! Like, poured it down her throat . . . as she lay . . . dead on the gravel?'

'It's a dreadful thought, isn't it, but perfectly possible.'

Priya nodded silently, an appalled expression on her face. 'I suppose so,' she said. 'I guess when the post-mortem comes back we'll know more.'

'Or the police will know more, anyway.' Francis sliced into his Maryland crab cakes, then dipped a forkful into the gleaming orange splodge of Dewkesbury chilli jam that sat to one side.

'If only there was a draft of this alleged scoop,' he said, 'or even the start of what Grace had planned to write, on her laptop, that would be a huge help.'

'Presumably the police have got that too?'

'Yes, Fleur told me they took all Grace's stuff away in bags early this morning.'

'So come on,' said Priya, brightly. 'How were the love birds?'

Francis made a face. 'With Ranjit's help I found them snuggled up together in The Sun Rising. Put it this way, I don't think you need worry unduly about Conal's broken heart.'

'Ridiculous man,' said Priya, wincing visibly. 'He always was. So theatrical and sentimental. And then he wonders why I had doubts about his sincerity.'

'More to the point,' Francis continued, 'I found out why Grace had Fleur's video camera with her. She was filming those interviews for a show reel. To help her break into the *Sentinel*'s online operation. In return for the loan of the camera, Fleur was going to have the use of them for her film. So if the memory card survived the fall, that might be interesting. See who Grace spoke to on Sunday morning and what they said.'

'Yes,' Priya agreed.

'Whatever our wilder speculations,' said Francis, 'we've reached an impasse. We need to speak to the police as soon as possible. Find out proper answers to these questions. At least now we've got Matthew Ashcombe's evidence to offer them. Not to mention all your thoughts about Jonty.'

Meal over, they left the restaurant and walked back to the White Hart together. The rain had stopped. The pavements were still awash with dark puddles, but overhead the moon rode clear across a star-bright sky, a few fluffy, backlit outriders of cloud accompanying her on her way. Near the hotel, Priya slipped her hand into Francis's arm. They walked on together, saying nothing.

TWENTY-SEVEN

Tuesday 22nd July

Three hours later, Francis woke to hear a quiet sobbing coming from the double bed.

'What's wrong?' he asked into the darkness.

'It's nothing,' came Priya's voice. 'I'm sorry. I didn't mean to wake you.'

'That's OK.' He yawned, pulled himself up from the sofa and went over. Priya's hair was a black tangle against the white pillows; her big brown eyes shone in the light that filtered through the curtains from the street.

'I can't stop thinking about poor Grace,' she said. 'It's just so awful. She was so young.'

'She was. It's hard to believe that it's happened.'

He sat with her in silence. From somewhere nearby came the squeals of cats fighting.

'You know,' Priya said quietly. 'I didn't just lose my sister.'

'No,' said Francis; he imagined she was about to elaborate about the unborn baby.

'My father and brother too.'

'You're not serious?'

'In a car crash.'

'My God . . .'

'It was barely a year after the fire that killed Chinni. They were out together on the M42 on a foggy November night. The visibility was even worse because of smoke that drifted across from some fireworks display at a site next to the road. Bilal – that's my brother – always drove like a lunatic anyway. They smashed into a lorry and another piled in behind them and the Nissan was crushed like it had been in one of those machines they use for cars without insurance. Loads of others were involved. It made the national news.'

There was silence. Francis didn't know what to say. 'How terrible for you,' he managed. Then, feebly: 'You must miss them . . . dreadfully.'

'I do. Particularly my dad. He was always so great to us girls when we were little. He could be strict at times, but then again, he was always spoiling us too, laughing and joking with us. We were his little angels, Chinni and I. He used to call us that, his little English angels.'

'His little English angels.'

'Yes. That was his kind of sense of humour. He was joking, in a way, but in another he wasn't. He'd come over from India, you see, as a young man. He had an arranged marriage with my mother, who was from over here, and he missed . . . all that. Being at home, the extended family, friends, the weather . . .' She smiled. 'Even though that life was grindingly poor. Not that he hadn't wanted to come. He had. But I always got the feeling that the UK – or "UK" as he called it – wasn't all it was cracked up to be. He used to say that as a boy he'd been told the streets of England were paved with gold.' Priya chuckled. 'That was his exact expression. "Paved with gold." Like something from a fairy story. I don't think working in his father-in-law's garage ever quite lived up to it.'

'And your brother?' Francis asked.

Priya sighed. 'If you want to know the truth, we were never that close. Mum always spoilt Bilal terribly. You know, he could go out, but Chinni and I couldn't. He could have his music on loud, but we couldn't. When we were growing up, he was like the little prince in the house, and we had to scurry around after him. He didn't have Dad's gentleness either. He fancied himself as this kind of Asian hard man. He had a *bhangra* ringtone, loads of bling, all that. He was never going to be a mere mechanic like Dad, either. He'd decided that at about the age of eight. I actually used to like messing about in the workshop with Dad. It was fun. But Bilal was always above that. He was going to be a *bhangra* star, even if the silly tosser had no talent. When that didn't work out he became this, like, club promoter, organizing gigs around Derby. Then across to Nottingham and Leicester too. He always had some pretty blonde on his arm, even while the fat hypocrite thought his sisters should settle for the Punjabi farmer option. But that was typical, because he was also incredibly proud of our caste – *jat* – which is like the farmer, landowning class. Even though he'd only been to India once. I just thought it was silly. But there are loads like him. They get drunk at weddings and sing all these songs about how great they are to be *jats*. I always thought they were dickheads.'

'What about your mother?'

Priya made a face. 'She's basically never got over it. She talks about going back to her family in India, but I don't think she ever will.'

'I'm sorry,' said Francis. Then: 'Is she a burden to you?'

'She could be, I suppose. But I'm afraid I don't let her be. I'm not that much in touch with her now. We fell out badly after Dad died, because she wanted me to marry the guy who was meant for Chinni and I refused.'

'Where was he from? India too?'

'Yeah. He was the son of this, like, great old boyhood friend of Dad's. But basically, as far as I was concerned, he was just another Punjabi *jat* looking for a UK passport. If Dad and Bilal had been alive I'd probably have had to go along with it, but with them gone I didn't feel obliged any more. My uncles and cousins may tut-tut, and say this and that about me, but there's not a lot they can do.'

'No . . .'

'I suppose it's one of the things that's made me so ambitious. I want to do well for Chinni as much as anything else. It was always her dream to be a successful journalist. And I suppose, in a weird kind of way, I want to prove to Dad and Bilal that I can do it, even though they're not around to see it. D'you get that?'

'Yes,' Francis said quietly. 'I do.' Then: 'Did Bryce know . . . about all this?'

'No. I never told him much about my family. Conal neither. Now I'm wondering why I've told you.'

'It's OK,' said Francis. 'It's hardly a story I'm going to share.'

'You do understand, though. Why I just want to be Priya Kaur. My own person, getting on in the world, leaving all that shit behind.'

'Completely,' said Francis. 'For what it's worth, I never talk about Kate, either.'

'Why should you?' There was silence. Outside, the cats seemed to have resolved their differences. 'Have you ever got over it?' she asked.

'What happened in Egypt was a terrible, unbelievable thing. But after about a year of being in pieces, I realized I had to stop saying "what if?" and get on with my life. Without her. So I did. There comes a point when it's no use dwelling on a tragedy like that. You can take time out to remember it, when you want to, but otherwise you have to move forwards . . .'

'Exactly,' said Priya. 'You do.'

Another silence. 'You never found anyone else, did you?' she added.

'No,' said Francis, and with that, it was he who was in tears.

'It's OK,' she said, taking his hand.

'It's not OK,' he muttered. Gradually he got control of himself. He took several deep breaths and wiped his face on the corner of the sheet. 'I've tried,' he said. 'God help me, I've tried. This woman, that woman, but it's never right. And then I think: maybe I was just very, very lucky to meet someone I fitted so perfectly with when I was so young. Maybe that's not meant to happen twice in a lifetime . . .'

He stopped abruptly. He hated self-pity, in any manifestation.

'Maybe, Francis, deep down,' said Priya, 'you don't want it to happen. Maybe that's why these relationships never work out.'

'Don't think I haven't thought that too.'

They were alone together in a dark hotel bedroom in the middle of the night. Warm hands entwined. Now Priya was gently squeezing his palm, her thumb stroking the back of his forefinger.

'Come here,' she said quietly.

'No, Priya. Let's finish what we have to do first. OK?'

He withdrew his hand from hers and got to his feet, then leant over her and kissed her softly on the forehead. It wasn't that he didn't want her. Just the smell of her was doing powerful things to him. But the poor girl had only lost her boyfriend two nights ago. She was clearly still in shock. If there was going to be a time for this to develop in any constructive way, it shouldn't be now.

'OK,' she replied.

'It's important. This isn't some cosy little murder mystery, the sort I might write for my clever-clogs detective George Braithwaite, for the amusement of a bunch of readers who would freak out if they saw a road accident, let alone a murder. Actual people are dying here.'

'I know they are.'

'You didn't see Grace, flat out on the gravel, but believe me, it was a chilling sight.'

'That taped outline was enough for me . . .'

'Something horrible and evil is going on and I – we, Priya – might be in a position to do something about it.'

'Yes,' she said, quietly.

Francis returned to his sofa and let his head sink back onto the pillow he'd taken from the bed. He lay there for awhile thinking about Priya's story, which certainly explained why Conal had never met her family. The only question was: was it true? Or was it possible that this apparently lovely, switched-on young woman was some kind of fantasist? God knows, Francis had met that type before. Dated them, even. He remembered one highly strung – and very beautiful – ex of his who had specialized in making up convincing tall tales: about her past, her present, the works. Quite often, for no apparent reason at all. Francis had finally given up on her when she'd told him she'd gone to spend a weekend with an aunt in Paris and a friend had run into her at a fancy dress party in Balham.

But if Priya's story were true, why had she told him? Especially if it really were the case that neither Bryce nor Conal had ever known. In his journalistic days, when he'd specialized in long interviews for magazines, Francis had always been marked down as the guy who could pull the extra confession out of this or that actor or celebrity. So should he chalk it up to that? His famous empathy? Or was Priya, so bright and collected on the surface, much, much more traumatized by Bryce's death than she'd been letting on?

As for him, he was already regretting that he'd revealed as much as he had. But there it was; somehow she had pulled it from him. The truth was he felt better for it. Now, despite himself, he wanted to tell her more. He was feeling something he hadn't in a long while: an almost visceral desire to trust and be trusted; to get, as people always said so blandly, close to someone again.

He could get up and go over there now. He wanted to; god, did he want to.

Across the room the numbers on the digital clock glowed red. 3.12.

A surprisingly loud click. And it was 3.13. He put his hands together in a gesture of prayer and rolled over onto his side.

TWENTY-EIGHT

'So how can I help you?' asked Detective Chief Inspector Julie Morgan, after a little preliminary banter in which she'd volunteered, almost flirtatiously, that she was a fan of Francis's work. Now she leant forward from the black leather chair that was about the only decent bit of furniture in this makeshift incident room, tucked away at the back of a trading estate behind the Dewkesbury ring road. She was in her own screened-off corner, but it wasn't much protected from the noise beyond, where a string of six or so plain-clothes officers made phone calls and exchanged banter as they worked at computer screens. 'Or rather,' she added, 'how can you help us? I gather you have some new information.'

'We do,' said Francis, glancing over at Priya, who looked both businesslike and sexy this morning in a tight-fitting black suit and knee-high boots. In the cold light of day, he was proud of the self-control he'd exhibited in the small hours.

'OK,' said Julie, putting up steepled hands to cover her mouth, 'I'm listening.' Close up, she looked more life-battered than when seen from a distance. That mane of dark hair contained a good few grey strands; through her Touche Eclat the bags under her eyes were black.

'As you know,' Francis replied, 'Priya here was Bryce's girl-friend.'

'Yes, and we've been grateful for your cooperation and your very helpful statement, Ms Kaur. Which you now want to add to, is that right?'

'May I ask first,' Francis chipped in, 'are you still treating both these deaths as murder enquiries?'

'As a professional crime writer, Mr Meadowes, I'm sure you understand that all the details of our investigation have to remain confidential until we either arrest and charge suspects or else establish that there is no reason to pursue further enquiries.'

'I thought you might say that. But I imagine you are treating the two deaths as linked?'

DCI Julie's impatience was tangible. 'I'd love to spend the morning gassing with you about these cases, but as you see we're pretty frantic out here. I was told you had some important new information for us.'

'We do. In relation to that, have you had the post-mortem results for Grace yet?'

'I really can't comment, Mr Meadowes. Now please, what is this "crucial new evidence" you mentioned to DS Povey over the phone?'

'Priya, d'you want to tell the Chief Inspector what Bryce was planning to talk about on Sunday afternoon? To his eager public and any representatives of the national press who were in the audience?'

Francis enjoyed watching the DCI's face as Priya filled her in.

'I see,' said Julie, when she'd finished. 'And you seriously think that these revelations would have been damaging enough to make someone of Jonty Smallbone's calibre contemplate murder?'

'Yes,' said Francis.

'With all due respect, Mr Meadowes, this isn't a George Braithwaite novel. What you've given me is pure speculation. I was told you had evidence.'

'There should have been a copy of Bryce's speech in our room somewhere,' said Priya. 'As well as drafts on his laptop – and an accompanying PowerPoint presentation.'

'That should be easy enough to check.' DCI Julie pressed a button on her phone. 'Steve. Can you come round here, please.'

It was the same DS whom Francis had first seen in the dining room of the White Hart, the blond prop-forward with the thick eyebrows. No, Steve said, once the DCI had brought him up to speed, he wasn't aware of a hard copy of any speech having been found in Room 29. 'So what are we looking for on the laptop?' he asked.

'In his main Documents section Bryce had a folder called Talks,' Priya said. 'It would almost certainly have been in there, probably called something like *Mold Festival Talk* rather than *Celebrity and Hypocrisy*, which was the title in the programme.'

'OK, Steve,' said DCI Julie. 'Quick as you can on that, please. We'll see what he comes up with,' she said, once DS Wright had gone. 'But even if this speech does turn up or we find a draft on the computer, and it's as damning as you say it is, it's hardly evidence of murder, is it? At best, it's circumstantial.'

'Bear with us,' said Francis, 'because this leads directly to the second thing we wanted to share with you. Grace phoned her newspaper at three fifteen on Sunday afternoon to tell her editor that she was about to email a seriously damaging story about a major celebrity.'

Now they had got the DCI's full attention. 'So how did you know about this?' she asked.

'We spoke to the editor. Priya also works for the *Sentinel*, so we were able to do it informally.'

'And this editor hadn't thought of telling the police?'

'No,' said Priya. 'He's up in London. He wasn't sure whether he should.'

'Of course he should. When did he contact you about it?'

'He didn't. We contacted him.'

'I don't quite follow,' said Julie.

Francis looked over at Priya. She shrugged. But her eyes and pinched mouth said: *Tell her, whatever the consequences for the others.*

'We found out about all this,' Francis said, 'because we were talking to some of the young people who were out at Wyveridge on Sunday. Grace apparently came back to the Hall at around half three in a state of excitement and told them that she had this scoop and she was going upstairs to file it.'

'File it? I'm sorry. Where?'

'"File" is journo-speak for "send it to her newspaper",' said Francis.

'I see. And this was at half past three?'

'Around that time, yes.'

Julie had already pressed the buzzer on her desk. 'Brian. Could you come in here, please.'

Now DS Brian Povey appeared round the corner. Today he was casual in jeans and a blue T-shirt that read DIVE CAYMAN over some badly drawn tropical fish. He nodded a hello to Francis and Priya.

'You supervised the Wyveridge statements, didn't you?' Julie said.

'Yes, ma'am.'

'I thought you said there was nobody out there after one thirty except for the housekeeper and gardener.'

'That's what we were told.'

'I think a couple of the guys might have got their timings a bit wrong,' Priya said. 'One thirty is what they told us too, at first. Then they remembered that they'd left for town mid-afternoon.'

'They *remembered*,' said Julie scornfully. 'Who exactly are we talking about here?'

'I'd rather hold back on that information for the time being,' said Francis, looking over at Priya.

Julie sucked in her breath. Her fingers tapped impatiently on her desk. 'Your call,' she said. 'But we will obviously need to know at some point . . .'

'I appreciate that,' said Francis. *You scratch my back*, he thought. 'Now we realize,' he went on, 'that you guys took away pretty much all of Grace's stuff from the room she was sleeping in. So, may I ask, was there anything on her laptop that would show either that she'd started writing this email to her editor, or that she had in fact written it?'

'That's easily found out,' said Julie. 'What's the editor's name?'

'Matt . . . Matthew Ashcombe,' said Priya.

'Check that out for us, would you please, Brian?'

'Yes, ma'am.' The DS turned on his heel and departed.

DCI Julie turned back to Francis and Priya. 'OK,' she said, 'let's just see if I've got your theory right. You're saying that Jonty Smallbone, the well-known TV personality, having done away with Bryce in order to safeguard his priceless reputation, then goes out to Wyveridge Hall at tea time on Sunday and somehow persuades this young journalist to take hallucinogenic drugs. Having established a believable cause of death, he takes her up onto the battlements with him and pushes her off?'

'More or less,' Francis replied. So they *had* had Grace's post-mortem back; and by the sounds of it found hallucinogens in her bloodstream. Had Julie slipped up, or just decided it was time to cooperate? 'Though there wasn't necessarily any persuasion involved,' he added. 'Grace could have been given such drugs unwittingly – or even, more likely, after she died.'

'What are you saying?' said Julie. 'That the murderer fed them to her as she lay dead on the ground?'

'Seems like the most likely supposition. Given that all of them agree she wasn't a drug taker.'

'Interesting . . .' For a moment Francis thought Julie was about to share something else with them, but then the professional mask descended again. 'The main question then is this,' she continued. 'Whether Grace had taken drugs or not, knowingly or not, why did she agree to go up on the battlements with Jonty when she was supposed to be writing an urgent story for her newspaper? I mean, did she even know him?'

'She'd met him,' said Francis. 'At a party that was held at Wyveridge Hall on Saturday evening. She also interviewed him on Sunday morning about his reactions to Bryce's death. But you're right, she didn't know him well. However, there is a close

associate of his whom she might have been much more likely
to trust: Jonty's ghostwriter, Anna Copeland.'

'Anna!' said Priya, leaning forward. 'You think she was involved?'

'Hang on,' said DCI Julie. 'You've lost me. Who's this . . .?'

'Anna Copeland,' Francis repeated. 'She's a ghostwriter, who's
"worked with" Jonty on several of his books, including his most
recent, *Wild Stuff*.'

'You're saying she wrote it for him?' said Julie.

'In a word, yes. Now Anna has also been staying at the White
Hart, along with her new boyfriend, Marvin Blake, an ex-Marine
who's also a client of hers.'

'The black fellow?' said Julie, and then looked immediately
as if she wished she'd phrased it another way. 'I mean . . .'

Francis put her out of her misery. 'Muscly geezer who looks
as if he could strangle you with his bare hands – or in his case
his bare four fingers. He's a bit of a romantic departure for Anna.
Before that, she was, for a long while, the girlfriend of Bryce
Peabody.'

Now the DCI looked puzzled. 'My information was that
Bryce's, er, long-term partner was Scarlett – hang on, where's
my list?'

'Paton-Jones, yes,' said Francis. 'As Priya here can confirm,
Bryce's love life was a bit complicated. Besides his partner, he
also had a girlfriend.'

'I thought that was you, Ms Kaur?'

'Another one,' said Francis.

'Another one!'

'I replaced her,' said Priya.

'And the partner?'

'Both of them.' Priya explained about the open marriage, Anna, and her ultimatum.

'Crikey!' said DCI Julie, when she'd finished. 'Good for you.'

Priya shrugged and smiled weakly. 'It was a high-risk strategy. But it worked.'

'So how did Anna take that?' asked DCI Julie.

Priya looked over at Francis. 'You've spoken to her recently,' she said. 'You probably know better than me.'

'She was furious,' Francis said. 'She'd been Bryce's loyal bit on the side for five years and suddenly along comes Priya here and gets him to leave Scarlett within three weeks.'

DCI Julie whistled. 'Pretty gutting. So what did she do?'

Francis explained, sparing no detail, especially not the invasion of Bryce's workplace.

'OK,' said Julie, 'so she was happy for everyone to know she hated him. Doesn't make her a murderer, though, does it?'

'Not necessarily,' said Francis. 'However—'

The door had swung open. Steve Wright was back, hovering with a heavy-looking laptop. 'Yes, Steve?' said Julie.

'This is Bryce's Dell, ma'am. I've booted it up and given it a cursory search, but there's nothing under *Celebrity and Hyprocrisy* or *Mold Talks* or even anything with Mold in the title. I've also been through the inventory and we haven't found a hard copy of a speech either. Anywhere.'

'Could I just have a peep?' Priya looked hopefully at the DCI.

Julie nodded and Steve put the machine down on the edge of the desk. Priya's hands were shaking visibly and she was breathing deeply. For a moment Francis thought she might be about to break down again.

'Sorry,' she said. 'Seeing all these icons on his desktop. It's almost like he's back.'

'Take your time,' said DCI Julie.

Priya clicked open Documents and found a file called Talks and Lectures.

'Here it is,' she said, opening it; and there, listed, were all the things Bryce had done recently. *Critics Circle Lunch. Bath Festival. Ways With Words. Hay. Bogstandard After-Dinner (funny).* There was nothing about *Celebrity and Hypocrisy* or Mold. 'This is very odd,' she said. 'All the other festivals he's given talks at are here. I'll run a wider search for Celebrity.'

This brought up a raft of documents.

Celebrity autobiographies – the horror goes on

Too Many Celebrity Chefs Spoil the Jus

Celebrity Chocaholics

Nothing New Under The Sun – Celebs of the 1890s.

'Hang on, what's this?' said Priya. 'Double Standards of Celebrities. Author. Bryce Peabody. File: More Serious Work. Date created: 20/12 . . . that's way back last December. Date modified: 17/1. Let's have a look.'

She double-clicked and they all leant into the screen as it opened.

Celebrity culture is no longer optional. However much we struggle to avoid its cheesy embrace, it is there waiting for us. We can give up newspapers and magazines. We can give up radio and television. But wherever we turn, the tinsel gods and goddesses of Medialand pursue us, yelling from every white van parked on every corner, forcing their all too tedious 'secrets' upon us . . .

Francis's eyes flicked down the page. 'And as if all this wasn't enough,' he read out loud, 'there lies, at the heart of each and every one of these narratives, an undeniable hypocrisy . . . You're right, Priya. This is it. Don't you think?'

'The germ of it,' said Priya. 'Once Bryce realized it was going to be a talk rather than a piece he'd have transferred it to the Talks file.' She paused and looked around at the waiting trio. Her eyes were bright, her lips in a resolute pout. 'I'd say somebody's been at this computer. Deleted all the drafts of the talk itself, but didn't realize that this was there too, in a different file.'

'Mightn't Bryce have deleted these drafts himself?' asked Julie. 'Once he'd printed up his speech and was about to deliver it?'

'No way,' said Priya. 'For a start, he'd have wanted the latest one there, so he could add in any changes in the morning. And then, knowing Bryce, he'd have hung onto everything for ages anyway.'

She clicked on the icon in Talks which read *Bath Festival*. It opened to reveal a long list of files. 'See,' she said, '*Bath Festival 1, 2, 3* . . . Seventeen drafts of that one. All still there. And Bath was back in March.'

'So what are you saying?' asked Julie. 'That *Jonty* deleted them?'

Priya shrugged. 'It's a possibility, isn't it? And then removed the hard copy from the room.'

'Removing his motive at the same time,' said Francis.

Julie turned to the waiting DS. 'OK, Steve. Could you get this over to Dipika in Bristol, please. Right away. We're looking for anything with *Mold Talk* or *Celebrity and Hypocrisy* in the title.' She turned back to Francis and Priya. 'These techies are pretty

251

impressive. If a file has ever been registered on the hard disk they can usually find it.'

As Steve left the room with one laptop, Brian came in with another. This one was far smarter, a slim, brushed-aluminium machine. 'Grace Pritchard's Macbook, ma'am,' said Brian. 'I've had a quick shufti through her email, but there was nothing sent to anyone after nine forty-three a.m. on the Sunday. That was also the last time the Inbox was checked.'

'Sounds like she didn't even get to switch it on,' said Julie.

'And yet,' said Priya, 'Rory and co. told us she went straight upstairs from seeing them.'

'Rory and co.?' asked Julie.

Francis met Priya's eye. What was she playing at? But her shrug was only a little apologetic. 'She's going to have to know sooner or later,' she said.

'These are the young people who left Wyveridge mid-afternoon but told us otherwise?' said Julie.

'Yes,' said Priya.

'What do we have on that, Brian?'

The DS consulted his notebook. 'I was coming to that. The last people who claimed to be there, apart from Mrs Macpherson the housekeeper and Gunther Bachmeier the gardener, were three of the resident house party: Rory McCarthy, Neville Tanner and Eva Edelstein. Who all concurred on leaving for town at one thirty p.m. after a late breakfast.'

'Which you're now saying wasn't true?' Julie asked Priya.

'They left later. They saw Grace, basically.'

'You're sure about that?'

'Yes. Not that they wanted us to know that.'

'That would tie in with the housekeeper's evidence, ma'am,' said Brian. 'She told us there were people in the house when she knocked off at two.'

'You hadn't followed up this anomaly?'

'I'd only just got to it, ma'am.'

Julie gave him an impatient glance. 'OK, I think we'd better get onto those three, please, Brian. Right away. You can bring them in if you like.'

'Ma'am.' He turned on his heel.

'You're going to arrest them?' said Priya, when he'd gone.

'Lying on a police statement is perverting the course of justice. We don't necessarily have to charge them. Just make them aware we don't like timewasters and see how helpful they want to be, obviously without leaning on them in any way that might be prejudicial to their evidence.' She sat forward with a smile.

'Rory McCarthy in particular will take that threat very seriously indeed,' said Francis. 'As he's doing his pupillage in a barrister's chambers at present.'

'Is he now?' said Julie. 'So he knew exactly what he was up to – lying on a statement. You're making me wonder why he didn't want us to know that they'd seen Grace.'

'I don't think he was *involved*, if that's what you're thinking,' said Francis. 'Not directly, anyhow. Can we talk in total confidence?'

'Of course.'

'I think he had other worries. Relating to his future as a barrister.'

'Such as?'

'The recreational use of certain Class A substances, perhaps?'

This brought a bark of laughter from Julie. 'We know the place was awash with drugs. They flushed the whole lot down the toilet a few minutes before we got there. Little realising that the drainage system for Wyveridge runs into a big cesspit in the field below the house. But busting a few poshies for possession isn't really what I'm interested in just now. The question is, was that concern by itself enough to make Rory lie about the time he left for town? And presumably persuade his two buddies to lie also. Or was there more he didn't want us to know? You don't have any useful theories about that?'

'Not at the moment, no,' said Francis, not meeting Julie's eye, though he was aware of her looking slowly from him to Priya and back again. After a moment Julie said: 'Hopefully he may be able to tell us more when we talk to him.' She rubbed her hands briskly, then leant back in her chair. 'In the spirit of ongoing cooperation, I might as well tell you that we also had a call from Grace on Sunday afternoon.'

'Did you,' said Francis, leaning forward. 'Saying what?'

'That she had something important she wanted to share with us.'

'And you didn't take that seriously?'

'We were going to see her at six p.m. on Sunday. At the White Hart.' DCI Julie leant down and pulled up a large handbag from the floor, rummaged around and produced a pair of business cards. 'If there's anything else you happen to remember,' she said, 'my mobile number's on there.'

'Thanks,' said Francis, pulling out his wallet and producing a card of his own. 'Before we go,' he added. 'Is there any chance you could tell your uniformed guard dog out at Wyveridge to let us through? There's a few things inside the house I'd like to check out.'

'Which uniformed guard dog is that?'

'Shaven-headed gentleman. Looks as if he enjoys his food.'

The DCI laughed. 'Stan's nickname in the force is Pieman.' She considered them both for a few moments. 'OK,' she said, 'I'll make an exception for you. On the strict condition that anything you find, you share. Agreed?'

'Of course,' said Francis. 'May I also ask: was the memory card still in the video camera when you found it? And if so did it survive the fall?'

For a moment Julie looked taken aback. Then her face relaxed. 'What do you think?' she asked.

'On balance, not. But sometimes that kind of data can be quite resilient.'

'The card was there. We took it out hoping for the best and discovered the worst. It was irretrievably damaged. But not, the SOCO guys seemed to think, in the fall.'

'How d'you mean?' asked Priya.

'Somebody had tampered with it, either before or after it was chucked over. It had been stamped on, they thought, by some kind of hard shoe.'

'Oh my God!' said Priya. 'He wanted that footage destroyed.'

DCI Julie nodded at her. 'That's rather what we thought.'

'May I chance one final question,' Francis asked, as he rose to his feet.

DCI Julie was shaking her head in mock-wonder. 'Now I see where Braithwaite gets it from,' she said. 'OK then – try me.'

'Was the hallucinogenic drug in Grace's bloodstream psilocybin or lysergic acid diethylamide?'

Julie returned his gaze for several long seconds. 'Both drugs were present,' she said eventually. 'But the pathologist found that at the point of death the ingestion of neither of them was very well advanced.'

'I see,' said Francis.

Julie smiled and put her hands flat on the table. 'Since I'm being so helpful I might as well share this with you too. In strictest confidence, of course. When the SOCO guys examined Grace's body they found a splash of liquid on her dress which turned out to contain psilocybin. Which would tie in rather well with your theory about post-mortem ingestion, wouldn't it, Francis?'

'Certainly would,' Francis replied. He looked over at Priya, who was shaking her head in disbelief. 'Before we go,' he added, 'I think both of us would appreciate it if you didn't mention your sources to Rory and his friends.'

'Fine by me,' said Julie. 'Chatham House Rules all round. And do please let me know what else you find. However inconsequential it may seem.'

TWENTY-NINE

'Why didn't you tell her about Eva and the shroom tea?' asked Priya, as she and Francis sped back together towards Mold. The rain clouds had cleared away and it was another warm, sunny day, the clear blue sky dotted with occasional little fluffs of white.

'The three of them are in enough shit already, don't you think?' Francis raised an eyebrow at his companion. 'Anyway, we don't want to share everything with her just yet, do we? Hold on to a few bargaining chips. So what do you make of the post-mortem result? Sounds as if your hunch about Rory might have been right.'

'He's definitely hiding something.'

'You game to drop in at Wyveridge for a few minutes? Now we're allowed, I'd quite like to have a quick look at Grace's room, not to mention the battlements.'

'Will there be anything left to see?'

'Probably not. I'm assuming that's why Julie's letting us in. But you never know.'

This time there was no obstruction. Pieman had gone, to be replaced by chirpy Wendy. The radiophones had clearly been crackling, because Francis and Priya were let straight through, round past the diminished pile of coats and boots to the echoing empty hall. The sound of voices filtered along the corridor from the kitchen.

'Another late breakfast?' said Francis, leading on towards a powerful smell of toast and bacon. Rory, Neville, Eva, Ranjit, Carly and Adam were all sitting round the big oblong wooden table, open newspapers in front of them.

'Here comes the great detective,' said Rory snidely.

There was no point rising to this sort of thing; thanks to Priya, the guy would be getting his comeuppance all too soon. 'Morning everyone,' Francis said.

'We're digesting the latest newspaper stories,' said Ranjit, waving *The Times*, which was open at a headline that read ONGOING MYSTERY OF THE MOLD DEATHS. 'Nobody seems to have a clue what's going on – even the *Sentinel*. The *Guardian* has misspelt my name *and* Wyveridge. And have you seen the *Mail*?' He pushed over a double-page spread featuring a large picture of himself dressed as a maharajah. AT THE COURT OF THE INDIAN SVENGALI, read the headline. 'Teach me to leave silly photos on Facebook.'

'They neglect to mention that the Indian Svengali was born in Streatham,' said Carly.

'They're so phoney,' said Eva. 'All this crap about herbal cigarettes and natural highs. If they mean drugs, why don't they say so?'

'Yeah,' agreed Adam.

'Libel, obviously,' said Rory. 'Until one of us has been done for possession they're stuffed. And that's not going to happen any time soon.' He turned to Francis. 'So what have you come for now, Clouseau?'

'Just to have a look around. If it's OK with you guys, I'd quite like to see the room that Grace was sleeping in.'

'Nothing left, mate,' said Rory. 'The cozzers have cleaned it out. Laptop, clothes, the lot.'

Francis ignored this. 'Are you six the full quota?' he asked.

'Conal and Fleur are still in bed,' said Ranjit, casting an embarrassed glance in Priya's direction.

At which the door pushed open, and a tousled Fleur appeared, in a cream silk nightie, pink pyjama trousers and bare feet. 'Morning,' she said with a yawn. Then, seeing Francis and Priya, 'Oh, hi.' She shuffled towards the sideboard and took two mugs from a wooden mug-tree.

'Fleur,' said Ranjit, 'this is Francis Meadowes.'

'Yeah, we met . . . last night . . . in the pub . . . hiya.'

'And Priya Kaur.'

Fleur looked sheepish, but Priya had clearly decided to give the encounter maximum charm. 'Lovely to see you again,' she said, holding out a hand. In front of six pairs of eyes, Fleur returned the offensive with interest. 'And you,' she replied. Greeting complete, she turned to hover over the cafetière in the middle of the table. 'Any of this coffee going begging?'

'Help yourself,' said Ranjit.

'You were sharing a bedroom with Grace, I believe?' said Francis, as Fleur filled two cups and splashed in milk from a nearby bottle.

'Yes.'

'Would you mind showing us?'

'Oh, for God's sake!' muttered Rory.

But Fleur flashed Francis her wide smile. 'No problem. What – right away?'

'If that's OK with you.'

'Come up with me now, if you like.'

'Thanks,' said Francis. He followed her down the corridor and Priya tucked in behind. 'We don't need to be more than a couple of minutes,' he added, as they turned up onto the staircase. 'Just be really helpful to get a feel of the layout.'

'There's not much left, I'm afraid. The police took pretty much everything. Hang on,' she said, as they reached the landing, 'I'll just give Coney his coffee.'

She dived into a room off the main landing. '"Coney",' Priya mouthed, raising her eyebrows. From beyond the open door came the sotto mutterings of lovers. Then Fleur was back, a blue cashmere V-neck pulled down over her nightie.

'We were just along here,' she said.

At the end of the corridor was a room with tall windows that looked out over the gravel circle of the driveway. There were two single beds, stripped back to stained underblankets; two mattresses were stacked up against the wall. 'I was in here with Grace and two others.'

'And you slept where?' Francis asked.

'On a mattress under the window. Grace was in the bed by the wall.'

'So,' said Francis, looking around, 'were you aware exactly what bits and pieces of Grace's the police took away?'

'Her bag and laptop. And her handbag, of course. That was it, I think.' Fleur paused and looked down at the floor. 'Sorry, it's all been very hard to take.' She sat down with a thump on the bed nearer the window. 'To understand, really.' Now she was sobbing. Priya went over and put a supporting hand round her shoulder.

'It's OK,' she said.

'But it's *not* OK,' said Fleur, in a voice that was halfway between a squeal and a shout. 'How could those bastards do this to Grace? She was only twenty-four.'

Francis waited as she recovered herself. Priya was soothing her, gently stroking her neck. She had tears brimming in her eyes too, bless her.

'Do you think it was "those bastards" who did something to her?' Francis asked softly. 'Or do you think she did something to herself?'

'Like what? Freak out on some drugs trip, as people keep trying to suggest? Of course it was those bastards. I'm sorry. I know Grace really well. She doesn't do drugs any more. She's far too focused. She barely drinks.'

'Any more, you say? Implying . . .?'

'That she experimented at uni. Who didn't? But even in her wildest phase there were two things she never touched, never wanted to touch.'

'And they were?'

'She always said that she didn't want to risk trying heroin because you can get addicted with one hit. And LSD, because she was frightened she might have a bad trip. She used to say, "I'm mental enough as it is." Through her tears, Fleur was smiling. 'That was the whole point. She wouldn't have touched Rory's acid in a million years – or any magic mushrooms either.'

'Rory's acid?'

'He was the one who had it. Sorry, didn't you know that?'

'Did you tell the police this?' Francis asked.

'They weren't really listening. That fat guy taking the

statements was full of, like, "You never know the odd things even your close friends can do." But I do know. Even if someone had spiked Grace's cup of tea or something, she's just not the type to go jumping off roofs. If she'd realized what was happening to her, she'd have gone and sat it out in a safe place.'

'So you reckon she was pushed?'

'Without a doubt. What I don't understand is why she was up on the roof in the first place. She knew I'd already filmed that view.'

'And when did you do that?'

'On Saturday evening. With Carly. We were just looking around the house and we found the window by accident. Then early on Sunday morning I took Conal up there too. In the dawn.'

'Conal,' said Francis. 'Why?'

'He wanted to see it for himself. I'd shown him some of the film I'd shot. On playback. Of the party and stuff.'

'When?'

'Just before. We'd all been chilling in the main room by the fire.'

'Who else was there?'

'A few of the others who were still up. Ranjit and Carly. Eva and Neville for a bit.'

'So were they the only people who saw it?'

'Yeah. Apart from that wounded soldier guy and his girlfriend.'

'Anna and Marvin were still there at sunrise?'

'No, that was much earlier. Anna came over to me while I was first reviewing the footage and asked me what I'd been filming. So I showed them. They both seemed really interested.'

'I'll bet they did,' muttered Francis. 'When was that?'

'I don't know. Around midnight, probably.'

'So was everything you shot lost in the accident?'

'I don't know. The police took away my camera and obviously the memory card. But I'd already backed up the stuff from Saturday night onto my laptop.'

'And you've still got that?' said Francis, as levelly as he could.

'Yeah. Everything up until Sunday breakfast. What I don't have was what Grace filmed after that. So I've no idea who she spoke to in town. Or what they might have said. It's a shame, but obviously not so much of a shame as . . .'

For a moment it looked as if Fleur might be about to break down again, but after a few breaths she had got herself under control.

'I don't suppose you'd be able to show us the roof now,' Francis asked. 'Where you were filming from?'

'Why?'

'It would be really useful for us to get a feel . . .'

Fleur shrugged. 'If you want. Just let me get some proper shoes.'

At the end of the narrow top floor corridor, Francis and Priya scrambled out after her through the little side window onto the battlements. It wasn't large, perhaps two and a half foot by three, and not designed for easy access, perched as it was three feet above the staircase; so you had, as Mrs Mac had told him, to pull yourself up to get through.

The battlements weren't intended for recreation either. The slate roof came down to a thin strip of lead flashing – and that was it. Not that it was unduly dangerous; as Carly had said, it would have been hard to slip over by accident. The uprights – the merlons – were almost up to shoulder height, while the crenels in between were a good eighteen inches high. But it was still dizzying looking down, a good thirty feet to the terrace far below.

'Goodness!' said Francis, feeling a familiar rush of vertigo. 'Quite a view.'

'And Grace went over where?' asked Priya.

'Just along here. She didn't get far.' They followed Fleur along the flashing for ten yards or so, until they were right above Grace's body shape, still clearly marked out with blue and white tape on the gravel. 'You can see where she ended up.'

'The police have presumably scoured this ledge?'

'Yeah, the white suit brigade were up here for hours. And on the tower. Sunday evening and most of Monday. They weren't talking to anyone except themselves, so I've no idea whether they found anything.'

Francis looked round, then down again to the terrace. 'But there's no way she could have fallen from the tower, is there? It's too far along.'

'No,' Fleur agreed. 'It must have been from around here.'

If her murderer had got Grace in the right position, Francis thought, between two merlons, her knees by a crenel, it wouldn't have been too hard to push her over. If, that is, she'd been taken by surprise. One thing was clear. If she hadn't been off her face on drugs, Grace *must* have known and trusted her killer.

Safely downstairs again, Fleur agreed to show them the footage she had saved from Saturday night. She fast-forwarded through some wider shots of the landscape, then came to the party spread out below her on the lawn.

'Here we are,' she said, 'this is the stuff I did from the battlements while it was still light. Quite fun, seeing people moving from group to group. Look, there's a couple snogging behind the gazebo; they have no idea anyone's watching. After that I went back downstairs again.'

Now the camera was in the thick of it: heads turning, laughing; bare necks and backs; jewellery flashing; some people studiedly ignoring the lens, others making little self-conscious waves. The camera wobbled through a French window, past the table where the drinks were being served – garnering a quick thumbs-up from Ranjit – then swerved round to catch Bryce and Priya coming through from the hall.

'Oh yes, sorry, this is you.'

'I hadn't realized we were being filmed,' said Priya.

'I'm quite discreet when I need to be. The thing is to keep the camera low and check the picture through the monitor. It's only when you've got the viewfinder up by your eyes that people notice you.'

They watched as Ranjit spotted Bryce, then turned to give Priya an effusive double kiss. In the background, Conal crossed the frame and grabbed a flute of sparkling wine from the table. As he stepped out of the French windows, his head spun round to reveal an unmistakable glower of jealousy. Then he was gone.

'Gosh,' said Priya. 'It's all there, isn't it?'

'The camera never lies,' said Francis.

From outside came the sound of cars braking sharply on gravel. Then the single whoop of a siren. The three of them got up and ran to the window to see four uniformed police officers and two plain clothes emerging from two regular cars and an unmarked silver BMW.

'What do they want now?' Fleur asked.

'To talk to someone, by the looks of it,' said Francis; he exchanged a smile with Priya.

'D'you think we should go downstairs?' said Fleur.

'If they need you I'm sure they'll find you.'

They returned to the laptop. 'Oh, look,' said Fleur, slowing from fast-forward, 'here's Grace, talking to that soldier guy.'

'That's a conversation that's going well,' said Francis. 'Shame you weren't in earshot.' Whatever it was Grace had just said, Marv seemed hugely tickled.

'That's the problem with this kind of subject,' said Fleur. 'Too much ambient noise. That's his girlfriend, isn't it?'

'Yes. Anna Copeland. Also his ghostwriter.'

'Oh right. That's probably why Grace's doing such a number on them. It was one of her ambitions to be a ghostwriter. That or a famous columnist. She changed her mind about once a week. Now this is a good bit. When Rory suddenly pitches up and has a go at Bryce.' Her face fell as she realized what she'd said. 'Sorry, Priya.'

'It's fine . . . I'd like to see it.'

They watched as the encounter developed. As Fleur got in close, a few snatches of sentences could even be heard against the general party chatter. 'What gives you the right?' Rory was shouting, eyes wild.

'Already high as a kite,' said Priya.

'Off his face,' said Fleur. 'Most of the time.'

'Bryce does look worn out, though, doesn't he?' said Francis.

'He'd had a long day of it, one way and another,' said Priya.

They watched as Bryce said something final to Rory, then

turned, yawned mightily and walked off down the bank. Then the camera was back on Grace.

'Still chatting animatedly to Anna,' said Priya. 'Now here comes, oh my God, Family Man . . .'

'Good friends with Anna and Marv, you notice,' said Francis.

'Now Grace gets introduced,' said Fleur.

'What a cheeseball,' said Priya. 'His face really does light up, doesn't it?'

'He can't keep his eyes off her,' said Francis.

'There she is,' said Fleur. 'Going in for the kill with the note-book.'

'He's loving this,' said Francis.

'Classic Grace,' said Fleur, and her eyes were suddenly bright with tears. 'Look at that way she's nodding. She's pretending to listen while she thinks of her next question.'

'Here comes the wife,' said Francis.

'Scary-looking character,' said Fleur.

'Lady Macbeth,' said Priya.

'That is a priceless expression,' said Francis. 'Proud of him being Family Man, allowing him his little moment of adulation, but not too long with pretty young Grace, no, there she goes, moving in. That doesn't look like a woman who knowingly tolerates her husband's bad behaviour, does it, Priya?'

'Here's you again,' said Fleur to Priya. 'Jonty and Eva were persuading you to stay at the party. Bryce looks mighty pissed off, doesn't he . . .'

'I should have gone back with him then,' said Priya quietly.

'Hey, check this bit,' said Fleur.

Now she was five steps behind Bryce, as he paced alone along the terrace and on through the house. As he reached the gravel circle he ran towards a white car with ACE TAXIS MOLD 5555 on the side, which was just pulling out. He waved at it. It stopped. Then he was leaning into the driver's window. The camera zoomed in, so you could see a dark figure in the back bending forward.

'Goodness,' said Francis. 'It's Dickson.'

'Wow . . .' said Priya.

'Who else have you shown this to?' asked Francis.

'Just the people who saw it on Saturday night. And Grace, of course. We were laughing about it on Sunday morning. Thinking how well it worked with the earlier footage from Dickson's talk. That's one of the reasons Grace wanted to take the camera with her into the festival. She realized I had the chance of making a decent little film.'

'The police haven't seen this?'

'No. And they won't either, till I get my camera and memory card back.'

From outside, there was the crunch of feet on gravel. Then voices and the sound of car doors opening and slamming shut. The three of them were at the window in time to see Rory, handcuffed to DS Povey; Neville and Eva following on behind, escorted by uniforms.

'Oh my God!' said Fleur. 'They've arrested Rory.'

'Looks like it,' said Francis.

'Not for . . . the murders?'

'The three of them lied on their statements,' said Francis. 'Which is never a good idea. If they're lucky they'll get off with wasting police time. "Attempting to pervert the course of justice" is the more serious charge. Either way, they're probably in for a night in the cells, unless they've got a very good solicitor and there's a court sitting in Dewkesbury this afternoon.'

THIRTY

'So what now?' asked Priya, as she and Francis stood outside the front of the house ten minutes later. The police had departed at speed, leaving visible tyre scars across the mass of tiny, variously coloured stones.

'Since we're allowed,' said Francis, 'I wouldn't mind a little stroll in the grounds to clear my head. Want to come along?'

'Sure,' said Priya.

They crossed the lawn and came to the bridge over the ha-ha. The field beyond was empty.

'Where have the cows gone?'

'To another field, I imagine,' said Francis. 'Unless they ate some shrooms and went on a wild trip.'

'Very funny, Francis. So, did you notice anything I didn't in that room?'

'Pretty useless, wasn't it? I'd been hoping we might find something the police had missed. But we were way too late for that.'

'Worth seeing the video material, though?'

'Certainly was,' said Francis. 'Shame Fleur didn't get a chance to download the Sunday morning footage too. I wonder what it was that our murderer didn't want anyone seeing.'

'Maybe something in an interview that gave him away. Or a

sequence from Saturday night. Grace being on such friendly terms with Anna and Marv . . . then introduced to *him* . . .'

'Yes,' said Francis, thoughtfully. They walked on together down the field. 'OK,' he continued, 'let's go back to basics and establish where we are. Rory and his pals are now, or soon will be, with DCI Julie. She is obviously not allowed to use any leverage on him, for fear of risking any case she builds up being thrown out by the courts. But none the less I suspect she'll get him to admit that a) the three of them were drinking "shroom tea" on Sunday afternoon, and b) that there was enough left in the pot to send Grace a bit doolally had she tried some.'

'D'you think she did?'

Francis shrugged. 'I don't.'

'So how about the psilocybin in her autopsy?'

'I stick by my original thought: that our murderer fed it to her. The question remains, why was Rory being so cagey?'

'That was definitely his LSD in her bloodstream, wouldn't you say?'

'I would,' Francis agreed.

'But you don't think he's . . . responsible?'

'For?'

'Pushing Grace off.'

Francis shook his head. 'No way. There's no motive. Unless he was working for or with Jonty, and I can't really see that. Anyway, if he'd been involved in her death, I don't think he'd have looked so worried.'

'Surely that's exactly what he'd have looked?'

'I don't think so. If he'd pushed her off those battlements himself, he'd have been acting his socks off to play the innocent.

However, if he's been a bit stupid leaving hallucinogens around, or selling someone a tab he shouldn't have, and then someone has died, of course he's going to look shit scared.'

They had reached the bottom of the field, where a fence marked off the woodland on the other side. Three strands of barbed wire ran along the horizontal wooden rails.

'After you,' said Francis.

'Is it OK to climb over?'

'Of course it is. Bit of barbed wire? Not a problem. I'll hold it down for you.'

'What if this land is private?'

Francis laughed. 'I suspect it all belongs to Wyveridge. Even if it doesn't, it's a little-known fact that there's no law against trespass in this country. As long as we don't damage anything – which we're not going to, are we?' With this, Francis hoisted Priya over onto a shady patch still covered with the brown, composting leaves of last autumn. He climbed over after her and they cut down through the shade of the trees towards the sunny open ground on the far side.

'Right,' said Francis, 'so the bottom line is that we know nothing for certain. However. Thanks to you, Priya, we appreciate that there is a man at this festival with a very valuable asset that needs protecting – his reputation: as a decent, ecologically minded, sharing, caring, family guy. Now there's no denying that, as a result of some things that have happened over this weekend, that reputation is still intact. One huge potential news story, very damaging to our man and his brand, has been replaced by another. Add to that the fact that if both these deaths really are murders, we're not dealing with a run-of-the-mill operative here. Bryce's death was made to look convincingly natural. So much so that Dr Webster and I – and possibly the police too – were almost fooled. When and if we're allowed to see the post-mortem results, things will hopefully be a bit clearer, but whoever it was bumped off Bryce, they did a good job.'

'Is one way of looking at it,' said Priya.

'Sorry, Priya. I didn't mean . . .'

'I understand what you're saying. Go on.'

'OK, so for the time being, the police have, quite publicly, pulled their resources off the Bryce case. Maybe our murderer – or murderers – are thinking they've got away with one crime, and may yet get away with another. So this, I think, is our way forward.'

'I'm not sure I follow you.'

'Our suspicions are centred on three people, none of whom have their eyes closed.'

'Jonty . . . and . . . Anna and Marv?'

'Exactly. They all know I've been snooping around, if only because I've spoken directly to all of them. Now what I think should happen is that someone, ideally not me, should let them know that my enquiries have drawn a blank; and that the police are coming round to the idea that Bryce died of a heart attack or an aneurysm, which may or may not be related to his fondness for ecstasy in the 1990s and his ongoing taste for cocaine. And that, unrelated to all that, Grace took some acid, had a bad trip and threw herself off the battlements. We can also let our suspects know that Rory has been arrested. And why.'

'So . . . we're suggesting that . . . Rory is potentially in the frame for . . . what?'

'No need to spell it out. The news of the arrest will be enough. Then watch the smile on the face of the tiger – or tigers – as they start to think they've got away with it. That's when people let things slip. Especially in the company of a young woman they find attractive.'

Priya smiled. 'You want me to talk to Jonty?' she said.

'It would certainly be interesting.'

'And Anna and Marv?'

'Let's start with Jonty.'

They were coming out of the woodland now, blinking in the bright sunshine. Beyond, the ground levelled and became grassy again, a wide strip running to the river. Down here, well below the little town, this was a much wider affair, a gleaming, eddying stretch of water perhaps forty feet across. On the far side were fields of corn, still damp and bent after the weeks of rain. On this side, the green meadow ended in a steep bank, below which was a band of reeds, their blond heads tossing in the light breeze. There were a few low bushes nestled into the bank, but no trees. Except one, that is, fifty yards or so downstream, at the point where the river made a sweeping bend before narrowing slightly. It was a magnificent oak, with a wide trunk spreading up to thick branches, eminently climbable.

'Now that,' said Francis, 'unless I'm very much mistaken, is the tree that your ex-boyfriend decided to sit in while he contemplated his rejection. I'm surprised he didn't know it was an oak, but there you are. Arboreal nomenclature isn't everyone's forte. The only remaining question is: how long did he spend up there, crying over spilt milk?'

'Hours probably,' Priya said. 'Knowing him.'

Francis looked over at her then, standing by the river in her neat little coat, her eyes bright, her long dark hair blowing to one side. For a moment, he paused. His younger, more impulsive self would have rushed over and taken her in his arms. But no, not now, not yet.

'Come on,' he said briskly. 'We'd best be getting back.'

THIRTY-ONE

Ace Taxis of Mold was not a huge operation. There was no office as such, just a phone, an answerphone and a ring-file of booking sheets in the kitchen of one of the smart new houses on the estate that had sprung up behind the public library and adjacent nursery, right off the main road which ran west out of town. Terry Jenkins drove the cab. His wife Sonia took the calls. Fortunately for Francis, Terry was at home having his lunch, before heading out to deal with the day's festival pick-ups and drop-offs.

Francis had been surprised to be let into the house at all, fully expecting a brush-off or a door slammed in his face. But no, when he'd explained why he was calling, Sonia was welcoming. She was a thin, rather nervy woman, dressed in black trousers and polo-neck, with heavy green eyeshadow above her dark eyes. Inviting Francis to step inside, she showed him along a parquet-floored corridor that smelt strongly of wood polish, past the kitchen, and into a lounge where shiny black leather sofas were grouped around a large flat-screen TV. In one corner of the room there was a trombone by a hefty sound system that looked as if it dated from the 1980s, complete with separate amplifier, tape and CD player, radio tuner and turntable for vinyl. A collection of such records was stacked on the big open shelves behind: plenty of obvious classics with a heavy preponderance of jazz. On narrower shelves above, there was an equally comprehensive stash of CDs.

'Fine selection of listening material you've got here,' said Francis, when Terry came through, still holding a mug of tea that read DADDIO in purple letters on the side. He was burly in his black T-shirt, his tight grey curls bouffant.

'The old vinyl. Should get rid of it really. Just can't bring myself to, somehow.'

'You're a practitioner too, by the looks of it?'

Terry smiled. 'I play in a little local band. We call ourselves the Four Musketeers. Weddings, bar mitzvahs, funerals, that kind of thing. But you can't make a proper living doing that down here.'

'Not enough bar mitzvahs?'

'You can say that again.'

'Hence the taxi business?'

'Spot on, mate.' Terry lowered his backside into a leather armchair. 'So how can I help you?'

Francis repeated the explanation he'd given Sonia.

'We don't really expect this kind of thing down here,' Terry said, 'even during festival time. I think a feller got drunk and punched another feller a couple of years ago. But that's about it. These literary types are pretty well behaved – that's why we like 'em. Now as to these two that you're talking about – I do remember them, as it happens. I picked 'em up from the Hall at around nine thirty on Saturday. I remember the time because I was kept waiting for about twenty minutes. I was about to give the guy up as a bad job. But I reckoned that if I stuck around I'd get another fare anyway. Big party going on. Sooner or later someone was going to want to go into town.'

'It was Bryce Peabody who called you out?'

'If that was his name. Sonia puts the calls through to my mobile, so I just pick 'em up as I'm driving round.'

'But then someone else came out?'

'Yes. Tallish chap. Not your typical arty-farty type. Cropped hair, muscly. Looked more like a bouncer than anything else.'

That was Dan all right. 'So he saw you there and helped himself . . .'

'He came over, yes, and I gave him the name and he confirmed that was him. But as I was turning round the circle to leave, this other shortarsed fellow comes running out in front of me, waving his arms in my headlights and shouting. He claimed it was his taxi. Then it turned out he knew the guy in the back, so after a bit of argy-bargy they agreed to go into town together.'

'Just describe how the other guy looked.'

'Bit older, I'd say. Short dark curls and quite a lived-in face, if you follow me. If you told me he used the old Grecian 2000 I wouldn't be surprised. So in he gets. They don't say a thing until we're halfway back to Mold. Then they start talking and suddenly it all kicks off. Screaming at each other, they were. I was supposed to be taking them up to the White Hart but I let them off at the bridge. I can't be dealing with fights.'

'But you got your fare?'

'More than, as it happened. It was like something out of Monty Python.' Terry grinned. 'I stopped the cab and told them to get out and they shut up immediately like a couple of naughty schoolboys. Then they had a right barney about who was paying, shoving tenners at me and telling me to keep the change. As I drove off, they got back to it.'

'Arguing?'

'Fighting, pretty much. The bouncer guy had the older one up against the wall of the bridge. I think he might have thrown a punch.'

'You didn't think of calling the police?'

'During the festival? You've got to be joking. Anyway, they were both grown men – I thought they could look after themselves.'

'You can't remember what they said – what started it?'

'To be honest, I can't. Bear in mind I'm working ten-hour shifts over the festival period.'

'Not even the odd line?'

'Come to think of it, there was one thing that did stick in my head. Something about "They're not yours".'

'"They're not yours",' Francis repeated slowly. 'Said by who? The bouncer?'

'It was him, you're right. The only reason I remember it is that it silenced them both for about half a minute, then they went back to it.'

'And you can't recall anything else?'

'Went in one ear and out the other. Most of it was to do with books, writers, who was good, who wasn't' – Terry grinned – 'not that I was bothering to listen . . .'

Francis's eyes scanned the row of publications above the CDs. There was Nelson Mandela's autobiography and *Bravo Two Zero* and a couple of books about jazz, then a long row of alphabetically arranged chick-lit novels, which he assumed were Sonia's. No, he decided, a fight about contemporary literature was hardly going to interest Terry.

'Just for the record,' he asked, 'how late do you normally carry on after midnight?'

'One o'clock's about the latest. There's not much call for taxis after that.'

'Even during festival time?'

'The pubs shut at eleven. You get the rush and then it quietens down.'

'What about last Saturday? How late did you stay out?'

'Not that late. I did a few more runs after that Wyveridge one, then I called it a night.'

'Finishing when?'

'Half twelve, oneish. Come to think of it, it was one when I got in, because I watched a bit of that *Jazz Greats* series they've got on BBC Four. Terrific stuff, have you seen it?'

'I'm afraid I haven't. But you'd have switched your phone off by then?'

'Once I'm in front of the TV, that's it. Sometimes I hear them come through on the main answerphone and I ignore them. I'm not greedy.'

As he drove off, ten minutes later, Francis wondered how much Terry Jenkins might have recalled of Dan and Bryce's conversation under torture. But a lurking suspicion of his had been resurrected and now he urgently needed to talk to someone else in the case. First he stopped to pick up two essential items: a sandwich and a pair of pliers. Fortunately Mold was one of those rare English towns that still had a basic collection of real shops: Simpson's Bakery, selling long filled rolls worthy of Subway; then, three doors down, two hardware merchants side by side – one of which, the father and son team of A & P Ness, had, unbeknownst to Francis, kept the local schoolboys in giggles for years.

THIRTY-TWO

It was 2.30 p.m. Andrew Motion was 'In Poetic Conversation' with Vikram Seth in the Big Tent; Will Self and Janet Street-Porter were discussing country walks in the Middle Tent; and Dan Dickson was chairing a panel of science fiction writers in the School Room. There was nobody in the Green Room except an old man who looked rather like Richard Ingrams, snoring quietly over a copy of the *Independent*. But of course! This was a literary festival, so it was Ingrams. Francis gave the snoozing satirist a respectful nod, then headed over to the shelves beyond the coffee machine to get what he needed. Without pausing, he picked out two of Laetitia's festival albums, 1998 and 1999, cut through their restraining brass cords with his new pair of pliers, then tiptoed off at speed towards the exit, looking neither to left nor right.

He found the Saab in the car park and sat in the passenger seat for five minutes, marking up various pages with yellow Post-It notes. Then he purred gently out of town, enjoying the latent power of the big engine as he kept strictly to the speed limit. Beyond the 30 mph sign, he put his foot down along the narrow green lanes. As he came out onto the wider open stretch of road before Tittlewell he heard the familiar trill of his mobile. He reached down to slide it out of his jacket pocket. DCI JULIE, read the screen. He guessed he'd better pull in before speaking to a police officer.

'Francis Meadowes.'

'No hands-free, Francis? It's Julie Morgan.'

'How can you tell?'

'Years of experience. Plus of course the delay. I hope you've stopped that car.'

'I have now. Fully legal. How can I help you?'

'As long as the key's in the ignition you're committing an offence, but we'll pass over that. I'm sorry to bother you, Francis. I just wanted to check something out.'

'OK.'

'We've had a statement from Bryce's long-term partner, Scarlett Paton-Jones, saying that on Sunday afternoon, between four thirty and six, you were interviewing her in her cottage outside Tittlewell.'

'I can confirm that, Julie. Though I'd put my arrival time a little later than four thirty. Sometime after five, I'd say. But if you're checking her alibi, she was there alone with her twin daughters when I turned up and her Turkish au pair didn't appear with her car till just before I left an hour later.'

'Thank you. That's very helpful.'

'So how are you getting on with Rory and the gang?'

'We're working through them as we speak.'

'Nothing you want to tell me?'

'In return for us agreeing not to prosecute, Rory's confessed to possession of LSD. The reason he was so freaked out is that he had three tabs in his wallet – and one of them had gone missing.'

'When was that?'

'Sometime on Sunday, he thinks. Before he went into the festival.'

'After Grace returned?'

'That's what he's not sure about.'

'So he says.'

'So he says. Funnily enough, I'm inclined to believe him. He's so desperate not to get a record, he's singing like the proverbial canary. Anyway, his story is that he left his wallet in his room, in a jacket on the back of a chair, but didn't notice what had gone missing till he got into Mold at teatime on Sunday.'

'He didn't take it himself and then forget about it?'

Julie laughed, but not for long. 'Apparently not. But he clearly thinks he's indirectly responsible for her death. Which would mean, if I decided to be uncharitable, that in addition to perverting the course of justice, and possession of two Class A substances, and a strong suspicion of supplying others with same, he might be looking at manslaughter. Not ideal for someone who wants to be taken on by a reputable chambers next year.'

'No wonder he was so nervy. Well, there's your second drug. The question is: how did it get from his wallet into her bloodstream?'

'Quite. While you're on, I thought you might be interested in something else that's come in: the preliminary result of the Bryce Peabody autopsy.'

Of course he would! Even down the line, Francis could tell that Julie was enjoying this.

'Fill me in.'

'Carbon dioxide levels in Bryce's blood confirm our suspicion that he was suffocated.'

'No . . .'

'More to the point,' Julie continued, 'some time on the Saturday evening he took – or was given – a powerful sedative, Zimovane. As I understand it from our police doctor, a good dose can render you insensible for several hours. There was a blister pack of this drug in his washbag, so it's not unduly suspicious – but I was rather hoping you might have Priya with you, see whether she could shed any light on his recent nocturnal habits. Because Scarlett told us he was a sound sleeper and never took pills.'

'Sorry, Julie, I'm on my own.' Francis contemplated telling her that he was on his way to Scarlett's right now, then decided against it.

'If you speak to Priya, tell her to give me a call, would you?'

'Will do. So how are the IT guys getting on with those laptops?'

'It's a painstaking business, dredging up files that have been deleted. I'll let you know as soon as we have anything.'

She clicked off. Francis sensed two things: she wasn't telling him everything; and she knew that he too was holding something back. Well, he thought, he was lucky she was being as open with him as she was; unless she had some other motive, she clearly valued his help. As for him, he would decide on whether to fill her in on what he'd seen in Fleur's film once he'd understood its full import.

He pulled out and gathered speed, on past the Black Bull and the gnarled tree. Outside the cottage the gate of the car boot was up. The front door was open. Scarlett was kneeling on the floor just inside, boxes and suitcases all around her.

'Are you leaving us?' Francis asked, walking in.

Scarlett turned. 'Hello. You again? No sooner do I get rid of the police than my private detective friend turns up.'

'Crime writer friend. So they've taken your statement?'

'Certainly have. And then stuck around. My Family Liaison Officer's been here since Sunday evening. Willing little bird called Patricia. A little too willing, if you ask me. Claimed to be offering me support, but was actually a big fat snoop. Until I had the brilliant idea of telling her I'd been talking to you on Sunday afternoon, I think they even had me in the frame for this other poor girl I've been reading about in the papers.'

'You haven't been into Mold then?'

'No. Couldn't face all that "I'm sorry for your loss" stuff when I don't even know what I feel myself. Luckily, Patricia was so desperate to be my friend I didn't even need to send Nurjan in to do the shopping.'

Francis looked around at the half-finished packing. 'Have you got time for a chat?'

'Are you any closer to an answer?'

'Maybe.'

'You're not going to tell me more than that?'

'Not unless you sit down with me.'

She looked at her watch. 'You'll need to keep it brief.'

They sat with a cafetière just inside the French doors to the garden. The sunshine had gone and the sky was now filled with dark grey cloud. A cool breeze was picking up. Down on the lawn Nurjan was still playing with the twins. Loud shrieks drifted up intermittently.

'You've told them?'

'When PC Patricia turned up it was hard not to.'

'How have they taken it?'

'I told them their daddy is in heaven, and that seems to be some consolation. But I don't think it's sunk in properly just yet. With me neither. I've surprised myself by not shedding a single tear. Is that awful?' She pressed her lips together in a tight smile. 'So, anyway, how can I help you?'

'I was going to ask,' Francis said, 'if you could tell me about your relationship with Dan Dickson.'

'I thought we'd covered this last time. I've known Dan for years. I always thought his success had more to do with self-belief and self-promotion than any profound talent. Bryce had an ongoing problem with him. What more is there to say?' She paused. 'Don't tell me you still suspect him of having anything to do with . . . all this? He may be a pretentious arse, but I hardly think he's a murderer.'

Francis shrugged. 'You haven't answered my question, have you?'

'I'm not sure I understand . . .'

'I'm afraid you understand all too well. Perhaps you're wondering how I found out. That you and Dan were an item. Off and on, but mostly on, for the best part of a year, before your kids were born, long before you and Bryce came up with the idea of an open marriage.'

You had to hand it to her, he thought, she was a splendid bluffer. 'I can't imagine who told you that,' she replied, and those pale blue eyes flashed. 'Mischievous misinformation, whoever it was. As I told you, I've known Dan for years. He was part of the same loose scene that I was, up in London in the 1990s. If you must know, he shacked up for a bit with a friend of mine, Tilly Bardwell. But no, never with me. He's not my type.'

Francis met her gaze levelly. 'Are you sure about that?'

Now Scarlett was on her feet. 'How dare you come to my house and accuse me of things that are not just hurtful, but completely untrue. I was trying to offer you some help. When I'm extremely busy trying to get off to London. But if this is going to be your tack, I shall have to ask you to finish your coffee and leave.'

Francis got up slowly. As he did so, he pulled from his bag one of the two albums he'd pinched from the Green Room – MOLD FESTIVAL YEARBOOK 1998. 'Laetitia was kind enough to show me this,' he said. 'A great idea, I must say. You get a real feel of how it must have been. Back in the day.' Francis opened it at one of the pages that he had marked with Post-it notes. 'How young you look. Bryce with barely a bag under his eyes, Dan with all his hair, you and Tilly as fresh as daisies. What great pals you clearly were. Staying out for the new lit fest at the same run-down cottage in Tittlewell, just the four of you. No kids, of course, to complicate things. It's an amazing machine, the camera, isn't it? Catches those telling little looks and gestures that even the best portrait painter would struggle with. Look at those lips of yours on Dan's hard stubble. The way your hand cradles round his neck. Tilly's face is a picture. Of brilliantly controlled jealousy. Did she know? What had happened – or was about to happen?'

Francis flipped to the next album. 'Here you all are again, the following year, lined up in the garden of the White Hart, having a great laugh by the looks of it. So what happened to change all that? Was it just that Dan's *Dispatches from the E Zone* rocketed him into the talent stratosphere while Bryce's debut never got off the ground? That must have been terribly galling for Bryce. To see Dan so lauded. Interviewed everywhere. Described as an *enfant terrible*, a description *he* had aspired to since college days.'

Francis turned to look at Scarlett; she was listening now, that was for sure. 'But was that all?' he continued. 'Or was Bryce's turning away from Dan something that you encouraged? Because you and he had fallen apart by then and you could no longer bear the sight of him? Or perhaps you could bear the sight of him too much. A sight which, unfortunately, met your eyes every day of your life.'

'I'm sorry, I've completely lost you,' Scarlett said, with a brittle laugh. 'Where is this absurd sequence of allegations going now?'

'I'm talking about the twins, of course.'

Now she looked scared.

Francis pressed on. 'They weren't Bryce's, were they? When you unexpectedly got pregnant, you panicked. You begged Dan to do the decent thing, make your relationship public, take them, and you, on. But he wouldn't, would he? He didn't want to be tied down. And he had his brand to think about, though you mightn't have called it that then. Dangerous, attractive, single, traveller, writer. He wasn't about to chuck that away to become knee-deep in nappies, was he?' Francis couldn't help a chuckle. 'Though perhaps if he'd known how lucrative the whole Family Man franchise would turn out to be, he might have gone for it.'

Scarlett was shaking her head. 'This is a ludicrous idea. If . . . *if* . . . I had been involved with Dan and he was the father of my children . . . why . . . why didn't I just tell everybody?'

'Because you realized that if you did, you'd have nothing. Here you were, this beautiful young woman who had entranced two literary lion cubs, and now the cub who was roaring like a proper king of the jungle suddenly wanted nothing to do with you. If you'd exposed him, and his rejection of you, you'd have lost not just face but Bryce. And you didn't want that, did you? Bryce had his Bloomsbury flat, money, a wide circle of friends that he shared with you. If you couldn't hold on to Dan, you'd sure as heck better hold on to Bryce. Where would you have been if he'd gone too? Most of your so-called joint friends would have taken his side. And then you'd have been a single mother of two struggling on child benefit and looking for a part-time job to keep you going. For all your nicely spoken manner, your family has no money; your father, the rural dean, was always above such things. Your career as a freelance journalist hadn't taken off; now the babies were going to make pursuing that a whole lot more difficult. So you told Bryce the twins were his and prayed that he would embrace fatherhood. Dan agreed to keep the secret and everything was tickety-boo. The girls were born. The Hampstead house was bought. Bryce proved to be, as you'd hoped, a doting dad. He was soon pushing them around the Heath in a double buggy while you were safe and comfortable. You met up regularly with his influential contacts. Before you knew it you had your column in the *Sentinel* about the day-to-day difficulties of being a mother. You had pin money and respect.'

Scarlett said nothing; but her face, tense and pale, spoke volumes.

'Then what happened? Within two years you'd agreed to an

open marriage. Was that really as consensual a decision as you made it out to be? In the frankly unlikely little sketch you gave me earlier . . .'

'Of course it was consensual,' said Scarlett angrily.

'You were initially jealous,' Francis continued, 'when you realized things had got far too serious with Anna Copeland. But you didn't chuck Bryce out, did you? You couldn't. Not being married, you had no leverage. The new house was in his name and so was this place. It was best just to let things roll along. The Anna thing would end one day, because he was never going to leave his beloved girls, was he? At least while he thought they were his. You knew him well enough to know that he was never going to give Anna the baby she wanted either, that that was just another of his famous promises.

'And then, suddenly, three months ago, along came Priya. To blow the whole thing apart. What had happened to your feckless philanderer? He seemed reformed, smitten, serious. About an obviously very determined young woman who could easily give him another family.

'Now you really had to fight. To cling on to what you could. Hampstead, this cottage, the money. You suddenly realized how few rights you had. Could you bear the thought of Priya, next year not just at the White Hart but out here too, in this place you loved so much? Sitting in this chair, with this window, this view. Pregnant perhaps with another little creature for Bryce to fall for. This time truly his. I don't think you could.'

Scarlett looked defeated. On the beautiful old clock on the mantelpiece Francis could hear the seconds ticking by. 'How do you know all this?' she asked.

'Looking at those albums helped me a lot,' he said. 'But don't forget also, in this tight little world you exist in, your business is rarely your own. There are others out there who've been keeping a close eye on what's going on.'

'Who precisely are you talking about?'

'I think I should keep my sources to myself.'

'Virginia – blinking – Westcott?'

'I really couldn't say.' For a would-be detective, Francis had a hopeless poker face.

'That interfering bitch! Of course it's her. Who else round here knows that my father was a rural dean. That Bryce always wanted to be an *enfant terrible*. God! She's just unable to leave him alone, isn't she? I suppose if you've heard it all from her there's no point denying it. I'm amazed, though, that she knew about the twins. I thought that was one thing Dan and I had managed to keep to ourselves . . .'

Francis looked down at the table. For a moment his eye fixed on the empty cafetière, with its dark sludge of coffee grounds below the curving spring of the plunger. 'You're right,' he said, 'I did get quite a lot of this story from Virginia. But she didn't tell me about the twins.'

'Who then?' Scarlett paused. 'Not Dan?'

'I worked that bit out for myself,' Francis said. 'Perhaps it was because when I drove out here the other afternoon I'd come straight from Dan, and there they were again, those same intense, questioning, alive brown eyes . . .'

'I see,' said Scarlett. Then: 'So you don't think Virginia knows?'

'She didn't say anything to me about it. And she was in a very confiding mood.'

'Come on, it can't just have been some vague resemblance of eyes. What else put you onto this?'

Francis explained about Fleur's video, about his interview with Terry – *"They're not yours."* 'Suddenly it all clicked into place. I knew Dan was pretty furious about Bryce's attack, but maybe he'd been goaded more than any of us realized.'

'I still don't see why he would have told him about the girls, though.'

'He'd been kicked, publicly, where it hurt and he had to get him back. He was drunk, and very, very angry. He went nuclear.'

There was silence in the room. As the clock ticked on, Scarlett seemed to be thinking it all through. 'Funnily enough,' she said, eventually, 'Dan used to look up to Bryce. Then, as you surmised, he had his success and all that changed. I found it sad. Two clever men, with a great friendship, spoilt by a silly competitiveness. We've only got one life, haven't we?'

Or no life at all, thought Francis. 'You don't think Dan could have taken it further?' he asked.

'How d'you mean?'

'That night.'

'What? Followed Bryce back to the White Hart and done him in? I really don't.'

'I agree with you. I think what we have there is the explanation of the bruise on Bryce's cheek, but nothing more. So who was it? Who really did have the motivation to kill him? Not you, I hope.'

'I thought you might be coming to this. As you've worked out so cleverly, I did have every reason. I was scared of what Priya might do; she'd got her claws so heavily into him. I've been a fool, letting us drift on as "boyfriend" and "girlfriend" all these years. If it had come to a fight, I probably wouldn't have been able to hold onto this place. And now he's dead – unless he's changed his will, which I'm ninety-five per cent sure he hasn't – this is mine, as is Hampstead and the Bloomsbury flat. So I appreciate it doesn't look good for me. But you have to believe me, it's not really my style to go round murdering people.'

'Why do I have to believe you?'

'What about that poor journalist girl? How did I get to her? When I was speaking to you. Have you got an answer to that?'

'I didn't get out here till five thirty. She was alone at Wyveridge from just after four o'clock. It's a fifteen-minute drive from here to there.'

'But Nurjan had the car. It's a bit more than a fifteen-minute walk, I think.'

'Your au pair turned up right at the end of our interview. You told me she'd been shopping in town. I didn't notice her carrying any bags when she got out.'

'Oh come on! They were in the car.' Scarlett chuckled dismissively. 'If you really want to think I've got something to do with this, what can I say? You have absolutely no evidence. So if you're done, I shall wish you goodbye. I have my packing to finish.'

'Are you off to London tonight?'

'As it happens, we're not. I always like to go first thing, when the roads are empty and the girls are half-asleep.'

'The police don't mind you going?'

'PC Patricia told me I was free to leave whenever.'

Francis shifted from foot to foot. 'May I quickly use your loo before I head off?'

'If you must. There's one on this floor at the far end. Or just up the stairs here. Second door on the left.'

Francis had been hoping she would say that. Once upstairs, he paced on down the corridor and into what was clearly the master bedroom. There was a king-sized bed, covered in a white waffle pattern eiderdown; beyond was the en suite bathroom. Francis hadn't dared to even imagine such a result, but there they were, on the top shelf of the mirrored cupboard, right above the sink: two packets of Zimovane, one half used.

Francis pulled out his mobile and took a quick photo; then a second, wider shot to establish where the cupboard was. Hadn't PC Patricia seen them? If she had, why were they not already in a plastic police evidence bag? Or had she not been briefed at that point on the Zimovane element? TIE, pah.

By the bed was a white phone. Francis picked it up quickly and dialled his own mobile, waited for the first buzz, then put it down. Heading back, he nipped into the other upstairs toilet and pulled the flush.

'One last question,' he asked, as Scarlett showed him out of the front door. 'When he was with you, did Bryce ever need to use sleeping pills?'

She gave him a very measured look. 'Funnily enough,' she said, 'PC Patricia asked me that too. No, for your information Bryce always slept like a log. I've had a few problems with insomnia myself, especially recently. But Bryce was infuriating in that way. Head on the pillow and he'd be gone.'

THIRTY-THREE

Francis was in luck. As befitted an author who regularly expressed contempt for the parochialism of the literary world, Dan Dickson was still in the Green Room an hour after his event, reading *The Bookseller* as he picked at a piece of carrot cake and sipped a mug of tea. The place was otherwise deserted.

Francis walked over. 'Hi Dan.'

The great sculpted head turned. 'Hi mate. You still around? I've just done my last gig. I was sitting here wondering whether to head to Dewkesbury station for the train back to the Smoke or have one last exotic night in the sticks.'

'You didn't drive down?'

'Never learnt, mate. Scares me, all those people racing around in metal boxes, separated only by a painted white line. I feel safer on the rails.'

'D'you mind if I join you for a moment?'

'Help yourself.' Dan gestured to the chair opposite and gave Francis the benefit of his toothy smile. 'Terrifying magazine, this. But good for us authors to read every now and then. Just so we understand our true status. Which is, these days, somewhere between a bar of soap and a factory-farmed chicken. You still on the sleuth?'

'A few more bits of the jigsaw to get into place. With which in mind, I wanted to ask you about your taxi ride into Mold on Saturday night.'

'My taxi ride into Mold?' Dan looked as if he were struggling to remember something entirely forgettable. His acting wasn't that good.

'With Bryce . . .'

Dan laughed. 'What on earth made you think I was with Bryce?'

'You were filmed getting into a taxi together outside Wyveridge Hall.'

'Filmed?'

'By one of the young people in Ranjit's house party.'

Dan's laugh was throaty in its scorn. 'You can't do anything these days, can you? It's not just CCTV, is it? Even way out in the country, at a private function, Big Brother is watching.'

'Little Sister in this case.'

Dan's face shifted a register. 'Not that poor girl?'

'Her friend.'

Dan was shaking his head. 'As I recall, I was already in the taxi, about to leave, when Bryce crashed in demanding a free lift.'

'That's not how the driver remembered it.'

'You've spoken to him too?'

'Terry Jenkins of Ace Taxis of Mold. Told me that by the time you got into town you were pretty much at each other's throats. He had to put you out on the bridge.'

For all of five seconds Dan said nothing, his mouth hanging open. Then the smile returned. 'You have done your homework.'

'Might I ask what you were arguing about?'

'This and that. I should never have let him in. Bryce always had this terrible problem with me. Ever since I became even vaguely successful he was like a dog with a bone. Once he started slagging me off he couldn't stop. Which was slightly galling on Saturday, considering that it was me who should have had an apology from him.'

'For his review?'

'Of course.'

'And that provoked you enough to want to fight him?'

'Were we actually fighting? I think your taxi driver mate might have been exaggerating.'

'Apparently you got so angry you told Bryce you were the father of his children.'

For a moment, Dan looked as if he'd been punched in the face. Then he burst out laughing. 'This cabbie told you that? Fascinating though the idea is, I'm afraid he misheard.'

'There's no point denying it. I've already spoken to Scarlett and she's confessed all. What I need to know now is exactly what you told Bryce on Saturday night.'

As Dan stared down at his heavy black boots, there was a distant rumble of thunder, away across the valley. He looked slowly up and met Francis's eye. 'Scarlett told you . . . what . . . exactly?' he asked.

'Your affair, Tilly Bardwell, the works.'

'OK, OK.' Dan held up his hands. 'Maybe I did say something to Bryce along those lines. I was a little tipsy. And yes, still furious with him about that frigging write-up. *Otherworld* is my best book yet. By far. How dare he slag me off like that. And then come barging in, quite deliberately, on my talk. Perhaps I did lose it a bit. I should never have told him about the twins. That was stupid. Nobody else knows, except Scarlett. I'm amazed she said anything.'

'I kind of forced it out of her.'

'But how did you know?'

'I guessed. It fitted everything else. And I'm afraid they've inherited your eyes.'

Dan looked simultaneously proud and sad. 'They have, haven't they?'

'May I ask. Why didn't you take them on? Become their father openly?'

'None of your fucking business.' They sat in silence for what seemed to Francis like five minutes, but was probably only one. 'I did consider it,' Dickson said eventually. 'But it wouldn't have worked. Scarlett and I had already split up when I got her pregnant.'

'How did you manage that then?'

Dickson laughed. 'Cheeky bastard, aren't you. You know the kind of thing. We'd parted, then we met up for one last shag and Sod's law she got up the duff.'

'So how did you know they were yours? If she was seeing Bryce too?'

'He was away that month. In Australia. Opining about international fiction at the Adelaide Festival. That's why we got together again. While the cat was away. To be honest, it wasn't just the once. No, I was never in any doubt the girls were mine.'

'And why wouldn't your relationship have worked?'

'How long have you got? We turned each other on mightily

but,' he yawned, as if exhausted by the very memory, 'she's very controlling, is Scarlett. Didn't want me doing this, didn't want me doing that. Even though she herself was cheating on Bryce, she used to get insanely jealous about any other birds I hung out with. So I knew, long term, it wasn't a runner. I actually, for my sins, wanted an abortion. Thought it would be cleaner. But she wouldn't countenance that, bless her. And when we discovered it was twins I was glad she'd persuaded me out of it. Ridiculous. Why should two dead foetuses be worse than one? Anyway, we came to an agreement. We'd stop seeing each other. She'd tell Bryce they were his. The whole thing would remain our secret and I'd give up all rights as a father.'

'And how did that work out in practice?'

'Not very well. You got kids?'

'No.'

'Put it this way, it's not been an easy secret to keep. I've thought about telling Bryce many times before. So we could at least work out some sort of arrangement. Whereby it was at least acknowledged. And I could see them properly from time to time. But whenever I talked to Scarlett about it, I came up against the same brick wall. My sacred promise. And our pact.'

'But on Saturday you cracked?'

'I guess I did. Perhaps because he'd been such an arsehole, earlier, and I wanted to get him where it hurt. Perhaps I just didn't want him swanning around thinking he was their dad any more. I saw them, you see, on Friday. Scarlett brought them in for that Michael Rosen event. They're so sweet and sophisticated now.'

'Do they know who you are?'

'I'm a friend of Mummy's. Uncle Dan. Who often seems to

be at the zoo when they're visiting. They asked me once if I *worked* at the zoo.'

'What happened when you told Bryce?'

'He didn't believe me at first. Then I gave him dates and details. Spelt it out for him. So he got it.'

'And he had you by the throat?'

'When we got out of the cab, yes. But then, once we'd traded a couple of blows, the whole thing seemed ridiculous. We're writers, not fighters. There we were, on the bridge, the river rushing by below, the full moon coming up over the trees. Suddenly he burst into tears. I ended up consoling him.'

'Then he went back to the White Hart?'

'Eventually.'

'Covered in bruises?'

'Nothing too serious. I clipped him on the cheek, I think.'

'What time was that?'

'Just after ten. I remember, because I offered to take the poor bastard for a drink. I thought the pubs might be closed, then I looked at my watch and was surprised how early it was.'

'He wasn't interested?'

'He said he wanted to be alone. He was tired.'

'When did you hear he was dead?'

'When I came down to breakfast. You were there, I think.'

'I was. You were in the company of a tall blonde.'

'My editor, Rachel Lightfoot. I'm not shagging her, if that's what you're thinking.'

'You didn't hear the commotion in the small hours?'

'I'm a heavy sleeper. Apparently the fire alarm went off and all sorts.'

'So when you found out . . . about Bryce . . . what did you think?'

'I had to hope it had nothing to do with what had happened between us.'

'Was that likely?'

'I suppose it was a possibility. He was very mournful when he left me. And one thing I've learned over the years is that people do sometimes do crazy things. But then again, Bryce was hardly low on self-esteem. The only worry that I did have was: had I perhaps hit him in a place that had triggered off a blood clot in his brain or something? All the next day I was wondering if I should fess up to what had happened, then that poor journo bird bit the dust . . .'

'And?'

'I didn't know what to think. But I no longer thought Bryce's sad demise had anything to do with me.'

Dan looked up at Francis and gave him an unassailable smile.

THIRTY-FOUR

Francis had just left the Green Room when his mobile rang. It was DCI Julie again.

'I thought you might be interested,' she said, 'to know that the techie girls and boys up in Bristol have finally got somewhere. There *were* drafts of that speech on Bryce's laptop. Lots of them. And an accompanying PowerPoint presentation. All deleted.'

'None of it flattering about our friend Jonty?'

'Definitely not. I've got the most up-to-date one in front of me. It's a complete demolition of his reputation. Backed up with some impressive evidence. Photos of girlfriends, some alarmingly young-looking. Two of a love child. The works. I think if Bryce had gone ahead with it, it would have caused a sensation.'

'Any chance you could bung it over to me on the email?'

'I'm afraid it'll have to stay in-house for the moment.'

'So what are you going to do?'

'That's for me to know.'

'You're focused on Jonty, though? Presumably?'

There was silence on the line. 'In strict confidence,' Julie said eventually, 'we're going to pull him in.'

'Jonty?'

'Yes. First thing in the morning. He's got his last event at lunchtime tomorrow, so I don't imagine he'll be going home before that. He'll be under surveillance in the meantime, obviously.'

'You've got enough evidence? I thought you said that the content of the talk was circumstantial.'

'But a very nice back-up for the purple thread we found on the battlements, right above the spot where Grace landed. It matches a Boden Classic Twill shirt that Jonty was wearing all Sunday. Sorry I didn't mention that before . . .'

'God . . .' muttered Francis.

'Not to mention the two blond hairs on the lead flashing currently being pushed through the Bristol DNA lab. I feel reasonably confident of the result, given that they were within inches of the thread. I think we can be fairly sure they don't belong to either Anna or her shaven-headed friend Marv.' The chuckle that came down the phone line was smug. 'Now there is one other thing,' Julie continued, 'I thought you might be interested in, which is raising a few questions over here.'

'Fire away.'

'As well as the numerous drafts of the speech on the laptop, our IT whizz Dipika found the times, both of the changes and of the deletions. The last modification to Bryce's final draft was made at eleven twenty-seven on the Saturday night. It was auto-recovered at eleven thirty-two and that saved text featured a long row of z's about halfway through the second page.'

Francis laughed. 'Bryce fell asleep on the job.'

'That's what we rather thought.'

'And the deletions were all done at once?'

'Yes, but d'you want to know when?'

'Go on.'

'Five fifteen.'

'But how . . . I mean . . . if Bryce—'

'Not p.m. . . . *a.m.*! The next morning.'

Francis gasped. 'They were deleted after the body was found . . .'

'So why hadn't Jonty done it before? Did he suddenly think, Oh no, if they find the laptop, they're going to find Bryce's talk, and then they're going to suspect me? There was time enough for him to get up there, I think, given that the body was found shortly after four and the ambulance didn't arrive till five thirty. I'm assuming the room was empty and unlocked?'

'Yes,' said Francis. 'It was. Apart from a short visit by me, and another by Priya when she went up there to change.'

'The rest of the time you two were both in your room, I think you said?'

'Yes.'

'Doing what?'

'Talking, mainly. Cathy the manageress was there for a bit. Then I was alone with Priya.'

'OK, so you and Priya could have quite easily been distracted while Jonty got past into number twenty-nine?'

'I suppose so.'

'That fits perfectly. Thanks, Francis.'

'No worries,' he replied. He clicked off his mobile and took a long, deep breath. Then he turned and walked slowly back down the tented corridor towards the Green Room. Dan had gone and it was now completely empty. He slumped onto a battered armchair in one corner. For two long minutes, he appeared to be in a deep trance. Then, abruptly, he had got to his feet and was walking at speed towards the White Hart. The sky was lowering now, a deep charcoal grey, the thunder rumbling closer.

There was no one in reception. And yes, there was the key to Priya's new room, 19, dangling from its hook on the board. He took it, then headed back up to his room to fetch his laptop.

Pushing open her door a minute later he saw Priya's squidgy leather bag, as yet unopened on the double bed. He clicked up the catch on the Yale so that nobody else could get in, then ran over and unzipped it. With shaking hands he sifted through the clothes: chiffon tops, leggings, bras, dresses, a pair of black pumps. But otherwise nothing but a book called *Where Soldiers Fear to Tread*, which a glance at the back cover told him was about Somalia. Well, well! Maybe Priya had been more hung up on Conal than she'd been admitting. Just inside the suitcase an old Derby address had been crossed out and replaced with a London one. Above that, in the same thick black laundry marker, was written P.K. JASWAL. The 'K' was presumably Kaur. So when Priya had come to London as a journalist, she'd taken the generic Sikh female name as her byline. But that was all. Damn.

What had he been thinking? Expecting to find? Then he noticed a pocket on the outside of the case and a promising bulge. He unzipped it eagerly. But it was only a travel brochure about Greek islands. He reached inside for one last ferret around. And as he did so, he noticed, tucked away at one end, a little buttoned pouch. Inside was a blue plastic memory stick. It had nothing on it but the printed word VERBATIM. Keeping an eye on the door, Francis booted up his laptop. Then slid the stick into a USB socket and clicked it open. He gasped. There were just two files on it: *Celebrity and Hypocrisy 10b* and *Celebrity and Hypocrisy PowerPoint*.

There it all was! Jonty's double life, no holds barred. If Bryce had stayed alive to deliver it, this speech would have destroyed him. The accompanying PowerPoint presentation was as compromising as DCI Julie had said it was. Skimming through photos of young women, some posed, some just observed, Francis paused on one image of a toddler holding up an ice cream. She had a familiar crooked smile and tell-tale big ears – unmistakably love child Amelie.

While he was copying the files onto his laptop, he paced back and forth across the room, eye on the Yale lock, thinking hard. He replaced the memory stick in the pouch, put Priya's clothes back as they had been and made his exit.

Downstairs Cathy was back in her office. 'Just replacing this key,' he said quietly.

'Thanks,' the manageress replied, barely looking up from her screen.

'Could I also trouble you for a couple of things?'

Five minutes later he was back in his room, straight on his mobile to DCI Julie.

'I was about to call you,' she said. 'We just searched Jonty's room and guess what we found at the bottom of his briefcase.'

'I've no idea.'

'The hard copy of Bryce's speech. Complete with annotations.'

'So that's where it ended up.'

'A final nail in his coffin, wouldn't you agree? So what can I do for you, Francis?'

'Is there any chance you could get out here to the White Hart for nine o'clock?'

'Why?'

'I'm organizing an impromptu "event". Extra to the festival programme.'

'Why?'

'You didn't want to talk to Priya and me this morning, did you? But you were glad you did, I think?'

'Perhaps I was.'

'Trust me then. But bear in mind, when I address the group I intend to assemble, we may have need of assistance. I should bring Steve and Brian with you at the very least.'

'Will this assembled company include Jonty Smallbone?'

'Yes.'

Silence on the line. 'I'm not intending to change my plans for the timing of this arrest, Francis.'

'Even if you thought our murderer might strike again?'

'As I told you, he's under surveillance.'

'While out drinking with Priya,' Francis said, 'at some hostelry in town.'

'Operational information I obviously can't share.' Julie's tone was a satisfactory mixture of the pissed-off and the impressed.

'Whether you come or not,' Francis said, 'I'll be going ahead with this event. I think you might find what I have to say of considerable interest.'

'You don't want to tell me now, save all of us a bit of trouble?'

'If you do come, you'll see exactly why I can't do that.'

'Very cryptic.' There was a long pause. Francis could almost hear the cogs of Julie's brain turning. Then, quietly: 'OK, we'll be there.'

Even as he put down the phone, lightning flashed outside,

followed immediately by a loud crash of thunder. The storm was upon them. As he stood by the window watching another fork of elemental fire snaking down to lose itself in the dark woods above the little town, Francis had a further revelation. Of course! How had he been so stupid? Unless his intuition was wrong this was the very last piece of the puzzle. He clicked through to Recent Calls on his phone and found Scarlett's number. But before he could press Call there was a knock on his door. And here was Priya, bright-eyed, wet from the rain, carrying a crumpled copy of the *Daily Mail*. The 'festival murders' were still dominating the front page.

'There you are,' said Francis. 'I was starting to worry about you.'

'With good reason. It's crazy out there. I need a towel.'

'How did you get on?' he asked, bringing one out from the bathroom.

'Well,' she said with a grin, as she ran it back and forth through her hair. 'I managed to do what you wanted, talk to Mr Jonty Smallbone, also known as Family Man.'

'And how did you accomplish that?'

'Easy-peasy. He was in the Green Room after his kids thing with some children's publisher, so I just sauntered over. I was disgracefully flirty, I'm afraid.' She giggled. 'In the end he made it clear to them that the business side of things was over and he wanted me all to himself. We shared a glass of Laetitia's festival plonk, then he invited me to go for a drink with him in town.'

'And you went?'

'Just the one. We're meeting later for dinner.'

'Well done. So where's the family?'

'Gone back to Peewit Farm. He's all on his own tonight. We're going to the Old Bakery. Why don't you come too?'

'And spoil his chances? Perhaps I should. Although I'm not sure he'd want a gooseberry in the shape of a coconut.'

'How d'you mean?'

'Never mind, silly joke. Tell me, did you manage to drop in anything with Jonty about the progress of the enquiry?'

'Of course I did! I said that you and I had been working closely with the police and that they now thought Bryce had died of natural causes. And that poor Grace's death was an unfortunate coincidence. She'd taken some of the hallucinogenic drugs which were all too available out at Wyveridge, gone crazy and jumped off the battlements all by herself.'

'And how did he take that?'

'"What did I tell you?" he said. "A classic case of rural coppers getting overexcited." So d'you think he thinks he's got away with it?'

'I've no idea,' Francis said. 'But it'll certainly be interesting what he says now. Quiz him about Anna and Marv. Exactly what were they up to on Sunday afternoon? Does he know? Does he look shifty when you ask him? Does he overcompensate?'

'Oh, do join us! Then you can ask him yourself . . .'

'I think it would be more productive to leave him to you. Anyway, I've got a couple of things I need to be getting on with. But what you can do for me, Priya, is bring him over here afterwards. For nine o'clock if you can manage that.'

'What – to this room?'

'No, downstairs. To the guest lounge. We'll be joined by a few others.'

'What are you planning now, Francis?'

'You'll have to wait and see.'

Now she looked sulky. 'I thought we were working on this together.'

'We are.' He went and sat by her on the bed. 'I'm extraordinarily grateful for everything you've done, Priya. And have still to do. I just don't want to put you in an impossible position. Not to mention a dangerous one.'

'You think I'm in danger having dinner with Jonty?'

'I don't, as it happens. DCI Julie has got him under surveillance. So look out for that burly rugger player tucking into the potted shrimps over the way. No, if you can just hang on you'll find out everything. And also see what a fantastic help you've been.'

'Don't you trust me enough to tell me now?'

'It's not that. I need you to concentrate on Jonty. More specifically on being your usual charming self, so that he a) reveals more than he means to and b) trots along here obediently with you at nine.'

'And if you tell me what you're up to, I won't be able to manage that?'

'Something like that . . .'

'What *are* you planning?'

'Priya! Stop probing. Just bring him here at the appointed hour.'

'I hate this. Have you got new evidence or something?'

Francis shrugged.

'Francis! You can't be so evasive. It's not fair.'

'OK. But I'll only share this with you under conditions of the very strictest secrecy.'

'Of course.'

He told her about the hard copy of Bryce's speech in Jonty's briefcase, then the purple thread and the two blond hairs.

'Wow,' she said, slowly. 'Why haven't they arrested him already?'

Francis shrugged. 'Who knows? Maybe they will if you bring him over tonight.'

'So the police are coming too?'

'Yes.'

She looked over at him, then crossed to where he stood and put her arms around him. He didn't move away.

'You're a lovely guy,' she said. 'You know that?'

Outside, at that moment, there was another flash of lightning, followed after a second and a half by a mighty clap of thunder.

'That felt close,' said Francis. He could feel her trembling. Then suddenly she was sobbing, warm tears on his shirt.

'I just can't believe it,' she said, looking up at him. 'Bryce . . . and Grace.'

'No,' he agreed. 'It's awful. Dreadful and shocking and awful.' He held her while she calmed herself.

'Come to bed,' she murmured.

He looked down at her and wondered for a moment if he had imagined this; but no, he hadn't.

'Not now,' he said. 'We've got work to do.'

'Can't it wait? Just a little?'

'Come on, Priya. You need your energies for Jonty.' He closed his eyes, leant forward, and kissed her on the forehead. Then he stepped reluctantly but firmly away. 'We're almost done now.'

THIRTY-FIVE

Two minutes to nine. There were perhaps twenty-five present, grouped on a loose double circle of sofas, armchairs and the padded straight-backed chairs which Cathy and Irina had brought in from the dining room. All the people Francis had phoned had turned up: Dan, Conal, Virginia, Anna and Marv, Priya and Jonty, even Scarlett, pale-faced on a beige and brown striped Parker Knoll in the corner. In the end it had taken just the one call to make her abandon her packing and come in. The police were here too, grouped round DCI Julie in a posse at the back. Despite himself, Francis felt reassured; if things went pear-shaped, this gang should be able to handle the flak. Just along from them was Terry from Ace Taxis, then Doctor Roger Webster, next to manageress Cathy.

This was not the way Francis had planned it – or wanted it. Braithwaite would have hated a set-up like this – as near as dammit to the traditional 'group denouement' of the Golden Age! But given what he had to do, here and now tonight, he couldn't see another way.

He took a deep breath, then stepped out and introduced himself, before launching straight in with an explanation of how he'd been woken on Sunday morning by Priya's screams. 'Before

I knew it,' he continued, 'I found I was having to take charge. Priya clearly needed looking after. And nobody knew better than I that a room containing a recently dead body needs to be preserved in as pristine a state as possible. We couldn't have all and sundry galumphing in there in their pyjamas.'

'Just you,' came a fluting, unmistakable voice.

'Yes, Virginia. And when I went up to room twenty-nine to see poor Bryce I made sure that I left as slight an imprint on the place as possible. But it was my decision to take a look at the body that precipitated me into the chain of events that leads me to be standing before you all tonight. Because what I saw, in the company of Dr Webster here, was what made me start to think that Bryce wasn't just another of those unfortunate people who'd been struck down in their prime by a heart attack, or perhaps an aneurysm or a stroke.'

'Do tell us what that was,' said Virginia.

'I'm coming to that.'

'Spoilsport.'

'Please. This is a serious business we're talking about. A double murder.'

'You really think that?'

'I really know that,' said Francis. That shut her up. Her mouth opened twice, like a hungry goldfish, then she was silent. 'But first,' he continued, 'let me take you through the people I was initially suspicious of.' He launched into a summary of what he'd been thinking before Grace died: Dan, insulted in print, but with no other obvious motive; Conal, who had publicly threatened to kill Bryce, but had almost certainly been too drunk to do so; Priya, the textbook prime suspect, but with a sound alibi and no motive;

Anna, cruelly treated by Bryce and a probable beneficiary of his will, staying in the same hotel, with an ex-Marine boyfriend; Scarlett, out at the cottage with kids, but with most to lose – and gain; and finally wild card Virginia, just down the corridor, whose feelings about the celebrated critic were clearly complex, to put it mildly.

'Now this was not a stabbing,' Francis went on, 'a shooting, or even a hanging. If it was murder it was trying very hard not to look like it. So what had happened, I wondered, to this man who lay with his eyes closed, the only marks on his body being a bruise on his right cheek and a love bite on his neck? If he hadn't died naturally, might he have been poisoned? Strangled? Suffocated? The bloodshot eyes we found when Dr Webster peeled his eyelids back suggested the last, though they could also, just as likely, have resulted from tiredness or discomfort from the contact lenses Bryce wore. But imagine for a moment that this redness had not had such an innocent cause, my guess was that some sort of sedative would have been involved. The other thing any murderer needed to be sure of was that his victim was alone in the room, which meant that Priya had to be well out of the way.

'The same was obviously true if he'd been strangled. Poisoning was a little different. If our killer had found a way to make sure that Bryce alone took poison, it didn't much matter where Priya was. However, unless he' – Francis paused and looked slowly round the packed room – 'or she, of course, had managed to get his hands on that apocryphal South American snake venom that acts immediately and leaves no trace, the post-mortem was in due course going to give him away. For that reason, I thought that option less likely.

'Indeed, after a busy day running around talking to all my

315

suspects, I was starting to think perhaps I'd been wrong in imagining that this death was suspicious at all. Maybe Bryce's postmortem would reveal no more than another sad case of a man in middle age struck down by natural causes.

'But at the very moment I was coming to this conclusion, there was a second death. This changed everything. Though a few were saying that Grace's bizarre fall was an awful coincidence, I instinctively felt that it wasn't. I was also – I thought – able to rule out no less than three of my potential culprits. For at the time this latest incident had occurred, I myself had been closeted with Scarlett in her cottage ten miles outside Mold. Then, driving back into town after this interview, I'd stopped at the Black Bull pub in Tittlewell, where I happened across Conal O'Hare having a quiet drink with Fleur Atkinson, Grace's close friend. Meanwhile, Virginia Westcott hadn't moved, by all accounts, from the Green Room where I'd left her after her talk.

'Just as I was simultaneously certain that foul play was afoot, yet despairing of my shortlist of suspects, Priya here presented me with another one. She confided to me that Bryce's hatchet job on Dan Dickson had only been the starter. The main course had been going to be his big event on Sunday – *Celebrity and Hypocrisy*. The central subject of that was one of our very best known TV faces, whom we are fortunate to have with us here tonight: Jonty Smallbone, Family Man.'

As his audience turned to check the famous face, Francis glanced over at the police line-up. Her sidekicks were as impassive as trained coppers should be, but on DCI Julie's lips was the flicker of the smile that accompanies a job well done. 'I've now had a chance to read Bryce's speech,' Francis continued, 'and I can tell you it had even more juice in it than his attack on Dan in the *Sentinel*. I'm not going to go into all the details here and now, but the burden of it was that Family Man's wholesome public image was not exactly borne out in the way he lived his life—'

'You can stop right there!' said Jonty, rising to his feet. His smarmy confidence had gone; his voice was a reedy quiver.

'I will, Jonty, don't worry. Of course,' Francis went on, as Family Man sank slowly back into his seat, 'Bryce's allegations never came to be made. But the idea that Jonty might have been involved, even if not directly, in Bryce's death, seemed to fit perfectly. And it answered one question that had been troubling me all along: if what you wanted to do was kill Bryce, why do it in the full glare of a festival? Especially if you wanted to make your murder look like a natural death, why not do it at some other time, when you'd be far more likely to get away with it? Because, obviously, if Jonty had only found out about this threat to his brand some time on Friday or Saturday, he'd have had to act fast. Whatever else happened, Bryce's event was scheduled to go ahead at three p.m. on Sunday. There would be journalists in the audience, quite apart from all those bloggers and tweeters. By teatime, the super-injunction that had kept the lid on Jonty's double life for so long would be next to worthless.'

Family Man was back on his feet again. 'Now listen here!' he said, 'you have absolutely—'

'Let Francis finish,' interrupted Priya.

'No foundation—'

'Ssshh!' came the collected hiss of the room, as Priya pulled him back down again.

'This new suspect,' Francis continued, 'also gave me answers to the main problem of the second murder: why Grace? Because, of course, as soon as she'd heard about Bryce's death, she had gone rushing into Mold to uncover all she could about what had happened. She did well. A day ahead of me she found out about the content of *Celebrity and Hypocrisy*. And she was on the brink of filing a piece to her newspaper about Jonty's real lifestyle when she met her horrid end.

'I was getting somewhere, but without access to any of the evidence the police had uncovered, I was stuck. So this morning, early, I called on DCI Julie Morgan, taking with me Priya here, whose support and feedback I'd been finding very helpful. This was, we both hoped, going to be a mutually beneficial meeting. We would alert the police to our suspicions about Jonty. In return, they might tell us what they had found at the crime scenes, not to mention on the two laptops they had taken away: Bryce's – and Grace's.

'We were in luck. After a little, entirely understandable, obstruction, DCI Julie was ready to cooperate. A cursory search of Bryce's laptop revealed that all the drafts of his attack on Jonty had been wiped. Someone had wanted the substance of this talk removed and they had done a thorough job. Sadly not quite thorough enough, because the police have some very skilful IT people working for them. Eventually the deleted speech was retrieved and, as Priya had suggested it would be, it was damning. Things weren't looking good for Jonty, were they? Yes, he'd been out late at the Wyveridge party on Saturday, but he'd also been one of those encouraging Priya to stick around, leaving Bryce to go back to his room alone. He and his wife Amber had then returned to the hotel some time before her. If he had somehow managed to put a sedative in something Bryce had eaten or drunk, say a glass of wine or one of the canapés he'd been handing round at the *Sentinel* party, all he had to do was let himself in to Room 29, hold a pillow over Bryce's face for five minutes, and that would be that. He could then search the room, remove any hard copy of the incriminating speech, wipe any drafts off the laptop and exit.'

'Ridiculous!' said Jonty loudly.

'He also, I felt sure, believed he could get away with it. There was a strong chance that the local medic and the police wouldn't pick up on the over-red eyes of someone whose lids had been carefully closed, who in any case wore contact lenses, and had helpfully indicated his discomfort by leaving a bottle of Optrex right by the bed. If the case did go to post-mortem and traces of sedative and high levels of carbon dioxide were found in the blood, then there was nothing whatever linking Jonty to Bryce. Once those files were deleted, he was out of the picture. Priya might have known the contents of the speech her boyfriend had been planning to make, but that would only ever be hearsay.

'Unfortunately for Jonty, though, circumstances intervened. Between leaving the party and getting back to the hotel Bryce had managed to get himself in a fight, and there was now a livid new bruise on his right cheek. When they saw the body, the young constables who were first on the scene were suspicious. More senior officers were called in, then Bryce's room was put in the tender care of scene-of-crime officers, with all their state-of-the-art forensic capabilities.

'At the same time, Grace was sniffing around, very publicly asking leading questions. Jonty was one of the first she spoke to on Sunday morning. So here was my thought: during the course of that interview, had Grace let on that Priya had told her what Bryce planned to reveal in his talk? Had she in fact gone so far as to challenge Jonty; to raise his double standards with him directly; even to suggest that he might have had something to do with Bryce's death?'

'There was only one problem with this theory. For Grace's death at least, Jonty had a watertight alibi. On the Sunday afternoon he'd been present at my event in the Big Tent, then highly visible in the Green Room afterwards. So if he had done it, how had he done it? Was it possible that he'd had an accomplice? His wife Amber perhaps, or maybe even Anna Copeland, who had ghostwritten his latest book *Wild Stuff* and was now a close associate and friend. She of course had with her her boyfriend Marv, an ex-Marine, who had spoken frankly in his talk about what it's like to kill a fellow human being, albeit in a war zone—'

'Now 'ang on a moment,' came Marvin's deep voice.

'Let me finish,' said Francis, holding up a hand.

'It's fine,' said Anna. 'This is so crazy I'd like to hear it.'

'Amen to that!' said Jonty.

'But unless it *was* his wife,' Francis continued, 'how on earth had Jonty persuaded such a person to help him? It was all very well getting Anna to write for you by proxy, but to murder by proxy? The incentive would have had to have been huge. Unless of course this accomplice had been part of the original murder, so now had to be involved in the cover-up.

'Now whoever Grace's killer was, he, she – or they – must have known her and been trusted by her. Because Grace would never have gone up to the battlements of Wyveridge with any old stranger, would she? And this person – or people – knew exactly what they were doing, taking Fleur's video camera with them, making it look as if Grace had been filming. At the same time the impact from the long drop was almost certainly going to wipe the memory card, and with it any incriminating footage from both Saturday night and Sunday morning.

'In our meeting this morning the police confirmed that the memory card had indeed been trashed. But not, they told us, in the fall. The card had been removed previously, stamped on until it no longer functioned, then replaced. Even as I was thinking about the implications of that, it occurred to me that Fleur might have outsmarted our murderer by backing up at least some of the footage on her computer. When I'd called out to Wyveridge on Sunday morning, I'd seen her camera right next to her laptop with images of the previous night's party on the screen. So after Priya and I had finished with the police we drove straight to Wyveridge.

'We were in luck. Despite our murderer's attempts to stop us, we were able to see all Fleur's film from Saturday night. This included Grace chatting and laughing with Anna, Marvin and Jonty, and Priya being persuaded by Jonty to stay at the party. If I could just understand how Jonty had got Anna and/or Marvin to do his dirty work for him, we would be in business. Did the fact that both Jonty and Marvin had once been in the Navy have anything to do with it? Or perhaps it simply came down to money. Jonty had plenty of that, while Anna and Marv had very little, and with Marv recently discharged, and Anna freelance, no regular income either. And if they were planning the baby Anna had wanted for so long—'

Family Man was on his feet again. 'I hate to cut you off in mid-flow,' he said, and now his tigerish smile was back on show, 'but there's only one problem with these highly entertaining speculations of yours. I didn't kill anyone. Yes, I may have tried to persuade Priya to stick around on Saturday night, but that was only because – I'm happy to admit it – she's a very attractive young woman and I was enjoying talking to her. And yes, I was, like half the rest of the White Hart's guests, interviewed on camera by Grace on Sunday morning. But she certainly never told me anything about what Bryce had planned to talk about that afternoon. The first inkling I had of that was when you and Priya spoke to me in the Green Room after my event on Monday, a full twenty-four hours after the poor girl met her death. My keen interest then, which I'm sure you remember, was not faked.

'How did I manage such a watertight alibi for Sunday after-noon? It was just what happened. I was here at the festival, attending interesting lectures. Yours included. And d'you want to know why you couldn't work out how I'd persuaded Anna or Marv to kill Grace? Because I didn't. Anna is an excellent writer and editor. She did, as you've guessed, pretty much write *Wild Stuff* for me. But her skills don't extend to murder. Just because Marv was in the Special Boat Service doesn't make him an assassin either. What a highly offensive suggestion!'

'I appreciate that you weren't Bryce's murderer, Jonty,' Francis said slowly. 'Or Grace's.' Out of the corner of his eye he clocked the faces of the police line-up. Both her sergeants were looking round at DCI Julie, who was saying nothing, her lips pursed as she stared at Francis with an expression that was half intense curiosity as to what he was about to say now, half fury at being betrayed. 'And my apologies also,' he went on, 'to Anna and Marvin. But my earlier misconceptions do have some relevance. Because if I hadn't been looking on Fleur's film for evidence of Jonty's likely accomplice, I wouldn't have come across some other footage which gave me a crucial lead in another aspect of this case: Bryce leaving the Wyveridge party and doing so in a taxi with . . . Dan Dickson.'

Heads turned towards the great iconoclast, inscrutable in his black leather chair.

'Now, suddenly,' Francis continued, 'I had a chance to get to the bottom of a witness report of Bryce and Dan fighting on the Mold bridge at ten p.m. on that fatal Saturday evening . . .'

'Didn't you believe me?' That Pathé News voice again.

'I did, Virginia. But as you said yourself, you were too far away from them to know what they'd been fighting about. But if they'd shared a taxi back from Wyveridge together, there would have been a witness – the driver, Terry Jenkins. When I called on him at his house, he told me the pair had indeed been quarrelling, though he couldn't recall what about. However, there was one snippet of overheard dialogue he repeated to me which confirmed a suspicion that I'd already had when I'd looked through the festival albums – one that involved Bryce's paternity of his beloved girls.'

Francis looked out around the room. The eyes of the assembled company were bright and attentive. Over in her wingback chair, Scarlett's mouth was a taut line, her gaze impassive.

'Things were happening fast,' Francis continued, as he looked directly at her. 'Even as I drove out to Scarlett's cottage, wondering if she would still be there, DCI Morgan called to fill me in on the results of Bryce's autopsy. Carbon dioxide levels in his blood indicated that he *had* been suffocated. Prior to that, sedated. With a powerful prescription drug called Zimovane.

'At the cottage, Scarlett was packing to leave. When I confronted her with my suspicions, that she and Dan had once had an affair, and that it was he, not Bryce, who was the father of the twins, she tried to deny it. When she realized that was pointless, she agreed things didn't look good for her. As I left, I pretended I needed to visit the loo before I drove back into Mold. Once upstairs, I had a quick look around Scarlett's en suite. And there, tucked away at the top of a cupboard above the sink, were two packets of . . . Zimovane.'

Now the ssshhers were open-mouthed; you could almost hear the intake of breath across the room, as heads slowly turned in the direction of Bryce's long-term partner.

'Perversely,' Francis went on, 'as soon as I gave it two minutes' thought, the presence of this sedative made me realize that it was less, not more likely that Scarlett was involved. For surely no competent murderer would sedate their victim with a drug that they then left lying around their bathroom. There was of course the possibility that these packets were old ones belonging to Bryce. But, when Scarlett confirmed to me what she'd already told the police, that Bryce never used sleeping pills, it occurred to me that someone might have been actively trying to frame her.

'As I drove at speed towards Mold my head was buzzing with all the possibilities. Back in the Green Room at the festival site I found Dan. Initially, he denied he'd been fighting with Bryce; but when I told him what I knew, he confessed all. And yes, he admitted, when he'd heard about Bryce's sudden death, he had been worried that he might have had something to do with it. At least until Grace died. Should I believe him? Was it possible that the fight was the start of something darker that had happened later that night?

'As I was walking back to the White Hart, my mobile rang

again. It was DCI Julie, confirming all the suspicions Priya and I had had about the deleted *Celebrity and Hypocrisy* files. They *had* been there on the laptop, she said, draft after draft, the last one auto-recovered at eleven thirty-two p.m. More interesting was what the police's IT people had found out about the timing of the deletions. They had been made at five fifteen a.m.'

Francis paused, enjoying the silence as this piece of information sank in. '*After* Priya had found the body, in the silent hour before the ambulance crew arrived. Suddenly everything that had been circling round at the back of my brain came together and I knew who had killed Bryce. It was, I suppose, just possible that Jonty or Anna or Marv had sneaked along to his room shortly after five, while you and I, Priya, were sitting huddled with shock in my bedroom. But why would they have waited till then? Because they'd forgotten to do the job earlier? Was that really likely when the removal of the incriminating evidence from the computer was central to the whole plan?

'How much more plausible was it that someone altogether closer to home had decided to delete those files, as part of her framing of the national treasure so damningly implicated by them? That same person had already demonstrated to me, and the police, that she was highly familiar with the contents of Bryce's laptop. If she knew how his documents were organized, why on earth shouldn't she have read everything he wrote? Long before. Giving her a chance to plan the perfect murder of the man she'd had in her sights for ten long years.'

As Francis's gaze settled on Priya, she looked straight back at him. The familiar humour had drained from her features. *If you think you can betray me now,* her taut face said, *this had better be good.*

THIRTY-SIX

'You pulled the wool over my eyes,' Francis continued, 'right from that first moment when you excused yourself from my room saying you wanted to say goodbye to Bryce. You were gone for much longer than you needed to be, but you were clever, even about that. You changed into different clothes, giving me a visible reason why you'd taken your time.

'On the evening before, Bryce was tired and returned to the hotel early. I'm afraid, Priya, the contrast between the Bryce I spoke to at the *Sentinel* party and the weary-looking man captured on Fleur's footage was all too marked. Once I saw that, I knew for sure that someone had drugged him. It was just that at first I hadn't realized it was you. Even though Jonty was handing out canapés at the *Sentinel* party, it was you who were beside Bryce all evening, you who had access to the Zimovane you had pinched from the cottage when you'd stayed there earlier in the week, then left in Bryce's washbag, to make it look to the police as if it were a sleeping pill he regularly used. It would have been the easiest thing in the world to fetch him a drink and slip one into it. Maybe it was in that glass of champagne you brought him right in front of me, while he was standing flirting with Grace at the *Sentinel* party. A present from

Laetitia, you said. But was there an extra little present from you in there too?

'Later, out at Wyveridge Hall, you chose not to go back to the hotel with him. You wanted to stay and enjoy the party, you said. Fair enough. In any case, Jonty was encouraging you to hang around, an exchange you were quite happy for Fleur to film. What could be better than an alibi by invitation, recorded on video, with the nice side-effect of implicating your preferred main suspect. Was that just fortuitous – or had you worked hard to get the result you wanted?

'As the evening wore on, there were plenty of cars going back into Mold, but you deliberately missed them all. And yes, it's not easy to get one of Mold's two taxi firms to come out at eleven, when they're busy doing runs from pubs. But by midnight in this little town, even during the festival, things have quietened down. Had you bothered to phone Ace Taxis, whose number you'd been given by Ranjit, you could have gone home then. Couldn't she, Terry?'

'She could,' came the gruff voice of the bouffant-haired jazz musician.

'Instead you waited. Until you could be sure that Bryce would have stopped working on his talk and had his second dose of Zimovane, which you had left waiting for him in a receptacle you knew he would find impossible to resist – a pillow chocolate. Unless something had gone very wrong with your plan, by the time you got back to your room Bryce would be out cold, all set for a firm application of the pillow before you let rip with your hotel-waking scream. You could, perhaps, have done without Conal's unscheduled attack on you. But despite appearances, that hardly threw you. And there was a bonus, as your ex put himself in line with the other suspects you had so carefully set up.

'Otherwise all went fine with your evening. You had, maybe, a slight panic when you realized that taxis in Mold stopped at one a.m. But you managed to keep your cool and a lift into town did eventually materialize. It was only when you got back to the hotel that things started to go wrong. Bryce had returned with the main set of keys and you couldn't make the spare outside door key, which you'd cleverly taken along with you, work. Why should it? It was the wrong one, given to you by Irina, the scatty Polish girl, who was as inept with keys as she was with everything else.

'So now you had to ring the doorbell. And, once Cathy had admitted you, pretty much sprint upstairs, let yourself into your room, check that Bryce was sufficiently sedated, suffocate him, then run outside and scream. Your original plan had also given you ample time to delete the files of Bryce's speech from the computer. Now, in a mad rush of blood to the head, you realized this was something you were going to have to sneak back and do later. Unless of course you aborted the whole thing. But no, you had worked so long and so carefully to set up your scenario that you couldn't back out now.

'Because of course Prime Suspect Jonty was only Plan B, the guy with the cast-iron motive if Plan A, Tragic and Unexpected Natural Death, failed. You had prepared the ground brilliantly for this, addressing that distinctive symptom of suffocation, bloodshot eyes, before Bryce had even died. Early on Saturday afternoon you took him off for a walk – or was it more? – in a cornfield and made sure he got dirt in his eyes, which gave him grief with his contact lenses. By the time he turned up at the *Sentinel* party people were noticing how red-eyed he looked, which fitted in neatly with the tiredness that swept over him once he'd had his first dose of Zimovane. As for the love bite you planted on his neck; what better evidence was there that you were seriously keen on him?

'The pillow chocolates that he found on your bed when he got in were ones left over from Friday. You had sliced them open and filled them with ground sedative. Did it matter that the earlier batch had pink sugar roses, while on Saturday the chef had moved on to purple? No. Bryce had never even seen the first lot. So all you had to do was get back to the room on the Saturday evening and make your switch.

'As it happened, I ran into your victim at the very moment you must have been doing this. Bryce was pacing up and down the lobby of the White Hart looking impatiently at his watch. What had you told him? That you needed to refresh your make-up, that you'd forgotten something in the room? It didn't matter, because he didn't suspect anything bad of his beloved Priya, did he? All went fine and the bait was laid. Your mistake came later, when in your hurry to get out into the corridor and scream, you failed to notice the choccie that Bryce had touchingly left out for you – on the side table. When I asked you about it subsequently, you claimed to have eaten it when you went up to the room to get your suitcase. You didn't, did you? It would have knocked you out. But I'd already seen it, with its pink rose, and wondered why it didn't match the others put out on Saturday night.

'Back to the action: as soon as you'd got round the corner from the front door, out of sight of Cathy, you sprinted up the stairs at speed. You let yourself into your room. Found Bryce was, as you'd hoped, out cold. What you hadn't anticipated was that he'd be out cold with a bruise on his cheek. What had happened? The temptation to abandon your plan was even stronger.

'But you'd waited so long, hadn't you? Even as you panicked, you decided you had to go through with it. So you held down the pillow, having first wrapped it in a towel so there would be no bite or saliva marks. Two minutes later Bryce was dead. You rinsed the towel through, wrung it out, and left it on the rail in the bathroom. Then you plumped the pillows, took the annotated hard copy of his speech from the bedside and slipped it into your bag, for disposal later. Why didn't you also take the pen he'd been using to correct it? Because it had a date and an inscription on it that might implicate yet another suspect – Virginia Westcott. If that turned out to be a misjudgement, the rest of your plan was brilliantly thought out. It was you who planted that half-empty bottle of Optrex by the bed, bang next to Bryce's contact lens case. If the police did follow up on this clue, they would discover that Bryce had already had red eyes the night before. It was hardly likely they would ever find out that he normally left his contact lenses in the bathroom at night.

'Then you ran outside and started screaming. A little later, after I'd been up to have a look at him, you went back to "say goodbye". It was then – at five fifteen a.m. – that you deleted the *Celebrity and Hypocrisy* files and shut down the laptop. You weren't to know that in due course a police IT expert would recover them and discover this damning timing.

'Nor was it your fault that when he turned up, the local medic cracked a feeble joke that made the rookie police suspicious, made them think they'd better cover their backsides and call in more senior officers. No worries, you had your back-up plan. With Bryce's talk erased, all you had to do was plant the idea of Jonty's guilt in a suitably gullible mind. Could you believe your luck when I presented myself? The crime writer who thought he was a detective. You accepted my offer of the bed in my room, then subtly slipped into the position of being the sounding board for my ideas, biding your time with my suspects before ingeniously planting your own.

'By that stage, Grace was dead. That had never been part of the plan and killing her was a terrible thing to have to do. But needs must. At first, you tried to use her. When she came and interviewed you in my room on Sunday morning, you did as you did with me, told her and her camera about Jonty's double life, giving her a magnificent scoop and simultaneously implicating him in the murder. But she was cleverer than I was, had somehow, at least in part, cottoned on to what you were up to. Did she confront you – or did you just realize from her line of questioning that she suspected you? Was that why you had to trash the video memory card – even if it did also contain your Saturday night alibi?

'Grace had arranged to speak to the police about her misgivings about you that Sunday evening at six p.m. Was her tragic mistake to wait until she'd emailed her scoop about Jonty to her newspaper before she did that? Whatever, the delay gave you your chance. You couldn't obviously repeat what you'd done to Bryce, but you quickly came up with another idea.

'Grace's murder wasn't something you had a lot of time to plan. She'd told you she was going back to Wyveridge to write and file her story. It occurred to you that if you could get her up onto the battlements, you could push her off and make it look like an accident. If you took the camera with you, it might seem as if she'd slipped while filming. The upside of this method was that once she was over, you had no worries about the body, either getting rid of it or what might be found in the post-mortem.

'So early on Sunday afternoon you drove her out there, in the car you had now inherited from Bryce. As well as offering her a lift, you had agreed to provide her with the compromising detail of the Jonty story. The ace up your sleeve was that you'd kept a digital copy of Bryce's speech on a memory stick. Even if she had her suspicions about you, she needed that.

'Once you got out to Wyveridge, you found the place wasn't as empty as you'd hoped. There was noise from the kitchen, so you sent Grace down to find out who was there. She was so desperate to get her story off to her newspaper, she was happy to go along with your insistence that your presence in the house remained a secret. What did you tell her? That you couldn't face them all so soon after Bryce's death? That you didn't want Eva back on your case? I'm sure you were convincing. And when she told you that it was indeed Rory, Eva and Neville loitering around having tea, you had a brainwave. You knew from your earlier conversation with Birgit that Rory had LSD in his possession. If you could somehow get hold of this, without him realising, that would provide a convincing reason why Grace might have fallen – or jumped – from the battlements. Leaving her with Bryce's speech, you sneaked up to Rory's room and found his wallet in his trademark velvet jacket on the back of his chair. The tabs were there, just as Birgit had described them – white postage stamps with a strawberry motif.

'So how were you going to persuade Grace to take one? You weren't. Once Rory and his pals had finally left for the festival, a cup of tea and a slice of the cake she had brought to Wyveridge herself was a thoughtful thing to bring her as she worked on her piece. You had one too. She wasn't to know that hers had been doctored.

'Somehow you then got her up on the battlements. Did you wait until the drug kicked in before you did that, or did you do it while she was still unaware of what she'd taken? That I don't know the answer to, nor exactly how you persuaded her to go. What I do know is that chucking over the video camera after her was inspired. Not only did that suggest that Grace might have been filming, and cover up your destruction of the memory card, but you also made it look as if your chosen prime suspect had been repeating his tricks. What had been on there that Jonty didn't want anyone to see, the police would wonder. As it happened, very little, but that didn't matter, because by that stage the blond hairs and the threads of purple shirt you'd taken from him later that Sunday morning and brought with you to plant on the lead roofing would have worked their magic. When you told me that the consolatory hug Jonty had given you had been "long enough", I hadn't quite realized the full import of your words.

'But now,' Francis continued, 'when Grace was lying dead on the gravel, and you were free to go, you did what many a murderer is guilty of. As you checked desperately through your actions, worrying if you'd missed anything that might incriminate you, you had a bright idea. Why not give her a dose of that shroom tea that was conveniently still sitting on the kitchen table? A combination of that and acid was surely going to convince the pathologists that poor Grace had been in a crazy enough state to jump from the roof. In the heat of the moment, that struck you as a brilliant addition, even if that was one of the things that made me so suspicious: two hallucinogens taken by a woman who didn't like drugs. The splash on her cotton dress was another mistake you couldn't have bargained for. You must have been panicking, your hands shaking, shocked and appalled by what you'd done.

'You returned in Bryce's car to Mold, your alibi still, just, intact. Because of course your cover story was that you'd been "at" my talk. How was I expected to spot you in that big tent, especially if you weren't there? Earlier, in my room, you had read my note cards. Later, you discussed my talk and the questions afterwards with Rory and the others in the pub. It was just a shame that this evening, when I made a reference to one of these, about me being a coconut, you didn't pick up on it.

'I wonder how you felt as both I and the police fell for this story of yours, hook, line and sinker? I even followed your lead in looking at Jonty's book and spotting his chapter on Wild Highs. Comically, I thought the idea that Grace might have been tripping on shrooms was mine. You led me by the nose on that, just as you did on everything else. As a result, I'd pretty much decided Jonty was our man, even though I was convinced he must have had an accomplice for the second murder. However. Trying to keep, like my detective George Braithwaite, an open mind, I continued to follow up all my other leads and suspicions at the same time. For a while, I must admit, I also had doubts about Scarlett, and when I found her packing for London this afternoon, I began to wonder whether you'd led me to bark up the wrong tree.

'Then came the call from Detective Chief Inspector Julie, about the timing of the deletions, and suddenly everything made sense. So many niggling little loose ends that I'd been trying to fit to unlikely suppositions hung together. One of the reasons

I'd been so set earlier on the idea of Jonty as murderer was that I could never understand why this crime had been committed here at a festival in the full glare of publicity. I'd been stuck on the assumption that it had to be done in a hurry. But there was a better explanation. In London, wherever really except for here, you, Priya, would have been prime suspect. But by doing it at Mold, where Bryce was surrounded by upset exes, as well as enemies old and new, you were putting yourself well down the list. If the case against Jonty failed, there was Scarlett and her Zimovane; then Conal, Dan and maybe even Virginia. And that mattered, didn't it? It was clear to me that even though you'd decided you had to kill him, you really didn't want to be caught.

'I needed to back up this sudden blinding conviction that it was you who'd done it, so I raced back to the hotel and let myself into your room. At that point I didn't know what I was going to find, but I thought there might be something. When my initial search was a failure, for a moment I wondered if my intuition was at fault. Then on a second search I found a memory stick. When I plugged it into my laptop and opened it up, there they were: *Celebrity and Hypocrisy* and the accompanying PowerPoint presentation. The talks you had repeatedly told me you'd never even seen, let alone kept. And why had you kept them? Because you yourself had deleted them from Bryce's computer.

'Everything fitted. Even a call from Julie telling me that the hard copy of Bryce's speech had been found in Jonty's briefcase didn't put me off. You'd already shown your propensity for planting evidence. My only problem was the one which had been there from the start – motive. Why on earth would you, Priya Kaur, with your whole life ahead of you, want to murder anyone, let alone this man who offered you so much? Bryce had taken you on and made you his protégée on the newspaper, you pretty much ran the section now. As for his personal life, you had successfully ousted both his long-term partner and his girlfriend. He lived in a nice place and had plenty of money. You had enthused to me about his charisma, how he was not just talented and knowledgeable, but kind and thoughtful too . . .

'If there was no clue in your relationship, I had to look elsewhere. Now it had occurred to me early on that you hadn't talked much about your family. Why should you? I'd only known you a couple of days. But even Conal, who had been involved with you for several months, didn't seem to know that much about them either. Then yesterday afternoon, while we were out at Wyveridge, looking at the outline of poor Grace's body on the gravel, you broke down and told me the tragic story of how your pregnant sister Chinni had died in a house fire. Later, in the small hours, you opened up further . . .'

The room was rapt as Francis repeated what Priya had told him about the car crash that had killed her father and brother. 'As I lay there in the darkness,' he went on, 'my first thought was that you might be some sort of fantasist, telling tall tales to draw attention and sympathy to yourself. Lord knows, I've met such types before . . .'

'Haven't we all,' chipped in Virginia.

'Only later,' Francis continued, 'did it dawn on me that the problem with your story wasn't that it was or wasn't true, but that there had been a reason for this chapter of apparent accidents . . .'

He paused and looked around the room.

'While I'd been rummaging around your suitcase looking for

that hard copy of Bryce's speech I'd noticed that just inside, on the soft underside of the leather, was written the name P.K. JASWAL. OK, so when you'd moved down to London you had dropped the family surname and adopted your second name, the generic Sikh female Kaur – it means "princess", I believe.'

Francis only glanced at Priya with this question. She wasn't looking at him, her sloe-dark eyes directed straight ahead of her. He wasn't expecting an answer and he didn't get one.

'Fair enough. Kaur is snappier, easier to remember. Why wouldn't you want that as a byline for your new life as a journalist? But was there another reason why you wanted to leave Jaswal behind? Did the tragic story you told me last night conceal an altogether darker one? Of, to start with, a pregnant young woman who died in a fire, not accidentally, but deliberately, precisely *because* she was pregnant.

'Chinni had been lined up, as is still traditional with many families in the world you come from, for a *Rishta*, an arranged marriage, with a young man from a similar caste to you. A *jat*, you explained, the landowning farmer caste. He was from the same area of the Punjab as your father, the son of an old friend. Chinni was only going to meet him just before her wedding day, out in India, so it was hardly likely she'd have become pregnant by him. No, the problem, surely, was that she was pregnant by someone else: a man, who knew, from a lower caste than *jat* – or worse, some local English guy. Chinni, you told me, had always stood up to your parents, was not going to be put off by what she saw as their old-fashioned ideas.

'But it was more than just ideas, wasn't it, it was honour. *Izzat*, in Punjabi. The strict code that I learned about when I was researching my last but one novel, *A Matter of Honour*. *Izzat* meant that your family name would have been so dragged down in public shame within your community that disowning his pregnant daughter was something your father would have felt obliged to do. And if she continued to make trouble, to insist she was going to have this shameful baby, a worse fate for her would have to be considered. Your hard man brother Bilal, with all his pride in his caste and his ideas about honour, would have gone along with that. And helped in the execution, too . . .

'As lightning forked outside,' Francis went on, 'as bright as the awful – and, now I realized, intentional – fire that had killed your sister, I had a further flash of inspiration. When Scarlett and I had been talking on Sunday afternoon, she told me *en passant* that Bryce had once been involved with another young Asian woman – one of his students when he was teaching at Birkbeck. He had ended the relationship, she said, almost jokingly, when her brothers had found out . . .

'Was it possible that this previous girlfriend had been your sister? Was this the link that made sense of everything? I was just about to phone Scarlett when in you walked, bright-eyed and excited with your progress with Jonty. Now it was my turn to dissemble, as I played along with you and held off on my call. As soon as you'd gone I dialled Scarlett's number. Could she, I asked, by any chance remember the name of the young Asian woman whom Bryce had dated over ten years ago? Of course she could! She knew Bryce's lovers like the kings and queens of England. His first Asian dalliance had been called Chinni Jaswal.

'The man who had got her pregnant wasn't, as I'd casually assumed, some feckless youth from Derby, but her lecturer from her journalism course in London. Had he stood by her, even offered to marry her and given her baby a respectable home, there would have been serious ructions with your family, but in the end his high status and wealth might have been enough to save your father's honour as Chinni abandoned her *Rishta*.

'But, as we know, this lecturer already had a long-term partner and, at the time, two baby daughters. From his point of view, the whole thing was a mess: if he did the right thing by Chinni he stood to lose both his job and his family. It was a no-brainer. He backed out. I'm sure he did so gracefully enough. Perhaps he even offered money for the abortion, as he'd done at least once before . . .'

Francis paused. This wasn't the time to bring up Virginia's personal tragedy of long ago, even if she would have let him. Instead he turned back to the woman he had got so close to in the last three days.

'When you and I, Priya,' he continued, 'sat in my hotel room early on Sunday morning, waiting for the ambulance and the police, we talked briefly about death. You told me you had only seen one dead body in your life. Your grandfather. And perhaps that was true, because the car crash that killed your father and brother didn't leave much in the shape of remains, did it? But were they just unlucky to hit that bank of fog and smoke on the M42 on that November night, exactly a year after Chinni had died, or had someone helped their deaths along? Did the prospect of marrying the same Punjabi farmer meant for Chinni, combined with revenge for your poor beloved sister, make you consider doing what would have been very easy for a girl trained in mechanics by her father, fixing the brakes of the family car

– a couple of pinholes in the front and rear cables, was it, so they would give out some way along the journey? Perhaps you hadn't even been sure you wanted them to die, but you wanted to punish them, that's for sure.'

All eyes were now on Priya. Her gaze was back on Francis, defiant; her mouth set.

'Only once Chinni's death had been avenged within your family,' Francis went on, 'did it somehow become more important that you reach the last man in the case, that treacherous lecturer who had let your sister down, fatally as it turned out. Even if he hadn't realized the seriousness of what he'd done, he was still guilty, wasn't he?

'It was easy enough to find out who Bryce was. But getting to him was going to be a different matter, because he came not just from a different city, but a different world. It was a world you started to get closer to, as you followed your sister up the education ladder to a course in journalism, in London, too.

'By the time you had got to that stage, Bryce had moved on from teaching. He was now a big name on the *Sentinel*. Anything bad that happened to him was hardly going to go unnoticed. In any case, what were you going to do? Visit him at his flat? Arrange an accident for him at work? Even if you did think of something, how on earth were you going to get away with it? So perhaps for some time your revenge on Bryce remained a fantasy; an obsessive one, but not one you were ever really going to do anything about.

'But then, at one of the parties you had now started getting invited to, out of college, an up-and-coming journo in your own right, you met someone who knew Bryce – one Conal O'Hare. Was the relationship you started with him cynical? Were you just using him to get close to your victim? Or perhaps things were more complex and your feelings for this talented Irishman were genuine? They only cooled when you started to doubt his commitment, when you decided he was more of a passionate fly-by-night than a reliable partner . . .'

Francis glanced over at Conal and Fleur, hands clasped together on their chintz couch. He needed to say nothing more.

'Now I totally understand,' he continued, 'how you could have got involved with a successful travel writer a few years older than you, who had nothing to do with your sister's case, who bore no blame. But when it came to Bryce, why, *how* did you go so far as to go out with him, and for some weeks? The only answer I can come up with is this: because you wanted to get away with your crime. Your revenge was personal, but you didn't want it to ruin your life. As you told me the other night, your sister's death had made you more ambitious, not less. And if you were in a relationship with Bryce, it would seem completely unlikely that you would do away with this man who had employed you, opened doors for you, set you up. This was one of the main reasons why I kept putting the suspicions I had about you to one side. Because the motive just wasn't there.

'But tell me, was there a moment when you too came under his legendary spell? Were you able to understand why your sister had fallen for this brilliant, intemperate, quixotic man; and why she had wanted to have his child? Were you even tempted to abandon your obsession, sober up and just seize the life she could have had? Or didn't you care? Had your mission for what you saw as justice taken you so far outside the norms of human behaviour that sleeping with your victim, softening him up over a few weeks for your final *coup de grâce*, was just what you had to do to achieve your ends?'

The only sound in the room was the muted laughter and chatter from the now reopened bar, and over it Whitney Houston's 'I Will Always Love You' ringing out inappropriately from the juke box.

'Whatever the answers to these questions, Saturday night was the end of a long-planned act of vengeance, wasn't it, Priya Kaur Jaswal? Bryce Peabody, that serial breaker of promises to loved ones, finally got his comeuppance.' Francis looked around the group and allowed himself a little smile. 'Though some might say he got what he'd always said he wanted: to feel the impact of something real from outside the parochial world he had existed in for so long.'

There was a nervous ripple of laughter from the assembled group. The young woman in the turquoise cheongsam didn't join in. She stared straight in front of her, out of the window to the deep green shadows of the garden beyond. The sun had set, and the apple trees were turning to silhouettes in the gloaming. Priya's head turned, and her lovely dark eyes scanned the room, taking in Bryce's scorned exes, and at the back another, more powerful woman, DCI Julie, looking sternly ahead of her, her male subordinates grim-faced on either side. For several long seconds Priya seemed undecided, staring forlornly at Francis as if, even after this awful denunciation and betrayal, he might announce another twist in the tale and rescue her. Then she tilted up that chin.

'I've no idea,' she said, levelly, 'what on earth you're talking about.'

She got to her feet, pushed hurriedly past a stunned-looking Jonty Smallbone, and without looking round, made straight for the door.

AFTERWORD

Wednesday 23rd July

The whole festival was buzzing with talk of what had happened the previous evening. After a showdown in the White Hart, the police had (apparently) arrested none other than Bryce's 'Asian babe' girlfriend for the murder. What a bizarre turn-up for the books! Nobody could believe it, or (to be honest) quite follow the motive. Something to do with 'honour killing', which was still, wasn't it, a very real issue in parts of the Asian community, however hard it was for outsiders to believe in or understand; that family members might murder each other to prevent some bizarre, outdated idea of 'shame'. Was it possible that such things still took place in twenty-first century England? Apparently, it was.

But life itself must go on – particularly literary life. This sunny late July morning was an important one for Mold. Laetitia Humble, after much lobbying in London, had scored a coup. This year, for the first time, it was from Mold-on-Wold that the Booker Prize longlist was to be announced, at 11 a.m. in the packed Big Tent.

Towards the back, a fifty-something female with an odd,

badger-like streak of white in her otherwise glossy dark hair was fidgeting in her seat. Last night had been riveting, unexpected, *novelistic* almost (could this be her next subject?), but this morning Virginia could hardly contain herself, as Laetitia stood behind the microphone to read out the names of the lucky contenders. They proceeded in scrupulous alphabetical order, each accompanied on the big screen by an author photograph.

No, she told herself, as the roll call of the acceptably brilliant was read out. No, I do not stand a snowball's chance in hell. Nice of Erica to put me up for it, but no, I must accept my fate.

'John Banville,' read Laetitia, 'Julian Barnes . . . A.S. Byatt . . . Peter Carey . . . J.M. Coetzee . . . Dan Dickson . . . Hilary Mantel . . . David Mitchell . . . Rose Tremain . . .'

How absurd it was to even hope that *Sickle Moon Rises* might be amongst this glittering crowd. Why had she bothered to turn up? Her books were not the kind to win prizes. They were, let's face it, better than that. More lasting, deeper than the transient fluff of the zeitgeist. As she so often remarked at dinner parties, Shakespeare had never won a prize. Trollope neither. Virginia's eye was fixed on a harsher, fairer judge than that haphazard team of modish quasi-intellectuals who made up the Booker panel.

Posterity.

With Sarah Waters they had reached eleven – out of twelve. Virginia's heart was, as she might have put it in one of her novels, in her mouth. They were at the end of the alphabet, a place she had never enjoyed being, from school days onwards. Catch her another time and she'd have told you at length how authors whose surnames began with A, B, C were bound to do better than those unfortunate to be cursed with V, W, Y or Z, always at the wrong end of the bookshops' shelves.

Laetitia's lips parted.

'Virginia . . .' she began, and at that moment, the badger woman saw her literary life flash before her. Right from the very start and the two unpublished novels she had written in her early twenties in Cambridge and London, before her Parisian-set debut, *Entente Cordiale*, had put her firmly on the map. The six titles since, each one a long-drawn-out labour of love. And now . . .

'Westcott,' she heard, as if in a dream. And then: '*Sickle Moon Rises*.'

'Oh my giddy . . . *God*!' squealed Virginia, despite her best intentions. It was true, it was true, it was true. The sniff of a prize. After all these years. And not just any old prize. The Booker, no less. Oh, oh, OH . . . and OH again. And what a dreadful shame that her ancient rival in the world of letters, Bryce Peabody, that evasive bastard, father of her murdered child, whose death in truth she wished she'd had the courage to have a hand in herself, was not around to see *this*.

Five yards behind her, Francis Meadowes heard her little scream and smiled. He had grown almost fond of her over the past three days and was happy that she should at last be allowed her little moment of triumph. He doubted she would make the shortlist.

He was heading back to London soon, eager to leave the bizarre events of the last four days behind him. He doubted that he would ever forget the look that Priya had given him as she leapt to her feet and left the games room at speed. Not that she had got far. DS Povey and DS Wright had been right behind her, and Francis had heard that almost ritual mantra of arrest as if in a dream. 'You do not have to say anything. However, it may harm your defence if you do not mention when questioned something that you later rely on . . .'

He felt sick at heart for her. She who had overreached herself so insanely, acting on who knows what twisted sense of honour or revenge. For a moment there, down by the river, he had felt his heart reopen, he had seen a future. And then, so quickly afterwards, he had realized the truth. And what alternative had there been for him then?

Now he would go on his way up the long and beautiful valley, onto the A roads and the motorway and the M25 and the crowded North Circular and back to his flat and his life in London. He could console himself with this: that real life did occasionally throw up the kinds of scenarios he had started to doubt were credible. Maybe George Braithwaite wasn't such a busted flush after all.

ACKNOWLEDGEMENTS

I am grateful to the organizers of the Shetland Literary Festival for inviting me to speak, as it was there, at a jolly dinner with Scottish crime writers, that it first occurred to me that I might attempt a whodunnit. Various kind friends read the manuscript in its different stages, made useful suggestions and offered encouragement: Heather Brooke, Oliver Butcher, Sue Cooke, Stephanie Cross, Victoria Hodder, Jeff Hudson, Linda Hughes, Susan Jenkins, Philip Kerr, Miles Mantle, Stephen McCrum, Duncan Minshull, Jackie Nelson, Peta Nightingale, Debra Potel, Joanna Swinnerton, Katrin Williams, Antony and Verity Woodward. Roger Stephenson gave me good tips on the life of a country doctor and DCI John Carr advised me on police procedures and made helpful suggestions. Guy Martin put me right on libel law. My agent Mark Lucas offered useful advice on structure and Steve Gove did a fine job of copyediting. Tina Seskis inspired me to go the independent route and went out of her way to help me with the publishing process. Katie Roden of Fixabook gave me an excellent steer on cover design, while Laura Bamber came up with the goods. Finally of course thanks to my wife Jo, who comes back after a long day's work with tricky authors only to find one waiting for her at home.

AUTHOR'S NOTE

Word of mouth is crucial for all authors: traditional, hybrid and indie. If you enjoyed this book, please consider leaving a review at Amazon, even if it's only a line or two.

You can find out more about me and my work at my website – markmccrum.com – where you can also read my blog and contact me. Alternatively you can follow me on Twitter (@McCrumMark) or Facebook: facebook.com/Author-MarkMcCrum.

Enjoy The Festival Murders? Read on for the opening chapter of the second gripping Francis Meadowes mystery, *Cruising to Murder . . .*

What had just happened? She was gasping for air, choking out saltwater, pain in her chest – oh God, such pain. A big wave slapped her from the side and now she was swallowing more. No, she wasn't going under. *Wasn't*. She struck out with her arms, strong swimmer that she was, but she could hardly move them for the stabbing agony. She had broken something hitting the water. Cracked a rib, must have done.

She remembered the sea racing up towards her: black, glittering with moonlight. She remembered screaming, at the top of her voice, all the way down.

Then nothing. She spluttered as she gulped the warm air. She tried to yell again, but she could hardly hear herself against the noisy waves. It didn't matter anyway. The ship was far away now. A little silhouette coming in and out of view, a few tiny lights showing.

How had she got here? Drunk, yes, she had been that, all evening she'd been drinking. Cocktails, wine, brandy, champagne, on and on till she tipped over, as always, into stupid oblivion. But she hadn't *fallen*, she was sure of that. She had been holding the rails, looking out at the silver path beneath the moon, when she had felt that sudden push from behind. Hoist, more like.

Firm hands on her waist, flip, that thump of her head on the ship's side, and then suddenly nothing . . . but the long, terrifying plunge.

So who, who had done that to her? And why? Because she'd had her suspicions about Eve? And Rising Star? That had to be it. She should never have asked those questions. She should have said more to Don . . .

Useless speculations raced through her brain as she fought to stay on the surface, hyperventilating as she floundered in the huge swell. They would see her. *No*. They would turn back and rescue her. *No*. A lifebuoy would be dropped. *No*.

The choking had stopped. She was going down, a beautiful woman in a gold cocktail dress, falling into the depths like a scuba diver without a BCD.

Under the water, no longer trying to breathe, she opened her eyes. The moonlight was still strong, shining through the turquoise sea from the shimmering surface above her. She was flooded with memories. Her mother, Luisa, gone when she was a little girl, just a mass of dark hair and a white dress in a green garden. Father Jorge, playing his guitar to her, ever nimble fingers, that silly little song, 'Chumba chumba cha-cha', how that had defined her life, taken it over really. And then when he was gone, so suddenly . . . boys . . . men . . . beautiful Diego, all those nights of sobbing. *Papita* in his white suit, making her laugh again.

Even under water she was crying for her lost life, salt tears into the salt sea.

So this is how I die.

ONE

'Oh, yes, that rotting shark, dis-*gus*-ting!' the large Englishwoman was all but shouting. Despite the rattling of the minibus, Francis couldn't help listening as she swapped stories with the two tanned American guys sitting opposite her. They were discussing unpleasant local delicacies from around the world. The shark was what they insisted on giving you in Iceland; washed down with this 'local firewater' that 'kind of took the taste away but then again didn't'.

Cue laughter. But had she ever been to Malaysia and tried Durian fruit, asked the younger American. 'Oh my *gad*, the smell of it! It's like a *gym sock.*'

'What did that guy in Taiping say, Damian?' the other replied. 'That after you'd eaten it your breath smelt like you'd been French kissing your dead grandmother.'

The Americans were chortling, but the Englishwoman wasn't to be outdone.

'You remember those widgetty grubs we were offered at Uluru, Gerald?' she said, turning to her companion, a skinny fellow with a trim grey goatee. 'So gross, weren't they?'

'We didn't eat them, Shirley,' he pointed out.

'We just *couldn't*,' she admitted. She had three, if not four chins, wobbling below a face like a pink blancmange. Trying not to stare at her, Francis found himself wondering what she might have looked like when she and Gerald were young. She had a dainty nose buried in there somewhere, and intense, rather beautiful pale blue eyes.

'*Ooh-loo-roo*,' asked Damian, 'where's that?'

'In Australia. Haven't you been? It's the most sacred Aboriginal site in the world.'

'You mean, like, Ayer's *Ruck*?'

'The Aborigines call it Uluru,' Shirley replied, a tad self-righteously, but she clearly wasn't going to spoil her fun new friendship over a matter of parochial PC. As the Americans fought back with turkey testicles in Hong Kong and deep-fried guinea pig in Argentina, Francis tuned out. Through the tinted windows, under the cloudless cobalt sky, was the here and now of Africa; to each side of the potholed coast road, stalls on the orange earth, selling everything from bananas to motorcycle tyres. *Happy Corner Shop Bar. In God We Trust Butcher.* There was one ramshackle outlet that had fifty identical Pepsi bottles for sale. Women, swathed in colourful robes, walked languorously through the late-morning heat, carrying their goods and shopping on their heads; on individual braided topknots was balanced everything from a huge white enamel bowl full of pineapples to a teetering pile of black bin bags.

Over the other side of the coach, the competitive travel-boasting had advanced from delicacies to destinations. The worn tarmac coast road had degenerated to a rutted dirt track, so

Francis strained to hear over the bumping and clattering. The Americans were now enthusing about Burma: '. . . temples laid out on the plain . . . totally awesome . . . you can take a balloon at dawn.' Shirley fought back with Georgia: 'Not the American one, the Caucasus . . . stunning frescoes . . . you just walk in.' But Brad and Damian had been in Antarctica which had been amazing: '. . . like, armies of penguins . . . you have no idea how huge the icebergs . . .'

But – oh no – Shirley had been to Chernobyl. 'They only let you in for two hours. And you have to wash all your clothes afterwards. But it's extraordinary. Incredibly spooky. Wasn't it, Gerald?'

Brad and Damian couldn't top Chernobyl, but they didn't have to, because suddenly the minibus had turned on to smooth cement and they were into Tema docks, driving past tall stacks of oblong containers in red, rust-brown, pale blue, grey – MAERSK, MOL, CGM stencilled on their corrugated sides. Assorted vessels were moored up along the quay. Gulls swooped and squawked among tall masts. The fresh, salty tang of the ocean was mixed with the industrial whiff of engine oil. At one end, dominating the rest, was the gleaming bulk of a cruise liner.

'That's our ship!' Shirley cried, stating the obvious excitedly.

The minibus came to a halt in its shadow. Francis had been told that the *Golden Adventurer* was not large. Indeed, one of its merits, the PR people back in London had stressed, was that it was comparatively nimble, could go to places that more sizeable cruise ships could not. But to Francis, as he stepped out and stood looking up at it, it seemed substantial enough, with its five long rows of windows above the waterline. Portholes in the black hull, then above the encircling red line, where every surface was a gleaming white, small, round-cornered square windows, then much bigger ones, with sliding doors and slim, flush balconies, then another layer with a surrounding walkway. Above that, tall white railings circled the open-top deck, which bristled with masts and funnels and satellite dishes.

As the new arrivals got out and gathered in a loose gaggle on the quay, a silver Mercedes drew up beside them. The front door swung open and a uniformed chauffeur sprang out, ran round and opened the left rear door, from which disgorged an elderly woman in a large and floppy straw hat, a dark-blue, silk knee-length dress, navy tights and tan leather espadrille wedges. The old fellow that followed her, helped out by the chauffeur, was correspondingly dapper: blue blazer over checked grey trousers, shiny brown brogues, Panama hat. He smiled round at the waiting group and then followed his urgently beckoning partner over to the narrow gangway that led steeply up to the walkway three decks above.

At the foot of this stood a Filipino crew member in a crisp white shirt and pressed dark trousers.

'This way, please, ladies and gentlemen,' he said, grinning as he gestured upwards.

As the others stepped on to it, one by one, the gangway wobbled visibly. Big Shirley looked terrified, holding tight to the rails as she manoeuvred herself carefully to the top, where there were more smiling staff to take her hands and pull her on board. A fresh-faced blonde with her hair up stood with a circular silver tray holding flutes of champagne. Another stockier greeter, with tight brown curls and a rather tense smile, offered flannels from a neat pile. Francis took one, gratefully. It was cool on his skin, delicately scented. Sandalwood, he rather thought.

'Sparkling apple juice?' asked the blonde. 'Or a Bellini?'

Why not? It was after noon already and Francis had woken early in his unfamiliar hotel room. He took a Bellini and waited in line as the newcomers handed over their passports and were registered at a desk in a gloomy reception area with patterned blue and gold wallpaper and deep blue carpets. The elegant elderly couple – she still in the hat – were being given the royal treatment by a handsome fellow with four-stripe epaulettes on his white shirt and thick blond hair swept back from his forehead.

'So good to see you again, Mr and Mrs Forbes-*Are-lee* . . .'

His accent was almost cornily French; while Mrs Forbes-Harley was American, from somewhere on the East Coast, Francis thought; distinctly *refained* anyway.

'And you, Gregoire. How have you been keeping?'

After a minute or so of this, as Gregoire moved seamlessly on to a little old lady with a grey bun, Mrs Forbes-Harley turned round to take in Francis. Close up, her lipstick gleamed a deep maroon against the wrinkly brown crepe of the surrounding skin. Her coiffed blue-grey curls trembled as she smiled, revealing incongruous but magnificent white teeth.

'They treat you so well on this ship,' she said. 'This is our seventh time. We love it. I'm Daphne, by the way.'

'Francis,' said Francis, taking her extended hand.

'Good to meet you, Francis. And where do you hail from?'

'London.'

'London, England? Oh, we love London. Brown's Hotel in Piccadilly, d'you know it?' She pronounced it as if 'a dilly' were some kind of exotic flower. 'It's one of our favourite hidey holes.' She gestured at her companion. 'This is my husband, Henry.'

'Nice to see you again,' said the old man, vaguely. Then he focused and smiled charmingly. 'It's Tom, isn't it?'

Daphne gave Francis an apologetic moue. 'You – haven't – *met* – him, Henry,' she said slowly, as if speaking to a small child.

The old man looked taken aback. 'Don't we know each other?' He paused, as if retrieving some distant memory. 'From Antarctica?'

'No, honey. *Francis* is new on this ship. We've never seen him before.' She switched on a thousand-volt smile. 'Are you travelling on your own, Francis?'

'I am.'

He could have told her that he was a crime writer and had been invited to lecture; and that in return Goldencruise had offered him the ten days for free. But he decided to enjoy being a man of mystery, for the time being at least. What was he? Newly divorced? An inveterate single? Gay? Wealthy, obviously.

'Do please consider us to be your friends,' said Daphne.

Now Gregoire was making an announcement: about the cabins, which were, he said, in the final stages of preparation, and would be ready for occupation immediately after lunch. 'So please, feel free to go on up to the restaurant, one deck above us 'ere, which is now open.'

With remarkable speed the passengers got moving. Francis heard the rising crescendo of Shirley's laugh dwindling away down the corridor.

He stayed where he was, taking a seat on a blue velveteen banquette, sipping his Bellini, noting that the peach juice was mixed with real champagne. No half-measures in this luxury zone. Below, on the quay, a few final bits and pieces were being loaded on to the ship; square crates hauled up on tense, quivering blue nylon ropes to the open top deck above. Urgent shouts accompanied the work; but none of them, thankfully, were for Francis.

He was glad to be away; to have escaped, even if only briefly, the pressures and distractions of his life in London. Not to mention the demise of his latest relationship, with the stimulating, sexy, but in the end impossibly solipsistic Chloe G—. What had happened to him? The temporary fame that had settled on him after he, a mere B-list crime writer, had solved the 'litfest murders' of Mold-on-Wold had led him to a strange place. For an autumn and a spring, he had found himself lionized. In public, there were requests to appear on TV and radio shows, to contribute his thoughts to this or that desperate rag: *Of what quality in yourself are you most proud? What advice do you have for an aspiring writer? Has your colour ever held you back? Wine or beer? Steak or sushi?* In private, there were invitations to little dinners in London suburbs, where he was often seated next to a suitable 'single' female, generally equally put out to be so obviously matchmade. On the couple of occasions he had followed up these thoughtful introductions of his married friends, he had found that things were not as simple as they seemed and there was a present or past attachment lurking. Chloe had been one such. In her late thirties, allegedly looking for someone to settle down with but in reality hung up on another, older man who had messed her around for years. In the end it had been easier not to try and compete; to back out and put a stop to intimacy and its complications. At least for a while. Back to lonely but straightforward celibacy.

After ten minutes or so, Francis got to his feet and followed the others through, out of the reception area and into a central landing from where circular stairs went up and down. He passed a young man with a bushy blond beard peering into a cupboard with a torch. Up one floor at the entrance to the restaurant, a maître'd in black tie was waiting to receive him. Another Filipino, another clean white smile. *James* said the name tag on his lapel.

'Good afternoon, sir. Please, take a seat.' James gestured through to the swathe of empty tables. There were bigger windows up here, mirrors on the walls and a lighter colour scheme, cream and gold, so it was altogether brighter. Shirley and Gerald and the two American guys were lunching together, but Francis didn't feel ready to butt into such gregarious hilarity. He walked over and found a table in one corner, with a view out in two directions: to the quays and containers and assorted masts of the docked ships one way; and then, to the other, beyond a distant breakwater, the open sea. He took out his notebook and settled in for some quiet thinking time.

But now James was upon him, beaming. A couple of yards behind stood a tall, red-faced gentleman with thick white hair and a matching moustache. He seemed to be twitching slightly.

'Would you like company, sir?' James asked.

To refuse would surely be churlish.

'Of course,' Francis replied. 'Why not?'

He smiled up at his new acquaintance, who grunted loudly as he bent to take a seat at a right angle from him. Klaus was his name and he was from Hamburg, Germany. A surgeon, though now retired. 'I must apologize in advance for my school English,' he said.

'Please don't. I have no German at all.'

'In the world as it is, you have no need to.' Klaus chuckled as he picked up the menu. Now was Francis having wine? Good. Was he familiar at all with German wines? No? So perhaps he would allow Klaus to choose?

There were, Klaus said, after he had tasted the Spätlese and they had clinked glasses, in his opinion three stages of an individual's life. The first, until about twenty-five, thirty even, was learning. The second, from thirty to maybe sixty, was working. And the third, which some unimaginative persons called retirement, was living. 'At last,' he grinned, 'you have got shot of your responsibilities. You have, if you have been at all clever, accumulated some nest egg or so. So now you have the freedom to do what you have always wanted.'

In this living phase Klaus was now in, he loved to travel. Sometimes his wife came with him; quite often she stayed behind in Hamburg. Klaus liked it either way, though each was different. 'When I cruise with Helga, it is all very nice, but we sit together at meals, and we have a drink after dinner in the bar before retiring to our cabin. When I am on my own, I get to know strangers. I explore. I am more, how-to-say, adventurous.'

He really did say 'how-to-say' and his th's were z's, like some character from a bad sitcom. Under the friendly surface, there was something, in the look from his cool grey eyes, if not menacing, at least controlling. You got the sense that Klaus was not a man who was used to being thwarted.

So had Francis ever been on a cruise before? he asked. No?

OK, so perhaps he should explain that there were cruises and cruises. On a standard cruise around the Med, you would find all types, and perhaps all ages too. Such things were starter cruises. Then there were the huge American leisure ships, ten, twenty times the size of this, with passenger numbers in the thousands, which went from island to island in the Caribbean.

'Horrible,' said Klaus, grimacing. 'Thankfully, I have never been on one.'

And then there was this kind of cruise, which was, how-to-say, top-end, but also for the more experienced cruiser, the traveller, if you like. Had Francis ever heard of the Century Club? No? To be a member you had to have visited over one hundred different countries. Not just states, or subdivisions of countries, like Wales or Scotland, but proper separate nations.

'And have you got your hundred?' Francis asked.

'No. I am not concerned with such nonsense. But there are plenty who are. And if you take this particular trip, the whole way from Cape Town to Dakar, you would be able to add at least twelve to your list. So you will find some who are here just for that.'

'How many countries have you been to?'

Klaus sat back. 'Sixty, maybe seventy. But then I do not have an obsession with stamps in my passport. What is the point of going to Monaco for two hours just to get the stamp? What do you learn? No, it is all very stupid.'

Klaus had travelled with the Goldencruise group before, he explained. To the Antarctic, another how-to-say adventurous location. And then before that along the north coast of Australia. 'The Kimberley, they call it, after one of your British colonial administrators. A very wild area. Plenty of crocodiles but no people. There were some Aborigines there once, but those convicts poisoned most of them.' He laughed, challengingly, but Francis wasn't going to rise to this sort of provocative non-PC; he always preferred to listen and let people reveal themselves.

As their starters arrived, there were loud shouts from below as moorings were untied; then a wobble as the ship moved away from the quay and out into the harbour.

'At last we are sailing,' said Klaus, raising his glass again.

It felt good to be on the move, the port receding as the view from the windows changed to the open blue of sea and sky. They passed fishing boats heading out beyond the long stone breakwater, each with its halo of circling white birds.

At the welcome drinks that evening, Francis wore a cream linen suit. He had bought it on a whim in a January sale and never quite found the right occasion to wear it at home. Now, he felt, it came into its own. He looked round at the dressed-up groups of guests gathered in the wood-panelled Panorama Lounge. They were mostly from what Klaus would have called the 'living' third of life: white-haired, bald, turkey-necked, liver-spotted. The best plastic surgeons in the world couldn't totally turn back the clock, though valiant attempts had been made here and there.

Francis wondered if he had the nerve to go and chat to one of the exceptions: a tall, middle-aged Asian guy with shoulder-length dark hair, magnificently turned out in a crimson and gold salwar kameez, who was standing next to a portly white fellow in a double-breasted Prince of Wales check. He decided he didn't quite, not yet, then found himself exchanging smiles with the dark-haired young woman he had noticed during the afternoon's mandatory safety briefing up on the top deck, when the guests had been shown their emergency muster stations and how to put on their lifejackets (as well as being warned to keep their blinds down at night because of the 'slight risk' of piracy). Her name was Sadie and her older companion was not her mother, as Francis had imagined, but her *ant*. Aunt Marion's husband Saul had had to drop out of the cruise at the very last moment but fortunately Sadie was working in South Africa for nine months so had been able to fly up and take his place.

'My husband the workaholic,' Marion grumbled, flashing chunky diamonds as her bony fingers seized a smoked salmon tartlet from a passing tray. 'I only wish he knew what he was missing out on.'

When dinner was called, Marion invited Francis to join them. Head waiter James put the trio on a table for six and then brought three singles over. First, the old lady with the grey bun who had been behind Francis at check-in, all sparkly and smiley now in an eau-de-Nil top criss-crossed with threads of silver; she was English too, it turned out, and her name was Eve. Then a pink-cheeked American with a head as shiny as a billiard ball – Joe. And finally, crisp in a navy blazer with brass buttons, Klaus. He took the last place between Marion and Sadie. Having introduced himself to Sadie, he gave Francis a man-to-man nod which pretty much said, *A very attractive woman I see. You are the younger man. All yours for now.* He then turned politely to the aunt.

So Francis settled in with Sadie. Her missing uncle Saul was some big-shot on Wall Street and – she rolled her lovely brown eyes – he was always doing this. Aunt Marion only forgave him because he earned such pots of money. It was obscene, to be honest, how much he pulled in. Not that she, Sadie, usually got the benefit of his holiday no-shows. But because she was in Cape Town *anyways* it made sense. She was working for the Peace Corps on an education project down there. It was in this township, Khayelitsha, which was like this huge sprawling area of shacks that most whites never saw, except when they flew over it into the airport. Some of the classrooms were actually in ship's containers. 'Like the ones we saw in dock back there? You wouldn't believe the poverty?' She had that sing-song rising inflection more usual with Australians or Californians than East Coast Americans.

The starters arrived. Roasted goat's cheese with herb salad for Sadie; steamed monkfish medallions for Francis. Accepting another top-up of Chenin Blanc, Sadie started telling Francis about her South African boyfriend, Louis, who was like the most exciting guy in the Cape Town NGO sector; but then, she giggled, it was only Cape Town. She couldn't really imagine him being her boyfriend in New York. In fact, to be totally honest, she was wondering what to do about him.

With the arrival of the *intermezzo*, Klaus swung round and joined in. 'Did I hear you two talking about the Peace Corps?' he asked and he was off, starting with the interesting info that George W. Bush had, counterintuitively, actually doubled its size during his so-called war on terror. Francis was aware that on his left Eve had been dropped by the bald American and was eating her curried cream of clam soup by herself. So he left Klaus and Sadie to it and turned to her, introducing himself by offering her a glass of wine.

'Thank you, but I won't,' she said. 'I gave it up *many* years ago.'

Eve had thoughtful green eyes above a puckered, amused mouth. She lived, yes, in the UK, in a little town called Malmesbury – did Francis know it? Just north of the M4 near Bath. Her husband, Alfred, had passed away seven years ago and after that she hadn't seen the point of sitting around at home thinking about their life together, so she'd decided to do something completely different. She went on a cruise, just a little one, up to the Norwegian fjords. 'And then I got a taste for it, and there was no stopping me. Now I do three or four a year.'

'I'm impressed,' said Francis.

'So you should be!' She laughed. 'I've been all over. The South Seas. That was extraordinary. All these tiny islands with vast tracts of ocean between them. You feel wonderfully remote. Then I went to Greenland last summer, and I loved that so much I followed it up with Antarctica at Christmas. Got to see these places while you've got the chance, don't you think? You wouldn't believe the colours you get in the icebergs. And the wildlife is quite magnificent. Polar bears in the north, penguins down south. Such funny little creatures. Like so many pompous Rotarians heading off for a black tie dinner. To see them out there in the wild is such a joy.'

Next year she had signed up to do the Russian Far East and Indonesia. 'I've always wanted to visit Kamchatka, ever since I played Risk as a child. And it may sound silly, but I've a hankering to see Komodo dragons.' She loved Goldencruise. 'They do this very nice thing where the ships aren't too big, so you can get to know the other passengers. And the staff and crew. They become your friends too, believe it or not.'

'I see,' said Francis.

'You don't believe me, do you? Poor, lonely, deluded creature, you're thinking. Imagining the staff are her friends.' Eve's eyes twinkled. 'But sometimes, Francis, people tell an old bird like me things they can't tell anyone else.'

'Such as?'

'Personal things. Troubles they might have at home. That sort of stuff. You know, I like those sorts of confidences. It makes me feel useful again. And if you travel with the same ship, you see the same people. Lovely Gregoire, waiting to greet you with a kiss at the top of the gangway when you arrive. It somehow makes you feel safe . . .'

The funny thing was, she went on, that she had never travelled at all until she was seventy. In her middle age she had looked after her elderly mother for years. 'I was a carer, basically, though we didn't call it that in those days. Not a lot of fun, looking back. Mummy got needier and needier, until it came to a point where I gladly would have smothered her. And I missed out on children. Which was a shame. Then, when Mummy finally shuf-fled off her mortal coil, I met darling Alfred, at a bridge night, and my life changed again. He was a lovely man, but not a traveller in the leisure sense. He spent so much time going round the world for business that he was happiest on the golf course back home when he had time off.'

Somehow it didn't seem polite to ask where the money had come from: Mummy, or Alfred? Had Alfred been the charming adventurer, latching on to a lonely middle-aged woman with inherited wealth? Or quite the reverse?

'I realize I'm very fortunate,' Eve said. 'To be as old as I am and still to have my health and sanity. So many don't, do they? Living in la-la land, unable to recognize their friends and relatives. Ghastly. And yes, to be comfortably off with it. But when you get to my age you realize you can't change the way the world works. I give to charity, of course; but then I also make the most of things, because if I don't, who's going to? And when I do finally pop off there'll be some very happy donkeys in Somerset.'

A blackberry and apple sorbet arrived. Then, with the main courses, the conversation became general. It emerged that the bald American was a soldier; *Colonel* Joe, no less.

'Did you see action?' Sadie asked; a trifle mischievously, Francis thought.

'Nothing like the boys do these days.' Colonel Joe paused, then puffed out his barrel chest. 'No, ma'am, I was more what they called a Cold Warrior.'

Francis caught Sadie's eye for a second; her lips quivered, but there was no open laughter. Colonel Joe was serious, as he was, too, about the risk of piracy, which had been rather *scooted over*, he thought, during the safety briefing earlier. Over half the world's attacks took place, he said, either off the coast of Somalia or in the Gulf of Guinea, which is where they were right now.

'This adds a certain how-to-say frisson to our dinner, does it not?' said Klaus.

'It would be more than a freakin' frisson if any of these guys got on board,' said the colonel. 'They're famous for their ruthlessness.'

'Stop it, you two, you're frightening me,' said Eve. 'Goldencruise surely wouldn't take a risk with this sort of thing, would they?'

'That expedition leader guy did say they had made preparations,' said Sadie.

'Preparations!' scoffed Colonel Joe. 'But cruise ships are not allowed to dock if they're carrying weapons, so I don't know what they'd do if there really was an attack.'

'They have search lights,' said Klaus, authoritatively. 'Very powerful ones. And loudspeakers. And water hoses and such.'

'Loudspeakers,' scoffed Colonel Joe. '"Will you please remove your Kalashnikovs from the ship."' He mimicked a tannoy announcement and then laughed. 'I don't see a bunch of war-hardened n— Africans taking much notice of that.' He had swerved off the N-word just in time. Presumably for my benefit, Francis thought.

After the meal, Francis accepted Sadie and Marion's suggestion of a digestif in the Panorama Lounge. Klaus was close behind them, adding himself to the group by asking what people would like to drink. This was a somewhat bogus way in, as everyone knew the cruise was all-inclusive, so it wasn't as if he were standing a round.

There was a pianist in black tie tinkling away in the corner, a pint-sized Filipino doing shmaltzy covers of popular classics, but not many from the dining room had come up this first evening of the second leg. The fabulously dressed Asian and his portly chum were there, drinking up at the bar with another odd couple: a short, tanned old fellow with suspiciously jet-black hair straggling down over the collar of his blue Hawaiian shirt and a much younger woman whose glowing caramel skin was set off beautifully by a tight silver lamé dress. They were all laughing extra-loudly, as if at a sequence of private jokes.

In Francis's little group, Klaus rather dominated the conversation, revealing yet another area of expertise: where to find Club Class flights on the cheap.

'Excuse me,' said Sadie. 'I'm just going for a walk on deck. Clear my head. Would you like to join me, Francis?'

How could he refuse? As he got to his feet Klaus gave him a sophisticated look: that of a man whose dominance of the conversation has been usurped by half the listeners leaving, but who is determined not to show that he minds, even a little; added to that, the ill-disguised envy of an older man who watches a younger one being invited away for who knows what reason by an attractive woman.

'Mind how you go,' he said, raising his whisky glass and giving Francis a wink. 'Remember – no lights. No torches, not even smartphones.' He cackled, proprietorially.

One floor up, on deck six, Francis held open the double doors. A whoosh of night air greeted them, warmer and more humid than the air-conditioned interior. At this level a gangway ran right around the ship, passing the steel wall that enclosed the theatre and then, ahead of that, up by the bow, the big, curved-glass windows of the Observation Lounge, all blinds down tonight. At the stern was an open area of deck with another bar, though that, too, was dark and closed.

'Shall we go up to the top deck?' said Sadie. Francis followed the swish of her cocktail dress as she climbed the clanging steel steps. Above, they found the open space of deck seven, the two big lifeboats on either side dark silhouettes against the brilliant night sky.

Sadie all but ran to the stern, where she grasped the white railings.

'Sorry,' she said, after a moment, turning, smiling. 'My *ant* was doing my head in down there.'

'I thought it was Klaus who was being the bore.'

'Oh, yeah, he was, for sure.' She giggled. 'But it's just the way she sits there and takes it, all twinkly-eyed, expressing interest in something she has no interest in *at all*. She's loaded. Why would she give a toss about cheap flights? She and Saul always fly First. When he joins her, which he doesn't, because he's usually having an affair. Really, everybody knows except her, it's tragic. But I mean, why does she even bother to pretend to be one of the real-traveller gang? It's so phoney.'

'She's just being polite, surely.'

'Oh, sure she is. I'm sorry. I shouldn't be getting annoyed by her at this stage of the holiday. She's been very kind, asking me along. It's just, like, we're sharing a cabin and, I don't know how she does it, she manages to get right on my last nerve within about an hour of me first seeing her. Anyways, this is better.' She let out a long, powerful sigh. 'Just look at that.'

Below them, beyond the deserted tables of the darkened deck six bar, the white wake of the ship bubbled away in a flat, narrowing line into the blue-black night. To the side, the sheer drop down to the ocean was dizzying.

'You wouldn't want to fall in there, would you?' she said.

Francis shivered and held the rails tightly too, his old vertigo kicking in. 'You wouldn't,' he agreed.

Sadie flung her profile upwards. She had a lovely retroussé nose above those frankly rather sensual lips. 'Check these stars,' she said, turning. 'So bright out here, you feel you could reach out and touch them.' She sighed. 'That's the thing I like most about Africa. The night sky. And the sunsets,' she added.

'And the space,' said Francis. 'Just the vastness of it.'

'You've been to this continent before?'

'I lived here. Some years ago.'

'You never mentioned that.'

'Nobody asked me.'

'Even when Klaus was telling us about his great expedition to the tree where Stanley met Livingstone.'

'Yes, well, there is a virtue in not sharing everything, don't you think?'

'I'd say.' She turned and gave him a long, approving look. 'You're very English, you know that.'

'Shall I take that as a compliment?'

She laughed. 'You should. That's exactly the sort of thing I mean. "Shall I take that as a compliment?"' she repeated, in a poor imitation of his accent. 'Very Downton Abbey. So where were you in Africa? What were you doing?'

'Something a bit like you, I suppose. Helping out in a school in Swaziland. It was only for six months. After I left college.'

'When was that?'

'A while ago.'

Francis was vain enough not to want to say how much of a while. But without dating his experience, he gave Sadie the gist of it. How, too, he had hoped to identify with the heritage of his Botswanan birth father, but had soon realized that what he had in common with the kids he was teaching had nothing to do with skin colour. Indeed, the whole experience had made him realize just how British he was.

When they went back down to the bar, half an hour later, Klaus and Marion had gone off to bed.

'Separately, I hope,' laughed Sadie.

The glamorous Asian and the old white guy with the suspect hair were the only ones left at the bar. His shapely younger partner, if that's what she was, was out on the little circular dance floor, twirling round and round to the music on her own. She looked sad, and not entirely sober, stumbling a little on some of her turns.

'Lively scene,' said Sadie. 'You want a nightcap?'

'Maybe I'll pass on that.' Francis yawned. 'There's an early start tomorrow.'

'Yes, Togo, exciting. A bit of real Africa.'

They went out together past the library and down two decks to discover they were sleeping on the same corridor.

'I'm right opposite you,' Sadie said, inserting her keycard in the wall slot with a giggle.

'See you in the morning,' Francis replied.

'If those pirates keep away.' She winked.

He fell asleep to the soft rolling motion of the ship; the low hum of the distant engine; the gentle rustle of the sea on the hull. He imagined what it might be like, making love to a woman, in this bed, with these soothing sounds in the background. But no. That was absolutely not what he'd come for.